About the Author

Beryl Nicklas Henshaw lives in rural Wales where she worked 'doing sums' as she tells her grandchildren (in accounts departments). On her retirement in 2002 she finally found the time to test her creative skills. Nothing too domestic, so she enrolled on a creative writing accredited course which set her on a new and fascinating path. She has short stories in several anthologies but *Kindred Spirits* is her first full length novel. The first chapters she used in her dissertation at university in which she graduated with an MA in creative writing.

Kindred Spirits

Beryl Nicklas Henshaw

Kindred Spirits

Olympia Publishers
London

www.olympiapublishers.com
OLYMPIA PAPERBACK EDITION

A CIP catalogue record for this title is
available from the British Library.

ISBN: 978-1-78830-098-8

This is a work of fiction.
Names, characters, places and incidents originate from the writer's
imagination. Any resemblance to actual persons, living or dead, is purely
coincidental.

First Published in 2018

Olympia Publishers
60 Cannon Street
London
EC4N 6NP

Printed in Great Britain

Dedication

I dedicate this book to the memory of Alison Nicklas whose research into our family tree was invaluable and inspirational.

Acknowledgments

Grateful thanks to my husband, Dave, for helping with my research, and reading my work with a critique's hat on and to all family members and friends who have offered encouragement.

To my sister Margaret Seabrook for editing my work for me.

To Richard Jones (AKA 'Red Reg') who tutored the accredited course I joined. His exercises re the 'Doolough Tragedy' and the 'San Patricios' intrigued me and planted the kernel of a story in my mind.

To Professor Dic Edwards of Trinity St David University, Lampeter for being so supportive with his comments and my fellow students who listened to each chapter as I read out my work each week and gave kindly advice.

INTRODUCTION

Saolaítear na daoine uile saor agus comhionann ina ndínit agus ina gcearta. Tá bua an réasúin agus an choinsiasa acu agus dlíd iad féin d'iompar de mheon bráithreachais i leith a chéile.

Translation:
All human beings are born free and equal in dignity and rights. They are endowed with reason and conscience and should act towards one another in a spirit of brotherhood.

PART ONE
JOHN'S STORY

CHAPTER ONE
DUBLIN OCTOBER 1843

The crowd was noisy but good humoured as they waited for Daniel O'Connell to appear. John Walsh, and his younger brother Daniel, had learnt from their priest, Father Murphy, about Daniel O'Connell, first Catholic Member of Parliament at Westminster, who had refused to swear allegiance to the English crown. O'Connell had become a hero to all the Catholics seeking emancipation which was granted in 1829. His fame had grown, and he had drawn enormous crowds wherever he spoke.

John and Daniel had left home against the wishes of their parents to follow their hero. They had walked for many a long day from County Mayo to the Hill of Tara and had been overwhelmed by the sight of so many supporters gathered there. O'Connell had chosen the site for his rousing speech, in favour of an Irish parliament, with inspiration. The Kings of Ireland had once been crowned on this very hill and the patriotic Irish who heard his speeches caused the authorities to fear a revolution. The meeting had inspired the two youths who had then walked on to Dublin, finding casual work in exchange for food and board on their way. An enormous rally was planned near Dublin and the military were called upon to safeguard the city. When the brothers arrived, the sound of men singing hymns in Gaelic reverberated around the packed square, their faces shining, confident that with the huge number of protestors gathered they must surely win the day.

The joyous singing faded as the cheerful mob fell silent and everyone strained to hear what was happening. O'Connell made his way through the crowd and climbed onto the temporary stage. Holding up his right hand and staring into the distance, he indicated to the crowd he was about to speak.

"Brethren, although we have gathered here today in a peaceful demonstration, the Government has prepared for a violent confrontation. There are cannons ready, warships in the harbour and troops on standby, bayonets fixed. I fear that although we may not be outnumbered, we are not prepared for a fight. So I beseech you all, go home, return to whichever corner of our beloved country from which you hail. Now is not our time."

As he spoke, officers of the crown climbed onto the stage and grabbed him by the arm to lead him away. His supporters swarmed around them, shouting abuse at the officers who raised their batons as a warning, pushed their way out of the gathering and led him away. As O'Connell had rightly said, they were not equipped for a fight with the military or police. The crowd stood their ground but soon the shouts turned to low murmurs when they saw their protests were in vain. They slowly drifted away, furious at the treatment of their hero, but unable to assist him.

John and Daniel followed the crowd as they shuffled past, and debated what to do next.

"I'm done with this hellhole. A man has a right surely to self-governance?" John was fifteen and Daniel was thirteen.

Daniel asked, "Maybe O'Connell will start afresh when he is released from prison?"

John kicked a loose stone in anger and replied,

"What can we be expected to do against such a fearsome army? No, I aim to get myself to America, get a new life. I've heard tales of fortunes to be made if you're hard-working. I will turn my hand to anything that's within the law."

"But who d'you know there? Where will you go and what will you do for money?"

"Ah, Father Murphy told me of a place in New York where Irish Catholics are made welcome, lodgings found, help getting work. I'll do just fine. I have a letter from him to the priest in New York. I never told Ma an' Da, they would have talked me out of it, I know."

"What shall I tell them? They will expect us both back."

"Listen Dan, I am just another mouth to feed. There's no work, the cottage is too tiny for us all. It'll be best all round."

"Can't I come with you? One fewer again to feed?"

"But Dan, you are only thirteen, just left school, Ma and Da can use you on the land. No, tell them I'll make my fortune, send them money, and as the little ones grow up maybe then you can join me. How's that sound?"

The tears filled Dan's eyes and he wiped them away with his threadbare jacket sleeve. With a slight incline of his head, he indicated to John that he understood and he agreed to go home. John fought back his own tears as he put his arm around his younger brother and hugged him close to soothe the sobbing boy. He had been earning his keep since leaving school at thirteen by helping with harvests, gathering seaweed from the shore and labouring for a local landowner. From his meagre wages, he had kept a little back for himself each week, hidden in an old broken jug deep in the stone wall at the back of the cottage. He hoped he had sufficient to pay for a fare to America. If not, he would work his passage if possible.

"Here, Dan."

John unwrapped the binding of sackcloth from around his waist and took out a pouch containing coins.

"Spend this sparingly and it will help you get more than halfway home, maybe pay for a cart ride or two? Anyways, it'll feed you part of the way."

Dan frowned, puzzled. He took the money and thanked his big brother.

"Where'd you get this? We never earned this on the road!"

"Ah, well now, it was just my emergency fund. You must do the same when you get home. Anything you get paid for a job, put a bit aside. In fact, use the old jug I used, it's tucked away safe in the wall at the back by the pig sty. But be sure to help Ma and Da too, pay for your keep now. Promise?"

His brother nodded. His face brightened. The prospect of walking back to County Mayo alone with no money had frightened the poor boy.

Then they hugged again, went separate ways with John watching Daniel as he walked west out of Dublin until he was out of sight before he himself headed for the docks.

***

The quayside of Dublin was noisy, smelly, busy and exciting. A forest of ships' masts filled the skyline with strange flags of many countries fluttering from their mizzenmasts. John pulled his cap firmly on his head, secured his body belt with his hard-earned cash safely inside, and threw his sack of belongings over his shoulder before exploring the dockside. Men were shouting instructions or warnings as dockers discharged the cargo from berthed ships. Barrels were rolled and stacked, bales piled high, and coal was collected on waiting carts from chutes on board the vessels, creating clouds of heavy black dust.

John ducked suddenly as a net of bales swung over his head and a man shouted,

"Eh, you! Silly little bugger! Clear off before your head's knocked off!"

The boy dived to safety then watched, fascinated, as the man expertly guided the rope sling of bales down onto the quayside below.

A shrill whistle startled him, then he watched as the men finished what they were doing and climbed down from the ship. A wizened old man, sitting in a small wooden hut, was tending a blazing brazier over which hung a steaming iron kettle, just coming to the boil. He spat on his fingers before removing the hot lid and threw in a handful of loose tea. By the time the queue of thirsty men stood before him, the tea was ready to pour. Each man took from his belt his own enamel mug and had it filled with the welcome brew.

John spotted the man who had shouted at him approach and wondered whether he should run.

"Eh, you again. Come 'ere."

Walking towards the docker, John expected trouble.

"Where 'ya from, lad?"

"County Mayo, sir."

The docker chuckled.

"I'm no sir, lad. Me name's Tim McIvor. Are ya thirsty?"

"Well…"

"Speak up lad! Want a cup of tea? Wait while I drink mine then you can use me mug."

John's face lit up. He was so relieved. He'd been expecting to be sent packing.

"Ere, sit on that crate there, I'll sit by ya just now."

McIvor took his clay pipe from his pocket and with a splinter of wood he used the fire in the brazier to light it.

His mug refilled in one hand and his pipe in the other, Tim McIvor settled beside John and handed him the steaming tea. John smiled and thanked him. Tim puffed on his pipe and looked down at the boy gulping the brew.

"You lookin' for a job, lad?"

"No sir, Mr McIvor. I'm wanting to sail to America."

"America? That's a long way. How about Liverpool?"

"No, really I want to get to America. I've been told it's a land to make your fortune if you work hard. And I can do that I promise you."

Tim drew on his pipe in silence while John drank his tea.

"See this ship we're unloading? Alhambra's 'er name. Magnificent, isn't she? Well, she sails for America in two days' time when she's reloaded. I could maybe speak to the Captain, see if he needs a cabin boy. Like that?"

"Oh sir! I mean, Mr McIvor, would you? That'd be so good!"

"Ah well, now, see, he and the crew are up in the pubs while we unload so if you come back tomorrow, to this very hut, midday, we should get to see him. What d'ya say?"

"Blessed Mary and Joseph! I can't thank you enough! I'll wait right here till then!"

"Ah, now then. That's not possible unless… I'll have a word with the cocky watchman, see if he's got a spare corner in his shed for you tonight."

McIvor stood up, stretching his weary legs.

"Back to work for me. You keep yourself safe now."

John drained the dregs of tea, shook the mug upside down and handed it back, then thanked the man again and found himself a quiet corner until evening.

Around him feral cats, fat on rats and mice, dodged the feet of the workmen, as they hunted their next meal. He was fighting the desire to sleep when the whistle sounded for the end of the working day. John watched the dockers and riggers, their faces black with coal dust and sweat, throw their canvas bags over their shoulders and leave the docks. Their heavy hobnailed boots made the cobbles sing as they trudged out of the gates and headed to the nearest pub before returning home. Soon the quayside was deserted, but for John and shadowy feline figures. The sound of the wind cracking the rigging on the ships and the creaking of the swaying hulls on the water with the slap slap of the waves against the stone quayside made him drowsy and he closed his eyes. He was dreaming of his family back home in County Mayo when a shadow fell across him, rousing him.

The sky had darkened and the figure looming over him filled him with fear. The night watchman, in an old army coat tied with string and his hat pulled low obscuring his face, stood before him, eyed him up and down, grunted, nodded his head and indicated to John to follow him. He led him to a heap of straw in the hut, kicking out at escaping cats.

"You doss down there. I'll be doin' me rounds now and then so don't be alarmed if you wake in the night and find me gone."

With a heavy stick in one hand and a lantern in the other, Old Bill went in search of miscreants.

John shook the straw into a comfortable shape and curled up with his possessions safely tucked under his body. He slept soundly, relieved that his adventure so far was proving to be less difficult than he had imagined. He awoke only when the morning activities of the dock started noisily around him.

"'Ere boy, now you're awake you can earn your breakfast. Take this bucket and see there against the warehouse wall? The pump? Fill it and I'll get the brew on."

He helped Old Bill, the watchman, by stoking the fire, filling the kettle and going to the dock-gate shop for bread and baccy, the hearty breakfast of every docker.

The old man and the boy sat in silence while they ate their bread and watched the dock labourers file in. Bill grunted the occasional greeting as the men passed then he left John to sit watching while he went back inside to lie down.

Later, the midday whistle blew and once again the men congregated for steaming mugs of tea.

Tim McIvor took John to one side.

"I've 'ad a word with the captain. He said you can go on board now while the work's stopped. See the gangplank?"

John looked to where Tim pointed. He nodded.

"Climb aboard there, tell the man on deck at the top Tim McIvor sent you and he'll take you to the captain's cabin."

Tim held out his hand to shake John's.

"Good luck in the New World boy, and when you've made your fortune, remember old Tim McIvor."

Tears filled John's eyes. He'd only met this man yesterday but already he felt he owed his future to him.

"Go on with you now, before he changes his mind. God's blessing boy."

***

John looked up the steep gangplank and, grasping the ropes on either side firmly, he began to climb. On deck a sailor was busy coiling a rope, oblivious to the boy's presence.

John coughed politely.

The sailor stopped what he was doing and, screwing up his eyes against the midday sun, he looked up.

"What you doin' on board?"

"Please sir, Mr McIvor sent me to see the captain."

He had realised by calling all these hard-working men 'Sir', it softened their attitude towards him. It was a lesson he would remember.

"Oh, Tim, did 'e now. Follow me then, lad."

John followed the sailor, careful not to trip over ropes. Beneath his feet, the vessel rocked gently and he stumbled until he found his balance. They walked along the scrubbed deck to the captain's cabin.

"He's in here preparing the charts. Speak only when you're spoken to, right?"

The sailor knocked on the cabin door. A gruff voice shouted, "Who is it?"

"A young lad, Cap'n, looking for work."

The door opened and a huge man filled the doorway. He was grey haired with a beard and bright blue eyes which studied the scrawny lad standing before him. His navy jacket had four tarnished gold bands on the sleeves and his navy trousers were shiny with age. He stood aside to allow John to enter and the sailor returned to his duties. John removed his cap, adjusted his sack on his shoulder and stood tall.

Captain Foster stroked his beard.

"Hmm. Right. Want to be a sailor, eh?"

"Well, not exactly, sir, Captain. But I do want to get to America."

"So what services can you offer me in return for a passage to America?"

"Pardon, sir, Captain?"

"What work can you do?"

"Anything. Wash dishes, help cook dinner, scrub, polish, wash clothes, just about anything, sir."

"Hmm. Do you get seasick?"

"No, sir"

This was not dishonest. He'd never been seasick because he'd never been to sea.

"Right."

The captain looked round his cabin. The brass portholes were not as shiny as they could be, the charts needed sorting and his bed was unmade.

"Can you read?"

"Yes sir, Captain."

Captain Foster pushed a chart across the table to him.

"What can you read there?"

The chart was a complete mystery to John but he could read Irish Sea, Atlantic Ocean and the date in one corner, 1832, which he did, out loud.

"Good. Good. Pity you don't want to be a sailor. I could make something out of you. A lot of the crew can't read. See all this brass? I want you to polish it till it shines like candlesticks on the altar in your church, right? Then make my bed so neat and tidy I won't want to mess it up by sleeping in it. But first, stow these charts in that special cabinet there. They are all marked with numbers in the corner, see? So stow them numerically."

John looked puzzled.

"In number order, just like hymns in a hymn book."

John nodded. His English was improving day by day. He now understood why his parents had sent him to the National School where only English was allowed instead of the hedge school set up by Gaelic-speaking Irishmen.

"I will ask the mate to give you some cleaning materials and then I'll be leaving you to get on with it, I have much to do before we sail tomorrow."

John looked around the cabin after the captain had left, taking in the mahogany bunk, the desk with brass handles and the oil lamp swinging on a gimbal. Pictures of sailing ships in full sail hung on the panelled bulkheads.

He jumped when the door burst open and a man with a furrowed brow and a turned-down mouth entered. Dermot O'Leary eyed the boy up and down.

"So, what mischief are you leaving behind? Why the need to get to America?"

He handed John a wooden box containing polish and cotton rags.

"No mischief, sir, just a need to find work, make something of myself. My Da's small plot won't give work for all of us boys, so being the eldest, I left room for the young 'uns."

Dermot frowned. He didn't trust these country boys, being a Dubliner born and bred himself.

Boys this age were always trouble in his eyes. He would be watching this one.

"Right. Make a start, I'll be checkin' your work so put your elbow into it."

He stalked out of the cabin, slamming the door behind him.

Hunger began to gnaw at John's stomach. He'd eaten nothing since the chunk of bread given him by old Bill. He started with the brass polishing. He rubbed away at the portholes until they gleamed. Captain Foster had not mentioned the desk drawer handles but John gave them a quick polish too. Then he turned his attention to the bunk. At home, the whole family had slept in one cramped room with little bedding, relying on the closeness of each other for warmth. This bed had sheets as well as blankets, two feather pillows and a decorative counterpane. Never having made a bed before, he stripped it down to the mattress, spread the sheets and smoothed them, shook the pillows and replaced the blankets, tucking in the corners. Then he carefully threw the counterpane over the bed. Captain Foster would be able to see at a glance he had done his best; the linen sheet was turned down over the soft blankets and the pillows plumped up. He had just finished returning the charts to the cabinet and was checking he had not omitted any tasks when Captain Foster startled him as he threw open the door. The big man walked around in silence, his hands clasped behind his back. He inspected the brass, opened the drawers to check the charts were in place and smiled when he saw how welcoming his bed looked.

"Hmm, not bad, not bad at all. Well, you've done a good job here, no mistake, I'm satisfied. Now, are you hungry?"

"Yes sir, Captain, to be truthful I am."

"Follow me. You can meet your shipmates."

They descended a ladder to the deck below the main deck and entered the mess. The chatter and laughter ceased as the captain's presence was noticed.

"Dermot you've met. You call him Mr O'Leary. He'll introduce you to the rest of the crew. This here is young John – what's your family name, lad?"

"Me name's John Walsh and I'm from County Mayo."

John looked around the seated men tucking into their dinners and was pleased to see a few lads not much older than himself.

Men of all ages sat on benches either side of the plank table and weighed him up and down in silence.

"Shove up, lad."

Captain Foster spoke to the boy sitting at the end of one of the benches.

"Make room for a little one. Get him a dish someone." One of the youngsters climbed out of his seat and took a tin plate from a shelf for John.

"Thank you."

It was all John could say. He was a little overwhelmed and feeling awkward.

"I'll fill your dish, boy, there's plenty to go round."

Kevin the cook, with a cloth thrown over his shoulder and a 'kerchief on his head, ladled out a portion of the steaming contents from a pan on the stove. The stew smelled good and John was soon eating ravenously.

Captain Foster returned to his cabin followed by a crew member carrying a jug of stew to be served in the captain's private quarters.

The talk around the table resumed.

"'Ow old are ya, son?" asked a bald man with his front teeth missing.

"Fifteen, sir."

The men fell about laughing, even toothless Adam.

"Sir Adam I am, to be sure. Yes, sounds good, you carry on calling me Sir Adam and we'll get along just fine. What has brought you to Dublin and to this ship? Got a young lass in trouble did ya? Steal from the landlord? Tell us, boy."

The men had finished eating and sat with smiles on their faces, enjoying the brief spell from work.

"No lass is in trouble from me, nor no lad."

This brought a roar of laughter and the men rocked in their seats.

"Nor am I a thief. But my Ma and Da do have a large family to feed and being the eldest, I left home to find work in America."

"America, is it, you want to go? Well, it takes a month and a half, with a good following wind and no storms. Have you sailed before?"

Kevin the cook asked him.

"Never, sir, not even in a curach. But I learn fast."

The bosun, Big Bob O'Neal, spoke next.

"You'll need to lad, we don't carry passengers on this boat. Least ways not freeloaders, only fee payin' passengers and them not too often, thank God. Right lads, back to work."

The benches were pushed back as the crew members stood to leave.

Kevin turned to John.

"You, young John, you can help Padraig wash the pots and straighten up the galley, got to be shipshape before we sail."

Padraig, one of the other young boys, showed John what went where. As he did so, Kevin began telling him about his first day at sea.

"I was full o'meself, thought I knew it all, listened for years to an old uncle with his salty tales. But, lad, I can tell you my first day rollin' an' buckin', my breakfast an' me soon parted company. No shame, mind, if you do get sick, no shame at all. Many a Cap'n still gets sick in the quiet of their cabin. I know, I get to see their unfinished meals."

The two boys and the cook worked well together. John hung up the pans, stowed the plates and cutlery in such a way they wouldn't fly around in bad weather and Kevin taught him how to keep the fire lit.

"Now we clear the officers' mess, they should be all done too."

For the officers, there was a little more comfort. The table seated six, crockery was used instead of enamel dishes, but the benches were bare wood same as for the crew.

The smell of stew mingled with the smell of tobacco and oil from the lamp. John wound up the wick carefully until the flame burnt clean. Kevin nodded, approving of the boy's initiative and wiped down the table top.

"Please, sir, Kevin sir, where do I sleep tonight?"

"Good question. We hot-bunk, two to a bunk, take turns see? We should just about squeeze you in with the other youngsters. If you snore mind, they're likely to push you out onto the floor!" He winked as he said this and John smiled back.

Later, when he was wedged between the bulkhead and the thinnest boy, Micky, John remembered how he had slept with Daniel and Patrick, so close that if one turned the others did too without waking. The water slapping the side of the boat, the craft swinging gently at her moorings and the heavy breathing of sleeping crew members soon lulled him into a deep sleep, too exhausted to remain homesick.

CHAPTER TWO
AT SEA

Next morning, he awoke in the dark foc'sle to the sound of loud hammering on the door and Dermot O'Leary shouting,

"Get up you lazy lot of layabouts. Leave your fleas in peace an' let's be 'avin' ya." Everyone leapt from their bunks. The early morning light crept through the cramped, sweaty sleeping quarters. A gust of wind blew in through the open hatchway, freshening the air and waking the half-asleep crew. They all went out on deck to prepare to sail. Alhambra was sailing on the morning tide and breakfast would have to wait. A quick swig of drinking water was all the refreshment allowed before the crew ran to their positions, ready to heave on board the ropes being released by the dockside crew. A paddle tug, black smoke billowing from her funnel and the wash from her paddles churning the water to a white froth, came alongside and connected up to the bow to tow them out to sea. The wind was light so the captain shouted through his megaphone to the master on the tug that he would require towage without sail until they reached Tuskar Rock off the coast of Wexford, where he expected to pick up a fair wind.

As they sailed with the east coast of Ireland on their starboard side for a full day, John was still able to see his beloved Ireland. There was no time to admire the view, even though the sails were not yet hoisted. The ropes were stowed in the lockers fore and aft, the decks had to be scrubbed using stone and sand, hatch boards were put in place and covers pulled over the hatch boards while the ship's carpenter drove in wedges to hold the canvases down. John watched in fascination until he heard his name being called.

Big Bob, the bosun, was beckoning him from the deckhouse.

"See these lamps, boy? Micky here will show you how to trim them. Know about trimming lamps do you?"

"Sir, Mr O'Neal, d'you mean trim the wicks like we do at home? I've done that, sir."

"Right. Do this lot and top up the paraffin. Any smoked glasses, get a bucket of sea water and wash them. Not the fresh water, understand? That's as precious as gold, remember that. Micky will be watching mind, see you do a good job. Micky, keep an eye on him, see he's not bragging."

Micky, another youngster, winked at John.

Nearby, one of the other deckhands, Jack, was helping the sailmaker repair sails while Padraig sat with a basket of potatoes to peel for Kevin who was busy stirring porridge on the old coal-fired range.

They had a hurried meal, taken in two watches while the ship was still under tow.

The sun was sinking in the west when they passed Conningbeg lightship, the tug still billowing smoke and paddles flashing in the setting sun. Captain Foster felt a light breeze on his face, then shouted,

"Make sail, Mr O'Leary."

"Aye aye, sir. Hands aloft you lubbers. Jump to it."

Men leapt to the shrouds and climbed like monkeys up to the yards. John gazed skywards, watching them until they were at least a hundred feet above the decks with their feet on the footropes as they pulled the gaskets free and let the sails fall to catch the wind.

Once the wind filled the sails, Captain Foster ordered O'Leary to hail the tug and let the tug master know he was about to let him go. The tug's hawser was freed by the foredeck crew then the tug's whistle blew to indicate he was all clear and about to turn back for Dublin. With a good following wind they entered St George's Channel and out into the Western Approaches to the Atlantic.

Alhambra sailed from Ireland heading south to the Canary Islands to pick up the North East Trade Winds and Canaries Current which would take them on to the East coast of America and ultimately New York. John stood on the stern, the spray washing away his tears, as Tuskar Rock faded into the distance and he strained to catch a last glimpse of Ireland, not sure if he would ever see her shores again. The final rays of the sun shone on the rippled sea like a path to America then disappeared below the horizon. John stood still, thrilled to be starting a new life, one he had dreamed of since he first heard of "The Americas".

After a four-hour watch, John was exhausted but he had enjoyed all the challenges thrown at him. He had taken his turn with the other men pulling on the main halyard to increase the height of the sails. The ship cut through the sea, rolling gently as the wind filled the canvas. He soon mastered the gait of a sailor by steadying himself as he walked the length of the deck, holding onto whatever came within hands reach. As he passed the door to the galley, Kevin emerged carrying an empty pail.

"Ah, just the fella. Here, fill this for me won't you? Be sure to draw the water from the freshwater pump here outside the galley then take it and fill the pan on the bogey while I see how Padraig's gettin' on peelin' more spuds. The little bugger will peel 'em away to nothin' if I don't check."

As the pail filled, John didn't hear Mr O'Leary approach.

"Right lad. When that job's done I've another for you. See up there?"

John stopped pumping to look aloft in the direction of the mate's pointing finger. Through the rigging and the full-blown sails, he saw the maintop, a platform half way up the main mast where crew members could act as lookouts. The other boys had bragged about climbing to the maintop and regarded it as a test of their manhood.

"Aye, sir."

Get up there, see what you can see, and holler down to me, got that?"

"Aye, sir, right away."

The lower rigging was no trouble to climb and he experienced just a gentle rocking motion of the ship as he climbed, but as he went higher the rocking increased and he clung on for dear life. By the time he reached the maintop, he was being flung backwards and forwards as the bow rose and fell and his legs trembled with the strain of maintaining his balance. His breakfast was quarrelling with his stomach when he finally reached the platform and stood upright. He held tight with one hand, and with the other shielding his eyes from the sun, he scanned the horizon in all directions. Below, the first mate was looking upwards, hands on hips, and John could just hear him shout, "Well?"

"Nothing but sea to see, sir."

"Sure? No land?"

"No land, sir, in any direction."

"Then down you come, sharp as you can, boy."

With the task accomplished, John found his legs had turned to jelly and he was shaking with fear. His head began to spin and he felt quite faint when he looked down.

"Come on lad, no hanging about. Get yourself down here, now!"

He lowered one leg cautiously until he felt the rigging beneath one foot, then the other, swaying violently from side to side. He felt Alhambra was doing her best to shake him loose, but his fingers gripped the ropes as he climbed down. With both feet planted once more on the deck, he exhaled the breath he had been holding and stumbled towards Mr O'Leary.

The first mate surprised John by slapping him on the back and smiling.

"Mmm. You did alright. I may have misjudged you, boy. I knew you'd see no land, we are well off the coast of France in the Bay of Biscay. With this fair weather we will not see shore until we pass Spain then Portugal. Ever heard of these places, boy?"

"I've heard of France, sir, all the fighting and that, and didn't Columbus sail from Spain to find the Americas?"

"Oh, so you've had learning have you? Well, when we've passed those countries we will carry on south for Africa to The Canaries. That's where Africa meets Europe on its way to America see? Got your legs back yet?"

John released his grip on the mizzen stay and stood, feet apart, upright and nodded.

"Now, go and see if cook needs you. Well done."

He blushed with pride at receiving praise from the surly mate and returned to the galley.

The daily routine continued without incident all the way to Las Palmas where the Alhambra reduced sail as she made the approach into port. John watched a small sailing vessel approach and draw alongside. A man climbed up the side of Alhambra.

"Who's he?" John asked Padraig.

"Every foreign port we call at, a ship's agent comes on board to check our vessel is free from disease. If she was not, she would have to fly a quarantine flag."

Padraig enjoyed the rare privilege of being the source of knowledge. A local officer also climbed aboard to assist the Alhambra into port and guide her alongside to drop anchor.

John and Padraig were kept busy along with all the other members of the crew carrying boxes, crates and sacks full of food stores, casks of fresh water and ale, and locally caught fresh fish for salting to last the voyage.

The replenishing of stores was undertaken very efficiently with the help of the shore gang and soon Captain Foster gave instructions to the first mate to weigh anchor.

O'Leary barked his orders, "O'Toole, Murphy, get that anchor up quick as you like. The rest of you stand by to raise the sails when the captain gives the order."

As soon as Alhambra's anchor was secured on the cathead she followed the pilot boat out into deep water where the full crew raised her sails to catch the Canary Current. The north-easterly trade winds would carry her south of the Sargasso Sea before crossing the Atlantic.

***

Alhambra made good speed as the winds filled her sails. The crew were kept busy mending torn canvas, replacing old rigging and helping the ship's carpenter carry out repairs to the bulwarks where necessary. On the fifth day out from The Canaries, the wind dropped. John woke in his bunk, puzzled. Something was different. The lamp hanging from the deckhead was still. The only sound he heard was the gentle creaking of the ship and muted voices from the deck. He threw back his blanket, pulled on his boots and rubbing the sleep from his eyes, he joined his shipmates.

Overhead, the sails hung limp, as men climbed the rigging to furl them. The captain walked the deck, his hands clasped behind him with an expression on his face which caused his men to give him a wide berth. John found Padraig on the afterdeck with a line over the side, fishing.

"What's to do? Why are we still?"

"Can you not see? The wind has dropped, not a breath. See? The sails are empty; we're in the doldrums so we are."

"Doldrums? What are the doldrums?"

"Like I said, no wind. We get becalmed an' go nowhere. So, we take advantage and fish for fresh supplies. You ever fished, John?"

"Aye, but only in a river, never at sea. Mind, I can cast a line."

"'Ere, 'ave a go of this then, see if you get lucky."

Close by, Mister O'Leary ignored the youngsters as he felt a pull on his line. He struggled with it then cried out,

"Give me a hand here someone. This one's a right big bugger."

Padraig ran to help him heave the catch up on deck.

"What's that? That's no fish you've caught, Mister O'Leary."

Lying on deck was an enormous white bird, squawking and flailing his huge wings as he swung his head from side to side, attempting to free himself from the line. O'Leary took a marlinspike from his belt and clubbed the bird into silence. Captain Foster arrived to find out what all the excitement was about.

"Mr O'Leary! Who pulled this poor creature from the sea?"

"I did, Captain, sir, he took my line. I was hoping for a big fish so I was, but got this ugly bugger instead."

"That 'ugly bugger' is an albatross, you fool, rare in these waters but I have known of one stray further north than he ought. Well, as he's here he can make a dinner for tonight. Tell Kevin to have it plucked and prepared."

The captain continued his stroll around the ship's deck.

When Kevin saw the albatross, he cursed the first mate for his foolishness.

"That bastard! Doesn't he know it's unlucky to kill an albatross? Every sailor knows that. Now we're for it an' I have the misfortune to serve him up to us all. Just be sure to say a little grace before you eat him, get the Almighty on our side, but what He will think of us killing one of his special creatures I'm sure I don't know."

The bird was delicious, a little on the fishy side, but a welcome change for the crew. One old salt bagged the feet of the bird, said he remembered a sailor on one of his voyages making purses from them. The feathers were used to plump up the mattress on O'Leary's bunk, the captain having declined them for his own.

Captain Foster and Mr O'Leary walked around the ship checking for any damage to the rigging, masts and sails, deciding which repairs were most urgent. Once the captain had returned to his cabin, the first mate issued orders to the other officers to form work crews to take advantage of their enforced lull.

The youngsters had performed their everyday duties, the lamps were all trimmed and filled, the galley scrubbed, and the sleeping quarters tidied. Big Bill approached them.

"Now then, can't have idle hands on a ship, time you all did a bit of learning. You three know a little more than John here, but as I show you the ropes you can tell me how much you know and how much you still need to know."

Big Bill had with him some odds and ends of rope, salvaged during earlier repairs. He lowered himself onto the deck beside them, with his back to the deckhouse, and told them to sit around him.

The four boys, John, Padraig, Micky and Jack, watched carefully as Big Bill began to show them a variety of useful knots. Each one was demonstrated once, then handed to one of the boys to attempt as the others watched, advising if they thought mistakes were being made. When he thought they were becoming proficient, Big Bill stood up, arching his back for relief after sitting so long, and told them to keep practising.

"I never knew there was so much to being a sailor," John said. He had always been game to learn new skills and now, to become experienced at tying the knots he had seen in the rigging, was proving a welcome challenge.

"Beats bein' beaten at home," Padraig said, his face wearing a frown as he concentrated on whipping the end of his rope.

"What! You were beaten? Who by?" asked Micky, holding up his reef knot for inspection.

"My old man, bastard that he was. He took to drinkin' after me Ma died and me an' me sister used to hide from 'im when 'e staggered 'ome. I ran away to sea an' our Maggy found work in a big 'ouse as a maid."

Padraig bent his head as he struggled to complete whipping the end of his rope. John pretended not to notice the other boy's tears.

"Well, for me, it was just the family grew too big for the house so being the eldest, I left home. I do miss my Ma and Da, an' all my brothers and sisters though. But then, this ship is like home a bit, now I have all of you as friends."

"Where you from then, John?" asked Jack.

"A little village, Ballybray, in County Mayo, near Ballycastle. D'you know of Ballycastle at all?"

"No, I'm from Dublin, don't even know of County Mayo. Is it far from Dublin?"

John sat back and looked at the still sea around them.

"We live not far from the sea, in a corner of Mayo on a bit of land with potatoes growin' in plenty, a pig fattenin' in the yard an' hens scratchin'an'cluckin'. We are four boys, three girls an' me Ma an' Da."

John paused while he attempted to pull the line through on his whipping. His tongue stuck out as he concentrated. When he had succeeded, he continued his tale of home.

"We were so cramped we had to sleep head to toe; one turned, we all turned. Kept us warm though on chilly nights."

John sighed and bent to continue with his work.

"You sure you want to leave them? Sounds like you're missin' them already. As for me, I was brought up by nuns. Never knew my family," said Jack, cursing as he had to undo his rope once more.

"Micky, where are you from? You're keepin' pretty quiet."

Padraig nudged Micky, making him lose his grip.

"Bugger, now look what you've done. I ain't from nowhere special. The sea is now me home so any port can welcome me."

Micky stood up to go and relieve himself. The others didn't need to know he'd been in trouble with the law. He should have been shipped to Australia but he slipped the clutches of the officers taking him to the ship filled with convicts and had hidden aboard Alhambra before her last voyage to America. Captain Foster had lost two crew members to illness that trip and had released Micky from his confinement with a chance to redeem himself. The boy had never looked back.

The following few days passed slowly, water was rationed for the duration of the time in the doldrums, causing grumbling amongst the crew. Still, all the maintenance work was completed, fresh fish was being salted, and the four young crew members had shown they were all keen learners and becoming expert at knots.

CHAPTER THREE
MID-OCEAN

Next morning, a thick cold mist descended, and the men spoke in subdued tones. All around, the sea was motionless, until a sudden squall raised the sleeping white horses and the sea began to boil. Several hours later the squall had developed into a full-blown gale, screaming through the rigging. As it reached hurricane force, the mizzen topgallant and royal mast carried away, and all hands were called on deck to furl the sails, leaving just the double-reefed topsails. The ship was pitching and tossing and almost put on her beam ends when the cry "man overboard" rang out. O'Leary had left the charthouse just as the ship lurched. He had grabbed for the rail but a huge wave washed him over the side. John struggled along the deck to reach the point where Dermot had gone over. A feeble cry of help caused him to peer down over the ship's side.

"He's here, hanging on! Help me someone, get him back on board!"

The ship threw John backwards as he lost his grip with one hand, but somehow he regained his feet and caught hold of the mate's hand as he clung to the rail while his body crashed against the ship's side.

"I've got him but need help. Quick somebody, help!"

Padraig was washed along the deck, frantically holding on to the ship's lifelines-ropes rigged along the bulwarks.

He pulled himself upright and leaned over to feel for O'Leary's other hand. When both boys had good purchase on the sorry fellow, they heaved him back on deck.

The first mate lay in a heap at their feet and they were unsure if he was alive or dead.

Slowly he stirred, coughed up sea water, and shook himself.

"Well, glory be, if it isn't the two boys. D'you know, you just saved my life? I was losing my grip and the sea was pullin' me in. I think I even heard Davey Jones call my name. I thank you both with all my heart. You will make good seamen one day, to be sure."

They helped him to his feet, pleased at his fine words. Between them they held him and steadied themselves as they made their way to the ladder leading below.

The second mate, on the wheel, struggled to hold the ship steady, but lost his grip and the ship turned against the wind. All this happened so quickly while the captain was still below, but feeling the ship had swung around, Captain Foster emerged and took the wheel with the struggling mate. Between the two men they saved the ship just in time by turning the stern to the wind as mountainous seas ran astern of them and the wind drove them on. Once all the crew were accounted for, the captain put two men on the wheel while he returned to his charts and they continued on, sailing under three reefed topsails with the sea still high. Vittles were served cold, the crew grabbing a bite whenever time and work allowed. After an exhausting few days, the wind eased and they sailed under full sail with the skies clear and a full moon overhead.

The crew enjoyed brief respite, however. They had rested their weary bodies and enjoyed hot meals once again then the wind began to pick up once more. The storm returned and the sea rose rapidly. The main brace of the stern-sail on the starboard quarter snapped, "just like a carrot," said Kevin, and the mainstay sail carried away, followed by the jib sail. Captain Foster used his megaphone to order the full crew to reduce all sails. The men struggled to maintain their balance as they worked aloft, fighting with the resisting canvas, while the boat thrashed and ploughed into the churning sea as if to shake them from their precarious footholds. Their best sea legs were required that day.

Two men still fought with the wheel, endeavouring to maintain their course, while mountainous following seas built up on the stern. The captain was fearful that they might broach to, go beam on to the waves, and the ship would be lost. A great roar was heard, followed by a crack like thunder and the main top gallant sail was rent from top to bottom as the gale continued to increase. This was followed by the fore topgallant sail ripping, and three ropes holding the main royals snapped asunder as if they were no more than darning thread. The gale once more reached hurricane force with torrential rain adding to the men's wretchedness. All sails remained furled with the mainsail double reefed, the foresail triple reefed, and also the foretopsail hanging in shreds. No man slept that day or night as they worked all hours pumping bilges to stop the steady influx of water.

The next day as dawn broke, the storm began to abate and the men were allowed short breaks from their duties of repairing the masts and rigging and fetching spare sails from the sail locker. Three crew members were sent below to check the cargo in the hold. The crates of crockery stowed in Liverpool before her arrival in Dublin had shifted, but were undamaged, while the barrels of finest whiskey remained secure with just a little seeping from one. The men allowed the leak to drain into a pewter jug for a short spell, before plugging the hole with a cloth soaked in tallow. They would save this as a reward for later. Bales of Irish linen, damask and Donegal Tweed cloth were damp in patches but mostly sound. However, the crates carrying the Waterford crystal had broken free and careered around the hold. On investigating the contents of one, Micky Murphy, the second mate, held aloft pieces of broken glassware, unable to find one item still whole.

"It could have been much worse, that was one hell of a storm. We're all lucky still to be livin' and breathin', praise be to God for that. What's a bit of glass then, just for the posh people to sip daintily from, no more, no less."

The cargo was lashed securely and the jug of whiskey was carried carefully aloft to be shared over their meal.

The voyage continued with a good wind, with speed reaching sixteen knots at times. The captain calculated they would arrive on time, so full water rations were restored. When the sailor shouted from the topmast that he could see land, the crew were ordered to scrub the poop and side decks of the ship. Mattresses were hauled on deck to air while the bunks were cleaned and the sleeping quarters washed down, ready for the Government Inspector who would come aboard on arrival at New York.

The shores of Ireland were just a distant memory when, six weeks after leaving Dublin, John and the crew all stood out on deck to witness the first glimpse of New York. John's elation was tempered with apprehension. He could not countenance what was in store for him, but with God's help, he was determined to give it his best shot.

The ship was approached by officials and boarded while at anchor. One was taken by Mr O'Leary to inspect the vessel while the other stood before the captain with a list of requirements. Captain Foster was courteous, as always, to the officious gentleman, patiently answering his questions.

"How many crew members do you carry?"

"I have a crew list prepared for you." Captain Foster handed the list over.

"I see you have thirty-five men on board including boys. Do you know if any of them plan to stay in America now they are here?"

"I do believe one of the youngsters hopes to settle here. First mate, find John for me will you?"

John stood before the captain, folding and unfolding his cap in his hands, with a worried expression on his face.

"Now John, am I right in saying you hope to stay here after we sail?"

"Yes sir, Captain sir. I am to meet with the priest at the Church of the Immigrants. He will be expecting me, as my priest back home in Ireland has forwarded a letter to him, and I carry a copy with me."

"Let me see it."

The overweight official, his face still flushed from the climb aboard, took from his pocket a pair of spectacles as John handed him the creased paper taken from his jacket pocket.

Once he had read it several times, the official handed it back to the boy.

"Captain, if there are no more immigrants, I suggest we take this young lad and his belongings to shore with us and see him on his way. Does that suggestion suit you, sir?"

Captain Foster took John to one side, signalling to the other man to spare him a minute with the boy.

"Now then, John, I want to be sure you are still keen on staying in America. If you have changed your mind, I will tell you now you can sail with me; learn seamanship, make a career of the sea. Now, tell me truthfully before these men get impatient."

Without hesitation John replied, "Thank you for your kind offer, Captain sir, but my mind is made up. I have planned and dreamed of this day for two long years. I want to go."

Captain Foster clapped him on his shoulder and told him to collect his belongings.

Padraig and Kevin helped him and told him he would be missed. John fought back tears then followed the Americans down the rope ladder to their waiting vessel. Once they left the shelter of Alhambra and headed for shore, he raised his hand in farewell to his comrades, a lump rising in his throat at yet another departure.

CHAPTER FOUR
NEW YORK

The oars dipped and rose as the boat carrying Mr Cornelius Taylor, Mr Henry Perrot and young John Walsh left Alhambra behind. John had never been so close to the water since he last went fishing back in Ireland and he sat gripping the seat to hold himself steady. The Inspector watched him, and seeing the boy was nervous, he reached and patted his leg.

"Well young man, what awaits you in your new venture? Have you family or friends here in America?"

"No sir. I am to meet with Padre Felix Varela of the Church of the Immigrants. He will know of me from the letter my priest back home sent him. I carry a copy."

"Of course, I saw it on board Alhambra. I have heard of Father Varela. He is a good man who has dedicated himself to helping Irish immigrants. I am told he even speaks your Gaelic tongue. Well, you are in luck, we can take you directly to him, we pass his church on our way, so never fear we will abandon you friendless in the city."

At this, Henry Perrot raised an eyebrow but saw Cornelius wink, and understood. After all, it would be a short detour only and he was happy to see the boy safely welcomed by the priest.

John fought back tears of relief as he thanked the inspector. The thought of having to find his way through the streets of New York had terrified him.

The boat pulled alongside the jetty and John watched as the oarsmen raised their oars, gliding alongside to allow one crew member to step out and fasten the rope to a mooring ring on the quayside. The three passengers climbed out, the boat rocking as the portly inspector struggled to disembark, failing to retain his dignity in the process. One of the oarsmen assisted him with a shove to his posterior and the red-faced gentleman turned to grunt a thank you. Henry Perrot was a lean and fit man and boarded the jetty gracefully then turned and offered his hand to John. As John clung onto his knotted bag of belongings with one hand, he accepted the proffered hand and was soon on the jetty. He was both nervous and exhilarated as he watched the boat pull away. He was now in America. He shook his head and smiled at his two companions.

"Now then John, we must find a cab. Ever travelled by horse-drawn cab, boy?"

"Never sir, though I have sat on many a horse-drawn cart. Bumpy it was too."

Cornelius Taylor laughed, causing his bulbous belly to shake under his ill-fitting waistcoat.

"Ah, this will be a more comfortable experience by far. Henry, be so good as to flag down a cab will you? I will rest my weary legs."

He perched with his voluminous bottom overhanging on a nearby bollard.

John gazed in wonder at the dockside of New York. He remembered how impressed he had been with the Dublin quayside. Here too, there were many ships, with masts obscuring the sky and the sound of the rigging melodic above the activities of the dock workers. Sailing ships were disembarking passengers, loading and unloading cargo, while small boats carried crew to and from vessels anchored in deeper water awaiting permission to come alongside. New-fangled steam ships blew smoke from their funnels, impressing the sailors on the sailing ships. John heard for the first time languages alien to him as passers-by spoke in Italian, German and Yiddish.

An approaching cab driver responded to Henry's upraised arm and the two steaming horses pulling the cab slowed to a stop, their hooves ringing on the cobblestones. John was fascinated by the driver. He had never seen a black man before though he had heard tell of them. When the driver smiled, John saw the whitest teeth he had ever seen, and when the man removed his cap to scratch his head he revealed his tightly curled hair.

"So, where to? The harbour master's office? Or will it be straight home?"

He had carried the two men before but he looked at John as he spoke.

"Stop by the office first then home via the Church of the Immigrants. We have another friend for Father Varela, just arrived from Ireland."

Henry climbed into the cab and pulled his superior in. John followed and was just able to squeeze in beside them. He was relaxing now, enjoying his new life, his anxieties had evaporated, replaced by excitement and awe. The cab driver urged the horses into a trot.

After pausing for Henry to call briefly at the harbourmaster's office, the journey took them through busy streets with shops and bars, laundries and stabling yards. Stalls were set up selling hot food and drink, second-hand clothes, boots and shoes and hawkers noisily shouted their wares.

Two children standing beside their mother as she called out "Hot corn, hot corn" moved closer to her as the cab passed them by and caught John's eye. For a moment he thought of his young brothers and sisters back home and he swallowed in an effort to prevent a lump forming in his throat. He drew himself up to remind himself that now he was a man, no longer a boy.

He was then distracted by a scruffy youth picking the pocket of a passing man who walked on, blissfully unaware of the theft. John was ready to shout out to the victim but the horses broke into a trot as the driver urged them on with his whip. This was no part of the city to linger. The streets became narrower, still busy with people but now the crowds had sullen faces, eyes darting about looking to make mischief or avert it. Women with babes wrapped in shawls strapped around their scrawny chests shuffled by, thin cries from some babes, others sleeping. Bare-footed children dressed in rags clung to the skirts of their mothers, their dirt-grained faces streaked with runs of pale flesh exposed by spilt tears.

The horses slowed once more to a walk.

"Where do you want me to stop, sir?" the driver shouted.

Cornelius heaved himself to the open window and recognising the street they were in, called out.

"Just around the corner. This is Chamber Street where you will find the old Dutch Reform Church, now known as the Church of the Immigrants. The rectory where the priest will be expecting us is at 23 Reade Street."

"Aye sir, I know it well. He is well known in these parts, a good man."

The cab turned into Reade Street and slowed to a halt. The weary horses snorted and tossed their heads. John moved forward in his seat in anticipation.

"Henry, be a good chap and alert the priest to our arrival. Now then John, remember to be effusive in your gratitude to this most noble of men. Gather up your belongings and go with Mr Perrot. I will remain here should the priest need to speak with me."

Cornelius held out his hand to John.

"I wish you good fortune, keep your wits about you, remain honest and work hard. Our country welcomes those who have aspirations to do well but try to steer clear of the lowlife who fill the tenements of Five Points, the roughest district in New York. It's full of villains and rogues."

He shook John's hand, clapped him on the shoulder and watched as the boy climbed down from the cab. John turned and thanked him, raised a hand in farewell and followed his escort.

He looked up at the clapboard house, its paint peeling from the woodwork and followed Henry Perrot up the steps to the front porch. It was now evening and daylight was fading. Henry raised the heavy knocker and let it fall, the sound echoing around them. Above the door, a glazed fanlight slowly filled with a soft light and they heard bolts being drawn back before the door opened and the light illuminated the porch. The oil lamp was carried by a tall, swarthy man dressed in sombre clothes wearing a large crucifix around his neck. Father Felix Varela smiled at John then spoke to Henry Perrot.

"Well now, who do we have here? I do believe this is young John Walsh from County Mayo, parishioner of Father Alastar Murphy?"

"Good evening, Father, yes you are correct, sir," replied Henry

"We have brought him directly to you from the Alhambra, at present at anchor awaiting a berth to unload her cargo. This young man impressed the captain so much, he was allowed to work his passage to fulfil his dream of settling in America. We saw no need to wait another day so Inspector Cornelius Taylor and myself, having been satisfied with our inspection of the vessel, offered to bring him to you according to his instructions in a letter he carries from his parish priest. So, here he stands."

"And so he does."

Father Varela shook first Henry's hand then grasped John's hand.

"Father Murphy recommends you well, young man. I understand that you read and write, fully conversant with the English language? And how is your Gaelic, boy?"

John was not sure how he should address a foreign priest.

"Your Holiness, the Gaeilge as we call it, is the language of the hearth at home with my parents and brothers and sisters but we were all schooled in English."

"John, only the Pope is called Your Holiness. Father is all you need call me, just as you do Father Murphy. Now, believe it or not, I speak a little Gaeilge, as you call it, myself. 'Fáilte go dtí Meiriceá is féidir, leat teacht ar sonas fíor anseo.' How was that then, did you fully understand or did I err in any way?"

"You welcomed me to America then said may I find true happiness here."

The priest laughed triumphantly.

"My lessons in the Irish language have served me well. Many of my new parishioners have only the Irish and so I took pains to learn a little to help them feel at home here, so far from your beautiful country. Now, take this lamp while I speak with the Inspector."

The boy took the opportunity to take in his surroundings whilst the three men said their farewells. The cab driver gave the horses a gentle flick with his whip and tugged gently on the reins to turn them back the way they had come. John held on tight to the sputtering lamp and wished he could have a hug from his Mam just then, or a pat on his head from his Pa. Tears stung his eyes so he wiped them away with his sleeve as he heard the priest walking back to the house.

Father Varela took the lamp from him and ushered the boy in. The hallway was dim and sparsely furnished, just a hallstand against the wall and a small table at the far end on which the priest stood the lamp. The patterned floor tiles were scrubbed clean and the walls were decorated with pictures of places strange to him. On either side of the passage were closed doors but the one leading to the rear of the house was ajar, allowing the lamplight to spread into the kitchen.

"Go in, go in, a bright fire burns in the grate to warm you. Now then, I imagine it is some time since you have eaten?"

Before John could reply, Father Varela said, "Yes, I am sure it is. Me too! I have some Irish stew to welcome you, how d'you fancy that then? My housekeeper, lovely woman with whom I try to converse in the Irish, made a lovely pot and left it to keep hot on the trivet by the fire. Warm yourself while I fill two bowls then we will sit at the table and become better acquainted."

As the priest ladled the steaming stew into the bowls, John looked around the room. The kitchen range shone black, with gleaming brass handles and threw out such a heat he stood back near to the table. A chenille tablecloth was partially covered by a smaller white cloth spread diagonally. Two smaller cloths were placed for each diner. John was to find out the purpose of these when he sat down. Father Varela took bread from a cupboard and spoons from a drawer in the dresser which was laden with fine dishes on its shelves then beckoned John to sit.

They sat with heads bowed as the priest said grace.

"Tiarna gabhaimid buichas leat as ár n-arán laithúil."

John was all too familiar with the simple prayer from school but there it had been said in English.

"Lord, we thank you for our daily bread."

Then the priest took hold of his napkin, shook it loose and laid it on his lap. John had never seen napkins before but he copied his host.

"Now tuck in boy, pretend you're at your Grandma's."

John needed no second bidding. The stew was better than any he had ever tasted. Back home they often had 'blind stew', a pot with no meat in, with whatever root vegetables their mother had to add to the potatoes. The meat in this stew was beef, juicy and tender, other ingredients were unfamiliar to him but he ate it all ravenously. He devoured every last mouthful then the priest offered him some bread.

"Here, mop your dish clean with this, the juice is too good to leave to the washing."

Both bowls were soon clean enough to put back on the shelf but John knew better than to do that. He stood up and carried the dishes into the scullery where he found a stone sink with a wooden draining board and a handpump. The hot water was from a large black kettle with a brass tap which hung close to the fire. Such luxury! At home a bucketful of water drawn from the well outside would have hung over the fire to be used for pot-washing once the cooking pot had been removed.

"Before you wash the pots, sit back down until we have had a drink. Now, you are too young for ale but I have some buttermilk or water from the tap. Which would you prefer?"

John could not resist the urge to try the kitchen pump so he was allowed to fill a beaker with fresh water. He was too polite to say it tasted strange, not at all like the water from the well at home, but he drank it down. As they sat enjoying the warmth from the fire and the full feeling in their bellies, Father Varela's head drooped on his chest and gentle snoring filled the silence. John stood up quietly and took the beakers into the scullery to wash them. Then he too tried to stifle a yawn. The priest stirred, rubbed his eyes and sat up straight.

"Well, I think bed is calling. Come, let me show you where you will be sleeping."

He lit two candles with a spill from the fire, poked the fire until it was just a small glow in the grate and blew out the oil lamp. Smoke curled lazily from the glass as John picked up his belongings and took a candle from the priest. Father Varela led the way up the bare stairs which creaked as they climbed them. Shadows followed them like unseen guests, filling John with dread. This house was so much bigger than the small cottage he had left behind. There, one candle sufficed to light the gloom. Here, the priest lit yet another candle to sit on a coffer on the landing through the night so the forbidding atmosphere was soon bathed in a warm glow.

John was shown into a small room with a bed covered in a pretty patchwork quilt, a bedside table for his candle and a chair for him to put his clothes. Never before had he known such comfort. Father Varela pulled the heavy curtains to hide the dark sky outside.

"How will this serve you? Cosy enough d'you think? I trust you will sleep well and when you arise in the morning you will find a bathroom next door. The bowl and jug are ready for use so after washing and dressing, return to the kitchen for breakfast. There you will meet my housekeeper, Widow Pierce, name of Molly. She comes every day to keep me fed and tidy. Now, God bless you and may the angels watch you in your sleep."

After the priest closed the bedroom door John undressed down to his worn undergarments then knelt beside the bed to pray for the safekeeping of his family, so far away.

CHAPTER FIVE
FIVE POINTS

A thin shaft of light penetrated a gap in the drawn curtains and nudged at John's eyelids as he lay sleeping. John screwed his eyes shut tight. The ship was still, no gentle rocking, no noisy shouts from the mate or grumbles from the crew. He opened his eyes to unfamiliar surroundings then remembered he was no longer at sea, sleeping in a bunk in the cramped fo'c'sle where the living quarters for the crew were, but in a warm bed in a room such as he had never ever slept in. He threw back the covers and shivered as his bare feet hit the floorboards and crossed to the window to draw back the curtains. Not used to seeing rooftops of other buildings, he stood and watched in wonder as birds alighted on nearby chimneys calling a greeting to him before flying away.

His need of the bathroom was urgent and he went into the next-door room to use the chamber pot before pouring water from the jug into the bowl and washing quickly. A towel hung on a rail; such luxury to have one for his sole use, not shared between the other members of his family. After drying himself he returned to the bedroom and dressed in a change of clothes from his bag then made his way downstairs to the kitchen where he could hear the priest talking and laughing and the voice of a woman answering. Two faces turned to him as he entered. Widow Pierce stood by the fire, a short, stout woman dressed in a black high-necked dress with long sleeves over which she wore her uniform, a crisp white pinafore. She held out her arms to John.

"Dear boy. What excitement it is to have you with us. Now then, I'm starved of news of Ireland so I am. Tell me, what d'you know of Wexford?"

Before John could escape from her hug she went on,

"Come and sit here at the table. Father has just finished his breakfast but he saved some porridge for you so sit, sit, you can stand to grow later."

"Pleased to meet you, Mrs Pierce, but I must tell you I know nothing of Wexford. I'm from County Mayo but I have been to Dublin where I was taken on as a crew member on the Alhambra, which I left yesterday."

"Well, would you hear the boy Father, he's been to Dublin! Capital city an' all! What was it like? Big? Noisy? Full of the posh people I imagine?"

"Now Molly, let the boy have his porridge before it gets cold. Then we can all get to know one another."

John sat at the table and picked up his spoon then recalled the previous night when the priest had said grace. He quickly remembered his manners, laid down the spoon and recited the same prayer while the priest and his housekeeper stood by.

"Oh, my lovely boy. That brings back memories of my boy...such a long time ago now. He was about your age, fifteen, sixteen when I lost him to the fever."

Molly dabbed away the tears welling in her eyes. She poured tea for John and herself; the priest shook his head at her offer of a cup but stood by listening to his young guest.

"Tell me more of Dublin."

She sat close to him, watching with a satisfied smile as he emptied his dish.

"Me and my younger brother, Daniel, went to Dublin to hear our hero speak, Daniel O'Connell. D'you know of him Mrs Pierce?"

"Aye, he's known here too boy for his standing up for justice."

"Well, he was arrested just as he was about to talk to the huge crowd. That's when I made up my mind to leave Ireland. And here I am."

"What of your brother, Daniel? Did he not want to come too?"

"Oh yes, ma'am, but he's just thirteen and far too young."

Molly winked at the priest.

"I persuaded him to return home and maybe sail himself in a few years' time."

Father Felix joined the conversation.

"Well, John, whenever he chooses to come he will receive the same welcome here in my house as you have had, be sure to write to him and tell him. In fact, now you have breakfasted I suggest you write a letter to your parents telling them of your safe arrival. They're sure to be worried sick, waiting for news of you."

The priest left the warmth of the kitchen and went to fetch paper and pen from his book-lined study along the hall. While he was gone, Molly went about her chores so John took the dishes into the scullery and washed them in a bowl of water ready - pulled from the pump.

"Here we are, use as many sheets of paper as you need. You have written with a pen before or just pencils?"

John wiped his damp hands on his jacket as he entered the kitchen.

"We did a lot of work on slates, Father, but I have written on paper with both ink pen and pencil."

"Which would you prefer then? Pencil? Good choice, you can write quicker with a pencil and so write a longer letter. I have a quick errand to run then when we are both done we will visit Five Points. You will have your eyes opened wide there boy, I guarantee. It is the part of New York where many immigrants first find lodgings. Now, where is my scarf? This November air is chilly and Mrs Pierce insists I wrap up warm."

Father Varela left John to his letter writing and went to fetch his cape from the hallstand. John heard the front door slam as the priest went out so he settled himself to his letter home.

Dear Mother and Father,

(John decided such an important letter as his first written in America warranted full and proper titles.)

You will be pleased, I feel sure, to know that I am safely arrived in The Americas.

The priest here, Father Felix Varela has made me very welcome and he thinks I should have no trouble finding a good paying job seeing as I can read and write in English. For that I know I have you both to thank, and I want you to know I truly appreciate the sacrifices you must have made to have us all schooled. My sea crossing was not without danger but you can be proud of your son who left Ireland a boy and arrived in America a man, having proven to my fellow crew members, the mate, the bosun and especially Captain Foster, that I have both courage and skills. In fact, the captain offered me a chance to remain as a member of his crew but sailing is not the life for me.

So far, this land appears to be a place of opportunity and I intend to do the very best I can to be successful. Today Father Varela is going to take me with him around his parish and I can't wait to meet my fellow Irishmen and learn how they have fared.

Tell Daniel to keep working hard at home and at school. The priest has assured me that my brother will receive the same welcome I had should he too choose to come here. Thank Father Murphy for me too, it is so comforting to know I can write to you through him and that he is willing for me to keep contact this way. He and Father Varela would get on very well. Give Eliza and Beatrice a big hug from me, kiss little Margaret and if the boys are not too big for one, give them the same.

I will write again soon. If you can spare a few moments to reply with your news, be sure your eldest son will be waiting for it.

May God take care of you all.

Your loving son,

John

He was reading through his letter when he heard the front door open then close as the priest returned carrying a large bundle tied with string.

"Well, that was a most satisfactory excursion John."

The bundle was placed on the kitchen table and the string removed. Neatly folded clothes for all ages were prevented from falling to the floor by John.

"The more prosperous of my parishioners, of which there are too few sadly, collect from their friends and families unwanted garments, some in need of a little repair but otherwise of excellent quality. Let's see now, what we may find to suit you, young John, to supplement your bagful from home."

Father Varela rummaged through the pile and held up a pair of britches, brown in colour made from a thick woollen material.

"I do believe the fabric used for these is tweed, maybe from Donegal, very popular here in America. What d'you think? Stand still while I hold them against you, see how the fit is. Well now, John, they seem ideal, just in need of a button replacing. Try them boy, while I see what else we have."

John blushed as he removed his own pants, glad that the priest was busy examining garments, setting aside some, and was oblivious to the boy's embarrassment at revealing his worn, patched undergarments. He stepped quickly into the tweed britches and was pleased with the fit. He beamed with delight when Father Varela glanced over his shoulder then turned to look the boy up and down.

"If I didn't know better, I would say they were made for you. Look, here is a jacket, patched elbows but that is a sign of a virtuous well-to-do family, waste not want not."

John took it, but when he discovered the sleeves were too long and the pockets almost out of reach, he shook his head with disappointment and began to remove it.

"No, no, wait. Look, just turn the sleeves back. There, is that not better? Before you know it you will grow into it, I promise."

"I feel so grand! Can they really be mine?"

"Of course, keep them on for today, see how you get on. If you find you like them, well they will be yours. Right, we will repackage the rest and carry it between us to meet some of the tenement dwellers who are most needy. I will just find Molly to let her know we will be out most of the day."

While John was alone, he examined his new clothes then dashed upstairs to fetch his cap and scarf. Then he and the priest bade farewell to Molly and left the house.

For a November day it was quite mild, the sun broke through the clouds and warmed John's face. As they walked, Father Varela told John of his plans.

"There is a printer I know who may well have work he can offer you. With your ability to read and write in English, you have a distinct advantage over many of the Irish immigrants who mostly use the Gaelic and have scant education. You will also need lodgings as I am sure you understand that my home is just a temporary refuge for you. There is a constant stream of people arriving from Europe and I do my best to assist as many of them as well as I am able."

They arrived at the corner of Reade Street and turned left into Broadway. John was awestruck as they passed fine big houses with so many windows hung with lace curtains and polished knockers on the doors. A couple had just left one house and the man hailed a passing cab. They were dressed in such fine clothes, the gentleman in a well-fitting suit with a cravat at his neck and a silver-topped cane held up for the cab driver to spot them, while the lady wore a full- skirted dress with a paisley shawl and carried a dainty parasol. John heard the cab driver ask, "Stewart's Department Store as usual sir?"

The gentleman nodded and helped his wife into the cab, the horses were told "walk on" and off they went.

A horse-drawn omnibus passed them full of elegantly dressed passengers. Carts laden with goods, men on horseback and other pedestrians filled the street and raised John's expectations of how his life was going to be so different. They passed inviting-looking bars and cafés full of laughing customers behind cut-glass windows which gleamed in the sunshine, sitting at tables with their friends sipping cups of tea or chocolate and eating dainty sandwiches. An imposing building caught John's attention as they approached it and Father Varela rested his hand on his shoulder, slowing him to a stop.

"Here we have a fine theatre, John, known as 'Niblo's Garden'. You can see the attractions on these advertising posters."

The boy's eyes widened when he saw pictures of ladies in short-skirted dresses displaying their ankles for all to see while hiding their faces by large feather fans, and men in frock suits with tophats held aloft.

"I believe it is called 'Burlesque and Variety' though I have never been a patron, not at all. Still, carriages and stagecoaches come from all over New York carrying the well-heeled citizens to be entertained here and the theatre helps other businesses and creates work. It is too expensive for my parishioners to enjoy, for which I am grateful. The building was once a popular café renowned for its excellent ice-cream and lemonade. A little musical entertainment on occasions added to its popularity which led the owner to build the Grand Saloon, a proper theatre."

John had never seen the like before. Smart, uniformed men stood at the entrance to ensure that no unwelcome unwashed urchins tried to sneak in.

They turned into Anthony Street, also a street for the prosperous, but as they neared the end they passed a house unloved and derelict which was being demolished. A woman, dressed in ragged clothes accompanied by two boys also in rags, staggered from the building almost bent double under their burden of salvaged timber.

"This family will sell the timber for firewood, maybe make enough from the sale to pay their rent and put a little food on their table. Hey, take care!"

The priest shouted as the family almost walked under an omnibus. The black driver cursed them and caught one of the boys with his whip in his effort to steer the horses clear.

As they walked, John noticed a significant decline in the grandeur of the properties they passed. The run-down dwellings had rum or grog shops on the lower floor with living quarters above. They were crowded with rough-looking men, some already intoxicated even though it was not yet midday. Women with children pulling at their skirts wore blank, pitiful expressions while the children were mostly bare-footed with matted hair and unwashed faces. They waited for their errant husbands to pass on what little money they had left for food. The priest had passed many times and the women knew it was unwise to beg from him but the children held out their hands anyway.

Father Varela sighed.

"Oh John, if you only knew how it pains me to walk by and leave those small outstretched hands empty but they are far too great in number I'm afraid. I do my best but it will never ever be enough."

With his head bowed, the priest strode on until they reached Orange Street.

"Well, here we are at the infamous Five Points. This iniquitous collection of poor dwellings is an abominable district which draws the poorest, meanest people when they arrive on our shores. Stay close by me, come, I will carry our precious bundle from here. Watch your pockets are not felt, for any trifle, even one of no value will be lifted by nimble fingers if you do not take care."

This street was narrow, the cobbles hardly visible under the garbage strewn about. Stalls selling such a variety of goods such as John had ever seen lined both sides of the road leaving very little room for passage. Second-hand clothes were piled on one stall with the stallholder eyeing Father Varela's bundle with hope. Another sold old bedding, old boots and other damaged household goods. Bruised apples were piled on the next stall and bundles of kindling on a stall with a young girl offering them to disinterested passers-by. A brazier burned and John heard the cry "hot corn, get your hot corn now" and watched, curious as a man purchased some and walked away, blowing on the cob then gnawing it as John would on a bone.

"We are to visit a family in Mulberry Street. A poor woman and her young children have been left destitute after her husband was murdered."

"Murdered!" exclaimed John. "What a dreadful thing to happen! Was the killer hanged?"

"Oh John, I fear I must tell you it is a wicked place here, murders are just everyday occurrences and the police are so afraid of the tenants, they fear for their own safety so justice is seldom served."

They turned into Cross Street which had a grocery shop on one corner with the sale of rum being its most lucrative trade. On the opposite corner, women and children waited with buckets to take turns collecting water from the pump which served the neighbourhood.

"The tenements here have no running water or indeed no sanitation. How much better it would be if the residents drank the water they draw rather than the grog they buy."

Cross Street was lined on both sides by tall grim-looking buildings opening directly onto the street. As they passed open doors, disgusting smells wafted out from the dark interiors making John cough and bury his nose in his sleeve. Father Varela looked down at him.

"These obnoxious smells are so prevalent we must all get used to them I'm afraid. Now, here we are at Mulberry Street."

Nothing could have prepared John for the dwellings here. Three-storey tenements with timber balconies running the length of each floor, partitions between the individual living quarters providing an open space where washing was drying, and men and women hung over the rails shouting and cursing the people below. Rag pickers sat in one corner of the yard, sorting their morning's pickings. Rags, bones, glass and metal could be sold to paper and soap producers, to metal workers and other manufacturers. Children played in the filth while others received beatings from angry parents. To access the tenements, a wooden outdoor staircase of dubious strength must be climbed, almost all of the steps occupied by sullen, wary tenants, their dull eyes weighing up the possibility of mugging the two outsiders. Fortunately, Father Varela's cassock provided protection but the stout walking stick he carried was also a deterrent.

John resisted holding his nose even though the stench was overpowering. They climbed to the top floor and at one of the open doors the priest knocked and called, "Mrs Kelly? Are you there Mrs Kelly?"

He nudged the door wide open but little light penetrated the darkness within. They walked cautiously in, taking care as they had difficulty making out if there was furniture they might bump into. Embers glowed in the stove offering a feeble light until their eyes became accustomed to the gloom.

A woman sat close to the stove nursing a sleeping child. Movement from a bed in the corner alerted them to two older children, huddled under old overcoats.

"Are you alright, Mrs Kelly? No one sick I hope?"

The woman shook her head.

"No, Father, not sick. Well, only sick of being hungry. The few coins I had were taken by the landlord with me being overdue on the rent. The kids had lean pickings in the streets last evening so we have not eaten for two days. Except the baby, I still have milk for her, so I have."

John remembered his chubby little sister, now a toddler and fed well on bacon and potatoes.

"Well, maybe what I have here will be of use to you. There may be one or two garments suitable for yourself and the children, then any of no use I feel sure you can sell."

The dim light was enough for John to see the delight on the woman's face. She stood up and carefully lay the baby on the bed with her brothers and put her finger to her lips to be sure they would make no noise to waken the little girl. Then she rummaged through the priest's bundle, lifting clothing up and carefully replacing it before examining more. A long-sleeved, high-necked navy dress made from heavy cotton took her attention and she held it against her skinny body.

"I think that will serve you well, Mrs Kelly; and here, look, a beautiful fringed shawl to wear with it now that December is almost here. As for the men's clothes, sadly I know you have no need of them but they should fetch a good price. I leave them all for you to do with as you will."

The priest put his hand in his pocket and offered some coins to Mrs Kelly.

"Here, I can give you the price of some bread and maybe a jug of milk to give you the strength to go out and do your selling. Please take it with the Lord's blessing."

John felt such pride at the priest's kind gesture. He smiled at the poor woman's tears of joy.

"Bless you, Father, whatever would I do without your help? I'm not even able to come to Mass just now but you still visit. Still, it is my cross and I shall bear it for the sake of my children. But tell me something Father, who is this smiling young man you have with you? Is he training for the Priesthood maybe?"

John spoke before Father Varela could answer.

"No, Mrs Kelly, not at all. I have just yesterday arrived here in America from Ireland and Father Varela has been so welcoming, took me into his house and tells me he might help find me work."

"I wish you all the luck in the world. Do you have a skill maybe?"

"Only my schooling. I can read and write in English."

"Fancy! Well now, you should have no trouble getting hired. Few tenants here speak much English let alone read and write it. Can you tell me, what news from Ireland for a woman so far from family and friends in Cork? I do so much miss the place."

"Ireland is fine just now, Mrs Kelly, but brothers and sisters keep coming and the family home grows no bigger so I thought I would make a fresh start along with so many others having to leave Ireland. I do not know Cork but I could well have sailed from there. It's just that I was in Dublin and made my mind up there and then to find a ship. I was fortunate to be taken on as a crew member so my passage was free which means I do have a little money until I get work."

The sound of footsteps on the stairs interrupted the talk of Ireland. A huge black man, even taller for wearing a stove-pipe hat, entered the room, removing his hat out of both courtesy and necessity to fit through the door.

Mrs Kelly ushered him in to stand by the dying embers of the fire.

"Father Varela, John, this is Mr Jonah Brown who tried in vain to save my husband Joe's life the night he was murdered. He carried him home when he came across him lying in a narrow passageway and found his way after asking directions from anyone who knew Joe."

The priest held out his hand and Jonah smiled at the two strangers. His smile lit up his dark features and John could not take his eyes off him.

"Good to meet you, Mr Jonah Brown, it is always a pleasure to meet a man with such a big heart. Did you know Joe before that night?"

Jonah turned his hat in his hand and shook his head, his smile fading.

"No, not at all. I just wish I had been on the scene sooner to deal with the thugs who left him for dead. And him with a young family too. I am here with a request for you Mrs Kelly. With the priest here to advise you, I would ask you if you would consider having me as a lodger for a short time? I work nights so you and the children would not be inconvenienced and I would be no trouble to you in the day, asleep in the corner."

The woman looked at Father Varela.

"This is not uncommon, Father, the rooms here house several families, but would the Church frown on a widow woman taking another man into her home?"

The priest asked Jonah, "What is your work that keeps you out all night? Good honest work I'm sure, but I'm curious to know?"

"I am indeed honestly employed. I act as a watchman at the docks, taken for my height and threatening looks."

Here he scowled showing a mean face. His laughter rumbled through his frame and his shoulders shook.

"If they only knew the softness of my heart. But my lodgings have become uncomfortably crowded and I thought me and Mrs Kelly could both benefit from sharing."

"What about the children? Will they be wary of you?"

The older of Mrs Kelly's sons, Stewart, spoke up.

"We have seen this man when we go rag-picking, Ma. He has always smiled and told us of the best places to search. We like him!"

John saw how the big man looked with affection on the children and how they smiled back at him.

"I see no reason, Mrs Kelly, why this arrangement would not suit you both. Have my blessing by all means and be assured the church will not judge you harshly."

Mrs Kelly's face lost its strained expression and she beamed with delight.

"That's settled then! Shake my hand, Mr Brown, and consider yourself my tenant. And thank you, Father, for your support. Now that is settled, when will you be joining us, Mr Brown?"

"Well, Ma'am, I can fetch my few belongings and be back within the hour. Would it be too forward of me to ask you to call me Jonah? Naturally, you will still be Mrs Kelly to me?"

"Eileen is my name Jonah, but yes, I agree you should always call me Mrs Kelly if you don't mind. That way there will be no unnecessary gossip from the neighbours."

Father Varela held out his hand to Jonah.

"Glad you can be of help to one another in a true Christian spirit. I think our work here is done, John, so we will leave these good people as I have somewhere else I need to take you. Until next time, Mrs Kelly, boys, Mr Jonah Brown."

CHAPTER SIX
JACOBS PRINTERS

The priest and John walked back towards Cross Street.

"I have someone to introduce you to, John, Mr Jacobs, who has a small business on Anthony Street. He is a printer by trade and his business is prospering but he often complains to me he has more work than he can manage yet he has difficulty finding anyone suitable to become an apprentice, there being a lack of educated youngsters in these parts. How do you feel about the prospect of learning a little about printing, young man?"

As they walked, John found keeping pace with the priest quite a challenge. Father Varela was accustomed to leaving the vicinity of Five Points as fast as he was able once his mission there was completed.

"I think I should like that very much, Father. I have noticed that there are many people living here but few of them working. Is there no work for them or are they not interested in working?"

"They come in such numbers, John. The few of them who arrive with sufficient funds soon move on. This is a vast country with so much opportunity for a man to make himself a comfortable living. However, those who arrive destitute are fortunate if they get a roof over their heads and food for their bellies. When they do make a little money by an odd day's labouring or searching for scrap to sell, the men often squander the few coins they earn, drinking in one of the many rum shops while their wives struggle at home with children to look after. If they are lucky, the women may have some sewing work they take in to help with their rent money. Yes, they do pay rent for the squalid hovels they are forced to live in. You should be grateful that your parents had you educated, because you have such an advantage."

"In my letter home I did just that, Father. I thanked them both and I promise I will make the best of my good fortune."

They soon arrived at the printing shop. John was disappointed, it was nowhere as grand as he had expected. He knew nothing of print shops but in his mind he had imagined an imposing building with a shop window on the ground floor displaying books, leaflets and the like. Instead, the entrance to the three-storey building was a plain wooden door with a sign 'Jacobs Printer' in old-fashioned lettering nailed to it. A small, dusty window alongside the door revealed the interior was dimly lit and he could hear the regular sound of machinery from within. Father Varela knocked with his stick on the door several times until the sound of the printing press ceased. The door was opened by an elderly man with a permanent stoop whose face lit up with pleasure when he saw the priest.

"Felix, how good to see you. Please, come in, come in. You have company today I see. Well, let me shut the door and we can become acquainted inside."

The hallway was piled high with freshly printed pamphlets and it was a squeeze to pass them. Mr Jacobs ushered them into his busy workshop and led them through the back to his living quarters.

The smell of ink filled the room, not an unpleasant smell and one that John would carry on his clothes like a badge in the coming months.

"Do you recall bemoaning to me the lack of young, willing, smart young men you would hire if you could? Well, here is John Walsh, just arrived from Ireland and in need of work. Now, he is not just in need of work but comes equipped for work; he can both read and write in English! Does this not astonish you?"

The elderly printer beamed.

"Now, that news excites me. Shall we have some tea and we can discuss the boy's possible employment?"

As the elderly man swung the kettle back over the fire to return to the boil, John looked around. The room had everything a man could want for comfort. In front of the fire stood two old, shabby leather chairs. Mr Jacobs asked the priest to sit in one and he fetched a small stool for John. The steam from the kettle soon prompted the printer to heave himself out of his chair and with the gait of a man suffering from arthritis, he poured the boiling water into a large china teapot. From the corner of the room which served as a kitchen, he fetched three pretty china cups and saucers.

"How do you like your tea, John? Felix and I drink it as it is but I do have a little milk if that is your preference?"

"With milk, please, sir, if it is no trouble," replied John.

"Not a bit of trouble, a growing boy needs his milk. Our growing is long done isn't it, Felix? I myself am at the shrinking age now."

After sipping from the steaming cup of the strong black brew, Mr Jacobs quizzed John.

So, you have an education and you can read and write in English?"

"Yes sir, I was taught at a school where our native language was forbidden so we soon learnt English."

"Good, good, well some good can come from persecution I suppose. How about you read for me, I think I can find something suitable. Wait while I search through my books. I have the Talmud of course, but it is not in English."

Father Varela spoke up.

"I carry my missal, perhaps you can read from that, John?"

The small worn prayer book was produced from the pocket of the priest's robe and handed to John.

John was familiar with the Latin words and began to read but was interrupted by Mr Jacobs.

"No, no, I do not mean to be offensive but I need to hear your English. Wait, I'm sure to find something. Here, have you heard of Charles Dickens, John? He is very famous now, oh yes, even here. I have a book which suits me well, Oliver Twist...now then Chapter Twenty-Five, about Mr Fagin."

John found the chapter and began reading, stumbling over one or two words unfamiliar to him.

"While these things were passing in the country workhouse, Mr Fagin sat in the old den – the same from which Oliver had been removed by the girl – brooding over a dull, smoky fire. He held a pair of bellows upon his knee, with which he had apparently been end..."

"Let me see," said Felix. "Endeavouring."

"*Endeavouring,*" continued John, "*to rouse it into more cheerful action.*"

"Excellent, well done, you read very well. Maybe when you come to work for me you would care to read to me if we have a quiet spell? My eyes find the print too small these days. I shall be hiring you for your eyes do you know that? As well as your skills in English!"

As they sat by the fire drinking their tea, old Ben Jacobs asked John when he thought he might start in his new job.

John turned to Felix for advice.

"Well, John, as I have told you, there will soon be new immigrants needing my assistance, so the sooner we find you lodgings the sooner you can start."

Old Ben's face lit up.

"Now, about the boy's lodgings; as you can see, I live here alone, just here on the ground floor, in fact. It is a few years since I ventured up the stairs so I cannot vouch for the suitability of the rooms but you are welcome to see for yourself. Would you care to? Just be careful on the stairs, although a nimble boy like you should find no difficulties with them."

The old man stood up and beckoned for them to follow.

He pointed to where a steep staircase was partly hidden behind an old curtain.

"There are two rooms which, as far as I can remember, still have one or two pieces of furniture. Go and explore, see for yourself."

John did not hesitate and he climbed the stairs to where a hatch over his head required a strong arm to lift it, offering access to the upper floor. Old Ben Jacobs and Felix stood at the foot of the stairs and watched as he disappeared from view. They smiled as they heard him walking around on the bare floorboards.

The rooms were gloomy, very little light penetrated the small windows. John carefully swept aside the draped cobwebs covering the windows and the last rays of the evening sun lit the dark corners.

"Do you need a lamp? Can you see well enough?" called Ben.

"No sir, I can see just fine. There is a small iron bedstead and a chest of drawers. If I may, I would love to make this my lodging."

John remembered the little stone house in Ireland. The whole family had shared a room not much larger than this. He imagined his mother's joy if she had such a place to make her own.

"I would be more than comfortable here, I am speechless!"

Felix looked up to see John peering down and beamed with delight.

"I never imagined all your problems could be solved so easily! Well, come on down and discuss it with Mr Jacobs."

They returned to sit by the fire and Ben Jacobs asked what was required to make the rooms fit for John.

"I know I have spare bedding somewhere, if you can come back tomorrow you can find them maybe. Also, I could tell from your footsteps the floorboards are bare, I can promise you there will be a rug or two. A good sweep and dusting shouldn't take you long. I know you will ask about rent. Well now, let me see, you pay me with your company and as each day ends I will ask you to read to me. There will be errands to run, too, besides your daily work duties for which of course you will receive a wage. Can we shake on a good deal for us both?"

Ben Jacobs held out his arthritic hand and John took it and gave it a firm shake, smiling broadly.

"Easy boy, you don't know your own strength, mind my poor old bones. Now Felix, does it suit you if John comes here to live and work tomorrow?"

"This is more than we could have hoped for eh, John? This arrangement will suit you both."

"Take my hand too, Ben, I will be more gentle than John!"

Felix turned to John.

"I think if we go home now and have supper which I know Molly will have left prepared for us, you can sleep tonight in last night's bed then you can return after breakfast tomorrow. Does that sound agreeable to you, Ben?"

"Yes, yes," said Mr Jacobs. "I will see you tomorrow, John."

He rubbed his hands together, delighted at the day's events then stood up to show his visitors out. Dusk was falling as the priest and the boy walked briskly without stopping back to the church house. They had no desire to be caught in the notorious Five Points after dark.

The hall light cast a welcoming glow as they approached the priest's front door. Once inside, Father Varela removed his cape and scarf, hung them on the hallstand and replaced his cane in with the umbrellas. John hung his newly acquired coat up and they both went through into the kitchen. Molly Pierce had left their supper warming in the oven and left for home before darkness fell, as was her custom.

After they had eaten the meat and potato pie followed by rice pudding, John took the dishes into the scullery to wash and then he returned to the fireside and was about to speak when he saw Felix had his head dropped onto his chest, gently snoring. The fire had burnt low in the grate so to be sure it would still be lit for Mrs Pierce the next morning, he stoked it carefully and closed the damper. The priest stirred but remained asleep so John turned the lamps down low and took himself off to bed.

He lay awake for some time, imagining his new position as a printer's apprentice – how grand that sounded and he smiled, picturing the delight on his parents' faces if he could only tell them in person. The thought of his home and family in Ireland saddened him so he turned his thoughts to his new lodgings. The two rooms he would occupy would be like a palace after he had swept and mopped, dusted and polished, and made it all spick and span. He fell asleep dreaming of his bright future.

Father Varela woke up several hours later to find himself alone and the dishes and fire seen to. He blew out the lamps and retired to bed. Upstairs, he peeped around the door of John's room. The sleeping boy never heard the creak of the priest's footfall on the landing or noticed the dim light turn to darkness as the lamp outside his room was extinguished.

***

At breakfast the following day, the priest and John discussed the lodgings.

Father, I am to have two rooms all to myself and there is a bed so I shall want for nothing!"

"I'm pleased to hear it. Now, if I were to draw you a map of the route we took yesterday, do you think you could find your way without me? I have urgent church business and sick parishioners to visit."

John spooned the last of his porridge into his mouth before answering.

"I found my way to Dublin so I'm sure I will have no trouble with the help of your map finding Mr Jacobs' place again."

"Good. Oh, what about your belongings, can you carry them on your own?"

John nodded.

"I will do as I did in Ireland. I will wear as many garments as will be comfortable. I don't have much but the rest I can carry in a bundle. I've seen tinkers with sticks over their shoulders to carry their goods. Maybe you have a spare stick I could borrow?"

The priest wiped his mouth on his napkin, pushed away his chair and stood up.

"Come with me. Let's see what is in the stand in the hall."

John copied the priest, wiping his mouth after gulping down the last of his tea and followed Father Varela.

The umbrella stand was of blue and white porcelain and held an assortment of umbrellas and walking canes. The priest drew one or two out and turned them in his hands. He chose a large black umbrella and was about to open it to check it for faults when John quickly stopped him. "No, no sir, Father sir, you must never open an umbrella indoors, it brings bad luck!"

Felix laughed but to pacify the boy he took it out of the front door.

69

"Is it still unlucky on the front porch, John? I think not."

The umbrella opened with a little effort on the priest's part but after checking it carefully no moth holes or tears were found. The handle had a carved head of a grim-looking man with fierce eyes. It reminded John of Mr O'Leary, the mate on the Alhambra so he knew from experience a frightening face need not be feared.

"How about this one then? Will it carry your bundle? The hooked nose will ensure the knot won't slip."

He handed it to John to try it. After opening and shutting it several times John thanked the priest for the loan.

"That's settled then, you may keep this one, I have several more as you can see. It never fails to amaze me how many members of my congregation forget their canes, their umbrellas and even gloves as they leave church. Some get reunited with their owners but these belong to parishioners who attend Mass rarely or to others who have moved on, to bright futures or other places including heaven and sadly, some even to hell."

Mrs Pierce came downstairs to find the door open and John talking to Father Varela on the front porch.

"What's this then, the wind is blowing through the house! Can you not come in and keep the heat from escaping!"

"John is leaving us today, Molly. Gather your things, John, and I will draw the map I promised."

Mrs Pierce busied herself in the kitchen until she heard John come downstairs. She met him at the foot of the stairs and hugged him to her bosom.

"Well, my boy, I wish you all the very best of luck in your new position. It's been a real pleasure meeting you, so it has. No doubt I will see you at Mass some day? Oh, wait now, I have something for you."

She hurried back to the kitchen and came back with a packet in her hands.

"Here are some griddle scones I baked, you can share them with Mr Jacobs. Hold still, I will put them in your pocket for you, I can see you have your hands full."

He was so overwhelmed with all the kindness that John felt a lump rise in his throat and tears prick his eyes.

"Go on now, boy, before I keep you for myself. Be a good boy, learn from your master and give him no reason to scold you. God bless you, John."

A wet kiss was planted on his cheek then he headed back to the door which Father Varela held open.

"Goodbye until I see you in church. Thank you, Father, for all your kindness."

Felix shook John's free hand then watched him walk down the street until he turned a corner and was out of sight.

The priest turned his mind to the arrival of the next ship carrying immigrants needing his help then hurried inside to fetch his cape.

CHAPTER SEVEN
JOHN'S EMPLOYMENT

John walked with the map in his left hand and his umbrella carrying his possessions in their bundle slung over his right shoulder. He had no fear of the damp November air chilling his bones as the several layers of clothes he wore kept him warm.

The streets were already busy with horse-drawn carriages and omnibuses weaving through the crowds of pedestrians. Drivers sounded their horns and shouted abuse while the horses, with ears back and steaming nostrils, obeyed the whip and the pull on the reins. John kept into the side of the road as best he could, stepping over the occasional drunk sleeping off the excesses of the previous night's visit to the grog shop. Stallholders shouted their wares, mothers snatched at the hands of wandering children then clipped them around the ears for their carelessness.

The morning mist had lifted by the time he reached the printing shop and sunshine broke through the clouds. He stopped and studied the building. The sign hung crooked on the door and the windows hardly served to allow light in they were so dirty with dust from the road. He decided that one of his duties would be to clean the property inside and out. He found the door ajar a little so as he pushed it open he called out to the old printer to announce his presence.

"Mr Jacobs, sir? It is John. May I come in?"

The sound of the printing press drowned his words so John pushed the door shut and walked further into the shop. The old man had his back to John as he worked so the boy waited, watching the printing press as it worked rhythmically before slowing to a stop. John coughed loudly to attract the old printer's attention.

"Ah, John, you are here. Good. I have a commission I must finish so while I do that I suggest you make your rooms comfortable, eh? Follow me, I will show you where you can find everything you need."

John followed the old man as he shuffled through to his living quarters.

"When we are both done, we will eat. Now, here you have a broom, a mop and bucket and if you look under the stone sink there, see, behind the curtain, you should find blocks of soap, a scrubbing brush and cloths for use as dusters."

"Please sir, I want to thank you properly for your kindness. I cannot tell you how excited I am to have found both work and lodging so soon after landing. I promise you I will work hard and be no trouble."

"I know that, my boy, I have not lived to this great age without learning how to tell a good man from a bad. Take what you need, the kettle is on the hob ready for you but first go up the steep stairs and open the hatch, save you struggling."

The old man turned to a tallboy standing against the wall. It was almost as tall as John and had three small drawers with six large drawers below.

"The top drawers are empty but in the lower drawers you will find spare bedding I no longer use. Help yourself to anything you need. Now, let me think. Where are the spare blankets? You get what you want while I have a rummage."

John did as he was told. With his bundle still over his shoulder and the map safely in his pocket, he climbed the stairs and pushed the trap door open. He swung his bundle free and carried it to the bed then removed both jackets he was wearing and hung them on a strong wooden peg protruding from the roof timbers. He struggled out of one pair of trousers and folded them with his other clothes.

When he returned to the ground floor, he found Mr Jacobs on his knees trying to free a trunk from under his bed. He pulled it a little way then rested.

"May I help you, sir? Let me pull it out for you"

The old man did not argue, he acknowledged the young boy was strong while he was weak. The trunk was made from metal with a lock in the lid.

"I have a bundle of keys somewhere," the old man sighed.

"Where do you imagine they might be John? Any ideas?"

"We had no use for keys, sir, back home in Ireland. Our doors were never locked, but I saved from my earnings to come here by putting the coins into an old brown jug hidden in a crack in the pigsty wall. But you don't have a pigsty…"

"Of course. That's it. A teapot, I have another one somewhere. Can you search among the crockery and china in the dresser cupboards, John? I know I have far more crockery than I need for my daily use but it was my wife's pride and joy, she brought it with us when we left our homeland so I have kept it."

John opened the cupboard doors and found pretty china stacked on the shelves. He searched in bowls and jugs, finding nothing but at the back he spotted a teapot. He lifted it carefully out and something made a chinking noise inside. He removed the lid and upturned it to shake out the contents. Several bunches of keys fell out along with a soft velvet pouch with a drawstring top.

The old man picked up the pouch and stroked it with his bony fingers before teasing the drawstring free. Fumbling to extract the contents, he shook with emotion as he tipped several rings out into his hand. He sat in silence for a while unable to speak. When he did speak there was a tremor in his voice.

"Do you know what I have here, John? Ruth's rings, my wife and I were betrothed and married with these rings."

He turned the rings over in his hands.

"See how small her hands were? Such delicate fingers she had. We had a happy marriage but sadly never blessed with children. Such a shame, Ruth loved children but it was not meant to be."

He straightened his shoulders as best he could with his bent spine and said, "Enough of reminiscing, back to the here and now. Let me see the keys. I remember this one," he held an old iron key out. "I think this fits the trunk. Try it boy."

The key fitted the lock but resisted John's efforts to turn it. He tried with both hands and slowly, with a grinding noise, the key turned in the lock and they were able to lift the lid. Inside, the contents were hidden beneath a fringed shawl. Mr Jacobs lifted the shawl out gently and wrapped it around his shoulders reciting softly, "Barukh atah Adonai, Eloheinu, melekh ha'olam asher kidishanu b'mitz'votav v'tzivanu l'hit'ateif ba-tzitzit."

He glanced at John who was looking puzzled.

"That means in English, 'Blessed are you, Lord, our God, sovereign of the universe, Who has sanctified us with His commandments and commanded us to wrap ourselves in the tzitzit.'

"This was, is, my prayer shawl, John, called a tallit. I have had no use for it since Ruth's death. My visits to the synagogue ceased there and then. My faith was tested and found wanting."

He brushed his hand over the shawl and repeated the prayer once more before putting it to one side.

Books, a framed faded painting of a landscape from Jacob's homeland and an elaborated candle holder rested on folded blankets.

Ben picked up the candlestick.

"Have you seen one of these, John? It is a candle holder called a menorah. We would light it every Sabbath to bring joyous light into the home. See, it still has wax from the candles in it. Here, take it and put it safe, and the picture. The books I will look at later. Now then, we can see what state the blankets are in."

John carried the candlestick with care and laid it on the printer's bed with the painting.

"Shake out the blankets, John, let us check for moth holes, though I doubt moths could have found their way into the chest."

John unfolded both blankets and found them to be sound. He sniffed an unfamiliar smell.

Ben smiled.

"That is camphor wood you smell, cut from a tree grown far, far away. It repels moths and the like. Very useful. Did you have success finding sheets? Good, well I will get back to my work and let you prepare your rooms for comfort. Later, we shall eat."

John worked all morning in his rooms with the small windows open to help disperse the dust he raised with his sweeping. Then he mopped the floors, cleaned the windows, dusted the bedhead and chest of drawers before making up his bed and stowing his clothes in the drawers. When he was satisfied with his work he descended the ladder and found Mr Jacobs had finished work before him and was preparing a meal of bread and cheese.

John sat at the table and wondered if he should say grace as he had with Felix. He decided it would be polite to do so and he put his hands together, closed his eyes and said a prayer to himself. Mr Jacobs waited for him to finish before setting the food on the table.

"Help yourself, John, you do like cheese I hope? I eat it every day, never get bored with it. Here, have a slice or two of bread. The kettle won't be long now then perhaps you would make some tea? In the old pot of course."

John suddenly remembered the griddle cakes.

"Oh, excuse me, sir, I have something from Mrs Pierce."

He climbed the stairs to his rooms and was pleased to find he had not squashed the cakes. Back downstairs he unwrapped the gift and watched Mr Jacobs' face light up with pleasure.

"How kind, how thoughtful of Mrs Pierce. We shall have one each now and save some for tomorrow, what do you say, John? And as I think that we will soon be good friends we must be less formal. I would like you to call me Ben. No argument, I know I am old enough to be your grandfather. So, agreed? Ben it is then?"

They enjoyed each other's company as they ate lunch. Ben told the boy how he came to America after fleeing the land in which his family had lived peacefully for generations which was acquired by Russia. Jews were expected to convert to Orthodox Christianity or leave.

"That was back in 1821, so we sailed from Odessa with many others and settled here.

"Ruth was sad to leave her elderly parents but they were too frail to travel with us and blessed our departure. We never had contact with them after that. Maybe they moved elsewhere... maybe they died soon after. Eventually Ruth never spoke of them but I often saw tears on her cheeks when she prayed…"

They sat in silence for a while.

"It is a strange thing, but eating is so much more enjoyable when we have company, don't you think? Working alone, sleeping alone I can accept but dining alone I have always found to be a cheerless part of the day."

"I know what you mean, Ben, food tastes so much better when it is shared."

"But what of Ireland, John? Tell me about your family."

"Well, Ben, sir…"

"I have been knighted, eh? Sir Ben, sounds too pompous for me John, plain old Ben will do."

"I am from Count Mayo, on the west coast of Ireland. My parents have a small piece of land where we grow potatoes and cabbages and fatten pigs up for the rent money. I am the eldest child then there is Daniel, Eliza, Patrick, Bridget, Joseph, and baby Margaret. The small stone house is not big enough for so many so I chose to leave and here I am."

"Well, what a fine family! You will be missed I am sure but the house will still ring with the happy sound of children. How did you know Father Felix?"

"My priest, Father Murphy had heard of him from other Irish immigrants and of how he helped them when they arrived so he wrote to him telling me of my arrival. And here I am!"

After their meal, John cleared away the dishes and washed them while Ben sat quietly to digest his food. Soon the old man was dozing so John took the opportunity to clean the front window. The light flooded in, exposing the cobwebs and dust around the printing machine so while the machine was still, John dusted and polished it until he heard a movement behind him.

"Who would have thought this gloomy old place could look so good? Well done, John, good boy. Now I am rested, let me show you the workings of my old printing machine."

The printing press stood taller than John and just as long. Ben showed him the frame in which raised letters were set. He pointed out how to recognise the inverted letters then set him a task of laying out his own name. The pads were inked and a dampened sheet of paper placed between two frames.

"This one is called a frisket and the other is a tympan, you will soon learn the names for the different parts, John. So, let's print your name, eh? See if you have set the letters correctly. See this long handle? We call it 'the devil's tail'. Wind the handle and we shall see your first work as a printer's apprentice."

John turned the handle first one way then back again. Ben lifted the paper out from the frame while it was still damp and carefully laid it on a bench where they were both able to study it. JOHИ MALSH it read.

"Well, two letters wrong is not bad for a first attempt! You will improve with practice."

John then watched Ben work. It seemed so effortless so he tried to memorise the sequence of tasks. He helped by preparing the ink, dampening the sheets of paper and taking turns at winding the handle. By the time Ben was satisfied that he had completed his work for the day, the light from the window was almost gone and John was sent to light the lamps.

After supper, Ben asked John to read to him once more and he settled in one chair by the fire while the boy sat opposite him. Ben passed the copy of 'Oliver Twist' and asked John to start at the beginning. They passed a companionable hour before bedtime.

Bidding Ben a goodnight, John carried a candle to light his way upstairs to his cosy rooms. John said his prayers then climbed into bed and pulled the blankets up under his chin. He went to sleep trying to recite the machinery parts to himself.

The relationship between man and boy grew from respect to friendship as the months passed. Through the dark winter nights John needed no bidding to light the lamps or stoke the fire. His printing skills grew and his reading improved. Felix called when he was passing and brought more books for their enjoyment. John shopped for their food and soon learnt where the best stalls offered fresh fruit and vegetables. He found a butchers' shop rented by a fellow Irish man. The local baker knew old Ben well and would save loaves still warm from the oven for him. He always shopped in daylight on Ben's advice. The streets could be very dangerous after dark.

CHAPTER EIGHT
LEAVING NEW YORK 1845

Two years passed and John's skills on the old hand-operated press improved so he took over most of the work, allowing Ben to rest. The elderly man was becoming very frail but he was at hand to help John if he had any difficulties. The work was endless, printing posters for the theatre, wanted notices for the police force and pamphlets for would-be politicians. Very few of the wanted criminals were ever caught. The residents of Five Points served their own justice on murderers, thugs and child exploiters. They always shook their heads when shown a villain's portrait but as soon as the representatives of the law left, the tenement dwellers sought out the killers. Some of the killers were beyond the grasp of even these folk. Often as not, they were members of gangs which ran wild and became untouchable.

One of the posters John printed was a rough drawing of a brute, said to be of Irish descent, who had snatched a young girl of fourteen as she walked home from her work as a housemaid in Broadway. Witnesses claimed they saw a man and a girl arguing but took them for father and daughter. The man had dragged the girl away, protesting. Her bruised and battered body had been found two days later. She had been violated and the purse she always carried was not with the body. John had been on nodding terms with the girl, Josephine Conroy; she was often on her way home when John shopped late in the afternoon. He studied the drawing of the wanted man and memorised it.

Father Varela called for a brief visit one morning and found the old printer asleep in his bed while John worked the printing machine.

"Has Ben been unwell? He looks so grey lying there. How is he eating? Enough I hope?"

Ben opened his eyes at the sound of the priest's voice. He saw the concerned face studying him.

"I eat a little, Felix, my good friend John here insists I eat, be sure of that. Not that I have much appetite these days. John, be so good as to finish what you are doing then make Felix some tea, and yourself of course. None for me though."

His voice trailed off but he took hold of Felix's hand and spoke in a whisper.

"I would speak with you, Felix."

Then he called to John.

"John, run to the baker's, fetch some cake for our guest. I am sure Felix will watch the kettle for you."

John did as he was bid although he found it strange to be running an errand so early in the day and having to leave his work. He left the press idle and put on his jacket.

Ben pointed to the dresser.

"I think you will find coins there sufficient for a slab of cake. Hurry back, won't you?"

After the boy had gone, Ben asked Felix to prop him up in bed.

"Felix, my days are nearly done. I worry about John, he is too young to be left on his own and anyway the printing work is slowly being lost to the mechanical printers. Hand-operated machines are considered old-fashioned now. He told me he turned seventeen last week, did you know?"

Felix shook his head.

"He was putting the numbers on the frame for the date when he laughed and wished himself a happy birthday!"

"So we will celebrate with the cake he buys. But what about you, do you need me to fetch a doctor?"

"No, no need for a doctor. They can cure lots of ailments but there is no cure for the passage of time, is there? I seek peace of mind. Lying here has given me time to think. I want to be laid to rest with Ruth but I have not seen the Rabbi for many years. Would it be too much to ask you to call at the synagogue, find out if Rabbi Isaacs is still there and ask him to pay me a visit? Tell him I am in need of spiritual guidance. If he is a good man, he surely won't refuse me?"

Felix patted Ben's hand.

"I meet many members of the Jewish community as I visit parishioners. In fact, one man who has an old clothes stall often does business with me, Ely Cohen? Do you know him?"

Ben nodded.

"He keeps the Sabbath religiously even though it causes him to lose trade on the busiest day of the week. I will speak with him, ask him to pass on your message. As for John, what is to become of your business? I know you have no family here."

The kettle came to the boil so Felix went to spoon tea into the pot before filling it and standing it on a trivet before the fire to brew.

John was still not back so the two men resumed their conversation.

"The building is rented, Felix, a very low rent or I could never have made a living. The press, as I said, is old-fashioned and will soon be only good for the scrap heap. Whatever can I tell John? He will be out of work and home!"

Just then the door opened and John rushed in, his face flushed from running. He closed the door behind him and hurried to Ben's bedside.

"I saw him! I just saw that man the police are hunting for!"

He stopped for breath so Felix ushered him to a chair to get his breath back. The tea was poured and the cake, a little squashed from being grasped too firmly as John had run back to the shop, was divided between them.

"Take your time, boy, take your time. Here, drink this it will help compose you."

When his cup was half-drunk, John told them what he had seen.

"That picture, let me fetch a copy."

He went to the bench where the work done was waiting to be collected and found one he wanted.

"See him? I know him, he is often on the streets stirring up trouble. He never seems to work but always has money for the grog shops. Most good people steer clear of him and his bunch of loutish mates. I know his name too, Kevin Leary. What should I do?"

Ben and Felix looked troubled by the boy's predicament then Felix said, "Are you absolutely positive, John? You may be mistaken?"

"No, Father, honest to God, I know it is him. See his eyebrows join and half his teeth are missing, and he has red knotted curls for hair. He's not big but he has done street fighting for money and he lives in Bottle Alley or Bandit's Roost, down Mulberry Lane I'm told."

"Let us think as we eat."

They sat in silence enjoying the slab cake and finishing their tea. Even Ben had a little cake and when they were done Felix said,

"I suggest I take with me a copy of the wanted poster and find a constable or better still take it to the local police office. No offence meant, John, but I feel that the officers will take more notice of me than of you. Plus, they know me, some are even members of my church. Let us pray the poor girl's killer will be brought to justice. And Ben, I will consider a solution to your problem too. I will call as soon as I am able. The cake and tea were most welcome. Now, I will let myself out, I know John has things to do."

After John had washed the cups and plates, he left Ben to sleep once again and returned to the printing. Ben was so accustomed to the machine's soporific rhythm it did not disturb him at all.

It was two days later when Felix called on them again. He bid John slow down the press to listen to what he had to say.

"I have excellent news for you, John. The man you described was indeed the very man the police wanted. However, it took a large number of officers to go into Five Points in search of him. He was found in what is called a 'Den of Death', a cellar so badly ventilated with earth floors, so dark it breeds not just maladies of the body but low-life criminals. No good honest folk would go near the place so those who resist the law find it a place of shelter from the constabulary.

He is in custody while evidence is found to make a case against him. The purse he snatched was given in payment to a Godless woman for an act of moral sin. She in turn tried selling it and both she and the purse are now held by the police. I have not implicated you in any way, John. I said I had seen the man in my travels around the parish so you have no fear of being troubled by his fellow gang members. However, I must ask a favour of you if Ben is willing?"

"What is that, Felix?" asked Ben

"In my rush to bring the news, I forgot I was meant to collect meat and vegetables for Mrs Pierce. Do you have need to go shopping today, John?"

Ben answered for John.

"I fancy a little fish today, my appetite has improved a little. John needs to see the fishmonger, he can do your shopping too, eh, John?"

"I will fetch my jacket and a basket. Should I write a list?"

"Oh, I think you will have no need of a list, you know the contents of Mrs Pierce's stews; some lamb and vegetables and fish for Ben. Any fish in particular, Ben? Here is money, there should be plenty there."

"Something from a big fish, John, not too many bones, no herring as my eyesight prevents me spotting the fine bones."

So Felix and Ben were left alone to discuss what might become of John.

"Do you know, Ben, I have an idea for John which will get him away from Five Points into an environment where he will be in steady, government employment and be looked after into the bargain. There is a regiment of the United States Army which welcomes Irish recruits. If he were to enlist, he would have not only his officers but also the other soldiers to look out for him, he would get a uniform and regular satisfying meals. There is talk of trouble with Mexico so recruits are needed. Do you think John would care for a military career?"

"My knowledge of military affairs is limited but we have printed some leaflets recently about the annexation of Texas back in July. It caused a huge outcry at the time. Do they take Irish immigrants, Felix?"

"Yes, in fact they encourage them, the Irish are born fighters. John has the advantage of his education. He is a willing, polite boy and I sincerely believe he could do very well with a military career."

"That takes a weight off my mind. I have thought of him as a son these past months, he has brightened even the gloomiest of days. He is always so cheerful, willing and good company. Now, I would ask something of you. As you know, I have no family and few possessions but I would like to help John after I am gone…no, don't protest, I am content knowing my time is almost done. Here is something I have put in writing and you would do me a great honour if you would sign it for me. I leave most of my estate to the building fund for a new synagogue but the old printer, though no longer of any value as a press, must be worth a few dollars as scrap. I want John to have it, benefit from the scrap value. He deserves it."

Just then the door opened.

"Ah, here he is now. You have Mrs Pierce's shopping? Good."

Felix stood up and took the shopping from John.

"Now, I will leave you to your fish supper. I will call soon, Ben. I will see myself out, John, take care of our dear friend. Goodbye for now."

The priest called at Ely Cohen's stall on his way home and the news soon reached the Rabbi of the imminent demise of his old friend, Ben. Rabbi Samuel Isaacs had been saddened when Ben had forsaken his faith and ceased attending the synagogue. The Rabbi was a tailor and the makeshift synagogue was on the first floor of his shop in Elm Street. His was a poor, hardworking congregation of immigrants from Europe, mostly Poles, Russians and recently Germans.

He realised there was very little time so the Rabbi left his shop in the care of his eldest son, Saul, and took his younger son, Levi, with him. A shomer would be needed to ensure the rituals of death were observed.

John opened the door to the two Jewish gentlemen and after introductions were exchanged, he ushered them inside where Ben lay on his sick bed. John whispered

"He is not sleeping, he recites psalms occasionally but he will no longer accept food, just a little water. Is he dying, Rabbi?"

Rabbi Isaacs and his son wrapped themselves in their shawls and the Rabbi answered, "He is, boy, he is. I believe you are named John Walsh from Ireland? I have heard good things of you, John, and I know Ben has enjoyed your company these past months. It is not a sad time, life and death are all one in our faith."

Levi drew his father's attention to Ben. The Rabbi bent his head close to Ben's face. He held the frail wrist of his old friend then shook his head.

"Now, John, if you will pardon me, I must ask for privacy, I have the Viddui to recite with Ben. I believe you call it 'last rites'."

Upstairs in his room, John lay on the bed and stared at the ceiling as he listened to the muffled sound of familiar monotone recitation of psalms and prayers. After a long silence, there followed whispered instructions and the sound of Ben being moved. He later found the two men had gently lowered Ben onto the floor. A ripping sound followed and a blessing was recited.

"Baruch atah, Adonai Eloheinu, Melech Ha'olam, dayan ha emit." (Blessed are you, Adonai our God, Ruler of the world, whose judgements are righteous).

John heard his name called and hurried downstairs. He was surprised to see Ben on the floor and looked at the Rabbi for explanation.

"Our friend has passed, John. You must know your bible. In what you call The Old Testament in Genesis 3:19; 'for dust thou art and unto dust shalt thou return'. Ben lying on the floor symbolises the return to earth. I must go now to prepare the funeral but Levi here will remain with Mr Jacobs as is our custom. The dead must not be left alone, we call the guard a shomer. I will return with more assistants to prepare our old friend for burial. Would you be so kind as to stay here but keep the door locked? The business must be closed in respect of the dead."

John occupied himself tidying up the few leaflets he had printed before the press fell silent. Levi sat beside Ben, reciting prayers for the dead.

A knock on the door startled John and his relief was visible on his face when he saw the Rabbi accompanied by three other men. He had never been so close to death before, losing members of his family had happened when he was too young to be much moved by it.

"John, I suggest you take a walk, get some fresh air, we have to prepare Ben for his funeral. Take your time."

The washing of the body and the clothing of it in the simple white shroud and prayer shawl was a sight for Jewish eyes only. A plain wooden coffin was delivered by two more men and Ben was gently lifted into it and the coffin was sealed.

John walked without direction, his mind confused, and his hands deep in his pockets. His tearstained face he hid from curious eyes then eventually he made his way back to find Levi alone, still guarding the coffin. John's distress was obvious to Levi.

"I know this is a difficult time for you, John, but tomorrow we will bury Ben in the Jewish cemetery. For tonight, is there anyone who could take you in, just for one night?"

"I could go to Father Varela's, I'm sure he would let me stay the night. I do need to speak with him anyway, get his advice on what I should do now."

"Don't you concern yourself with Ben's departure any more. He was old, and until you came into his employment he was also very lonely. You have been a good friend to him, we all know that. I was about your age when his wife, Ruth, died and we have always hoped he would return to the synagogue. It is good that he called for my father in time for his final blessing, we can all take comfort from that. I would advise you to say your goodbye to Ben now, his funeral will be conducted in our old tongue and will be no place for a Christian. Please take no offence, it is just how things are."

John was relieved to hear this. He had been anxious about his presence at the funeral so he smiled at Levi and thanked him. He stood beside Ben's coffin and quietly said a prayer of his own. His hand caressed the wood then he turned to shake Levi's hand before fetching his coat and with his keys in his pocket he left the quiet darkness of the printing shop and closed the door behind him.

***

"Well, if it isn't my young man back," greeted Mrs Pierce when she opened Father Varela's door to John.

"Come in, Father is in his study, I was about to call him for supper. Go through to the kitchen, you can eat with us."

The familiar smell of the baking Mrs Pierce had done that day was so welcoming. John was sitting by the fire when Father Varela entered the room. He stood up and held out his hand to the priest.

"Sad times, John, sad times. I heard that old Ben has passed. Are you alright?"

"Thank you, Father, yes I'm just fine; I have a favour to ask though."

"Well, you know if it is in my power I will help you any way I can. What is it?"

John told the priest of the ritual of the shomer and how Ben was already sealed in his coffin. Also that Levi had advised him of the need for privacy for the overnight vigil and he asked if he could possibly spend the night once more with the priest.

"You're in luck John, we have no guests at present. The room you had is free, so of course you may stay. As it happens I'm glad you called, I have a proposition for you.

"Ben confided in me last time we talked that his shop is not owned by him, he has a landlord. He knew he was dying and he was concerned about you, where you would live, where you would work. His landlord will be finding a new tenant now. Here is a suggestion for you to think about; how would you feel about a military career?"

John sat forward in his chair and listened intently as the priest told him of trouble brewing in Mexico and the American Government's call for army recruits. Madison Barracks in New York were recruiting young men and now that John was seventeen years old and could read and write, a military career could solve all of his problems. Felix told him he would be provided with full uniform and immediately qualify for US Citizenship. John's enthusiasm was obvious by the huge smile on his face.

"Well, that sounds just grand, Father! I know nothing about soldiering though except for keeping out of the way of the British soldiers back home. How do I sign up? Where do I need to go? How soon can I go?"

Father Varela laughed at the boy's excitement.

"We'll waste no time, tomorrow we will take a cab to the barracks. I will accompany you, give you some moral support. Well, I am hungry, have you eaten yet today? No? Well let's find out what Molly has for us, shall we?"

Molly called to John for help to carry the food in and when they were all seated once again, the three of them bowed their heads and said grace. The mutton broth was followed by roast belly pork, mashed potatoes and steamed cabbage. John was almost too full for pudding but when Molly carried a bowl of stewed plums in, he managed to eat a small amount. As they ate, Felix told John about Ben's offer of the proceeds from the sale of the printing press. They agreed that the man to ask advice from was Jonah Brown, Mrs Kelly's lodger.

"John, maybe when we have finished eating you could find your way back to Mulberry Street to see Jonah, he is bound to know where to sell the press."

Finding Mulberry Street was not a problem. John now knew the roads, back alleys and tenements of Five Points well. He found the place where Mrs Kelly lived and made his way up the outside staircase, treading carefully, as each step was occupied by women sitting sewing, taking advantage of the daylight hours. Children played as they sorted through rags in the yard and old men lay sleeping amongst the rubbish. Mrs Kelly's door was open, as always, to ventilate the room but he knocked and waited.

A gruff voice cursed and the sound of someone shambling across the floor drew nearer. John had expected the voice of Mrs Kelly shouting, "Who is it?" but instead the huge figure of the black man filled the doorway, his face creased in a scowl. On seeing John, a broad smile lit up his face.

"Bless ma soul, if it ain't young Irish. What brings you here, I heard you have a respectable job with the old printer? I was just rousing from ma sleep after workin' all night. Mrs Kelly and the kids is all out."

"I came to see you, Mr Brown, sorry if I disturbed your sleep."

"Heck no, as I said, I was just rousing anyways, come on in, away from pryin' eyes an' inquisitive ears."

John followed Jonah into the darkness of the room and sat where the big man indicated, on a small chair by the stove. Jonah kneeled to rake the embers into life. "Gotta have the fire ready for cookin' on when Mrs Kelly returns. Now what can I do for you boy?"

John told him of Ben's death and how he could no longer live at the printing shop, how he planned to join the army, was going to enlist the next day and how Ben had told Father Varela that he, John, should have the printing press to sell and for him to keep the proceeds.

"Father Varela thinks you might know where and how to sell it? It must go this week as the landlord at the printing shop wants it out of the way."

"I just might be able to help you. Let me ask around this evening on my way to work and I will call by the priest's house tomorrow. How's that sound?"

***

That week was a busy time for John. He went to the barracks with Father Varela where he was measured, feet and teeth inspected, eyes tested and he was confirmed fit for service. He had forty-eight hours to 'sort out his affairs', then he was to return to the barracks.

That evening, Jonah was as good as his word. He told John to be at the printing shop the next morning when a handcart would arrive, pushed by a scrap dealer who would offer him a good price and take the printing press away.

The shop was eerily silent when John opened the door the following day. He saw everywhere was tidy, Ben's bed stripped, cupboards empty, all Ben's belongings gone except for the printing press. He climbed the stairs to fetch his few belongings and as he descended the stairs there was a knock on the door. There stood Jonah, huge grin on his face as usual with another big man with a handcart.

"Hello again, young Irish! This here is Mr Donovan, he deals in scrap. Can he see the printer?"

"Please, come in. Here it is, Mr Donovan, silent at last."

The stocky Irishman with arms as thick as thighs grunted a greeting to John as he walked around the machine, bending to look under it, inspecting the working parts and stroking his chin.

"I'll tell you what I'll do for you. It's a big lump of a machine, I grant you that, the wooden parts have no worm, the metal is sound... the shifting of it we can just about manage between us... If I were to say... fifteen dollars and I'll take it off your hands what would you say?"

Jonah, standing behind Donovan, winked at John and nodded his head showing his approval of the deal.

"That sounds fine to me, Mr Donovan, can I shake your hand on it?"

Mr Donovan seemed surprised at the ready acceptance of his offer. He was used to haggling so before John could change his mind, he pulled from his waistcoat pocket a bundle of dirty dollar bills and proceeded to count fifteen into John's hand. This was equal to three months' wages to John so he was delighted. Between the three of them, they dismantled the machine as much as they were able and loaded the parts onto the handcart. As they were doing this the landlord of the property arrived with a prospective new tenant so Jonah slapped John on the back, wished him the best of luck and helped Donovan push his laden handcart to his yard. John slung his belongings over his shoulder, patted his inside pocket of his jacket to ensure his new found wealth was safe and handed the keys of the printing shop to the landlord. He gave a last glance at the sign on the door and walked briskly back to the priest's house.

Father Varela advised John to bank most of the money and when John told him he wanted to send twenty dollars home to his family in Ireland, the priest blessed him for being such a good son. Later, with his banking done, John sat at the kitchen table while Mrs Pierce was busy in the scullery and wrote a letter to his parents.

Dear Mother and Father,

I hope this letter finds you all well. I am about to become a soldier in the US army, what do you think of that? Mr Jacobs, who employed me in his printing shop, has passed on and is now in a better place, God rest his soul. So I signed to join the Emmett Guards and we will be moving south to God alone knows where as trouble is expected with Mexico. When I know where, you can be sure I will write again. Tell Father Murphy I have sent some money to you from the proceeds of the sale of Mr Jacobs's printing press which he wanted me to have. We have heard over here that the crop has failed in Ireland, be sure to let me know you are all alright; I will be sad to have a full belly knowing you all are hungry. If Dan is still keen to come over, tell him he can either travel to New York as I did or I will write from my barracks when I am settled as it is likely to be somewhere in the Gulf of Mexico.

Give hugs and kisses to my brothers and sisters and let me know how you are doing. Write care of Father Varela, he will forward my mail.

From your loving son,
Soon to be Private Walsh, 5th Infantry, US Army
John

CHAPTER NINE
NEW ORLEANS 1845

Daniel had stayed home until he, too, was fifteen and old enough to leave.

He had helped his father plant the potatoes in the spring, repaired the pigsty, and built up the peat store, before telling his Ma and Pa his intentions.

"Look, the family is growing, our Pat is of an age to help Da, and so I'm off to find our John in America."

Patrick and Bridget had not argued with him: his announcement was not unexpected. They told him to do the same as John, have a word with Father Murphy for any contacts in America. John had kept in touch with his family through Father Murphy and had sent money home. His last transfer was through a bank in New Orleans, so Daniel decided to sail there to find his big brother. The ships for New Orleans sailed from Belfast, so once again the young boy undertook a long journey across Ireland, this time alone. With some help from John's money to his parents, and the little he had managed to save, he bought a ticket on a ship named 'Amoy', priced low, as passengers provided ballast for the return voyage of the vessel which had discharged her cargo of cotton in Liverpool. His priest had contacted Father Mullen of St Patrick's church in New Orleans who had scoured the local press for passenger lists to establish on which ship Daniel would arrive.

A woman in her twenties with three young sons was amongst the passengers and Daniel helped her carry her belongings on board. Jane McNulty found Daniel to be a good companion, especially with her boys, Mathew, aged five, Mark, four and Luke, two. Their friendship was of mutual benefit. Daniel missed his close family, and Jane, newly widowed, felt the young age of Daniel would not cause scandal. Watching him as he coaxed her frightened little boys to smile again eased her pain. When their accommodation was allocated, she had no hesitation in accepting a four berth bunk to share with her boys and Daniel. Jane slept with the three boys between herself and the polite young man. To the rest of the passengers, they seemed like any other family. The crossing was without incident and allowed the widow and Daniel to get to know each other well enough for Jane to trust him with her boys who were beginning to enjoy the sea trip.

***

On arrival in New Orleans, Daniel, with Jane and the three boys, headed for St Patrick's church to meet the parish priest, Father James Mullen. Father Murphy had advised the other priest of Daniel's impending arrival and asked for any information he might have about young John Walsh.

Father Varela had advised Father Mullen of John's enlistment in the army and James Mullen had contacted the military base. As a result, to Daniel's delight, John was waiting for him in the church, almost unrecognisable as his brother, now smartly dressed in his new army uniform. The two brothers hugged till they were breathless, and unashamedly wiped tears from their eyes.

"Dan, ah it's so good to see you! How in God's name did you find me? Did you have a good crossing? You came from Belfast, eh? Why was that? How long has it been since we parted in Dublin? Let me think – two whole years! How are Ma and Da, Eliza and Little Pat, Joe and young Bridget?"

Daniel smiled, waiting for a chance to answer his big brother's questions.

"Well, would you look at you, our John, looking so fine and soldier-like! Didn't you get letters back from Father Murphy? Your money has been most welcome and Da's just managing to keep the family in food, but the famine has taken its toll. Anyway, the crop is planted for this year, so God willing, they will not come to harm. Eliza is talking of leaving too when she is old enough. So with less mouths to feed, Ma an' Da should do just fine."

Daniel told John of the troubles back home in Ireland, of people losing all their crop to blight, unable to pay their landlords any rent and many turned out of their homes as a consequence, but he assured his brother that the family was managing to get by. Their father was working on the roads in the government programme which provided low-paid work for those in need.

John looked over Dan's shoulder at the young woman and three children standing close by and listening to their conversation. Dan turned and smiled at Jane.

"Oh, John, let me introduce my friends from the 'Amoy'. This is Jane McNulty with her three boys, Mathew, Mark and Luke. Sadly, she has been left a widow and is from County Wexford. We made friends on the boat, and with their company on the voyage, I felt I had family with me."

Jane held out her hand.

"Pleased to meet you, John, I have heard so much about you during the crossing. Daniel is like the young brother I never had. My grief is still raw, and his friendship towards the boys was a big help to me. He made them laugh again and sometimes me too."

John smiled at Jane and ruffled the boys' hair.

"Well now, thanks for looking after me young brother for me, and welcome to America. Let me tell you there is a good living to be made here for hardworking people so there is. I wish you all good fortune here."

Jane said, "I hope to find a position with a good Christian family, one where my boys will be welcome. I can sew, maybe someone will want me for a seamstress."

Her blue eyes flashed with embarrassment as she spoke. She was acutely aware that John thought she and Daniel were romantically attached.

Daniel interjected at this point.

"Your last money order was from a bank in New Orleans, our John, so as boats to this port sail from Belfast it was the only option. No point me going to New York only to find you gone."

"Father Mullen knew I had joined the army, I have attended Mass here and he likes to get acquainted with visiting members of his congregation. We are to be shipped out of New Orleans soon to a place called Corpus Christi. I was granted permission to meet you but I cannot stay long. Have you any plans for employment?"

"D'you think I could join your regiment, be a soldier with you?"

"Our Dan! You're not sixteen yet!"

"I will be next birthday and anyway, I'm so big for me age, me and you could be taken for twins so we could!"

John laughed and shrugged his shoulders.

"Look, for now with Father Mullen's help I have found some temporary lodgings for you. Sorry Jane, I didn't know about you, what do you plan to do?"

Jane looked at Father Mullen who had stood by, enjoying this joyful reunion and she spoke quietly to him.

"May I speak with you, Father, please?"

"Of course, of course, come with me."

The priest took her by the elbow and ushered the boys along with them.

"Come into the vestry and we'll have a chat. Say goodbye to Daniel and his brother, I know John has to get back to camp before too long."

The three young boys fought back tears as they hugged Daniel. The youngest, Luke, burst into tears and clung to Daniel so Jane had to gently pull him free as she sniffed away her own emotions. She shook Daniel's hand then held it in both hands.

"Good luck, Daniel. I can't thank you enough for being such a good friend to me and my boys. Maybe you could write to me through Father Mullen, let me know how you're doing? You can be sure I will write back."

Then suddenly Jane threw away her inhibitions and hugged first Daniel then John. Her eyes filled with tears which she brushed away before the little ones could see, then she and her three boys watched as the proud young soldier and his brother waved farewell and left the church.

John and Daniel walked briskly to the lodging house where Dan met fellow Irishmen, some speaking Gaelic so he felt he was back in Ireland. To hear the Gaelic spoken, so far from home, brought a lump to his throat. The lodgers welcomed Daniel but one warned him it got pretty cramped in the house, they had to hot-bed it, share the beds by working shifts. He could stay for one week only.

John interrupted.

"Sorry boys, but I must go now. Dan, I will ask about you joining up."

"What d'you think my chances will be, any good?"

"The papers are full of news of trouble brewing with Mexico and the government is recruiting like crazy. I think they will be so glad to get men they will not be too worried about a few months underage. Look, I've got to get back. Settle in here, I will let you know as soon as I have any news for you, good or bad."

So once again the two brothers parted, not too sure when they would meet again. Daniel was exhausted and bed beckoned but he tossed and turned on the old mattress he would share with a navvy working nights. He fell asleep just before dawn.

***

At the holding camp on the site of the Battle of New Orleans, John was granted permission to speak with his commanding officer, Captain Merrill, about Daniel.

The officer listened impatiently then interrupted the young soldier, "Tell your brother to get here as soon as he can, the recruiting officers will be staying on after we leave to enrol more troops. Every willing man and boy is needed. If he wants to be with you though, he must decide immediately for in a few days we board a ship to take us to Corpus Christi."

John saluted his officer.

"Thank you, sir. Permission to fetch my brother from his lodgings?"

"Make it snappy. Be back here for midday, you all have a lot of training to do." Captain Merrill dismissed John and walked briskly away.

Early next morning, John collected Daniel and took him back to camp where he passed the medical examination and satisfied the recruiting officers that he was fit and able. When asked his age, the colour rising in his cheeks was ignored when he said he was sixteen and this was accepted with no questions asked so he was enlisted there and then. He was issued with a uniform then he joined John and his fellow soldiers in the Fifth Infantry. The two brothers in their blue uniforms with dark blue caps now looked even more like they could be twins.

"Would you just look at us, Dan? Who would have thought two years ago we would be looking so grand in our uniforms? Soldiers! Wait till we tell our Da an' Ma! They will be so proud!"

"It's just great we are able to be together! We can look out for each other eh?"

They did not have to wait too long for their next sea journey. Left behind at the base was a small staff of officers for the next recruits' arrival. The newly-enlisted soldiers were transported to a berth at the dockside where their ship awaited them. None of the recruits had ever seen the like of it before. US Steamship 'Alabama' was a steam – powered paddle ship with a huge wheel either side of the hull. She had a tall black smoke stack, three masts and three decks and proudly flew the American flag at her stern.

"Good that we have our sea legs brother, eh? But did you ever see anything like this when you arrived in New Orleans?"

Daniel gazed up at the impressive size of the paddle steamer.

"Yes, but not this close up. They sail up the River Mississippi mostly, I never saw one like it crossing the ocean."

"Nor me, we only saw sailing ships. Oh, here we go, getting in line for boarding."

Before the men were allowed to embark, the Quartermaster Corp loaded the ship with all their equipment and stores, sufficient for the journey.

Then all the troops hoisted their full field packs squarely onto their backs and formed an orderly queue at the foot of the gangplank. As they watched the milling throng on the quayside, Daniel spotted Jane carrying Luke with Mathew and Mark at her side, she was waving to try to attract his attention. He nudged John and pointed to them, shouting their names. Both John and Daniel waved and blew kisses to them and Daniel was thrilled when Jane blew lots of kisses back. Behind them stood Father Mullen who mimed writing so Daniel mimed back to him, pretending to write on his brother's back. He felt much happier now that he saw Jane was smiling so much. He mimicked sewing to her and she nodded her head, holding on to her bonnet to prevent it flying off in the wind. When all the troops had embarked, the gangplank was heaved aboard and each soldier sought a space to sit, lowering their back packs to the deck. Over two hundred regulars and nearly as many volunteers with all the officers filled every deck and they all shouted "Hoorah" when the smoke stack belched black smoke and the steam whistle sounded one long blast to let everyone know the ship was about to leave. The men on board lined the rails to wave to the excited crowd ashore. Ladies in pretty dresses and poke bonnets waved back and blew kisses at the smiling troops while the gentlemen amongst the crowd raised their hats. The excitement of the moment was exhilarating, not one unsmiling face was to be seen; officers, men and crew were enjoying the moment as much as the crowds on shore. Slowly the distance between them widened, the paddles turned faster, throwing up spray which sparkled in the afternoon sunshine as the ship picked up speed. Everyone continued to call farewell as the ship pulled away and headed south to the Gulf of Mexico. The troops had been told their destination was Corpus Christi where they were joining the Army of Observation of General Zachary Taylor. They would need to transfer to shallower vessels at St Joseph's Island. This was all such an adventure to the two young Irish boys. Some of the troops had never been on a ship of any kind before and many of them were being parted from their breakfast and looking very green. John and Daniel felt like real old troopers and had no problem with the movement of the paddle-steamer.

"Have you thought, our Dan, so far we have sailed on three boats all beginning with the letter A. D'you think it's a lucky letter for us?"

Daniel grinned.

"We make our own luck John, nothing special in a letter. Unless it's a letter from home eh?"

"How long d'you think it takes for our letters to get back to Ireland? It took me nearly two months on the 'Alhambra' and you much the same, right?"

"Yes, but there's steamships crossing the Atlantic as well now, meant to be faster than sail so we might get an answer by Christmas. Meantime, we will write to Father Mullen to let him know where we are."

"And he can tell Jane, is that what you're thinking? You've got a soft spot for her I can tell, yes you have, don't deny it, you're blushing our Dan."

His younger brother laughed.

"I just want to know she is all right, you know? And the boys are settling down. They missed their dad, I know that much. Anyway, she signalled back to me she is sewing and she looked contented enough so I'm pleased for her."

The crossing to St Joseph's Island took five days and from there the men were shipped by shallow-drafted vessels each carrying a small number of men. The island was used as a depot for supplies shipped in from New York and New Orleans. Eventually, they all arrived at the camp at Corpus Christi, on the south bank of the Nueces River. The location was ideal, situated between the hills and the seashore and the new arrivals were awestruck by the order in camp. Neat rows of white tents awaited them. The proximity of the sea kept the camp virtually free from flies and mosquitos and except for the need to fetch wood from some distance, the site appeared to offer every comfort. Officers were able to buy ponies from the locals, some of which they used for hunting and their daily rations were supplemented with fish and shellfish from the sea and venison, beef, geese, cranes, hares and wild boar from the surrounding prairies. Other horses were needed for pulling the wagons and were trained by teamsters for this purpose.

The number of troops grew until there were four thousand plus two thousand civilian camp followers. The rumour that Mexican troops were now encamped on the Mexican shore at a place called Matamoros heightened the men's enthusiasm for conflict. If Mexico refused to agree to a peaceful settlement regarding the boundary between the two nations, General Taylor's army would become an Army of Occupation, taking over the land at the mouth and on the banks of the Rio Grande. Meanwhile, the soldiers would set to work building their fort when they were not engaged in military exercises.

CHAPTER TEN
CORPUS CHRISTI 1845

The Walsh boys found their new life exciting but they were surprised to find that contrary to their expectations, Irish recruits were not welcomed by the Americans who called themselves 'Nativists'. These were protestant settlers who made it abundantly clear that America should be free from Papists and they resented the wave of immigrants from European Catholic countries such as Ireland and Germany. The officers in particular gave them a hard time, punishing the recruits harshly for minor misdemeanours.

The routine of the camp was exhausting. A fort had to be erected which was directly opposite Matamoros and as the American soldiers laboured on building Fort Texas, they could see the Mexicans in their dark blue tunics wearing black shakos and hear them from across the river. Reveille sounded at four in the morning except for Sundays. The men would scramble from their two-man tents, fastening their tunics and straightening their caps for the roll call of the camp. At five o'clock they formed company mess lines ready to be served breakfast at six. The daily ration of food for each man was three quarters of a pound of Southern pork or bacon, one pound of beef, one pound of hardtack and strong coffee. John and Daniel tucked in heartily, it was far more meat than either boy was used to having. They had known real hunger back home in Ireland and so they kept silent when some of the men around them grumbled at the food. Around the perimeter of the camp were tents erected by the camp followers, purveyors of food and drink, women who did the camp washing, blacksmiths, wheelwrights, carpenters and harness-makers and other traders eager to make money from the military men. Cheap whiskey and brandy supplemented the diet of many a man.

After breakfast, any soldier with a health problem could visit the surgeon. With the sudden change in water and living conditions, outbreaks of dysentery laid men low for several days. At nine-thirty the men formed ranks on the drill field, a large plot cleared for this purpose and the hard work of the day began. Incessant marching, learning from the manual of arms and target practice at the butts until the men almost dropped from fatigue. Accompanying these drills was the sound of drums and fife bands perfecting the timing of each exercise. Just occasionally the two boys stole a glance at the dragoons drilling on their sturdy mounts, charging while carrying sabres and horse pistols, performing tight formations. A soldier close to them who had served in the British Army heard the boys commenting on the skill of the horsemen.

"Hello boys, I can tell you're from the old country, how long have you been over here then?"

John answered for both of them.

"I came in 1843, my younger brother, Daniel here, is new to America, arrived a few weeks back. What about yourself?"

John O'Reilly, a man of about twenty-five years of age, was vague in his answer.

"Well, I landed in Canada with the British Army then headed south where I was met off a boat and offered the chance of enlisting in this army and here I am. See these men here?"

He pointed at the artillery batteries practicing their manoeuvres,

"Just you watch them. I was a gunner myself, and let me tell you, the speed of these men is like none I've seen before. Watch now. Those guns are six-pounders and the crew are going through the drill of hitching them to the horses and getting ready to fire. That is skill!"

He fell silent while they all watched in admiration. The flying batteries were being put through their paces by Lieutenant Braxton Bragg whose reputation for being a bastard to his men was known throughout the camp.

"What part of Ireland are you from?" asked Daniel.

"Well now, I am from Galway, John O'Reilly's my name. And you two?"

"As you can see we are brothers, come from County Mayo. John here's my big brother and I am Daniel Walsh."

"A word of warning to you both then. If you want to get through all this," he raised his arm and swept his hand in an arc encompassing the whole camp, "you will need thick skins. Most of the officers are mean bastards, especially to us Irish. If you so much as raise an eyebrow when given an order, you can be punished severely. And dare get drunk or even just have the smell of drink on your breath and you'll wish you'd never touched a drop. One of their favourite punishments is bucking and gagging where they bind your legs with a stake of wood behind your knees and gag your mouth then you're left to sit outside your tent for hours as an example to others. Most of the officers are from West Point, the military academy. They all look down their noses at the rank and file, but they are particularly nasty to us Irish."

"Why is that? They were keen enough to enlist us," said John.

"They fear us for our faith. They think being Catholic we will get to outnumber the Protestants and if you know anything about the Pilgrim Fathers you will know why."

Their conversation was brought to an abrupt end when they spotted their commander, Lieutenant Colonel James McIntosh striding towards them. They rapidly jumped to attention and after he had passed, they continued with their manual of arms practice.

***

The days passed quickly. Every night the boys collapsed into their tents and slept soundly until reveille sounded once again. They witnessed some of the barbaric punishments handed out for minor offences but had never fallen foul of the officers themselves until one day, when Daniel was given an order to fetch wood with two other privates.

It was necessary to travel some way from camp in their search and when the three soldiers returned with what the officer considered to be paltry bundles of wood he was furious.

"What's the meaning of this? Where in hell have you been to take all this time? Men could starve waiting for a fire from you three lazy, idle bog-trotters! There's not enough here to boil a can of water on! Here, you four, over here sharpish. You know the punishment for dereliction of duty. Buck 'em and gag 'em, all three of them."

The young lieutenant stormed off.

The four given the order to see to the punishment carried out the instructions tight-lipped. Just a shake of the head from one of them was the only sign they sympathised with the three in trouble but they were all well aware that they would share the same fate if they were found to have been easy on the knots.

Daniel, Tim Hughes and Pat O'Toole were bound and gagged and their fellow soldiers were given strict orders not to converse with them, give them water or aid them in any way on pain of receiving the same punishment. The sun beat down on them even though it was now late September. Tim Hughes became delirious, driven mad from the exposure and when eventually they were freed, the harsh treatment had been more than he could bare and he was carried off to his tent.

Daniel was barely conscious when his brother came to his aid. John shook him gently.

"Hey, brother, I'm here, hang on there, let's get you out of the sun."

His young brother had difficulty opening his eyes. His lips were swollen and cracked from lack of water and his arms and legs were stiff and sore. There were deep welts where the ropes had bitten into his flesh.

John carefully lifted his young brother and carried him over his shoulder back to their tent. He passed a flask of water to Daniel who swigged some then poured the rest over his face. He brushed the angry tears from his eyes and thanked John.

John was enraged at the sight of Dan's injuries.

"That son of a bitch! Bastard! In Christ's name, Dan, what did you do to upset the monster?"

"We went in search of wood but this God-forsaken land suffers from a lack of trees. Honest, John, we got all there was but it was not enough. How are the others? Are they okay?"

John had seen one of the three soldiers being carried over to the surgeon's tent but as he didn't know the outcome, he reassured Daniel that they were all fine.

"Why do they treat us worse than animals? We work our butts off for them, ignore their vile comments about the bogs we came from, and for what?"

Daniel looked at the welts on his wrists and ankles and touched them hesitantly, wincing with the pain. His knees were cut and swollen from the stony ground.

"Leave me to sleep. I will be better by reveille, you go and see how the other two are."

John left him in peace, satisfied he could do no more and when he returned to their tent later he was relieved to find his brother sound asleep. He would leave it for now but tomorrow Daniel was going to have to be told that young Tim Hughes had not recovered consciousness but had died from heat stroke and the other soldier, Pat O'Toole, had gone missing.

The mood in the camp was in danger of turning to mutiny when timely news arrived that revived the troops' pride in their preparation for war. It was now mid-October and the officers reported to General Taylor that the troops were fully trained and ready for war. The General himself was popular with the rank and file of his army. He refused to wear a uniform, preferring instead to dress in blue canvas trousers, a long duster coat and a wide-brimmed hat. His only concession to military uniform was his army-issue boots. He was known to the men as 'Old Rough and Ready' while his horse was called 'Old Whitey'.

The General gathered the troops for inspection by Inspector General Payne. The Infantry, Dragoons and Artillery with their bronze field pieces marched onto the parade ground in full battle gear, some with bayonets fixed. They impressed the Inspector General with their display of defensive squares, long skirmish lines and dense assault columns. Then it was the turn of the cavalry to demonstrate their skills.

Inspector General Payne sent a glowing report to Washington stating that the Army of Observation was now ready for war.

***

The winter months brought a change in the weather with strong winds and heavy rain. In early April, there was a tropical storm and with many of the tents not made from the customary canvas due to a shortage of the regular fabric but from flimsy, inferior muslin, some failed to keep out the sleet and rain. The camp became waterlogged and all exercises ceased, leading to boredom and discontent by the men. Even though their supplies, including firewood, were now being shipped in rather than sourced locally, lighting fires became impossible and resentment of the officers' treatment grew. Men fell ill with pneumonia and many died without ever meeting the enemy. Funerals were a common occurrence yet still the Nativists selected the Irish for rougher treatment than others, even dragging them from their sickbeds to perform sentry duty. The only begrudged respite from the camp was when permission was granted to some of the men to attend Mass at a place called Kinney's Ranch, where a travelling Mexican priest soothed the weary men with the familiar Latin service and caused them to think nostalgically of Ireland.

Both John and Daniel suffered from dysentery but were still ordered to get back on duty. As they were young and strong they recovered and were fortunate enough to be given passes to attend Mass. There they met up again with John O'Reilly, once a sergeant in the British Army owing to his prowess as a gunner in the artillery. The three became firm friends; the two young soldiers respected the older man for his refusal to drink alcohol and they followed his example. They had seen the effect of drink on other men and the punishments for being drunk. Also they knew that men in drink were drawn to the camp-followers tents where they succumbed to the pleasures of the women of low morals. This distraction led to even longer queues each morning outside the surgeon's tent, with soldiers suffering from the first signs of syphilis. With disease rife, poor diet, unsatisfactory tents, poor sanitation and brackish water to drink, more than one in ten men were unfit for duty at any given time.

***

The two Walsh boys endured the rough treatment they suffered at the hands of the vindictive officers with stoicism, determined not to rise to the bullying until one day John was picked on for apparently ignoring an officer's order. The protests of John that he failed to hear the order over the noise from the rifle practice fell on deaf ears. It was Lieutenant Meade, the same officer who had punished Daniel. This time he sent John to spend time on the wooden horse. This was a contraption similar to one used for sawing wood only the man mounted on it would have his hands strapped behind his back with weights attached to his feet and, as with other punishments, no food or water was allowed for the duration. When the time came for their punishment to end, the soldier would be unable to stand without help.

Daniel watched as John was released and rushed to aid his brother when he collapsed to the ground.

"Here, our John, put your arm around my neck and we'll get you back to the tent. Don't give the bastard the satisfaction of seeing you on a stretcher."

All meals were finished but Daniel had been to one of the tents where food was sold and bought bread which he broke and fed to John.

After John had washed the bread down with water, he threw his cap and belt onto his bed in anger.

"This is no life, our Dan, we get treated like the worst criminals, there's no justice, none at all. But for the knowledge I'd lose my life, I would readily knock shit out of that little runt. I don't think I can take much more of this, I really can't."

Daniel was lost for words. He fully understood his brother's rage but did his best to pacify him.

"Just wait until we're fighting for real, John, then the jumped-up little ass-wipe officers will find us the best soldiers ever, you just see if they don't."

The tent flap was pulled aside and John O'Reilly's head appeared, barely visible against the darkening sky.

"How's your brother?" he asked Daniel

"Pissed off," answered John. "If I could get that son of a bitch alone on a dark night…"

He was interrupted.

"Ah, I'm with you in your thoughts but not in your proposed deeds. Look, from now on be sure to avoid crossing the bastards in any way. I have my own grievance with them. They know of my service in the British army where I was a sergeant, and I'd expected the officers in command would have promoted me by now. I've proved my gunnery skills but no. Cack-handed rednecks with barely the ability to present arms get made up to corporal. Still, that's not what I came about. I have a pass to attend Mass and I talked Merrill into making it out for all three of us. So at least tomorrow we can look forward to some respite from them and some comfort from the priest. OK, lads? After breakfast then."

O'Reilly pulled the tent flaps closed and left the two of them with a flicker of hope.

Sunday's reveille was later than on other days so by the time they had eaten breakfast the sun was climbing high in the sky. John found walking painful but he managed to keep up with his companions. As usual, the Mass was attended by other Catholic soldiers, devout or otherwise, taking advantage of an opportunity to leave camp and its fierce discipline for a few, brief hours. Before they headed back to camp, O'Reilly excused himself and went to have a private conversation with the priest. On their return to camp, they discussed the event earlier in the week when part of General Taylor's army had entered Santa Isobel where the army supplies depot was based and the acts of destruction and abuse by some of the soldiers had driven the locals away in fear.

"I heard that some of the officers tied their mounts to gravestones in the churchyard, tore down paintings of saints and grabbed terrified women off the streets to have their brutish way with them. They were heard to speak of the Mexicans as Papist peasantry. They have no respect for us Catholics, none at all."

As the older man talked, the two brothers, walking either side of him listened intently and saw an expression on O'Reilly's face that could only mean trouble. From the other side of the river the Mexican soldiers could be heard cursing or laughing as they worked to build their defences in readiness for the imminent battle.

The following week they attended Mass again but the following morning during roll call, they discovered John O'Reilly had gone absent without leave. They learnt he had swum across the Rio Grande and given himself up to the Mexicans. The boys missed him terribly but tight-lipped, they continued to keep their noses clean and performed their duties without any further incidents likely to incur the wrath of the officers.

Over the river, O'Reilly had been taken to General Ampudia for questioning. The tall Irishman made a strong impression on the General who decided that this man was no ordinary private as he learnt of O'Reilly's position in the British Army. Every question put to him by Ampudia was answered without hesitation and he was promptly offered a commission in the Mexican Army which he accepted immediately.

Lieutenant O'Reilly in his smart new uniform of dark blue jacket with scarlet collar, white canvas trousers and a black cap struck a handsome figure, drawing admiring glances from the pretty Mexican women. Now he was appreciated for his talents as a gunner and the fact that he was Irish was an advantage after the contempt he had been used to. He was made a battery commander of an artillery division.

Just two weeks after O'Reilly deserted under cover of darkness, three men had entered the US army camp and distributed leaflets quietly to sleeping men. The text of the leaflet was from a speech by General Mariano Arista to men of Taylor's Army.

"Soldiers! You have been enlisted in time of peace to serve in that army for a specific term, but your obligation never implied that you were bound to violate the laws of God, and the most sacred rights of friends! The United States government, contrary to the wishes of a majority of all honest and honourable Americans, has ordered you to take forcible possession of the territory of a friendly neighbour, who has never given her consent to such occupation. In other words, while the treaty of peace and commerce between Mexico and the United States is in full force, the United States, presuming on her strength and prosperity, and on our supposed imbecility and cowardice, attempts to make you the blind instruments of her unholy and mad ambition and forces you to appear as the hateful robbers of our dear homes, and the unprovoked violators of our dearest feelings as men and patriots. Such villainy and outrage I know are perfectly repugnant to the noble sentiments of any; and it is base and foul to rush you onto certain death, in order to aggrandize a few lawless individuals, in defiance of the laws of God and man! It is to no purpose if they tell you that the law for the annexation of Texas justifies your occupation of the Rio Bravo del Norte; for by this act they rob us of a great part of territory...and it is barbarous to send a handful of men on such an errand against a powerful and warlike nation. Besides, the most of you are Europeans, and we are the declared friends of a majority of the nations of Europe. The North Americans are ambitious, overbearing, and insolent, as a nation, and they will only make use of you as vile tools to carry out their abominable plans of pillage and rapine. I warn you, in the name of justice, honour, and your own interests and self-respect, to abandon their desperate and unholy cause, and become peaceful Mexican citizens. I guarantee you, in such case, a half section of land, or 320 acres, to settle upon, gratis (free). Be wise, then, and just and honourable, and take no part in murdering us who have no unkind feeling for you. Lands shall be given to officers, sergeants, and corporals according to rank, privates receiving 320 acres, as stated.

If in time of action you wish to espouse our cause, throw away your arms and run to us, we will embrace you as true friends and Christians.

It is not decent or prudent to say more. But should any of you render any important service to Mexico, you shall accordingly be considered and preferred.

Headquarters at Matamoros, April 20, 1846, M. ARISTA

CHAPTER ELEVEN
ACROSS THE RIO GRANDE

It was the last week in April when John and Daniel learned of O'Reilly's brief visit. They found one of the leaflets tucked under the opening of their tent. Reveille had just sounded so John pushed the leaflet under the blanket as he made his bed, stuck his cap on his head and they both hurried off for roll call. The day's work was as arduous as usual with men whispering secretly of the under-darkness visitors and the leaflets they had left behind. The officers kept a keen watch on the men but nobody was caught in conversation so no punishments given out that day. Exhausted, the two brothers returned to their tent and collapsed onto their beds. As John lay down, the paper was disturbed. He was about to screw it up thinking it was rubbish blown into the tent but Daniel snatched it from him. John closed his eyes as Daniel began to read the speech by Arista out loud.

"Eh, our John, listen to this! No, honest, you must listen."

When he reached the part where any soldier willing to leave the US Army would be guaranteed land in Mexico, John sat up and rested on his elbow.

"Let me read it."

Daniel passed over the crumpled paper and watched John's reaction as he read it in silence.

"Look, did you notice this?"

John pointed to the bottom corner of the leaflet.

"See! The initials JOR? That will be for John O'Reilly, don't you think? So now we know he is safe and not taken by the currents in the Rio Grande."

"He must have joined the Mexican Army then. I wonder if he's still a private?"

"Doesn't matter. It says here even privates get 320 acres. Eh, between you and me that's 640 acres! Bloody hell! Imagine that back home, what we could grow, what animals we could keep! This has got to be an offer like no other and certainly better than the Americans have promised."

They slipped out of their tents and went for their nightly ablutions where the talk from other soldiers was also about the Mexican promise. That night they got little sleep as they talked quietly of the benefits or perils of following O'Reilly. When reveille sounded next morning they were woken with a start. John thought at first he had dreamt the whole thing until he saw Daniel hiding the leaflet in his boot before heading out to roll call once again.

Around the camp that day, whenever an opportunity arose, small groups of men huddled in quiet discussion about the contents of the leaflet. The officers, remembering the earlier leaflets, posted American-only sentries, in an effort to discourage any attempts at desertion.

It was not until John and Daniel prepared for bed that night that they could talk to each other and discuss the offer in detail.

"What d'you say, our Dan, I've read this over and over and I am all for going. How about you?"

"Don't you think it's too risky?"

Daniel pulled his boots off and began to undress while John sat on his bed still fully dressed with his face flushed with excitement.

"Staying here's a poor option. We get treated like muck, ridiculed for being Irish and Catholic, punished harshly for no good reason and like John O'Reilly said, overlooked for promotion. I for one think it's a risk worth taking."

"What about the swim? We've only ever swum in the waves on the shore back home. D'you think we can do it?"

"Listen, it's not that far! You can hear conversations from the other bank, and others have done it. We can go after dark, just take what's necessary and when we get over on the other side, we go looking for O'Reilly. I reckon he's already made some good connections over there to have been trusted to return to camp like he did with these."

He waved the crumpled leaflet.

Daniel listened in silence and took his time answering.

"Well, I didn't come all this way to find you to see you just take off without me. So count me in."

John leapt from his bed and clapped his brother on the back.

"That's great news! I knew you'd see sense. But listen, I think we should wait a few days, let the heat die down, the bastards are expecting us to go and are just waiting for an excuse to take pot-shots at any of us trying. We'll let them think we haven't taken the bait then get permission to go to Mass again, but instead of heading off to Kinney's ranch we'll make our way to the bend in the river out of sight of the camp and wait for darkness."

The two boys did just that on the following Sunday. They remained hidden by the side of the river until after dark, knowing they would not be missed until reveille next morning. Stripped of all heavy items of uniform, including their boots, and with their documents and money rolled in a square of oilcloth, they waded silently into the river and once they were accustomed to the current, they struck out for the opposite shore. As they swam they heard shouts from the river bank they had just left.

"Oy! You two! Where in hell's name d'you think you're going? Turn around or we shoot."

A sentry called to his fellow sentry.

"Hey, you there, look. Two of the chicken bastards are making a getaway. What's the bet they're Irish? I've hailed them to turn around or we'd shoot so you get shootin' too."

The two swimmers heard gunshots and swam with even more vigour to get out of range. The shots and shouts kept coming but luckily the American soldiers failed to hit their targets. Daniel reached the other bank first and helped John out. They collapsed in the mud just long enough to get their breath back and climbed out of sight of the cursing shooters.

The sound of the shots had alerted the interest of the Mexicans who, with their weapons at the ready, warily approached the two dripping men.

John and Daniel raised their hands in submission and prayed they would be questioned rather than shot.

"What you swim for? Hands up, hands up. Answer!"

The two boys pointed to their bare feet and showed they carried no weapons.

They remembered the name on the leaflet.

"General Arista, he welcomes us. We want to fight with you, we are friends of John O'Reilly. You know him?"

The Mexican soldiers talked among themselves and the boys heard 'Lieutenant Riley' mentioned. This sounded promising.

"Come with us. Keep hands over head."

The walk without boots was painful and they shivered in their wet clothes but they followed the Mexicans without argument.

When they reached the plaza in Matamoros they were encouraged with the nudge of a rifle to cross to an imposing building where sentries standing to attention either side of the enormous doors crossed their weapons, barring entry.

The discussion between their captors and the sentries was obviously about them but hearing the mention again of Lieutenant Riley, the soldiers shouldered their arms and the sentries stood at ease.

The heavy wooden doors swung open and they were marched inside. An officer sitting in the entrance hall writing raised his head and stood up when he saw the two captives.

One of the Mexican soldiers left John and Daniel in the charge of the other soldiers and crossed the hall to explain to the seated officer what was happening. The officer nodded as he listened and looked across at the two unkempt, barefooted men with a disdainful expression on his face. Again, the mention of Riley prompted a change in his attitude. He pointed to a door and signalled for them all to follow him. As they waited for the knock on the door to be acknowledged, the two Irishmen glanced at their surroundings. The walls were covered in portraits of men in magnificent uniforms, some on horseback. Heavy chandeliers hung from the ceiling and wall lights flickered all around. As the door opened, the boys could not hide their delight at seeing John O'Reilly standing before them, a wide grin on his handsome face.

"Well, fancy! What do we have here now? A couple of young urchins, eh? Or is it a fine pair of fighting men prepared to fight with God and justice on their side? Will you just look at the pair of you, we must get you some dry clothes but first come inside and meet General Arista. I take it you read the leaflet I left for you? Come and tell him what is happening in Taylor's camp then he will be sure to agree to you enlisting and wearing a whole new uniform."

They stood before a tall man in the uniform of a General who looked them up and down. Riley (this is the name the Mexicans used) told General Arista how he knew these boys well and that they should be welcomed into his army. The news of the reaction to the leaflet pleased the General who laughed heartily when he heard how the American Army would only allow American-born sentries on night duty for fear of losing more men to the Mexicans.

"Well done, Lieutenant Riley, let us pray this is the few before the many. John and Daniel are your names? Well, if you are friends of Riley here you come with good recommendation. He has earned rapid promotion and so might you if you work as diligently for our cause as he has. But you must not stand here any longer in your wet clothes. Lieutenant Riley will take you to get uniforms and then to the sleeping quarters. Tomorrow we will ascertain your skills and find posts for you."

So, relieved to have made the crossing in safety and being welcomed so magnanimously, John and Daniel saluted the General then followed their friend out.

Once they left the General's Headquarters, O'Reilly hugged his two friends.

"God, but it's good to see you both, so it is! Have no fear you made the wrong choice, you will soon find for yourselves that in this army you are not despised, in fact, you will be made very welcome.

The pay is better too, and just wait until you see the pretty senoritas, they are particularly friendly!"

They walked briskly to the barracks where O'Reilly was saluted by the soldiers. He already had a limited knowledge of the Spanish language and he soon had the Mexicans nodding, going off to the stores and bringing with them several uniforms for the two Irish boys to try on. When two had been found to suit their sizes, they followed O'Reilly once more to the sleeping quarters.

"Now, when you are dried and dressed I will take you to the mess for chow. When did you last eat?"

"Last meal of the day yesterday, nothing since then. We are both starving."

John looked at Dan who nodded his head in agreement.

"Right. Now chow is a lot different here, different but very tasty. It might upset your bellies for a day or two until you get used to it so be warned! Hope you like things spicy boys!"

"Ah, we've strong stomachs haven't we, Dan? From the smell of the cooking, I can't wait to try it!"

As they passed an open window, their mouths watered in anticipation. Inside the mess hall were soldiers seated at trestle tables, laughing as they tucked in to food alien to the two boys from Ireland. O'Reilly led them to the serving hatch and recommended they start with something quite simple. Following John O'Reilly's example, the boys chose bowls of steaming soup with bread and found seats.

As they ate they tried to identify the ingredients in their bowls. Whatever it was it was certainly tasty, and soon the bowls were almost empty and the bread was used to wipe the bowls clean.

"That was good, so tasty but we never ate anything like it before. What was in it?"

O'Reilly grinned

"You like beef? Pork? Well, both of those meats were used in this dish, cooked with tomatoes, corn and onions."

"We had very little meat back home in Ireland, mostly pork or bacon and if we were lucky, a trotter to share. This is fancy-folk food to us!"

"Well, pig's trotters are used for your soup with tripe, the cow's belly, ever had it?"

Both boys shook their heads.

"The meat is cooked long and slow in large amounts because then it is often served cold next day for breakfast. Did you find it too spicy? The peppers can be quite fiery."

"Yes, but not unpleasant, the bread helped take the fire away."

There was still bread on the table and the boys were not prepared to leave it uneaten.

"Take it, take it, find a space in your pocket but now I must take you to the bunkhouse and return to being an officer. We will have to observe protocol from now on, you will be expected to salute me."

The Lieutenant winked at the two boys and took them back to the sleeping quarters. Some men were already in their hammocks and would have leapt to attention but O'Reilly signalled them to remain at ease.

"Ever slept in a hammock? Oh, maybe on your passage over?"

They both shook their heads, wondering how on earth men could sleep in such contraptions.

"There's a skill in climbing in but I will leave you to find out for yourselves. I must be off to my own bed. Tomorrow you will be just two of my soldiers but have no fear, I know your mettle. You will get along fine and be at home as quite a number of these soldiers are also from Ireland, others from Germany so you will hear several languages spoken. Still, the drill is much the same, you'll soon pick it up. Now, have a good night's rest and I expect to see you at reveille."

CHAPTER TWELVE
MATAMOROS

Men were deserting daily from Fort Texas. Some were shot as they attempted to swim to the Mexican shore. Even so, Lieutenant Riley soon had almost fifty Irish soldiers to swell the ranks of the Mexican Army.

The daily routine still consisted of rifle practice and artillery manoeuvres but in the evening the men were free to spend time becoming acquainted with the locals of Matamoros, mingling with the friendly inhabitants in the bars and cafés. The stunningly beautiful women were fascinated by the red-headed Irish men; they were such a contrast to all their dark haired Mexican counterparts. Equally, the Irish soldiers were most appreciative of the dark-skinned, brown-eyed beauties. News of the welcome they received reached the American camp, leading to even more men deserting to try their luck.

One Sunday evening, John and Daniel attended Vigil Mass and they were overwhelmed by the magnificent decoration in the Cathedral. The gold plasterwork ceiling was supported by Grecian columns, the floor was red marble and a huge crucifix hung over the altar. Back home, their small parish church was very humble. There, the crucifix stood on the altar table with brass candlesticks either side, all polished by the ladies of the congregation but so plain in contrast to the cathedral with its extravagant use of gold everywhere.

Nearby sat two girls of similar age to themselves who whispered behind their fans as they made eye contact with the two boys.

After the service the congregation streamed out, some heading home but many joining the people walking lazily around the plaza de Mercado in the evening sun. The market building was brick-built with a clock tower and arcades opening onto the plaza. Bands were playing, stallholders selling ice-cream, chocolate, brandy and beer sat lazily waiting for customers while Indian women in their ornate costumes sat in the shade of the arcades with their wares spread about them. The boys had never before seen such produce. The colourful fruit and vegetables displayed were corn cobs, bananas, pineapples and oranges while another trader had dried beans of different sizes, coffee beans and maize flour. They breathed in the rich smells and began to feel hungry.

"Shall we sit here, have a drink?"

Daniel had spotted empty tables outside a café.

"Sounds a great idea to me, what d'you fancy?"

"The coffee is meant to be good here, the locals seem to enjoy it anyway."

The café was filled with couples, families and soldiers eating and drinking watching a Mexican nearby dressed in flamboyant clothes and a wide-brimmed hat strumming a guitar while his female companion, in a flame-coloured dress, danced a flamenco. The enthusiastic spectators clapped to the beat.

A waiter arrived to take their order and stood patiently waiting while John nudged Daniel.

"Would you look at him!"

John O'Reilly was walking around the square with a very attractive lady on his arm. She was dressed exquisitely, in a full skirted rose-pink dress with a black lace shawl and a lace mantilla held in place on her head by an ornate comb.

"Lieutenant Riley sure knows how to pick 'em."

Daniel looked in the direction John was pointing.

"He looks like a cat who found the cream! Good luck to him, I say, he deserves a dose of it for sure. Look at his fancy uniform, sword an' all."

Dan then nudged John.

"Look, here come the two girls from the church heading our way."

The waiter had grown impatient and attended to other seated clients.

Before Dan had time to stop John, his brother raised his hand and waved to attract the attention of the girls. The senoritas were in white dresses over which they wore brightly-coloured shawls and in their glossy hair were tall combs from which tendrils of curls escaped. They quickly raised their fans to hide their shyness.

John stood up and beckoned to them to join him and his brother. However, the girls chose the table next to theirs and smiled before fanning coquettishly again.

"I think they like us, Dan. How about we join them? I think they are playing hard to get, leaving the running to us."

"Ay, why not? The worst they can do is get up and leave."

Dan stood beside John at the two empty chairs at the girls table.

"May we join you? I am John, this is my brother, Daniel."

Before waiting for a reply, John sat down. Daniel remained standing until the two girls giggled and nodded.

"Hola, Bienvenedos. Me llamo Maria, ella Paulina."

"Sit down, our Dan, they really do like us. Can you speak English?"

"No hablo Ingles," Paulina said, shaking her head.

"Yo hablo un poco de Ingles," and as Maria said this she indicated with her finger and thumb that she knew a little English.

The boys looked at one another. Communication might be difficult but not impossible.

"We buy you a coffee?" John asked.

"No, champurrado please," Maria spoke for both girls.

They sat in silence until they caught the waiter's eye. He stood before them, pad in hand, ready to take their order.

John held up two fingers.

"Two coffees and two…"

He looked to Maria for help so she broke into Spanish to ask for the girl's choice.

When the barman returned he placed the two dark cups of coffee in front of the boys and two bowls of steaming champurrado. As the boys leaned forward to see what was in the girls' bowls, they smelt the contents. It was such a rich, warm, sweet aroma, one they had not experienced before.

"Mmmm, smells good."

Dan looked to Maria to enlighten them.

"Champurrado is… erm… el chocolata ?"

The boys still shook their heads. It had never reached their corner of Ireland, well not for the likes of them at least.

The waiter put the bill in front of John, so John pulled out some dollar bills and offered some to the waiter. Maria looked across and spoke rapidly to the waiter who took a dollar bill and went back inside. The girls whispered to each other and frowned but they relaxed when the waiter returned with change in pesos.

As they became more comfortable with their new friends, the girls pointed out interesting passers-by to the boys. A woman was making her way across the square with sombreros of every size piled on her head and a variety of baskets hooked on each arm. When she reached the stone archways around the market building she lowered the baskets to the ground and stretched, relieved to be free from her heavy burden. She spread her poncho on the ground and arranged the baskets around her then settled down to await customers, confident that they would come to her. The hats remained in place and she didn't have long to wait before a customer arrived to barter for one. A passing baker with a basket full of rolls was also doing good trade, stopping when people hailed him.

Maria pointed at a man as he struggled past, carrying a dozen or more cages all fastened together. Inside were song birds, cockatoos and some held large fire beetles. The brothers were unable to understand the girls as they tried to convey to the two of them the purpose of the beetles. Just then, a lady stopped the hawker to purchase one of the beetles in its small bamboo cage and the man deftly released the fire beetle to be captured under her mantilla as she lifted it. Then the beetle, without any bidding, glowed with phosphorescence and so lit the gathering darkness for its new owner to find her way home.

The four friends laughed with delight at the display. Before the hawker could continue on his way, a Mexican gentleman with two young daughters was persuaded to purchase a songbird from him. As they took their time choosing which bird they wanted, the young girls ignored the audience sat at the nearby table. When they saw their father was becoming impatient, their choice was finally agreed upon and one small cage was parted from the others. Money changed hands and the satisfied trader took up his load again then walked slowly on while his customers carried their cage between them whilst attempting to encourage the bird to sing.

An elderly man staggered through the plaza, almost bent double under his burden of faggots strapped to his back with a sturdy leather belt fastening them around his chest and shoulders. With his head down, he made his way slowly through the crowds. He appeared not to want to sell his load but was carrying it home for his family.

The crowds began to disperse as darkness fell and John and Daniel reluctantly stood up when the two girls did. With her faltering English, Maria, after rapid discussion with Paulina, arranged to meet the boys again one evening in the plaza. Not sure what was expected of them, the boys shook hands with the girls then stood and watched as they walked away across the plaza, their skirts swaying, before they turned to wave farewell then disappeared from view. Daniel sighed, contented.

"Hey, our John, I think we made a favourable impression there, don't you? I think Paulina was giving you the glad eye, so she was! As for me, I liked the way Maria's cheeks dimpled as she smiled!"

"Well, I liked both girls too, they seemed nice and friendly, if a little shy."

The brothers drained the last of their coffee then headed back to barracks with broad smiles and lots to talk about.

***

It was April and Lieutenant Riley had organised a company of forty-eight Irish men including John and Daniel. Their training period was brief. The new recruits to the Mexican army had barely become accustomed to the Mexican procedures before the first battle ensued when General Arista, who had replaced General Ampudia as Commander, sent troops to lay siege to Fort Texas on May 4th. The Mexicans kept bombarding the Americans with cannon fire from dawn to mid-morning. One of the American casualties fatally injured was Major Brown, who had been left in charge of the fort. On May 9th, General Arista took cavalry and field pieces in an attempt to head off General Zac Taylor en route from Point Isobel as he was returning to the fort with supplies. Unfortunately for the Mexican soldiers with Arista, which included the newly-formed Legion of Foreigners under Lt Riley's command, the Americans had superior artillery, the 'flying artillery' which had so impressed O'Reilly before he had deserted.

The excitement was exhilarating. Daniel looked at his older brother carrying his rifle to see if he was nervous but John grinned and winked back at him.

"Let's go to it, our Dan, we've got the better of them in numbers and we are fighting with men defending their country's freedom."

He could just about hear Dan whispering a prayer.

"May the hand of God protect me and the shield of God defend me."

To which John replied, "Amen."

The order came to fix bayonets, this battle was to be at close quarters.

A cannon fired with tremendous noise from the opposition. No going back. Guns on both sides fired constantly but the flying batteries of the American troops proved lethal. Their infantry formed a defensive square as the Mexican cavalry drew near. The two Irish boys watched as the men on horseback in their colourful uniforms moved forward, lances dipped. Then the front line of the cavalry stopped and fired their guns before wheeling round and falling in at the rear allowing the second line to do the same. When they were at point-blank range, they put away their guns and raised their lances to attack the square of enemy soldiers. The Americans fired, guns roared, horses reared up in fear and many of the Mexican Lancers were dismounted. Then they regrouped and charged again, unhitching two cannons to fire on the square once more. The Americans retaliated until eventually the bugle sounded retreat for the Mexican Lancers.

During the fighting, a discarded wad from one of the guns set fire to the grass on the plain and soon a fire raged, swept by the wind and preventing further engagement. Under cover of smoke, both sides took advantage and re-formed. Now the flying batteries of the Americans had a new target, the Mexican Infantry. The fighting continued until night fell then both sides ceased fighting in order to go to the assistance of their groaning, wounded colleagues and recover the bodies of the dead. The surgeons, with the assistance of volunteers, did their best to make men comfortable who were beyond saving, some with limbs missing or gaping holes in their stomachs which bled too profusely to be staunched. Others worked frantically on the men who could be saved, stopping the bleeding of gaping wounds as best as they were able, stitching and bandaging them, before they were carried on carts back to their base camp. It was almost dawn before the weary soldiers still able to walk lay exhausted on their weapons and tried to get some sleep.

The following morning, General Arista pulled his troops away from Palo Alto upstream to Resaca de la Palma, which lay between Taylor's army and Fort Texas. Lt Riley was with the troops besieging the fort and when he had seen the smoke from the fire the previous day, he wondered how his two young friends had fared. His orders were to recommence the bombardment of the fort at daybreak.

The new position of Arista's troops provided excellent cover for his infantry. A dried-up riverbed, full of vegetation, was an ideal hiding place from which his men could face the enemy. The battle soon began again with hand to hand combat with guns, bayonets and swords wreaking havoc and carnage once more on both sides. The Americans, with their heavy artillery, approached the Mexicans from behind, taking them completely by surprise and causing some of the Mexicans to make a dash for the Rio Grande to escape. However, the Americans were merciless, attacking the fleeing men with renewed vigour and bayoneting many, leaving them dead or dying. Those who made it to the river attempted to swim across as few boats were available. Finally, the brave Mexican artillery abandoned their cannons and joined the exodus of Mexican soldiers.

The battle was over and had been indecisive with neither side the winner but two hundred and sixty-two Mexicans were killed while the Americans lost thirty-nine. Although the American loss was far less than the Mexicans', when the news reached President Polk in Washington the government lost no time in declaring war on Mexico on May 13th.

***

Out of respect for Major Brown, Fort Texas was renamed Fort Brown in his memory.

Men were still deserting from the American army, some fleeing from the territory to find their way home but others, Irish, German and other Europeans, joined the Mexicans. Lt Riley had the task of questioning them and reporting any news back to General Arista.

"Sir."

Lt Riley saluted and stood to attention.

Arista signalled for the lieutenant to sit and Riley removed his cap, put it under his arm and sat down.

"Well, what news have you? Anything vital to our cause to disclose?"

"With respect, sir, some of what I was told may be speculation but on the other hand, the officers are prone to boasting and these men learnt some disturbing facts."

"Go on, go on, tell me, I need to know."

"It seems that Washington has authorised ten million dollars for the military while volunteers are joining in large numbers. Their navy is blockading your Mexican ports, preventing supplies from sympathetic nations to your cause, our cause, from being landed."

General Arista stood up and paced backwards and forwards with his hands behind his back. He was a tall, elegant man, most striking in his general's uniform but his handsome face wore a worried frown and he was silent for a while. He was well aware that Mexican forces outnumbered the Americans but many of his soldiers were peasants with little training, dressed in poor clothing and on minimum rations. Hardly the tough fighting men he needed.

"I am considering withdrawing, we need to regroup, and I think that your foreign troops should stay together, be one unit. As they have shown their indomitable spirit, I suggest we give them a new name, not just be called a Legion of Foreigners. Any suggestions?"

Lieutenant Riley hardly hesitated before replying.

"Sir, you may or may not have heard of the Patron Saint of Ireland, Saint Patrick. I know all your Irish soldiers will fight to the death for Saint Patrick, can we use his name at all?"

"Saint Patrick? San Patricio? What if I was to form the 'San Patricio Battalion', it could be made up of all you Irish soldiers and the other foreign nationals? Maybe have your own banner? Mm, yes, I like it, I like it a lot. Right, that's settled, now, I have much to see to. Go and tell your men the news, you are dismissed Lieutenant Riley."

The tall redheaded Irishman stood up, saluted and left the General to his work.

***

John and Daniel had experienced for the first time the carnage of battle. Men had died, others seriously wounded with some losing limbs. Dan had tried to assist a soldier on horseback caught by his foot in the stirrup as he had been dragged across the stony ground but the terrified horse had reared up on his hind legs and caught Dan with his flailing hooves. His shirt had been caked in blood but the wound was superficial and required no stitching. The noise and smell of battle, the smoke from the guns, the shrieks of pain from the dying men and the clash of close-quarter combat with bayonets had spurred the young soldiers on. Their retreat had been inevitable. In their haste, equipment had been abandoned, cannons hurled into the Rio Grande and he and John had been among the frightened Mexican troops who fled for their lives.

Early next day, the troops prepared to retreat across three hundred miles of desert and scrub, transporting what was salvaged of their artillery and wagons of supplies. They limped, exhausted into Linares in Nuevo León to re-form and count their losses.

CHAPTER THIRTEEN
LINARES MAY 1846

The fleeing Mexicans left behind them all but their personal belongings, abandoning field packs, cannons they had spiked to prevent them being of use to their enemy, ammunition and even their wounded fellow soldiers who would have difficulty undertaking the long trek across parched lands dotted with cactus. The water they carried with them soon ran out and more men were lost to thirst and hunger. The weary troops had some relief when sudden rainfall eased their plight. However, some men succumbed to despair and found isolated places where they turned their guns on themselves.

John and Daniel were amongst those still barely alive when they saw in the distance the city of Linares, its white walls gleaming in the sunshine and the cathedral soaring over the single storey houses on narrow streets splashed with the gaudy bougainvillaea. Hardened soldiers, battle-weary, openly wept with relief. As they limped into the square, a fountain sparkled, water leaping into the air as if in joyous welcome to the parched, dusty men. They were soon pushing each other to get close enough to drink away their thirst before collapsing from exhaustion and lying bedraggled and weak around the low wall which surrounded the fountain. They had covered over two hundred miles across some of the roughest terrain they had ever experienced.

The concerned citizens of Linares had watched the troops arrive from the safety of their homes but they soon began to emerge with food and clothing for their brave soldiers. Shelter was found for them for the brief respite from marching before they left to head to Monterrey. Amongst the dozen or so men who were assigned a barn in which to rest, were John and Daniel Walsh.

Dan threw himself onto the welcoming pile of straw which would be their bed.

"Jesus, Mary and Joseph. How did we come to be here, our John? So far from Ireland, green and dewy, to a land of dry-throat sunshine and cold nights? How many men were lost? For what?"

John did not reply. He had no answer. His feet were blistered with weeping sores, his whole body ached from the long days of marching and he didn't want to think of Ireland with her soft rain and humble families making their living from small patches of ground with low walls of stones gathered from the fields in which the potatoes would grow. God willing. He fought back tears and a lump rose in his throat suppressing any words he might be inclined to voice.

Around them, other men muttered quietly while some just turned their backs on their stinking, flea-bitten comrades and faced the wall of the barn, feigning sleep. To fall asleep and not dream was all they wanted from life.

The sound of the church bells calling the faithful to morning mass stirred the soldiers from their deep sleep. Across the floor of the barn, the first shafts of daylight turned the straw to gold and accentuated the premature lines on the faces of the young men slowly sitting up, blinking in the soft light, and pushing their straggly hair away from their eyes. Those who still had boots to call their own had slept in them for fear of losing them to a bare-footed comrade.

The owner of the barn pushed open the door and winced as the overpowering stench of so many unwashed men caught his breath. Behind him followed two young boys and the three of them carried baskets filled with bread and fruit. They spoke no English but the Mexican soldiers among them nodded and even smiled as the farmer handed them the food and pointed to the stone trough half-full of water. He had told them they could wash in the trough, drinking water would be brought for them. The three disappeared but the two boys returned, one carrying a pitcher of water, the other a pitcher of milk.

As they ate, slowly despair was replaced with optimism and the men began to talk with some confidence at their current situation and even to laugh at the unruly sight of their companions.

"Mind my things while I clean up, eh? Then I'll do the same for you."

Daniel had eaten his fill and he wiped the remains of the milk from his mouth.

One of the soldiers said what they were all thinking.

"How long d'you think we'll be here for boys? Does anyone know? I could make myself quite at home. One of these small houses would suit me fine with a pretty Mexican girl to keep me warm at night, eh?"

The men slowly relaxed and enjoyed their respite from battle.

***

General Arista had been dismissed after a court martial had found him guilty of losing the battles at Palo Alto and Resaca de la Palma. The man who replaced him, General Francisco Mejia, was not popular with the troops. He had an arrogant demeanour and was contemptuous of the soldiers under his command, now almost 3000. He was to lead them, some without boots still, all wearing the filthy, ragged remains of their uniforms, to Monterrey.

It was July before the Mexican troops headed north for Monterrey, crossing the Sierra Madre Oriental with steep ravines and rocky walls, low temperatures and thin air which made breathing difficult. They climbed wearily through the forested slopes until, after covering one hundred miles, they caught sight of the city of Monterrey below them. The River Santa Catarina flowed swiftly through the city after torrential rain and the cathedral bells pealed a welcome. The Bishop's Palace, Obispado, stood guard over the city which from a distance appeared impenetrable. Cannons were positioned overlooking the road along which General Taylor was expected to approach. White painted haciendas shone in the sunshine and many of the men, relieved at reaching their journey's end, straightened their backs, raised their heads and marched with renewed vigour. The city was well fortified from all appearances and it was a happy band of men who entered the walls of the city.

Hope returned to the weary men. They were now free to attend Mass, mingle with the locals and enjoy some relief from soldiering. Sentries were posted to watch for any movement on the Marin road and by August their number had swelled with fresh troops arriving, bringing with them more cannon. Once again, their leader was replaced, this time by General Ampudia. The reinforcements raised the morale of the original troops who stood with the civilians cheering the men marching in with bands playing and flags flying. Now they truly felt they must be invincible. New bastions were built near the Marin road, buildings were fortified and even the church allowed the magazine to be stored within its walls.

John Riley was impressed with how readily his men had aided the Mexican troops and civilians prepared the city for withstanding an assault. One evening, when the two young Walsh boys rested after a day of piling sandbags on roofs, reinforcing doors and carrying ammunition into the cathedral, Lieutenant Riley sought them out. They stood and saluted him but he told them to resume their seated position. He sat with them in the shade of a tree with their backs to a low wall.

"Here, fresh water for you both."

He handed them a canteen of warm but refreshing water.

John drank from it and passed it to Dan.

"How are you enjoying military life then, you two? Does it fulfil your expectations? Come on now, be honest. We are just three men from the Emerald Isle enjoying some craic after a hard day's work."

Neither boys spoke immediately but glanced at each other, hoping the other would speak first.

Then Dan cleared his throat.

"Well, sir…"

"No need to call me sir when we are just in each other's company, Riley will do fine, seeing as we are two Johns."

"Well, Riley, I must confess that everything has been so different from anything or any place I've ever been. This time last year I had sailed from Ireland, met our John in New Orleans without so much as a plan in my head of where my future lay. What with the weather being so strange and the food even more strange, I have wondered if I should just be getting the first boat home. Yet here I am, shoulder to shoulder with Mexicans, fighting their bullying neighbours."

John Walsh interrupted.

"And don't forget we are brothers in faith with the Mexicans too. I never thought we would be treated so badly for our faith. It is good to be in a land of true believers, I say."

"Are you still keen to fight, though, boys? Remember, we are now fighting with the biggest army but we don't have the modern weapons the Americans have."

"But our cannons still fire good shot and our infantry out-numbers theirs."

Dan grew restless and stood up to begin pacing up and down.

Riley smiled and pressed the boy to be seated.

"I can promise you that this city will be hard to take. Her natural defences are impressive enough but with all the hard work improving the fortifications, we have made it damned hard for them when they arrive."

He stood up and stretched.

"There is also a good chance that more Americans will desert, some to head back home but some will no doubt join us. General Ampudia has prepared another leaflet for the enemy troops with promises they will find difficult to ignore. Now, I do believe it's time for vittles and bed for me."

The brothers bade him a restful night and headed to their own beds.

CHAPTER FOURTEEN
BATTLE OF MONTERREY September 1846

John Riley went looking for John and Daniel as they waited for the next advance of the Americans and he found them cleaning their guns. They looked up and were about to stand and salute him but he shook his head and sat down with them.

"We have learnt the Americans have now left their camp at Camargo and they are on their way to Monterrey. Now, what I want to know is – are you ready for them boys?"

"Yes, sir! We know from talking with our fellow soldiers we are as ready as we will ever be. Our defences are secure, they will have a tough time trying to break through to be sure."

John Walsh nodded in agreement with Daniel.

"Aye, we are all confident we will get the better of them. After all, are there not still men deserting them and coming over to our side? They tell us others are slipping away, no stomach for the fight and heading back home in droves."

"Don't pay too much attention to the tittle tattle of disillusioned troops, we know they are a hard enemy, and impatient to do battle."

He stood up and patted both brothers on the shoulder.

"Well, we have trained hard, weapons are ready and supplies are sufficient. God will be on our side you can be sure of that. Now remember, take no unnecessary risks, look out for one another. I intend to speak to all my men tonight, tell them to fight as if we are fighting for dear old Ireland herself. Be sure to rest up ready."

He left them and they watched as he spoke briefly to their comrades. Then quietness fell as men slept or sat deep in thought.

Dawn broke as the Americans attacked unexpectedly from both the north and the west. John and Daniel were among the troops fighting to maintain control of the supply road to Saltillo. The fighting was fierce and the Mexicans were slowly driven back into the city. The Mexican snipers on the rooftops inflicted heavy casualties on the enemy as they swarmed through the streets and soon the road was filled with fallen men, anguished cries mingling with the sound of gunfire. While this hindered the advancing troops, John and Daniel fled from the Teneria with the rest of their comrades and dodged the American snipers who had now taken over the roof positions. Lt Riley shouted,

"Men, let's see if we can make it to El Diablo. Go some of you while we cover your backs."

Not all of them were fortunate enough to join the soldiers already fighting gallantly to maintain control of the fortification. It was nightfall before the cannon fire ceased and the church bells could be heard ringing out for Evening Vespers. While some civilians knelt praying in the church, the troops of both sides sought out their wounded. The Mexican casualties were taken to the hospital in the city while the Americans had a makeshift field hospital outside the city walls. Other civilians had ignored the bells and were busy doing what they could for the exhausted soldiers. Young women were finding their way through the men sitting exhausted on the ground and offering them food from baskets laden with bread and fruit. John looked up as one young girl hovered over him, a shy smile lighting up her face. She proffered him some bread so he wiped the dirt and sweat from his face before he took it and thanked her, hungrily biting a chunk off.

"Thank you, you are an angel."

"No, no, I help. Give me a gun and I will be a soldier, like you, and fight for Mexico."

Her face wore a fierce expression.

"I bet you would, too. I don't think things will come to that where women have to fight."

The girl held out a canteen of water and he took it, nodding his gratitude before quenching his thirst and handing it back.

"What name are you? I know you came from a foreign place by your red hair."

"John. You have heard of Ireland?"

The girl shook her head.

"No? It is a small country, green from the soft rain, a long way across the Atlantic Ocean. This here is my brother, Daniel. How about you, what name do you go by?"

Daniel smiled at the girl as he took some bread from her basket.

"I am Francesca. What are you both doing so far from home?"

The boys finished eating before replying.

Daniel spoke first.

"Ah, now then, it's a long story. But we can tell you we are both pleased and proud to be here and maybe one day, when the fighting is all over, we will tell you about our voyages."

Francesca settled her basket comfortably on her arm.

"Be sure I will seek you out. My father is a doctor here and I have three sisters, no brothers sadly. We do what we can to make him proud. Now I must fetch more food, so many men to feed. Stay safe until we meet again."

She smiled and waved as she made her way between the seated soldiers.

"Well, brother, that's the nearest I have ever been to an angel for sure. And to think, I always imagined angels to be fair of skin and hair. She was so pretty with her beautiful brown eyes filled with passion and her dark curls framing her face."

Daniel laughed and pushed his brother.

"Our John, I do believe you are smitten once again! These dusky lasses will take your heart so they will. No red-headed Irish girl will stand a chance!"

The surviving troops slept fitfully that night with the anguished cries and groans of the wounded and dying replacing the sound of guns. They took some comfort from knowing that Monterrey was still in Mexican hands. For now at least.

Next morning before dawn, the American troops had climbed the western slope of Independencia Hill. Soaked to the skin from the relentless rain, they reached the summit by daybreak then rushed the Redoubt and took it, much to the surprise of the Mexicans. Meanwhile, Lt Col Francisco Berra, with two hundred men hid behind the walls of the Bishop's Palace. Soon the American artillery brigade was firing at them with twelve pound howitzers resulting in some Mexican soldiers charging at them and falling injured or dead as a result. Lt Riley shouted at his men to fall back to safety but only a few made it to the gates of the palace. By mid-afternoon the American infantry broke through the gates and swarmed into the inner courtyard to face the muskets of the Mexicans within who fought bravely, but the Americans triumphed and eventually outnumbered the Mexicans who retreated back to Monterrey, leaving in their haste their casualties to be dealt with by their foe. Soon the Mexican flag had been hauled down, to be replaced by 'Old Glory' the American flag, fluttering over the Bishop's Palace.

General Ampudia consulted his senior staff and reluctantly gave orders for an immediate withdrawal of his remaining troops back to the main city plaza. John and Daniel were among the defeated soldiers but many of their comrades had perished.

The next day, when American troops approached the Black Fort, part of the Northern defences, there was little resistance. It was only when they neared the city plaza that they came under heavy fire from the Mexicans and they too suffered casualties. They pressed on regardless, using the protection of the houses for cover. They smashed their way through the inner walls of the houses and fired at the enemy artillery from the safety of the buildings. Soon they were close to huddled groups of terrified civilians and the remaining Mexican troops.

That evening, General Ampudia, after further discussion with his senior officers, was ready to surrender and on the 25th September he did just that. General Zachary Taylor agreed to a withdrawal of the Mexican troops and allowed them to take with them their small arms and a battery of six guns. A cease fire was agreed to last eight weeks.

In their Mexican uniforms the Irish soldiers, with their Mexican comrades, joined the march out of the citadel. Lt John Riley sat aboard one of the caissons with his fellow battery commanders and waited for the infantry and cavalry to lead the march. Civilians wept as the column left to the sound of trumpets and drumrolls with banners carried proudly waving in the breeze. The American troops lined the route out of the city and watched in silence as their enemies left. It was not until the battery rolled slowly past them that angry shouts were heard. Hissing and booing, American soldiers recognised their former comrades leaving with the Mexicans. John O'Reilly and the other 'deserters' stared resolutely ahead as insults and invectives were hurled at them.

***

The retreat took the Mexicans south-west to Saltillo where they were able to replenish their supplies. From there they marched to meet their new commander, General Santa Anna, who was awaiting their arrival at San Luis Potasi. Battered, weary and dejected, they crossed the desert with just an occasional cactus or poor-looking palm tree to provide meagre shade. Initially, the Irish troops spoke to each other about their desire to see once more the lush green fields of Ireland with their low stone walls but as they marched, they soon fell silent. Their legs were weary and their backpacks heavy on their shoulders. With fair complexions now turned ruddy and blistering in the relentless sunshine, they looked a sorry sight. Talking was difficult with cracked, swollen lips and dry mouths. It was three weeks before they reached their destination.

As they entered the city of San Luis Potasi, they found the troops of Santa Anna already drilling and after a few days rest and with missing equipment replaced, Ampudia's men joined them. Soon Lt Riley had his men working so hard and expertly that his talents were brought to the attention of General Santa Anna who called for a meeting with him. John Riley was worried. He spoke with his two young friends.

"I don't know if I like the sound of this boys. Can it be that the general has no faith in his Irish troops? What can he have learnt of us that he needs to speak with me?"

He paced back and forth before the two youngsters, a concerned frown on his face.

John was optimistic.

"I can only think he has heard good things, surely? We all fought as if it was Ireland herself we were fighting for."

Daniel was not convinced though.

"Maybe he just sees us as deserters and as such we cannot be trusted?"

Riley stopped pacing and ran his fingers through his matted curls.

"My thoughts exactly. Well, take the bull by the horns, I guess. I will let you know later how it went."

"St Patrick himself will be with you to be sure, sir"

They saluted him and watched as their hero walked away.

Back at his quarters, Riley brushed down his uniform, adjusted his lieutenant's sword and tidied his hair before putting on his cap and made his way to the general's office.

General Santa Anna looked up from his paperwork as Lt Riley was shown in. He acknowledged the lieutenant's salute and stood to offer him a chair. Riley noticed the walking stick with which Santa Anna supported himself while he stood. He had been told that the general had lost his left leg fighting against the French and he was respected and adored by most Mexicans for his fierce fighting skills and ability to raise money and organise his troops with speed. The general was an imposing figure in his resplendent uniform.

When both men were seated, Santa Anna clasped his hands together on his portly stomach and looked Riley straight in the eye.

"I have heard only good things of you Lt Riley. Your ability as a soldier is well documented. Tell me of your past, how you came to leave the American army and join us. Be completely honest with me now."

Riley relaxed a little.

"Sir, I had served in the British army in Canada before heading south to America in search of a new life. When I found that the Irish were not welcome in America and so decent work was hard to find, I enlisted in the American army expecting my rank as sergeant in the British army to be recognised. We were promised American citizenship would be fast-tracked for us which was not strictly true. Our faith was against us. Any Irish Catholics were punished harshly for minor misdemeanours, the officers hated us and promotion through the ranks never happened, sir."

"So, were there other factors which caused you to change sides?"

"We learnt of atrocities being perpetrated on the Mexicans by the Americans because of their devout Catholicism and we could no longer support their actions."

"So it was not the promise of the land we offered that persuaded you all?"

"I will be honest with you, sir, it was a real enticement to many of the men but not the only reason they followed me."

General Santa Anna was silent for a moment.

"I heard you were responsible for recruiting men in significant numbers. You must be a born leader, Riley."

"I don't know about that, sir, but I did speak with passion and they needed little encouragement. After all, we share our faith with Mexico and we feel we are all now fighting for justice."

Santa Anna nodded his head. After a long pause he spoke.

"I have a proposition for you. I want you to train all your men in artillery skills as we know that is where your talents lie and your expertise in that field is well proven. Naturally you will serve under a Mexican officer, Captain Moreno, but he has been ordered to leave all training of the men to you. He speaks excellent English and I feel sure you two will get along fine. So, what do you think of my proposal?"

The general smiled at the lieutenant and waited for his response.

"I am deeply honoured for your trust in me and I assure you I will train any man in my charge to give his all. Do we keep the name we use for the battalion, sir?"

"San Patricio? Of course, what is the significance of the Saint?"

"He is the Patron Saint of Ireland, sir, and any Irishman's heart would swell with pride to serve in his name. If it is alright with you, sir, can we have our own banner too?"

"What did you have in mind, lieutenant?"

"Sir, the men would see a banner with the harp of Ireland and Saint Patrick himself featured on it as a beacon they would willingly follow."

Santa Anna struggled once again to stand up.

"Well, I will leave it to you to organise the making of your banner. I feel sure you are correct in believing your men will fight the better for sight of it."

"We will never let you down, sir."

The General held himself steady with one hand holding firmly to his desk as he offered his other hand to the younger man. Riley shook his hand then stood to attention and saluted. Santa Anna dismissed him and sat down as Riley left the room.

Later that evening, before they turned in for the night, Riley spoke to John and Daniel.

"I have interesting news, boys! We Irish are held in very high regard here, things are looking up! We have proved our support for Mexico in the best possible way and shown him what we are made of!"

John Walsh had no hesitation clapping him on his back.

"That is wonderful news! You must have made a huge impression on the general!"

Dan was a little more inhibited. After all, they were much lower in rank so he offered his hand for a handshake.

Riley gripped it tightly and thanked them for their support.

"We all impressed the general, not just myself. The amnesty with the Americans lasts eight weeks so we have a deal of work to do, then we must be ready for fighting once more."

The troops all threw themselves into the weeks of training, filling the days with drilling and exercises until they had honed their skills thoroughly. At weekends, they had lighter duties and were able to attend Mass in the magnificent Cathedral of Our Lady of Carmen. As in Monterrey, the Irish troops found the building so much more opulent than the small stone churches back home. The citizens were just as welcoming and called the red-haired Irish 'Los Colorados' for the colour of their hair and sunburnt complexions.

***

Before the New Year arrived, the Mexican army had welcomed even more deserters into its ranks and the foreign brigade numbered over one hundred men, mostly Irish but also some Germans and other Europeans.

One of the new Irish recruits had left the American army for the same reason as John Riley, he knew he had little chance of promotion. Patrick Dalton hailed from County Mayo and Riley told the two Walsh boys of his arrival. The three of them met in the mess room at dinner, all of them seated with other Irish soldiers and a couple from Germany. Dalton was regaling them with tales of his escape.

"Ah, well now, you see, we had all been washing our clothes in the Rio Grande and I rushed to get mine done so I could slip away. The dumb sergeant believed me when I said I was heading back to camp but as soon as I was out of sight I ducked into a cornfield and hid. After it was dark, I waded into the river and crossed into Mexico. Local rancheros are helping deserters and they supplied me with a mule and helped me on my way, and so here I am!"

Daniel waited while Patrick took a mouthful of food then asked him, "Whereabouts in County Mayo did you live? Me and me big brother here left Mayo ourselves."

"D'you know of Ballina? That's where what's left of my family live. Or did. I've lost touch with them but hell, they were glad to see me go. How about you boys, anybody back home to miss you?"

"We left our parents, two brothers and three sisters. We kept in touch at first through our parish priest but now it's not so easy. We wrote to them from Fort Texas but since we crossed over it's been difficult. Last we heard, they wrote they were all fine and wished us both well."

143

"And Lt Riley? Is he too grand for the likes of us now he's an officer?"

John looked surprised at the question.

"Hell no, you'll never find a more honest, decent man than the lieutenant. We get to call him John when we are alone with him but we take care to salute him and give him due respect most other times. He earned his promotion because of his skills with artillery."

"Did he now? Well wouldn't you know it, I am a dab hand with the old guns meself. Should I mention it, d'you think? Here he comes now."

Daniel stood to gain John Riley's attention.

"Lt Riley, sir? Our new recruit has something to ask you."

John Riley pushed his way between the crowded benches of men eating, talking and laughing until he reached their table. He stood at one end with his arms folded, his face expressionless. They fell silent.

"Well, be quick now, I am about to get my dinner too. What is it you want to say, Private Dalton?"

Patrick Dalton struggled to stand but Riley waved him to stay seated.

"Well, sir, the boys here were telling me how you gained promotion with your knowledge of artillery? Well, not boasting but I'm pretty good meself so I am and I would be grateful if you would consider me good enough to join the artillery?"

Riley unfolded his arms and stood with his hands held behind his back.

The rest of the men at the table stopped eating briefly as they waited for the reply.

"I'll tell you what I'll do. Tomorrow morning before your duties start I will take you to meet the general, he will be the one to decide. It will be down to you to make a good case for yourself so after breakfast be ready."

"Thank you, sir," said Dalton as Riley nodded his head and left them to finish their meal.

It was noon next day before John and Daniel saw Patrick Dalton. He ran to join them with a grin so wide the boys knew he must have good news.

"Ah, boys, boys! That Santa Anna! He's a man with understanding and a big heart. He did no less than ask me loads of questions about the Americans, quizzed me on gun handling then he said he was to make me a second lieutenant! Stuff you, Yankees! Just wait until we fight again, then they'll see what they lost, eh?"

***

In January the following year, General Santa Anna ordered his troops, now fully trained, to head north. The San Patricios were in the vanguard leading the troops out of San Luis Potosi, their new green banner flying proudly at the front. General Santa Anna galloped forward until he was ahead of them then he turned his horse to face his army. The troops slowed to a standstill and fell silent as he raised his hand before beginning his speech. They listened, their chests swelling with pride at being part of this magnificent fighting force until he ended his speech with the following words.

"Today you commence your march through thinly settled country, without supplies and without provisions; but you may be assured that very quickly you will be in possession of those of your enemy, and of his riches! And with them, all your wants will be remedied!"

He pointed north and saluted his troops as they progressed out of town to cries of 'Santa Anna! Santa Anna'. Bands began to play, families and sweethearts ran alongside the departing men, throwing flowers at their feet and blowing kisses. The sound of cheers faded as the troops marched onwards.

CHAPTER FIFTEEN
BATTLE OF BUENA VISTA February 1847

The march north took them across deserts, through ravines and up steep mountains. Thunderous storms raged, torrential rain lashed the weary men and some fell dead from exhaustion or slipped away unseen to head for home. When the remaining soldiers arrived at a point where the enemy could be seen in the distance, their spirits lifted. The army below them appeared to be a mismatched band of men and the Mexicans had the high ground and outnumbered the Americans.

When the fighting began it was onslaught after onslaught, first the Mexicans gaining ground then the Americans. Every possible weapon was employed from artillery to infantry with muskets and Lt Riley urged his gunners to keep firing at the American troops as they fell back. With horses dead and dying, guns had to be dragged back by worn out soldiers and soon the enemy were fleeing in order to re-form. Then it was the turn of the Mexicans to retreat to the shelter of ravines as the Americans stood their ground and bombarded them once more. Sprawled between the two armies was a patchwork carpet of bodies in a variety of uniforms from both sides lying amongst the fallen, dead or dying horses. As the fighting continued, the San Patricios held their ground under fierce attack. John Walsh looked around for sight of his young brother but it was impossible to distinguish one man from another. Night time came and the guns fell silent, just the sounds of dying filled the air as men moaned and called for their mothers, others blasphemed and swore at the uncaring God who had failed them when He was needed.

John went amongst the bodies calling out his brother's name, slipping on the spilled blood which joined Mexican to American in a ghastly blood-brotherhood. He saw one figure move slightly, a man of Daniel's build, lying face down, his tunic drenched in blood and when John turned him over gently he shuddered at the sight of the poor man's face. From one empty eye-socket to his jaw his face was missing. His other eye looked at John, wide eyed in abject fear until he recognised his big brother. Fighting the nausea at the horrific sight of young Daniel's injuries, John spoke gently to him.

"There now, our Dan, I am here with you now, I will take care of you."

Daniel was unable to speak but he cried out in pain as John carefully lifted him onto his shoulder. He struggled to carry the boy across the mound of bodies and made his way back to where the guns stood in silence as if admonishing the men.

Lt Riley tried in vain to count how many of his men had survived and how many had been brought in injured. He came across John Walsh tending what appeared to be a corpse. On closer examination he was shocked to see it was Daniel, lying on the ground, unrecognisable had it not been for the presence of his brother.

"God Almighty, John! In all my fighting days I have never seen carnage like this! Bastard Americans! The poor boy. Does he breathe still? He is so badly injured surely the Good Lord will take him in his mercy?"

The older brother leaned forward, tears falling from his eyes mingling with his brother's blood and glistening on Daniel's brow. He slowly closed the eyelid of the remaining eye now staring blankly back at him and fell onto his brother's chest, sobbing, his whole body shaking from emotion.

Riley knelt down beside him and put his arm around the grieving boy then between them they carried Daniel to where horse-drawn wagons were waiting to carry away the casualties. Close to where the battle had been fought, a place for a burial site was chosen. Working resolutely, no words spoken but with heavy hearts, the team assigned the task of burying the dead dug one shallow pit to contain the bodies of their comrades.

John took a last look at his young brother, having removed from his pockets his few personal belongings before covering him with soil as gently as if it was a blanket from home. He whispered a brief prayer before doing the same for other twisted, wrecked bodies.

Not one soldier slept in the Mexican camp that night. General Santa Anna gave the order to strike camp and after checking they had left no wounded soldiers behind to face whatever might befall them if left to the Americans, they slipped away under cover of darkness, returning beaten and bedraggled to San Luis Potosi. A roll call revealed more than a third of the San Patricios had lost their lives.

In March, the Americans took the port of Vera Cruz. Their supply line was now assured. In Mexico, the San Patricios were praised by Brigadier Mejia for the way they had fought and Lt John Riley was promoted to Captain. An uneasy truce gave both sides a chance to repair weapons, recruit more men and in the case of the Americans, care for the large number of soldiers struck down with yellow fever and dysentery. In April, General Scott ordered the camp to head to the mountains, away from the disease-carrying mosquitos, and where the climate was kinder. From the new vantage point they were able to see in the distance Santa Anna's army waiting for them in an excellent position at Cerro Gordo, guns aimed ready at the advancing enemy. General Scott swore when he spotted the flag of the San Patricios flying defiantly. He sent out scouts to look for a way around the Mexicans. A trail through the wooded hillside was hacked by the Americans and the troops were mustered to file along it to the Mexican base at La Atalya. This provided them with the opportunity to force the Mexicans back to El Telegrafo where the San Patricios with their sixteen pounders were ready.

"Stand your ground, boys, don't let the bastards get the better of us! Remember how they treated you before, if they capture any of us we will be hung as traitors! Aim steady and true, make every shot count!"

Captain John Riley led by example and the guns blazed, smoke swirled around the determined men but they had not reckoned with the Americans using a howitzer. The gun was used successfully at

Monterrey by the American army but the Mexicans had thought the terrain here at Cerro Gordo impassable for the guns. What they had not allowed for was the US Mountain Howitzer which could be broken down and carried on packhorses along with the boxes of ammunitions. The resulting casualties on the Mexican side were many and by nightfall they fell back and both sides had time to deal with their injured and dead.

General Scott now ordered another trail to be cut at El Telegrafo to enable him to attack Cerro Gordo from the north.

Exhausted from little sleep and endless duties, John and his comrades were woken early next morning by firing commencing once more from the American twenty-four pounders. It was followed by hand to hand combat and the Mexicans broke cover and fled down the hill. Captain Riley and his men abandoned their guns and escaped along the road to Jalopa. This battle was over by midday. Three thousand Mexicans were captured along with forty cannons which included the artillery of the San Patricios. The remaining straggling Mexican troops hoped they could make it to Mexico City.

Young John Walsh and his fellow Irishmen still had faith in their captain but they were a silent group of men as they headed north.

By May 15th, General Scott had garrisoned Jalapa, Perote and on May 28th, Puebla. Here his advance stalled because Mexicans had attacked the American supply lines.

General Santa Anna was now in Mexico City and by declaring Martial Law, he was able to increase his troops to 25,000.

The officers of the American Army still treated their immigrant, Irish soldiers with contempt, prompting Santa Anna to renew his appeal to disillusioned Irish soldiers to join with the Mexicans and once again promised land to any of the misused men who would change sides. As a result, the San Patricios numbers swelled once more with deserters, captured Irish and other foreign nationals who were persuaded to join them. They took the lull in fighting as an opportunity to drill and train the new soldiers along with the veterans, and once more they had some leisure time.

John had befriended one of the young deserters, Kevin Kelly from Wexford. As they explored the beautiful city, they chatted and laughed, two youngsters enjoying a brief spell of normality.

"What brought you to Mexico, Kevin?"

"Ah, wouldn't you know it, I came seeking fortune just like the next man. Things back home are just so bad right now with the potatoes getting the old blight again. Hundreds, no, thousands of Irish are getting out while they can, there's no food, no jobs, no hope. Me whole family got as far as Liverpool but that wasn't far enough for me."

"Well I'm just praying my family in Ballybray, County Mayo are as fine as they tell me. I last heard that my sister Eliza has also sailed for Liverpool so that is one less mouth to feed. I send them money when I can but fighting wars hinders a man, sure enough."

"Well, would you just look at this place!"

The two young soldiers had arrived at the Metropolitan Church. It was a magnificent building, soaring high above them. Their timing was perfect. As they considered entering through the huge doors, bells from the twin bell towers began to peal, calling the faithful to Mass. Slowly people began to make their way inside so they joined the crowd. Once inside they were stopped in their tracks as they gazed upwards. People behind them filtered around the awestruck spectating youths. The interior was beyond any sight either of them had seen.

"I thought I'd seen it all in Monterrey, but Holy Mary, this is something else, for sure."

"Just look at the altar! And look, look, there are chapels down both sides! D'you think they might have one to Saint Patrick maybe?"

"Ah, I doubt it but we'll have a closer look after the service. Where d'you fancy sitting, Kevin?"

"Ah, but it's so posh maybe we'd better sit as far back as we can. I wouldn't like some old Mexican lady to be draggin' me from me seat. If you watch, they seem to have their very own places."

A quiet side pew, half hidden from the Priest, suited the boys and after kneeling to pray they sat, caps in hand with their heads swivelling to take all the splendour in.

"They must be rich here in Mexico City, look at all the gold everywhere!"

John had been in Mexico long enough to learn from the Mexican soldiers some of the history of the country.

"They speak Spanish here because Spanish explorers came in search of gold and the Incas who lived here then had loads of the stuff! They gave tons of it to the Spanish but the Spaniards were greedy, so it's said, and wanted the lot."

"What happened?"

Kevin listened intently as John whispered the history lesson to him.

"The Spaniards had horses, guns and deadly diseases and the old Incas were no match for them."

The bells had stopped ringing and the clerics entered, incense swinging, passing the standing congregation as they made their way to the altar.

Although both boys had not attended any church service for some time, the incantations were familiar to them and they soon joined in. They were both deep in thought as they filed out of the church when the service ended, back into the spring sunshine. John had wiped tears from his eyes while he had his head bowed in prayer as he thought of Daniel. Kevin pretended he had not seen him.

Outside, the Zocalo, the main square was now a lot busier. People sat in the shade of the ash trees as they watched other citizens stroll by, admiring the flower gardens. A far cry from the sights John and Kevin had become used to of late. After a leisurely, refreshing diversion from their soldiering, the two young Irishmen returned to base. All the Mexican troops knew that the Americans were just seventy-five miles away in Puebla but the sickness was still rife amongst their troops. Santa Anna had prepared yet another leaflet entitled 'Mexicans to Catholic Irishmen' which was smuggled once again into the American camp. He hoped also that it would incite the people of Puebla to rise up against the foreign invaders when Santa Anna arrived with his army and hopefully leading to a victory for the Mexicans.

Captain Riley had been promoted to Major in June, so he had taken advantage of his status and negotiated a contract for his men with Santa Anna.

FOREIGN LEGION – SAN PATRICIOS COMPANIES

We, the undersigned foreigners, voluntarily contract ourselves to serve in the said Legion for the term of six months, counted from this date (July 1847), legally serving the Mexican Republic under the following conditions:

1. The Mexican Government will give us lands to cultivate at the conclusion of the war.

2. Those who do not wish to remain in this country will be embarked for Europe at the expense of the supreme government, which will also give them a gratification in money.

3. The Mexican government agrees to give to the Legion, during the time of their service, quarters, clothing, shoes, etc.

4. First sergeants will receive five reales daily, corporals three, and privates two and a half reales per day (eight reales in a peso, and a peso equal to a U.S. dollar).

***

Amongst Daniel's few possessions, John had found a scrap of paper on which Daniel had been writing a letter to Jane McNulty, back in New Orleans. As he read it his eyes filled with tears. His brother was writing a farewell letter, fearing the worst. Now it was down to John to add words confirming that indeed Daniel had lost his life. At the first opportunity he completed the letter and wrote one of his own to his parents back in Ireland. He had no idea how they were faring, he just hoped that their last letter had been truthful and that they were all well. At least the San Patricios were fortunate amongst the Mexican troops, they had received their pay while many Mexican soldiers had been made to wait. He found a bank from where he was able to transfer money to his family, care of Father Murphy.

My Dear Ma and Pa
Mexico City

I am sorry to be the bearer of bad news. Our Daniel was fighting alongside me in a fierce battle and was mown down by a cannon fired by the Americans. He did not suffer and died instantly. I buried him with fellow soldiers and said prayers from you for him. I am quite well though very let down by some of the Americans I have met especially the officers who made our lives hell. I am proud to fight for Mexico; she is second best country after Ireland. I have sent you some money as we hear disturbing news of yet more famine in Ireland. May God take good care of you all, I send my love to my brothers and sisters and pray the day will come when I shall see you all once more.

Your loving son,
John.

***

The peace treaty Santa Anna had been negotiating with the Americans collapsed but at least it had given him time to strengthen his numbers. By August, he was confident his troops could get the better of the American invaders. Major Riley and the San Patricios had left the safety of the city and were barricaded in an abandoned monastery. The men were drilled daily and were issued with Brown Bess flintlocks, guns some of them had been familiar with when they had served in the British Army. John and Kevin learnt fast. They were now firm pals, Kevin glad to be under the wing of the older boy while John found the younger boy's keenness so like Daniel's, his friendship eased his loss.

The boys were on sentry duty on the ninth of August, chatting to each other as they scanned the valley for movement.

"Eh, John, look."

Kevin pointed to dust clouds in the far distance.

"It's them! The Americans! Holy Mary there's an awful lot of them! Better tell the officers."

John replied,

"You go, I'll keep watching. Come back and let me know what's for us to do next."

Major Riley and Colonel Moreno accompanied Kevin back to his post. Colonel Moreno put his telescope to his eye and was silent for a short while before passing it to Major Riley.

"Looks like they're ready to do battle yet again. See for yourself."

"Private Walsh, Private McNulty, tell the buglers to sound the call to arms then join your battalion and await further orders."

"Yes, sir,"

Both boys stood to attention, saluted and ran quickly to find the buglers, easy to spot in their bright green coats and green shako plumes. With excitement and fear, they relayed the message and took up their positions alongside the guns. All the soldiers were preparing their weapons, buttoning up tunics and straightening their caps. They were as ready as they would ever be.

The advance of the enemy was still some way away but the gunners were ordered to fire their guns to warn all soldiers and citizens of the imminent danger. The night passed, very few men slept as they waited for the dawn. In the morning, the plaza filled with cheering crowds as military bands played, and civilians and soldiers sought good vantage points on rooftops from where they could watch the American army troops advancing towards them down the National Highway.

CHAPTER SIXTEEN
THE BATTLE FOR MEXICO CITY AUGUST 1847

John, Kevin and their comrades looked very smart in their new uniforms of dark blue tunics with red collars and cuffs and light blue trousers piped in red. On their heads, the privates wore caps adorned with red tassels.

Kevin grinned at John.

"Now what d'you think me Ma and Da would make of me now? Don't we just look grand? Never have I worn anything so fine before in all me life!"

"We look amazing! Even the British soldiers I saw back home never looked this good. We dress well and we fight well, that's what I think anyway."

John plucked a loose thread off his jacket.

"Shush, here comes the General."

All the troops stood to attention in perfect formation as Santa Anna reviewed his colourful men, stopping occasionally to share words of inspiration. As he climbed a podium to make a speech, the crowd of soldiers and civilians fell silent. His speech forecast an inevitable victory: they had the greater numbers, the city was well fortified and God was on the side of the Mexicans. Ravines lay to the right, and the Pedregal (a five mile wide volcanic field with boulders, shrubs and calcified lava which seemed an impossible terrain for an army to cross) was to the left. The cheers were deafening, hats were thrown in the air and bands began to play patriotic music.

The Irish among the soldiers never felt more Mexican.

From the safety of the monastery on August 19th, the men were alerted to watch from the walls a sight which made their spirits fall.

Heading back to Mexico City were some of their own troops, fleeing from the direction of Contreras. The general in command of these troops, General Valencia, had been taken completely by surprise when he saw that the Americans had hacked a pathway through the Pedregal. They had fought the Americans but were overcome, and lost the two guns they themselves had won from the enemy at Buena Vista. With the San Patricios banner flying proudly overhead, Major Riley inspected his troops, assuring himself of their readiness and shouting encouragement. He did not want the men to feel things were not going their way.

"We must all stand firm! Have your guns primed ready, we have the advantage so don't despair! Aim at the officers first!"

Some of the San Patricios were defending the bridgehead, their guns camouflaged from enemy sight. John saw Kevin cross himself as he held his muzzleloader ready.

They were soaked to the skin from the constant rainfall and shivering both from fear and cold when Major Riley gave an order for the men to feign death. As the Americans approached to within a hundred yards of what they thought were casualties, the 'dead' sprang to life and fired at the enemy soldiers. Smoke filled the air as the San Patricios charged, screaming obscenities.

John lunged at an American who was about to fire his gun and thrust his bayonet into him, withdrawing it from the screaming man just in time to lift his musket and fire at a mounted soldier, causing the horse to fall. The cavalry man landed in a twisted heap pinned beneath his injured steed. John brought the butt of his gun down on the screaming man's head and finished him off. He had no time to search out Kevin, it was every man for himself. Slowly the Irish were pushed back, ducking to avoid flailing hooves of the horses carrying sabre-bearing American cavalry units until they made it to the comparative safety of the monastery. Luck was not with them however, as the walls were being scaled by American troops and they were growing in number in the courtyard below. When the outer doors were breached by cannon fire, the Mexican command called for a cease-fire to be sounded. Major John Riley refused to surrender until an American officer of equal rank arrived. A general accepted the surrender and the Mexican flag was lowered and replaced by the Stars and Stripes. An American soldier took the San Patricio's flag and waved it defiantly at the captive Irishmen lying in the courtyard of the monastery. Overhead, a fierce storm raged, lightning illuminating the huddled pile of men. The spires of the churches in Mexico City shone briefly under each flash.

Out of more than three hundred men, all that was left of the San Patricios were ninety-six survivors including the men captured at Contreras. The fighting was over, now it was time for the Americans to seek revenge.

The prisoners were kept under guard at two locations, San Angel and Tacubaya. John Walsh and Kevin Kelly were amongst those held at San Angel along with John Riley. The Americans intended on charging all the prisoners with desertion, punishable with death but they had to accept with reluctance that only those who deserted after the formal declaration of war, could face the death sentence. However, the ones who had changed sides before this date would still receive the stiffest punishment permissible; fifty lashes, branding with the letter 'D' for deserter and to be held captive, doing hard labour until the war was declared officially over.

John whispered to Kevin as they sat with bound hands and feet.

"When was it you came over, Kevin? Was it in April or May? I've heard whispers we can be put to death."

Kevin tried in vain to loosen the ties around his wrists.

"I stuck it out until almost June but the bastard officers gave me no choice. I was gettin' punished just about every day and I thought they'd have my life, so I did. Anyways, I'd rather be hanged as a friend of Mexico and a foe of America."

He blinked away tears, unable to prevent them from running down his dust-ingrained face.

"Maybe we will be let off for being as young as we are? How old are you?"

Kevin replied, "Well, I've had my eighteenth birthday. How about you?"

"I am nineteen next birthday."

"How old was your brother Dan?"

"Seventeen, why?"

Kevin leaned close and whispered,

"From now on think of yourself as Daniel. I am tellin' you it will count in your favour. Before I left the American camp, there were arguments among the men for and against leaving to join the Mexicans. Some were concerned at the penalties they could expect if they were captured but they did say if you were under eighteen you would not be treated as a man."

"But what difference would that make? I could still be hung, surely?"

"Well, not in your case anyway because you defected early. But any other punishment should be more lenient."

John fell silent while he considered the suggestion. He thought of Daniel and what he would make of it. He recalled the dying moments of his brother and felt his presence. He imagined he heard him whisper, "Daniel is your name now, consider it is John who is dead and buried. Make things less grim for yourself with my blessing."

Next morning at roll call, he gave his name as Daniel Walsh and glanced across at the major to see how he would react. John Riley nodded in approval.

The men detained at San Angel learnt the fate of their fellow prisoners, all officers, court martialled at Tacubaya on August 23rd. Thirty had received the death penalty by hanging and eight were flogged and branded with a 'D' on the hip. The court martial at San Angel took place on August 26th, where twenty men were given the death sentence, three to be flogged and branded and six were fortunate enough to receive pardons as they had not deserted but had been taken captive by the Mexicans. Even though intense fighting broke out in Mexico City again, the executions were not postponed but were to be carried out on the morning of Friday 10th September.

The prisoners were woken early, those who had managed to sleep at all. They were a sorry looking sight with their heads shaved, hands bound and feet shackled as they shuffled, heads down in despair and not a murmur from any of them. They reached the Plaza of San Jacinta, usually a peaceful place with trees for shade but now the most prominent feature was the scaffold erected for the execution of those sentenced to death.

Major Riley raised his head, towering over his fellow prisoners. John, Kevin and the others awaiting their fate also stood erect and defiant. Even though they were a scruffy group of men, dirty and stinking from having been shackled for the past three weeks, they still had a dignified air about them. John Walsh felt his throat constrict with fear but he endeavoured not to show he was afraid. He had been fortunate to be sentenced to fifty lashes and to be branded on the hip. The court had accepted his brother's name and age. Kevin, however, was among the number to be hanged and his face was ashen as he struggled to control his emotions. Major Riley continued to look steadfastly straight ahead as they were led to the trees in front of the church where those to be flogged were bound, and each man tied with his face to the trunk of a tree.

The American officer in command, General Twiggs, had given orders that the flogging was to be carried out by Mexican muleteers, instructed to lay it on heavy or they would receive the same treatment.

With his cheek pressed up against the bark of the tree, John felt his shirt being torn from his back and he closed his eyes in preparation. At this point, one of the fourteen prisoners began to recite The Lord's Prayer and before he reached "Thy Kingdom come" the rest of the prisoners joined in and soon some of the crowd gathered for the spectacle added their voices while others bowed their heads in respect.

On the barked orders of an officer, the knotted leather whips began to lay into the captives. Cries of pain escaped from the pursed lips of men who tried so hard not to show their agony. Then the crowd grew restless as they counted the lashes. General Twiggs had miscounted and fifty-nine stripes crisscrossed the men's backs before the muleteers were ordered to cease.

Some of the victims had fainted, drooping against the trees with their knees buckled under them and the blood-stained ropes preventing them from falling to the ground. Members of the crowd gasped as they saw the flesh of the men shredded and bloody.

John opened his eyes when he felt the rope being untied and he fell to the ground. He was kicked until he stood upright and he fell in line with his bleeding comrades as they were led to where the fires burnt bright ready for the next punishment, the branding. He winced when he witnessed the first brandings on men with their trousers pulled down around their ankles to expose their hips in readiness. Then it was his turn.

"Holy Mother of Jesus," he cried as he felt the searing pain and smelt the burning of his own flesh. He was then pushed roughly to one side where his trousers were pulled up to cover his nudity. The groans of the men just punished turned to shouts of horror when they saw the prisoners who were branded on the face. Major John Riley was the last to receive his punishment and still he showed no emotion as the letter D was burnt into his cheek.

General Twiggs barked at the soldier carrying out the branding,

"You imbecile man! You had the brand upside down! Do it again! On the other cheek! But this time the correct way up!"

Major Riley now turned his head and stared General Twiggs straight in the eye. The general had a triumphant expression on his face as he heard the hiss of burning flesh.

Some of the civilians in the crowd bayed their disapproval but this was soon drowned out by the loud cheers from the American soldiers who were overjoyed that this particular deserter had got what he deserved. A double branding was definitely justice in their eyes.

The five Catholic priests who had been forced to watch the awful spectacle were now ordered to observe the hangings. The gallows had been prepared with sixteen nooses. Eight mule-drawn wagons carried two men each and as they stood waiting, the mules fidgeting, their handlers held tight to the reins to steady them. The priests approached to give the last rites and read prayers for the Sacrament of Extreme Unction as the drum roll began. The crowd fell silent.

Tears rolled unashamedly down John Walsh's face, not for himself but for his young friend, Kevin, standing with another condemned man on one of the carts. Kevin caught John's eye and winked before breaking into song, an old Irish folk song, Molly Malone, well known to the other men awaiting hanging. They joined in the singing, their voices strong as the sweet melody filled the square before the procession came to an abrupt end when the carts, on the orders of Twiggs, were led into position for each man to have a noose placed around his neck. The singers were strangled into silence as the men performed the dance of death.

On Saturday 14th September, a United States Marine Lieutenant hoisted the American flag over the National Palace in Mexico City. It would be the following June before all the prisoners held were finally released.

CHAPTER SEVENTEEN
WAR ENDS JUNE 1848

When the treaty of Guadalupe was signed to bring the war officially to a close, Mexico had lost two fifths of its territory. All the incarcerated men were released from their imprisonment in the Citadel. A lawyer, Carlos Franco, invited six of the San Patricios, including Major Riley, to share his home. He then contacted the Mexican Minister of War on their behalf and ensured the men received payment due to them. The men who had joined the Mexican side on the promise of land were also helped to realise their dream. A unit was formed in Querétaro and some of the Irish soldiers remained in the army along with American troops who requested permission to stay in Mexico to start ranches and businesses.

When the US Army finally withdrew from the Presidential Palace, the Honor Guard of US Marines was replaced by the San Patricios who took no time in raising the Mexican flag. The regiment had been restored to its original strength of two full companies including some US deserters and they were stationed at Querétaro to provide order in the war-ravaged country.

Major John Riley was promoted to Colonel in recognition of his leadership during the war but before long he was caught up in a revolt between the Royalists and the newly-formed government. Even though the Royalists were defeated, some of the Mexican troops, including Riley, were accused of plotting to overthrow the government and he was imprisoned with others but later found not guilty. The San Patricios, however, were disbanded in August and Colonel Riley was then stationed in Vera Cruz. While he was there, he appealed for help from the British Consulate as a British subject. His intention was to return home to Ireland where he had a wife and son, neither of whom he had seen for many years, along with other ex San Patricios.

Daniel Walsh now reverted to his true name of John and he decided to take up the offer of 320 acres of land. It was June when he went in search of the plot he had been allocated, not far from the town of Querétaro where the Haciendos lived on their large cattle ranches. Smaller farms bordered the much larger ranches and supplied fodder for the cattle and other crops. The land was good for growing wheat, barley, alfalfa, corn and beans and John had seen other local produce for sale at the market which he thought he might try to grow himself. Some vegetables he was familiar with such as carrots, lettuce, onions and cauliflower but broccoli and garlic were new to him. He realised he had a lot to learn and no time to lose if he was to harvest some crops before the year was out but he was excited at the challenge of it all. With his back pay he intended to invest in creating for himself a living not too dissimilar from his parents' place back home but much larger.

Many of the wealthy landowners were absentee farmers who left their land in the capable hands of managers while they travelled the world, returning occasionally to check all was well on their ranch. John was given directions to a smallholding close to a hacienda owned by a cattle breeder whose name was Signor Carlos Navarro.

When he rode out to the proposed site, it looked very promising. The ruins of a small dwelling stood on the land with a run-down barn still with its roof intact. John secured his horse and went to investigate the barn. Inside the walls the air was cool and musty, sunlight dancing on the disturbed dust caused by his entrance. The floor of the barn was compacted earth and John decided he could live in it temporarily while he rebuilt the single-storey dwelling to make his home.

As he inspected the plot from the back of his horse, Erin, he ventured close to the fence between what would be his land and that of Signor Navarro and he saw a figure on horseback watching him. He rode closer and waved his hand in salute. The greeting was returned and it was then he realised that the rider was a woman. She trotted over to speak with him.

"Buenos dias, senor."

John was struck dumb at first. The girl was maybe his age, with long dark hair, a smile which made her eyes sparkle and a mischievous expression on her beautiful face.

"Buenos dias, senorita. I am surveying this land with the intention of farming it. May I ask, are you from Hacienda San Diego?"

"Si, senor. My father is Signor Navarro. We speak in English? I learn English at my school. You are alone? No family?"

"I have been serving with the Mexican army and my reward is this plot. My family are all back home in Ireland. You know of Ireland?"

"Of course. You must be a San Patricio! You are famous throughout Mexico, I have read of you and my father has praised you many times."

John smiled and made himself more comfortable on his saddle.

"I have plans to rebuild the house while I live in the barn."

"I wish you well. Perhaps when you are living here you would pay us a visit? My parents and brother would love to meet you. I am Isabel Navarro by the way. And your name?"

John walked his horse close to the girl's mare and reached out to shake her gloved hand.

"John Walsh, pleased to make your acquaintance. Yes, I would be pleased to meet your family, maybe in a few weeks?"

"I will ride out in search of you, Senor Walsh. Encantada."

With a wave of her hat Isabel rode off, creating a cloud of dust. John was now convinced this was the place for him.

***

The day arrived when John left his lodgings for good and with a hired cart and driver carrying the bare essentials for his new life, he rode out to his new home. Once the cart was unloaded, he carried his few possessions into the barn and tied his horse to a post outside near a stone trough which he filled with oats.

It was still the rainy season and he had only just lit himself a small fire to cook on when the heavens opened. He cursed and realised one of his first jobs would be to build himself a fireplace on which to cook. His mat, which would serve as a bed for now, was all he had to sit on so he ate a meal of bread, cheese and a mug of water while he considered his new life. He felt good. He planned to keep a few goats and chickens, the land was fertile for growing vegetables and he had sufficient back pay from his military days to buy the timber and other building supplies he needed. The day had been long and as the rain did not ease, he decided to get a good night's rest and start first thing tomorrow. He spread a blanket on the mat and covered himself with his poncho.

John worked every morning ploughing his land, planting his vegetable seeds, tending his goats and chickens. After a simple midday meal followed by a siesta he began the rebuild of his small, single-storey house. He repaired the timber frame first using the remains of the fallen pieces of wood which were found scattered about the ruined building then measured the remains of the wall to establish how many adobe bricks he needed for rebuilding before riding into town to order them. The suppliers had ready-made bricks spread out under the sun to bake them dry and the owner of the yard advised him which to use for walls and which for the roof. In the days that followed as he waited for his delivery, he finished the window frames, and erected a porch. John had planned to build a fireplace indoors for cooking on but he was advised by helpful locals to have an oven made from adobe outside. He compromised and built a frame for a small lean-to which would serve as his kitchen and protect his oven from the rain.

It was not long before he received delivery of his bricks and after stacking them, he stripped down to his pants to cool himself with water from the well. As he ran his fingers through his wet hair and brushed it from his face, he saw two horsemen approaching. He picked up his sombrero to shade the sun from his eyes and watched the riders. One was Isabel. The other rider had pulled his horse to a standstill and watched Isabel continue riding towards John.

"Senor John Walsh! Buenos dias. You are busy I can see."

She smiled as she looked approvingly at his muscular physique. John reached for his cast off shirt and pulled it over his head.

"Welcome to my building site, as you can see I am about to begin repairing the walls. May I offer you and your companion a drink? I have coffee brewing on the fire."

"My companion? Oh, you mean my keeper!"

She laughed at the expression on John's face.

"Here in Mexico it is important that a single young lady is chaperoned when meeting with strangers. My parents insist. José will stay where he is."

Isabel climbed down from her horse and fastened him to the wooden frame of the house. She stood in the shade, watching John as he poured two mugs of coffee and handed her one.

"Forgive me, let me fetch you a chair."

John brought out one of his chairs from the barn and brushed the dust off it with his hand. Isabel sat down while he perched himself on the unfinished wall.

"I have come with an invitation for you. My mother and father would like to meet you and want me to ask you to dinner, maybe this evening? We eat at eight. My brother Roberto will also be there. Please accept, we should all be good neighbours, don't you think?"

He noticed again how she smiled with her eyes as well as her mouth. John felt awkward, sitting with this beautiful Mexican girl dressed in a most fashionable riding outfit while he wore mud-stained pants, a sweaty shirt and his hair hung damp on his neck like rats' tails. He paused as he tried to remember if he had a clean change of clothes.

"Well thank you, I would be delighted to come. I am in need of advice, perhaps your father can help me?"

Isabel stood and drained her cup before remounting her mare.

"He would consider it an honour, of course you must ask him anything, any problems you have we will all gladly help you resolve. Now, I must delay you no longer. I cannot wait to tell them you have accepted. Until this evening, goodbye again."

She turned her horse and kicked her into a canter.

As the dust settled, John returned to his building work for several hours before drawing water from his well to wash himself. He heated some for a shave, found his comb to tame his hair and went inside to change his clothes. With no mirror, he was unable to check his appearance but he had done his best. He shrugged his shoulders and saddled up. He rode at a gentle trot, slowing to a walk as he arrived at the imposing Hacienda San Diego.

The gates to Senor Navarro's property stood open and John rode into the courtyard where he found the family sitting waiting on the veranda. Carlos, his son, Roberto, and Isobel stood up as he approached then Roberto stepped down and took the reins of John's horse before the two young men shook hands.

"Welcome, neighbour. I am Roberto, please join my parents and Isabel while I secure your horse."

The tall young Mexican led Erin away as John climbed the steps to where Isobel and her parents were waiting. Carlos held out his hand, shaking John's and introducing his wife.

"John, we are pleased to welcome you as our neighbour. This is my wife, Rosa and Isabel you have already met."

Rosa was as beautiful as her daughter, elegantly dressed and wearing a lace mantilla on her head. She remained seated but smiled and held out her hand. John was not too sure of the protocol expected.

"How d'you do, ma'am, nice to make your acquaintance."

He had witnessed John O'Reilly lift a lady's hand to his lips but young John erred on the side of caution and shook Rosa's hand. Her smile broadened and he saw the strong resemblance between mother and daughter.

"Isabel tells us you are from Ireland? You fought with the San Patricios? We are proud to have you here. Now, can we offer you a refreshing drink of lemonade, something cool to wash away the dust of the evening while we wait for dinner? Isabel, please pour John a glass. Sit here, John, beside me"

He sat between Carlos and Rosa and thanked Isabel for his drink.

It was very pleasant sitting in the cool of the evening, listening to the crickets and watching the swift movements of the geckos on the walls and ceilings of the hacienda.

Roberto had joined them and helped himself to a glass of lemonade. He sat across the low table from John.

"What experience of farming do you have, John? Have you worked with cattle, grown crops?"

All eyes were turned on their guest.

"No. I was brought up on a tiny plot, not even as big as the one I have here. Our weather in Ireland is suited best to growing vegetables. We get a deal of rain so we do, and potatoes are the main crop. Then we kept a pig, chickens and a goat or two for milk."

Carlos asked,

"How many of you are there in your family, John?"

"My Dad and Mam, me, I'm the oldest, then Daniel, Eliza, young Patrick, Joseph, Bridget and baby Margaret."

He paused and lowered his head as he remembered his younger brother.

"Sadly, Daniel, who fought with me in the San Patricios, was killed. When the Americans took all survivors prisoner, to save myself from a hanging I pretended to be him as he was too young for the death penalty. I still have sleepless nights at my deceit."

Isabel reached out a comforting hand and patted his arm. She ignored her father's raised eyebrow at her familiarity.

"Daniel would be proud to know you took his name. Imagine your poor parents if they had lost both of you to our war here in Mexico? Better that one of you lives."

John brushed a tear from his eye and smiled a thank you.

"Well, we must eat. Here, John, you take my arm."

Rosa stood and led the family into dinner, ensuring that Isabel sat with Carlos and Roberto between her and the young Irish man.

In the high-ceilinged dining room, the air was cooler than on the veranda. A long table covered in a white lace tablecloth with fancy plates and cut-glass wine glasses set for five had a variety of appetising dishes waiting to be served. John refused nothing, only too eager to try the exotic food. During dinner, he was asked more questions about his time in Mexico and his plans for the future. Carlos was most interested when John told them of his friendship with Colonel John Riley.

"Your friend's leadership is renowned in these parts. We are deeply indebted to him. Where is he now?"

"He is still a military man based at Vera Cruz. We communicate rarely but he knows of my small place. I hope someday he might visit me."

"If ever he does, he will be greeted with a party we will hold here in his honour. You tell him that next time you write."

John consulted Carlos on which crops to grow and he was pleased to learn his choices so far were ideal. The evening passed in a most convivial way.

When John attempted to stifle a yawn, Carlos checked the wall clock then said, "I am sorry, you have laboured all day and need some rest. But before you go, you must try a favourite Mexican drink, tequila. It was first distilled by the Aztecs and it is very strong. We like to drink it with lime juice to temper its strength. Have you ever had it?"

John admitted he had never drunk alcohol of any sort on the advice of John Riley but he accepted a glass from Carlos to be sociable and so did Roberto. John noticed the ladies did not join them.

After his first sip he coughed at the burning sensation in the back of his throat. He remembered stories back home of the men who had their own distilleries for poteen hidden away where the customs and excise men had difficulty finding them. His father had disapproved of the drinking of poteen as he said "it addled a man's brains."

After pretending to sip again from his glass, he placed it on the table. He stood, preparing to leave.

"You are right, it has been a long day and I have enjoyed the evening, and thank you so much for inviting me."

He turned to Rosa.

"Ma'am, the food was delicious, I must try my hand at some of the dishes."

"So pleased you enjoyed them, John. I will ask Anna the cook to tell Isabel the recipes and she can pass them on to you. I wish you a safe ride home."

As the evening light was fading, Carlos and Roberto also got to their feet.

"I think now bed is calling and you must ride home before the blackness of night descends. Isabel, stay here with your mother while I see John safely on his way."

Roberto went to fetch Erin and John thanked him as he took the reins. He turned to the family, all standing now in the soft light from the oil lamps.

"I am most grateful for your warm hospitality. I feel I have made good friends tonight."

Carlos grasped John's hand and shook it.

"May it be the first of many such evenings, it has been a pleasure to talk with you and learn about your family. We will do it again soon, safe journey."

Rosa turned to go inside with a small wave while Isabel stood with her father and brother and watched John ride away before turning and following her mother indoors.

John dug his heels into Erin's flanks, raised his hat in farewell and urged his horse into a canter while Roberto shut the gates behind him and returned to the house.

A month passed before John heard once more the sound of an approaching horse. He finished laying the brick he had positioned on the roof and took his hat off to wipe the sweat from his brow before climbing down. As he replaced his hat, he saw through the dust stirred up by his visitor that it was Isabel, alone. She pulled her mare to a standstill and dismounted.

"I fancied a ride and so I decided to pay you a visit. I hope you don't mind?"

She shielded her eyes from the sun, her hat hung loose on the back of her neck.

John looked beyond her, expecting to see José again.

Isabel laughed.

"I am completely alone. My parents have gone into town, my brother is busy with the cattle and I was bored. I was curious to see how your building is progressing, will you show me?"

He felt in need of a break so he checked his last brick was positioned correctly before slapping the dust from his clothes.

"I was just about to get myself a drink. Would you like orange juice? Or maybe coffee, though I would need to light the fire."

"If it is not too much trouble a cup of coffee would suit me. May I see your house?"

"It is hardly a house yet but it will be finished soon and it will serve my needs."

Isabel went inside out of the sun.

The roof was almost finished and the small windows let in very little light. Once Isabel became accustomed to the gloom, she glanced around. Dried produce hung from pegs driven into the walls and a basket containing bread was attached to the roof timbers. In one corner of the single room John had built a small truckle bed. A table and two chairs completed the contents of the room.

Isabel went closer to the bed to inspect the picture hanging on the wall while John revived the last of the embers in the makeshift fireplace and put a pot of water on to boil.

"This picture, it is so beautiful, so green. Is it of a place dear to you?"

"Oh, that old thing. Yes, I found it while searching for books in English on a market stall in town. There was just one, a book of poems, and the stallholder, seeing I was interested in anything English, drew my attention to this picture. Sadly, it is not of Ireland but close. It shows a view in England. Almost as green as the Emerald Isle. It is the last thing I look at before I snuff out my candle each night."

Isabel looked closer at the scene of a gentle valley with heather-covered hills in the distance and a river winding through the fields. She pointed to the small cottage with smoke curling from the chimney.

"Does this resemble the one you told us about where you lived with your family?"

"Near enough."

John stirred some ground coffee beans into the pot.

"Come outside, I have a bench in the shade where we can drink our coffee."

Isabel hesitated at first then followed him out and sat beside him.

John felt awkward. He found Isabel extremely attractive but he realised her parents would be furious if they knew they were sitting side by side, unchaperoned. He drank his coffee quickly but she lingered over hers, sipping it slowly. They sat in silence until she passed him her empty cup and stood up, tugging her hat back on her head.

"Oh well, I suppose I should detain you no longer. Would you help me remount please?"

As he helped her back onto her mare, Isabel's breath was warm on his neck and her delicate perfume was very pleasing. She brushed her lips against his cheek then smiled when she saw him blush. He bent to check her stirrups, avoiding looking at her eyes. He had never known such feelings before, his heart raced in the presence of this beautiful, spirited girl.

"Perhaps I will ride this way again, John Walsh? If you have no objection?"

Her use of his full name stirred warm memories and he looked up at her and smiled.

"On condition you have the consent of your father, you will be welcome any time."

Her face lit up and she laughed then urged her horse forward, blowing John a kiss. She was soon galloping away and John watched until she was completely out of sight before returning to his roof.

***

John worked all the hours of daylight on his land and his house. He harvested his first crops of tomatoes, pulled a lettuce when he needed one and was very relieved to see his beans, sweet potatoes, onions and corn were growing nicely. His chickens laid well and the nanny goat he had bought had delivered a kid and gave milk for John and her offspring in abundance. He had taken Rosa's advice on how to dry his beans to store them through the winter.

The roof was finished on the house, windows were installed with shutters fitted to keep out the summer heat or the winter cold and his lean-to kitchen with the adobe oven served him well. He had also built a fireplace in one end of his living room for comfort. The furniture was arranged on a colourful, woollen rug woven by Mexican Indians and on his bed a newly purchased blanket.

As he had restored the small dwelling, he had thought about how to maximise the small space without it being too cluttered. He decided to fit shelving along one wall on which to display his pots and plates and underneath he planned to make cupboards for storage.

The first time he lit a fire in the grate he was thrilled to see when the flames burst into life, how they cast shadows which seemed to dance around the room, lighting up dark corners. At last the room looked cosy. He stood in the centre of the floor and turned slowly to admire his handiwork. With his arms folded and his legs apart he stood still, nodding his head, well satisfied with his work so far. He was a contented man.

***

Now that the pressure of work had eased, John felt it was time to relax a little and take a day off. It was a Sunday just before Christmas when he dressed in his tidy clothes, saddled up Erin and headed for town. The sense of freedom spurred John into a gallop and both horse and rider enjoyed the ride. John arrived in time to attend his first Mass in many months and his horse was tethered in a quiet road off the main square with other horses, buggies and traps.

The church, Iglesia de Santa Rosa de Viterbo, was even more imposing than others he had seen in Mexico and had a full congregation for Advent. John squeezed into a seat near the back of the church and looked around at the colourful outfits of the other worshippers. Everyone was in good spirits and the chatter only died down when the priest with his entourage walked in a dignified procession to the altar. As the service proceeded, John was able to follow it as the Mass was exactly as he remembered it back home. As he joined in the responses, he imagined his family were doing the same with Father Murphy leading them back in Ireland. He took comfort in the communal inclusion of his church, so relieved that he would never be a total stranger anywhere.

His mind only wandered when the priest read the sermon. He gazed upwards and was transfixed by the paintings covering the lofty ceiling. Everywhere the decorations were ornate. Behind the altar the screen had paintings of saints in richly carved frames. Above the screen was a magnificent pierced arch in gold and overlooking the congregation was a statue within a glazed cubicle attached high up on the wall. John was counting the richly carved pillars down each side of the aisle supporting the roof when he was drawn back to the service as it ended.

While the congregation filed out, John remained seated until most of the worshippers had left the church then made his way to the door. He noticed Isabel and her family talking to a group of friends and he was about to head to the plaza when Isabel spotted him and waved. Rosa looked to see who her daughter was waving to and she smiled at John and beckoned him to join them. Carlos continued talking to his Mexican friend but nodded a welcome to John before resting his hand on the boy's shoulder.

"Fernando, let me introduce you to our new neighbour, John Walsh from Ireland, but more recently from that proud regiment which fought so bravely for us, the San Patricios. He has accepted our government's offer of land and has been working extremely hard over the last six months or so, restoring the ruined house and barn and preparing and planting crops."

Fernando Delgado was another local rancher and he took John's hand between both of his and shook it with vigour.

"So nice to meet you, brave soldier. What you and your comrades did will never be forgotten by all Mexicans. Now, let me introduce you to my wife, Lorena, and our son, Raúl."

John blushed at the warm welcome and words of praise. Raúl was alone in keeping his distance and John felt his limp, brief handshake was just a reluctant gesture.

Isabel asked John what he thought of the church service.

"I felt quite at home, except for the splendour of the building. At home we have a humble stone church with very little ornamentation. Still, Mass is Mass wherever you go it seems."

"Are you staying for a while or do you need to rush back home?"

"No, I promised myself a day off and after I have been to the market to buy some essential stores, I intend to take a meal in one of the bars or a café and enjoy watching the people pass by."

"Well, maybe we will see you again later."

Her father shook his head.

"Isabel, we have been invited to dine with the Delgados. Please excuse us, John, we will see you again, you must come over when we celebrate Christmas. Adiós, my friend."

John smiled at Isabel who looked as if she was about to protest then thought better of it. He went to check on Erin and unstrapped a pannier which he carried over his shoulder before wandering back to the market. He enjoyed the noise of the sellers calling out to their customers, the smells of the produce piled high to tempt the shoppers and the gaudy displays of pots and dishes, woven blankets and ponchos and beautiful leather goods. He decided he would treat himself for Christmas and bought some new dishes and cutlery in case John Riley accepted his invitation. He hesitated at the stall selling beautiful linen and remembered the fancy table at the Navarro's place but imagining his mother would tell him it was an unnecessary extravagance, he chose instead to buy new towels and sweet smelling soap. His pannier was almost full, leaving just enough room for the chillies, tomatoes, olive oil and flour he bought. The cured meat stall tempted him so he bought slices of ham and several spiced sausages which would keep well. He had plenty of eggs from his hens and one goat was giving enough milk that he considered buying a butter churn but that would have to wait for another day. He did not want to overburden Erin.

After his shopping was done, he found a café with a few tables empty and he relieved himself of his heavy load then sat down and waited to catch the waiter's attention. Some tables had been pushed together to accommodate large family groups and John listened to the happy chatter of the children, his knowledge of the Spanish language was still poor but he was learning a little more each day.

"Lo qué puede yo consiguirle senor?"

John took a guess the waiter was asking what he wanted and answered,

"Carne guisada, por favour."

He had tried the spicy beef stew at the dinner with the Navaro's and found it very tasty.

"Quieres tomar algo?"

"Aguas frescas."

The waiter went away to return with the fruity drink. The beef dish came with a plate of bread and John thanked the waiter in English and was about to say "Obrigado" when the waiter interrupted him to say.

"Enjoy your food. I speak English too!"

As he cleared his plate, John heard a familiar voice behind him. He knew it was Isabel and he turned in his seat to confirm he was right.

"John Walsh! So this is where you disappeared to!"

Behind Isabel, her parents were talking to the Delgados while their son, Raúl, stood with a sulky expression, his arms folded glaring at John.

Isabel looked over her shoulder to see what had caught John's attention.

"Oh, the awful Raúl. He imagines one day he and I will be married but I have no intention of ever being his bride. Of course, my parents would be delighted if the two families were united, their hacienda is far more imposing than ours so they think it would be an excellent match. I find him just too awful, I cannot bear his company. Sadly, I see him more than I would like, he is friends with Roberto. They were at school together and often they go riding. Ugh, he makes me have creeps? Is that the correct saying?"

Isabel fanned herself vigorously as if to scatter her thoughts of Raúl from her mind.

"Anyway, it has been so nice to see you again and looking so relaxed after all your hard work. I imagine you will be very comfortable in your cosy home before Christmas? I must ride over to see for myself, perhaps with an invitation to share our Christmas Day?"

John remembered in time his invitation to John Riley and told Isabel.

"Of course, you have mentioned him before. Well, if he is unable to make it I am sure Papa and Mama will be pleased to see you."

Rosa called to Isabel.

"Isabel, come along, we are leaving now."

Rosa bowed her head to acknowledge John's presence but turned to bid farewell to their friends. Carlos glanced over his shoulder and raised his hand but turned away before Isabel blew John a kiss then followed her parents to their carriage.

John called the waiter over and paid for his food. He hoisted his pannier onto his back and went to collect Erin. On the ride home in the gathering darkness, his thoughts were of Isabel and her sulky suitor. He regretted leaving it so late to return as his farm was in complete darkness when he arrived back but fortunately Erin was able to find his way to the barn. John relieved him of his load, checked he had oats and water and closed the barn door. He went into his house and lit a lamp from the embers in the fireplace before unpacking his purchases.

As he undressed for bed, he promised himself that from now on he would spend less time daydreaming about Isabel. She was not meant for him, a poor Irish farmer. He cursed at his own stupidity. Any fanciful notions he had allowed to fill his head about her being his girl were well and truly dashed. Before climbing into bed he snuffed out his lamp, punched his pillow in frustration and tossed and turned before eventually falling into a restless sleep.

CHAPTER EIGHTEEN
Christmas 1848 Queretaro

A letter arrived for John from his friend Colonel John Riley to let him know he was heading west to visit him and he expected to arrive shortly after Christmas. Young John was excited at the news and looked forward to telling the Navarro family when he joined them to celebrate Christmas Eve.

As he approached the hacienda, he saw the veranda decorated with poinsettias, their rich green foliage topped with vivid red flowers. Amongst them stood a display of life-size figures made from clay depicting the Nativity scene. Isabel ran down the steps to greet him, holding her dress up above her ankles to prevent tripping as she crossed to where he had reined in his horse.

"John Walsh! Oh, it is so nice to have you here. We have been so busy the past nine days with posadas. Do you celebrate them in Ireland?"

John climbed down from Erin and began to lead him towards the stables with Isabel skipping along beside him.

"No, I have never heard of posadas, what are they?"

Isabel slowed to a walk.

"Well, what happens is each family goes from house to house to re-enact the scene where the Holy Family search for an inn to rest in, it is such fun! We carry candles and sing songs until the host, who pretends to be the innkeeper allows us in where a feast awaits us with games to play and pinatas full of sweets for the children. Such a shame you were not able to join us. Well, you are here now so when Erin is settled we will go in where the family are waiting."

In the hall every surface was brightly lit with candles and flowers were displayed in colourful pots.

Carlos crossed the floor with long strides to shake John's hand.

"So glad you could join us, John. No news of Colonel Riley yet?" John smiled.

"As a matter of fact, sir, I had a letter from him two days ago. He has left Vera Cruz and intends to stop overnight in Mexico City and hopes to arrive at my place soon after Christmas."

"What a shame he cannot share our Christmas. However, we will make him very welcome whenever he arrives. Now John, it is our tradition to attend Midnight Mass on Christmas Eve then return to a feast with suckling pig and other delights to be washed down with a Christmas punch. Roberto and Raúl have already left for the city on horseback so you can accompany us in our carriage if that is agreeable to you? Erin will be safe and warm here."

Isabel beamed at John.

"Oh John Walsh, it will be such fun! The church will be sparkling with candles and decked out in evergreen and bright flowers. The singing will take your breath away; everyone is so joyful. You can sit beside me so I can help you find the hymns."

John beamed with happiness. To sit with Isabel in the carriage and then in church was more than he could have wished for. Raúl was forgotten.

Carlos interrupted.

"Well, that is sorted. Shall we go?"

Rosa appeared wearing her black mantilla and a beautiful shawl over her exquisite dress and they were soon seated in the comfortable carriage. The groom ordered the horses on and they headed for town.

Everything about the evening was just as Isabel had described. John was grateful with her help with the hymns and the light touch of her hand on his while he held his hymnal awoke feelings in him he had never before experienced. She smiled at him and moved closer. John wanted the joyous occasion to last for ever.

They drove back to the ranch, chatting happily while Carlos and Rosa appeared to be sleeping, leaving the driving in the expert hands of Juan. The lights of the hacienda greeted them as they approached to find the servants had been busy preparing the feast.

"Help yourself to punch, John."

Carlos took a glass and filled it for Rosa.

"Is it strong?" John whispered to Isabel.

"No, not at all. It has a little rum maybe but it is mostly fruit juice with spices for flavouring. Try it."

John part-filled a glass and tasted it. As he sipped it, he found it very pleasant to drink so he filled his glass.

"How do you like our decorations, John?"

Carlos asked as he led John to the table.

"Do you decorate your homes back in Ireland for Christmas?"

"We never had decorations such as these, just a small Nativity scene with a candle. We did go to midnight Mass; well, except for my mother and the wee ones. Dad always took us and the walk there and back to church would tire us all out so we slept soundly until morning when small gifts had miraculously appeared overnight. Nothing too fancy, my parents had little money for extravagance but handmade toys for the young ones and knitted scarves and hats for the older ones put smiles on all our faces."

"Was there special food for Christmas Day?"

"If the year had been kind to us a goose might have been fattened but if not, a chicken was stuffed and served with potatoes, cabbage and turnips then for pudding we had apple cake made with hazelnuts which we had collected in the Autumn from the hedgerows before squirrels had them all and Ma stored them for Christmas. Ah, talking about it makes me wish I was there."

John was silent for a while as he composed himself. Carlos waited for John to continue.

"Of course, we enjoyed playing games and singing carols before bedtime. Here you have so much more but I would not exchange my large family for all the comforts of wealth."

"You have every reason to be proud of your family, it sounds like a perfect upbringing to me."

John appeared a little unsteady on his feet so Carlos took him by the elbow and led him towards the door.

"Oh, I forgot to tell you, sir, Colonel John Riley is on his way to visit me, he will be here in a couple of days."

"Well now, that is good news, John, you must be looking forward to seeing him again after all you both went through. Be sure to tell him he must ride over here with you and he will receive a very warm welcome from an extremely grateful Mexican. Now, young man, I suggest you take a little fresh air, you will feel much better for it."

John took a deep breath and answered.

"Yes, sir, I think you are right. I will check that Erin is content being as he is not in his own stable. Excuse me."

He made his way through the other guests and apologised when he thought he bumped into one on the veranda. The other person stood in silence then John realised it was one of the figures in the Nativity scene. He chuckled at his stupidity as he made his way to the stable block.

Inside, the stable was barely lit but he soon found Erin who snorted when he recognised the presence of his master. John stroked the horse's muzzle and whispered soothing words in his ear. He jumped when he heard someone was nearby. He screwed up his eyes trying to make out who the figure was.

"John Walsh. So this is where you are hiding."

Isabel came closer.

"Were you thinking of leaving without saying goodbye?"

"No, of course not. I needed air. That punch was strong and I am not used to alcohol."

He leaned against the stable partition to support himself.

"Look. Here is clean straw where you can rest a while."

John obediently allowed Isabel to lead him to the corner where he fell heavily into the bedding. When Isabel sat down beside him and pushed him gently to lie down he did not protest. She snuggled up against him.

Her hair was tied back but a few strands had escaped and fallen across her eyes. John brushed it from her face and told her how beautiful she looked.

She moved closer.

"It is so peaceful in here with just the sound of the horses moving now and then and the distant sound of music from the house. Are you happy, John Walsh?"

John had never felt happier in his life as he felt the closeness of Isabel and the effect of the punch arousing in him feelings new to him.

"I love the musky smell of the horses, don't you? My, but it is warm in here, don't you think?"

Isabel began to loosen the bodice of her dress. Now that his eyes were accustomed to the dim light, John watched Isabel as she felt for his hand and placed it on her breast.

"Can you feel my heartbeat, John Walsh? You make it beat so fast. Feel. Just here."

His fingers felt the hardness of her nipple through the flimsy fabric of her dress. She leaned over to kiss him then rolled over to straddle him. He was conscious of his hardness as they continued to kiss, each kiss more passionate than the last until Isabel diverted his kisses to her breasts which were now free from the constrictions of her bodice. She moaned in pleasure and began to move rhythmically against him, stopping only to lift her skirt and undo the buttons of his trousers. She rolled over and pulled him onto her, grasping his buttocks firmly as she moved in time with him. As they climaxed, John groaned with pleasure then they lay still, their chests rising and falling in union. John helped her adjust her dress then fastened his trouser buttons. Then the realisation of what they had just done hit him. He sobered up and pulled Isabel to her feet. Apologising, he carefully removed straw from her hair but Isabel stopped him by covering his mouth with her hand.

"That was your first time, right? I hope you will remember it forever, I have wanted you so much and now I have made you mine."

She shook straw from her dress and fastened her hair securely.

"Now we had better get back before we are missed. I will go first, you follow after five minutes."

Isabel kissed him once more then slipped quietly back to the house. John left shortly after her, turning his head when he heard what he thought were footsteps. He stood unmoving for a while before dismissing the noise as down to one of the horses then crossed the stable yard back to the house.

Isabel was chatting to one of the other guests and did not look his way. Carlos and Rosa approached him and Rosa asked him if he felt better for his fresh air. John blushed and nodded.

"I must leave now; my bed calls me. Thank you for making my Christmas so special."

They thanked him for his company and called to Roberto as he climbed the steps of the veranda.

"Roberto, John is about to leave. I am afraid he is not used to our punch. See him safely into his saddle, a slap on his horse's rump should be sufficient to send him in the direction of his home."

John protested that he would be fine but Roberto insisted on accompanying him as the festivities continued in the house.

CHAPTER NINETEEN
REUNION WITH JOHN O'REILLY 1849

The leather-buttoned seat was becoming more and more uncomfortable as the coach swayed from side to side on the road, not much more than a deeply rutted track. The transport of military vehicles during the war had not improved the roads of Mexico at all. Each time the wheels hit a stone or rough patch, the teeth of the passengers rattled in their heads and jarred their spines. Colonel John Riley was at a disadvantage because of his height, six feet two inches. His head scraped the roof and he was required to sit with his legs splayed out to avoid being knee to knee with the priest sitting opposite him. Beside him a buxom matron, sweating profusely, sat with a permanent frown creasing her forehead. Accompanying her was a timid young girl, crushed between her chaperone and the window of the coach. Two dark-skinned Mexicans of Indian blood sat next to the priest and neither of them had spoken throughout the journey except for the occasional curse at their discomfort. The initial polite conversation between the other passengers had ceased many miles back and the silence was only broken by the matron's tut-tutting as she fanned herself furiously and instructed the girl to sit upright.

It was late afternoon, two days after Christmas, when they arrived in Queretaro. As soon as the horses came to a halt at the staging post, Riley threw open the door and climbed down, arching his back, relieved to be out of the vehicle. The coachman's assistant was already unfastening the horses ready for stabling them. The coachman was on the roof of the coach throwing down the luggage to the passengers. He was a large man with a corpulent belly and a fierce expression so the matron resisted the protest she was about to make at his rough handling of her bags. Standing in the entrance of the hotel across the road, the proprietor weighed up whether any of these people would be likely to require a bed for the night. Deciding it could be a possibility he spat tobacco out of his mouth and sauntered across the road.

"Any of you folk in need of a comfortable bed for the night?"

The priest and the two women raised their hands. The two Mexicans ignored the hotelier and after collecting their bags they headed for the nearest bar. Riley shook his head and made his way to the livery stable to arrange the hire of a horse. The groom looked him up and down and led him to a stable where a black stallion was tossing his head and pawing the ground at being disturbed.

"This one here is a bit lively but you look like a man who can handle a frisky horse. He handles well for the right man, goes like the wind when urged on. His name is Nero."

The colonel stroked the horse, walked around him aware that Nero's ears were back. He patted him and said,

"He'll do just fine. I don't know how long I'll need him but I am heading for a small farm near the ranch, 'Los San Diego'. You know it?"

He slung his bags across the back of the horse behind the saddle.

"Navarro's place? Yeh, sure I know it. By your accent I'd say you might be looking for the young Irish man, am I right? He bought his horse from us. Take the road heading East out of town and follow it for about five, six miles. Pass the ranch gates and go a couple of miles on, you will see the place. It has a temporary sign with his name Walsh painted on it."

Riley adjusted the stirrups and mounted the restless horse, steadying him with a soft "whoa boy whoa."

When the horse settled and accepted his rider, Riley said,

"How much? Say for one week at least?"

The groom checked with his boss, asked for US dollars and a sum of $20 changed hands.

"Oh, Nero don't care for the whip by the way so you'll need to control him with your hands and your feet. He'll be kinda restless at first, so give him his head and he'll soon calm down. How does the saddle suit you? OK?"

John Riley adjusted himself in the saddle and shortened up the reins. Nero still had his ears back but he stood quietly waiting to go.

"The saddle's fine. I'll let you know before the week's out how long I need Nero."

"That's okay. Safe ride."

John turned the horse's head and rider and horse were soon out of the yard with John urging Nero into a canter. Once they were out on the open road, he urged his mount to a gallop and Nero responded immediately. The freedom was a pleasure to both horse and rider as they left the city behind.

***

In the darkness of his cottage, John Walsh groaned in pain as he turned over on his bed. His head hurt, his ribs were bruised and every part of him ached. As he lay trying to remember what had happened to him on Christmas Day morning, he thought he heard a rider approaching. The horse slowed to a stop and John sat up, reaching for his gun. He was not about to take a second beating, this time he was prepared. As he stumbled to his feet, he heard footsteps on his porch so he stood to one side of the door with his gun cocked ready. The sound of someone rapping loudly on his door took him by surprise. The previous time they had just burst in and attacked him. The latch was lifted, the door opened slowly and in the gloom John could just make out the figure of a tall man, his face hidden by his wide-brimmed hat and a poncho round his shoulders.

"Leave now! I'm armed!" John shouted.

A familiar voice answered, "Hey, it's me, O'Reilly. What the hell are you doing sitting in the dark?"

"Oh. Thank Christ, sir. I thought the bastards had come back for another go."

He put his gun against the wall and opened the door wide.

"Come in, I'll light the lamps."

He winced as he turned around.

"Are you alright, friend? Who are these bastards you were expecting?"

John lit the lamps and adjusted the flame so that he could see his friend clearly.

O'Reilly gasped when he saw John's injuries.

"Who the hell did this to you? And why? I thought your fighting days were over?"

"So did I, sir. Here I am making a modest living from my land but I seem to have got on the wrong side of some of my neighbours. Still, welcome, sir, you don't know how good it is to see you again."

"Drop the sir, eh? We are just two Irishmen in a foreign land."

John busied himself reviving the embers of his fire by blowing on them until flames licked around the charred remains when he added more wood. The coffee pot was almost full and soon steam curled from it.

"Here, sit down, the coffee won't be long. Are you hungry, I can fix you some food?"

"No, coffee will be fine. Where can I fasten my horse? He will need food and drink."

"Follow me, I have a barn where Erin, my horse, is stabled. It has room for another."

Erin watched, the whites of his eyes shining in the light of John's lamp as Nero was led in. Each horse sniffed at the other until Nero turned his attention to the oats John had given him.

"Right, that's the horses acquainted so let's catch up on each other's news."

Over several cups of coffee, John told O'Reilly about his Christmas. He was reluctant to tell him about Isabel but realised he should be honest with his friend. He made light of his canoodling with the girl but O'Reilly soon understood why the attack had taken place.

"What were you thinking of, taking advantage of your host's daughter?"

"No, honest, in fact it was the other way round! She pinned me down, what was I to do?"

"Is this girl pretty? Is she special to you? Answer truthfully now."

John sighed and gazed into the flames of the fire.

"Ah, well now, you know how it is. We had become good friends but I learnt that she was promised to another. I did my best to avoid her but she followed me to the stables and what with the punch 'n all I was easy to seduce, so I was. It was – I'm lost for words – she was so warm and loving, covered me in sweet kisses. Well, how was I to know we were being watched? It turned out that her brother's friend, the one who expects to marry Isabel though she says it will never happen, was in there, spying."

John sipped his coffee, pleased to have shared his tale with someone.

"You mean he saw you together, the whole time? Tell me, did Isabel suffer any pain?"

"No, not at all. She was the one of us that knew what to do!"

"Well, sounds like you were not her first then."

John frowned.

"What? Not a virgin? I just thought that with us both being a bit buckled like and the barn being so cosy and private…"

"Not exactly private. You had a spectator remember?"

The younger man wriggled with embarrassment. His warm memory of that night had been sullied.

"Are you telling me that this 'fiancé' is responsible for your injuries?"

"Him? That little squirt? Hell, no. Not on his own anyway. I could whip him with one hand behind my back. No, her big brother was with him, almost as tall as you and strong – he spends hours in the saddle checking on the cattle. He's fit and strong as I found out that night."

He straightened his back and winced with pain.

"Did they say anything to you as they beat you?"

"Oh, sure. They kept telling me with every blow to stay well away from Isabel and the hacienda or they would be back to burn my place down and ruin my crops. That's about it."

O'Reilly was silent for a while as he poked the fire and sent sparks flying. In the flickering light from the revived flames, John recognised the look of grim determination on his mentor's face. He had seen it so often during the war. O'Reilly stood up and stretched.

"Hell, I'm whacked. We will talk more in the morning, okay?"

He refused the offer of John's bed and made himself comfortable on the bed roll he had brought with him.

Next morning, John attended to the animals, still limping but able to get around while O'Reilly lit the fire in the lean-to. The two men enjoyed a breakfast of scrambled eggs, sliced ham and half a loaf of bread washed down with coffee topped with warm milk fresh from the goat. O'Reilly sat back in his chair with his long legs stretched out in front of him, his hands clasped across his full stomach.

"How are you liking being a farmer then, young John?"

"It's okay, it gets a bit lonely though. Isabel's family made me very welcome but I guess I won't be any more. Aw hell, I miss Ireland so I do, how about you?"

The big man stared past John into the distance before answering.

"Well, as I have resigned my commission and left the military for good it feels strange to be a civilian once again. As for Ireland, I have been away too long. I don't think I ever told you I have a wife and son back home. No? I am considering going back. I have sent money when I could and before I left Vera Cruz I called in the British Embassy to check on my status, after all we are considered to be British though it hurts my mouth to say so."

He fell silent again and young John waited without speaking, realising the other man had more to say.

"Have you heard the news from California that gold has been found? Yes, you must have done. Men are flooding there from all over the world. Americans, Mexicans, British even some from China would you believe! I've a mind to try my luck before going home for good."

O'Reilly waited for John to digest this idea.

"Considering everything, you being lonely, your dust-up with your neighbours and all, what d'you say to joining me in the hunt for gold?"

John looked into Big John's eyes and opened his mouth to speak but shut it without a word passing his lips. He gazed around at the place he now called home. The future had not alarmed him until now. He had expected that one day, even if he couldn't have Isabel, there would be another girl to take his eye, one who would be only too willing to share his modest living. Now though, with the added worry of aggressive neighbours, he realised life could get very uncomfortable for him.

He released a sigh.

"What about this place though? Everything I have is in this farm."

O'Reilly leaned forward in his chair and with his elbows on his knees he folded his arms. And looked across at John.

"I was thinking about that last night before I fell asleep. You told me in your last letter how Senor Navarro holds me in high esteem?"

John nodded.

"Well, I suggest I call on him alone. After introductions have been made I will engage him in private conversation. I will tell him of our near-death experiences in the service of his country, remind him of the debt owed to the San Patricios and while he is feeling obliged to us I will talk about your experience with his daughter."

"But you don't realise, her parents have her chaperoned, they will never listen to any excuses."

"You told me of times she called on you unaccompanied, right? Well, we let him know she is not the innocent young lady she pretends to be. She knew you were not a drinker but pressed you to try the punch knowing perfectly well how strong it was. Her father was aware you were not used to drink after you tried his tequila you said.

So, now we have her sharing the blame for what happened in the stable. After all, Senor Navarro was the one who suggested you take some air. He should have been more attentive to his daughter's whereabouts don't you think?"

"I still don't think he will forgive me."

"Listen, any man worth his salt will know it is nigh impossible for a young, hot-blooded male to spurn the advances of a beautiful young woman. After all, she didn't run back to the house screaming that you had attacked her, did she? So she is not blameless and he must believe that. I will tell him we are leaving for California on condition he buys you out, maybe give your farm to one of his farm hands and he will never see you again. More importantly, nor will Isabel and I will assure him that the incident will never be mentioned so nobody outside of his family except for the sulky suitor will be aware of her behaviour. What do you say?"

"Oh, I don't know. I can't see him agreeing to it. Why should he?"

"He will always fear that if you stay, her loss of virtue will become common knowledge. Don't forget, his son is implicated in your beating. I can bear witness to your injuries. I will remind him of how you grew from a boy to a man overnight while fighting so heroically. One incident in the straw with his daughter is a small price to pay. Settled then? I will ride over tomorrow while you recover from your bruises."

John stood up.

"Let me think about it, I'm not too sure it will work, okay?"

He excused himself and left the porch to hobble away while he considered the suggestion.

O'Reilly busied himself making fresh coffee until John returned and took his mug from his friend. He held it out and clinked it against the older man's cup.

"Here's to finding gold and going home."

"Good man, California here we come."

CHAPTER TWENTY
COUNTY MAYO 1849

Father Alastar Murphy watched as Patrick Walsh led his family from the church. He was disappointed that Bridget had not been with them. Perhaps she guessed his guilty secret and could no longer face him. If he had asked Patrick he would have made the usual excuses; baby not well, Bridget herself unwell. How could Patrick tell the priest what Bridget had confided in him? Her faith was being snuffed out, just like the flame on the altar candles after service. She told him she could no longer accept they had a Loving Father in Heaven, with all this dying going on around them. Through silent tears, she had said that all she felt now was emptiness and despair, and no amount of praying was helping. She still insisted he take the children to Mass though, as she knew the discipline of the church was good for them.

Patrick was a changed man. The handsome young fellow with a wicked twinkle in his eyes, unruly auburn curls which resisted any comb's attempt to control them, and his strong, muscular body, could have had any girl in the village. But Patrick had wooed Bridget and she never learnt of Alastar's feelings for her.

The three of them had been school friends, walked home together across the fields, stopping on hot summer days to paddle their feet cool in the brook, leaning over a wall to watch pigs snorting the ground, and talking of their schoolmaster.

Bridget was dark-skinned, like the gypsies who came by selling pegs and paper flowers. Her long black hair shone as it fell down her back when she pulled her ribbon free and her smile would melt any lad's heart. They had married young. Alastar had attended the wedding, congratulated them both and wished them well. Soon after, he applied to the Seminary to train for the priesthood. It was six years before he returned home by which time Bridget and Patrick had started a family, two sons and a daughter, with another one on the way. He had considered refusing the post in the local parish church, but just to be near Bridget and be part of her life persuaded him he had made the right choice.

So it was that on that day, as usual after Mass, when he had shaken the last hand of his departing parishioners, he turned back into the cool silence of the church and in his loneliness, he knelt before the Crucifix. His hands were clasped so tightly his knuckles were white, and he left marks on the backs of his hands from his fingernails. He offered his services to The Lord, promising Him his total devotion, and prayed for his calm resignation to return. If this still left him with thoughts of Bridget, he took himself off to the neighbouring parish, and slipped into the confessional to pour out his tormented thoughts. He knew full well that his friend, on the other side of the grille, was aware of his presence but never spoke of it. What priest after all did not suffer doubts, did not have feelings? It was not unknown for the clergy to have a lapse of faith now and then.

Father Murphy opened his eyes and looked up at the silent figure on the cross. Today was a day when his turmoil was not resolved. He stood up slowly, kissed his stole, genuflected, then turned and left the church. As he drew near the road, the horse-drawn clarence from the Big House was passing, and the family waved farewell to him. He raised his hand in acknowledgement but sighed when he saw the plump, smiling children, so different from Patrick's brood, all skin and bone now, clothes in tatters and their bewildered faces revealing haunted eyes. Patrick himself was unshaven, his hair down over his collar, and his clothes hung loose on his stooped frame. The priest's faith was being sorely tried.

Whenever the opportunity arose after Mass, Father Murphy would call to young Pat and Joseph. Waiting for a nod of approval from Patrick, he took them to the Manse. He checked to see that his housekeeper was not in the kitchen before beckoning them inside then he searched for whatever food could be spared, wrapped it in newspaper, and thrust it into the boys' eager hands. The joy on their faces helped dispel his disquiet. Patrick never asked why his family was singled out. The priest wondered if Patrick knew of his feelings for Bridget. As long as the Bishop let him remain in this parish, he would live with his suffering and guilt. He rarely met Bridget except for his rare visits to their cramped cottage with news of their two eldest sons in America and some money they had sent home. He had the unenviable task of breaking the news of Daniel's death in Mexico and watching Bridget fighting back her tears as Patrick held her close and stroked her head, neither of them noticing his departure. His desire to comfort Bridget was overwhelming and he returned to his church with a heavy heart to pray for them. He had no recent news of John and this caused them all great anxiety.

Many of his parishioners were leaving their small hovels with fields of rotting potatoes to find new lives overseas, some as close as Liverpool, others who had scraped the fare to America sailing away with heavy hearts. Despair hung like a heavy mist over the countryside.

***

In the thin shaft of early morning light through the crack in the shutters, Bridget Walsh saw the pain in her husband's eyes. Patrick leaned across, stifling his cough, and shook his wife, thinking she still slept. Her stomach lurched with fear as she sat up. The day they had dreaded had finally dawned. They both moved quietly around the crowded damp room. Slowly, bundles of rags, curled on the floor, stirred into life. The children rubbed their eyes, but uttered no word of complaint as they were helped into their clothes. Ripped sacking was wound around their feet, and when Bridget was satisfied the children were wrapped as well as they could be, she picked up the sleeping baby, Margaret, and held her to her breast, hoping that her restless night's sleep had not dried her milk. No word was spoken until they crowded out of the low stone building they called home.

Patrick felt so inadequate, useless. After years of struggle he had finally accepted that he could no longer provide for his family. He pulled the door closed behind them, remembering how he had carried Bridget over the threshold on the night of their wedding. They had worked so hard clearing their land of stones, building low walls to shelter the crops from the cruel Atlantic winds. It had been difficult work, but they had shared happy times, and at every child's birth they had rearranged the cramped rooms to accommodate just one more soul.

Bridget thought of Eliza, their eldest daughter. Like her two older brothers, Eliza had left home, and sailed for Liverpool in 1847. She wrote of her position in a large house, working as a servant. On her low wages she had little to send back to Ireland, but Bridget was thankful that two of the three children who had managed to escape from the grinding poverty they were now experiencing were not suffering the same.

***

Bridget refused to look back. With her head held high, ignoring the tears running down her cheeks, she walked ahead of the children so they would not witness her sorrow. Young Pat, now thirteen, held the hands of his younger siblings, Bridget aged ten and Joseph six. Pat had now left school but dreamed one day of becoming a teacher. His dreams were rapidly vanishing however with the past few years of disastrous crops. He had joined his father working on public works, road-building, to qualify the family for a small weekly wage. When Patrick senior had fallen ill and had to give up the labouring work, young Pat had tried to do the work of both of them, but it had not been enough. Now they were about to join other families presenting themselves to the authorities to be vetted as in need of relief. Pat felt so angry, so humiliated. He gripped the children's hands even harder, until Bridget tried to pull away with a pained cry so he put on a brave smile, bent down to kiss her better, and encouraged them on.

They walked through the field of rotten, stinking potatoes, blackened stalks on muddy ground reminding them of their plight. Patrick slowed to a halt when they reached the road.

"Right. Now then. I think the shortest way is up over the top, the downward path will be easier than the uphill climb."

Bridget hugged the baby to her.

"The little 'uns can't cross the mountain. Best go down to the shore and along that way."

The children, bewildered at being woken at dawn, cold in the March morning air, looked up at their Pa.

After a renewed fit of coughing, Patrick threw his arms wide,

"But that's much further!"

Bridget repositioned the baby across her chest.

"Yes, but if we end up carrying them it'll take us so much longer."

The first rays of daylight crept over the mountain, casting their shadows to walk before them. Patrick took hold of Joseph's hand, leaving young Pat in charge of his sister, Bridget.

"Right, right, as you say."

He attempted to sound cheerful but the children glanced at each other. Young Pat and Bridget followed behind. Pat's face was tense with emotion as he resisted arguing about the route chosen.

When they reached the shore, the slow-moving groups of other families could just be seen in the early light. Patrick led the way down to the hard sand near the water's edge as the wind tore at their ragged clothes and almost bowled over the little ones. Bridget pulled her shawl over the sleeping baby's head, and stumbled on.

The headland, which marked the point at which they must turn inland, kept its distance. The wind freshened, causing huge waves on the lough. Patrick looked down to find the water reaching his feet, so he turned and beckoned his family to follow him to the shoreline. They crossed the stones onto the bank as overhead dark clouds sped across the sky and rain lashed down to add to their discomfort. Patrick held onto his cap when the wind did its utmost to whip it away. Young Pat removed his hat and pushed it into his pocket, while Bridget and Joseph pulled their woolly caps tight to their heads.

Their mother tucked one corner of her shawl under the baby and pulled the other corner forward over her head to defy the wind. When they reached higher ground, they stopped briefly to catch their breath, and looked back. Distant figures appeared like wading birds, while the wind howled and the waves crashed. Then they realised that the bobbing seagulls riding the mountainous waves were not gulls at all. They watched in horror as the flailing forms of fellow travellers, raising their arms to the sky in prayer or admonishment, were carried back and forth, their ghastly screams just audible above the din of the storm. The plight of the poor lost souls was too much to bear. Patrick had tears streaming down his face, Bridget was howling and the children began to cry, never ever having witnessed their parents give way to their emotions. They had seen hard times, seen family members die, but they had never seen their Pa cry. Ma had cried when baby Mary had died, and again when Father Murphy arrived to tell them of the death of Daniel but even then nothing like this. Young Pat wiped his tears with the soaked sleeve of his coat and wondered whatever was going to become of them.

***

The mass exodus from the rural villages was necessary, as the government required families to present themselves to the authorities to prove they were indeed in need of Famine Relief. Everyone made their way as best they could, more than half-starved, as many had not eaten for days. They had been instructed to gather at Louisburgh workhouse for an issue of corn or possible admission to the workhouse.

The assembled group of wretched souls who had survived the journey huddled together for warmth, and waited patiently in the rain. When the heavy doors of the workhouse opened, they all crowded forward with hope in their eyes, whispering to each other. A large man, his size telling of a hearty appetite and regular meals, raised his hand for silence.

"This is awkward, very awkward. I have no authority to provide food for you. The two men on the Board of Guardians who you need to appeal to are in Delphi. You must find your way there."

Before they could protest he quickly went back inside and locked the doors.

Too exhausted to walk any further that day, the starving hoard slept as best they could through a cold wet night, before another long tiring walk to Delphi.

Patrick and Bridget were among the five hundred who set off once more, the children too confused and hungry to complain. Not all the sleeping families around them had woken to another bleak day. Many had given up and died where they lay.

In Delphi Lodge, Colonel Hograve and Captain Primrose ate a hearty lunch before having to confront the miserable peasants arriving in small groups.

As he wiped crumbs from his chin with his linen table napkin, Colonel Hograve stood up and left the table to take in the view.

"Good Lord, Primrose! Come, take a look at this!"

His fellow Inspector of the Poor drained his coffee cup and pushed his chair away from the highly polished table in the elegant dining room of the hunting lodge.

He joined Hograve at the window.

"How many were we told to expect? There must be six or seven hundred wretches out there waiting. What do we do?"

"Well, I for one, intend to enjoy another cup of this excellent coffee. Will you join me?"

Hograve strode back to his chair, picked up the coffee pot, and poured another cupful for himself.

Captain Primrose declined.

"Not for me, thank you all the same, sir. I will go out and ask them to be patient."

Captain Primrose was young, from a good family, but found his new position almost impossible. At home on his father's estate, the workers had comfortable homes, plenty of food and seemed content with their lot. His eyes had been opened to an alien world when he arrived in Ireland and saw the poor lives suffered by the peasants. His lunch had given him indigestion.

He marched across the lawn to the waiting crowd with little idea of what he would say to them. He stopped, and in his most authoritative voice, he asked them to be patient just a little longer.

"The Colonel is finishing his lunch."

The envy on their faces was apparent so he turned on his heels and went back indoors.

When Hograve had finished eating, he and Primrose discussed what could be done.

"We must tell them to return to Louisburgh, we can't possibly evaluate them here! No, no, they should never have been told to call on our help here. I will have something to say to whoever sent them, you can count on that!"

He crossed the lawn with the young captain beside him and addressed the crowd.

"You have been misinformed by whoever told you to come here that you would be assessed for your needs by us. Therefore, you must return to Louisburgh immediately and we will attend to you there."

The poor souls groaned as one, women and children sobbed, while the men had no energy for confrontation; they were spent, physically and mentally. The two military men turned and walked back to the house, slamming the door behind them.

Patrick Walsh coughed and fell to the ground. Bridget, with the baby lying still against her chest, fell on her knees beside him.

"Patrick! Patrick! Don't give up now, please stand and we will support each other. Get up, for pity's sake."

Young Pat looked on in horror. His Da was grey, eyes sunk in his sockets, struggling to his feet. Little Bridget and Joseph began to whimper so he hugged them both and did his best to comfort them, even though he was scared out of his wits himself.

Slowly Patrick stood upright, ceased coughing, and tried to smile.

"Now then, that coughing is done with. We'd better get back to Louisburgh as the soldiers told us. Ma, is baby all right? She is very quiet."

"She is sleeping. Take my arm will you now. Pat, keep tight hold of your brother and sister, the next stop we surely will get help."

The stillness of the baby worried her. She remembered the baby she had lost. Her family never knew how often she thought of Mary with her wide blue eyes and laboured breathing. Bridget had done everything she could for her sickly babe, but at just ten weeks old, she had convulsed and died. Now, she refused to cause yet more anxiety for her family by facing the knowledge baby Margaret, too, was gone. She tried praying to the Virgin Mary but her heart ached as she knew her prayers were in vain. Along with all the other weary travellers, they took the old goat track back to Louisburgh. The hills were dark and menacing, a mist lay all around until a wind blew through the valley and the waters of the lough heaved and crashed against the shores.

The slow moving column of people diminished in number as the weary fell, too exhausted to continue.

Patrick senior and baby Margaret never completed the journey. They were among the many who died along the way. Bridget laid them on the shore of Doolough, baby Margaret in the arms of her father. Young Bridget and Joseph cried. Pat, now the man of the family, had tears running down his cheeks, but Bridget's heart hardened, she had no tears left as she led them on, no comforting warmth of a baby on her chest now.

So many died on the way back to Louisburgh. The Walsh family, what remained of them, were among the few who were granted places in the workhouse, except for young Pat who was sent to work on the roads for a paltry wage. It would be some time before Bridget had news from Father Murphy that he had received further funds from her remaining son in America and that if she could return home she would have sufficient to see them through the next year.

Young Pat learnt his family was going home, so he left the workforce on the road-building program, and headed back to the little cottage they had abandoned not many months back.

CHAPTER TWENTY-ONE
LIVERPOOL 1849

"Eliza! Eliza! Oh where is that girl when I need her?" Adelaide Harper rose from her stool and crossed to her bedroom door, her silk dress rustling as she walked. She called her maid's name again. The pull on the bell had been ignored and this vexed her. From below, she heard footsteps running across the tiled hall then someone ascending the stairs. Adelaide returned to her dressing table and sat down as Eliza Walsh burst in, apologizing. Adelaide chastised her without looking at the young girl, so she failed to notice the swollen, tear-stained face.

"You really are most infuriating, Eliza. You know we are expecting guests this evening and I need help dressing. I do realise that it has been your day off but I require just half an hour of your time. Then you can retire for the night."

She handed Eliza her hairbrush, and while the girl brushed her hair she picked through her jewelry box, searching for a particular brooch. When she found the marcasite symbol of everlasting love, with two hearts entwined, each set with a pearl beneath a flamboyant bow, she sighed. It had been a gift from her husband on their betrothal. Although it had little monetary value, she cherished it as a reminder of their humble start in marriage. Now that Nathaniel was a successful businessman, their position in society had risen. Adelaide appreciated the gifts of diamonds, emeralds and other precious stones he had bought her over the years, but she treasured his first love token. Tonight she had a special reason for wearing it.

With Eliza's help, Adelaide dressed carefully until she was satisfied that she looked her best. Her grey silk dress was new; the dressmaker had delivered it that morning. As Adelaide moved, the light caught the silk and turned it from dark grey to flashing silver and she delighted in the sound the dress made. Her auburn hair was piled on top of her head, with wispy curls at her neck. She defied her female guest to look more elegant.

"Thank you, Eliza, you may go. I shall not need your help later, so the rest of the evening is yours."

"Oh, thank you, Ma'am. You do look handsome, if you don't mind my saying. Your gown is so beautiful."

Eliza had regained her composure and bobbed a curtsey as she left the room, but not before she saw her mistress flush with delight at the compliment.

A final glance in the cheval mirror satisfied Adelaide that she looked her best and she swept from the room, descending the stairs to join Nathaniel in the drawing room. She hesitated before opening the door and entered. Nathaniel was sitting at the fireside with his back to her, but when he turned to look over his shoulder, a gasp of approval escaped his lips. He stood up to admire his wife.

"My dear, how magnificent you look. I do like your dress. Is it new?"

"It was delivered today. Do you think it suits me? It's not too grey is it?"

"No, no. It is quite exquisite. It is silver, grey, black, as the light catches it."

As Adelaide moved nearer to the fire the silk shone with red, yellow and orange, reflecting the leaping flames. She fingered her brooch but Nathaniel didn't notice. She sighed as she sat down carefully to avoid crushing her dress.

A knock on the door prevented any further conversation and Tunstall, the butler, entered announcing:

"Mr and Mrs Frederick Winstanley have arrived. Shall I show them in, sir?"

Nathaniel stood up, nodding.

Jessica Winstanley breezed in followed by her husband. Jessica was much younger than Frederick, and people gossiped that it had been a marriage for money on her part. Poor Freddy, he was so besotted he didn't seem to care. She was certainly an asset to him, quick witted, charming and very glamorous. With her blond hair, smooth skin and perfect white teeth, she was not short of admirers, and so they received invitations to all the top society events. In stature, she was shorter than Adelaide and somehow caused the older woman to feel awkward by comparison. Not tonight, however.

"My dears, how nice to see you again."

Jessica offered her face for kissing to Adelaide then turned immediately to Nathaniel, holding his arm for longer than Adelaide thought was appropriate. Adelaide turned to greet Freddy.

Freddy grasped both her hands and shook them vigorously.

"Adelaide, darling, as usual you look delightful."

Adelaide relaxed and smiled. She liked Freddy, he was so unpretentious. He looked very much what he was, a gentleman farmer, who enjoyed being a farmer more than being a gentleman. He was a little taller than his wife, with ruddy cheeks, and hair that refused to remain tidy. It flopped over his face as he talked excitedly about his latest project. His tenants held him in high regard and enthusiastically fell in with his innovative new ideas about farming.

There was another knock on the door and Tunstall announced that dinner was served.

Adelaide and Freddy linked arms and led the way to the dining room. Jessica and Nathaniel did not follow immediately and Adelaide searched their faces for any trace of indiscretions as they entered. Seeing none, she dismissed her fears from her mind.

The evening passed pleasantly enough. Dinner was beautifully prepared and presented, and enjoyed by all. Just before midnight the guests departed, and snuffing out the candles, Adelaide and Nathanial retired to bed. Adelaide sat on the stool as she waited for Nathaniel to undo her buttons.

"Jessica looked absolutely radiant tonight, don't you think?"

She was unclipping her hair, allowing the dark curls to fall over her shoulders.

Nathaniel was struggling with his collar stud and didn't answer immediately. Eventually he triumphed over the stubborn, starched collar and flung it on his chair.

"Mm? What? Jessica? She looked the same as always. She dresses a little too flamboyantly for my taste."

He moved across to help Adelaide with the buttons on her gown.

"She doesn't have your good taste, my dear."

He bent and kissed the nape of her neck and she felt his breath on her skin. She felt a warm glow of pride as she studied his reflection in the mirror. Nathaniel was not handsome in the conventional way, but he had a presence, a confidence, which made him stand out. His hair was light brown and his moustache trimmed and neat. "Tonight she had an air of mischief about her, as if she had a secret she could scarcely contain. Did you not notice?"

She searched his face for a response.

"Ah. Well, Freddy has confided in me but he swore me to secrecy. They are expecting an addition to the family, but you must keep it confidential, Jessica doesn't know I know. You know Freddy, he couldn't help himself, it just came out."

Adelaide relaxed as Nathaniel struggled with the last button.

"Drat it, the button was loose and it's fallen off."

He bent to search for it but it was nowhere to be found.

"I'll have Eliza look for it in the morning."

She turned and was grasped in a firm embrace. The subject of Jessica was forgotten.

***

Next morning, while Nathaniel worked in the library, Adelaide dressed in a simple day dress and as she sat before her dressing table for Eliza to fasten up her hair, she saw the reflection of Eliza's face in the mirror wearing a worried expression.

"Is something troubling you, Eliza? Can I be of any help?"

She smiled as she said it, hoping Eliza would confide in her.

"Well, Eliza, I'm waiting."

Adelaide's voice cut through Eliza's musings.

"No, ma'am, I'm fine, really I am."

Eliza lied, unable to admit her concern for her family back in Ireland. It was humiliating to learn they had been threatened with the workhouse. How could she possibly tell anyone?

Adelaide stood up, straightening her skirt. She was too kind a person to pry but hoped that Eliza might open up later. The girl was obviously bothered about something, but she left her to hunt for the button, and went downstairs to write letters to her family.

The hiring of Eliza had been unusual. She had no references as she had not been in service before, but after reading about the famine in Ireland, Adelaide had had no hesitation in giving Eliza a position in the household and the young girl had learnt what was expected from her in no time.

Eliza searched the room until the missing button was found. As she placed it on the vanity tray on her mistress's dressing table, she caught sight of the brooch. She sat on the stool, turning the piece of jewellery in her hand. Her heart ached as she thought of her family's predicament back home in County Mayo, and on the spur of the moment, she pushed the brooch into her pocket. She hurried through the rest of her work and when she was finished, she made an excuse to Mrs Tunstall, the cook, slipped her shawl around her shoulders, and hurried from the house. She hoped she would not be missed as she headed for the pawnbroker's shop in town.

***

The bell tinkled over the shop door as Eliza entered. Inside, clocks ticked and whirred on the shelves and walls. Various stuffed animals and birds solemnly watched her from their glazed captivity. She shuddered with revulsion. She could never understand why people liked to display such macabre objects. From behind a dusty chenille curtain she could hear the shuffling feet of the proprietor, Mr Solomon. He was a stooped man of indeterminate age, with wisps of white hair escaping from the small cap he wore on his head. He peered over the half-glasses perched on the end of his nose. His stiff collar was grubby and his waistcoat shiny with age. A gold chain across his chest was attached to a pocket-watch which he took out as he approached the counter. This young woman was becoming a regular customer and he wondered what worthless trinket she had brought him this time.

He had little time for the majority of his customers. He knew that in most cases the bond he paid them went straight to the alehouses in town, but this girl perplexed him. She was obviously in service but had a quiet dignity about her. He had been more than generous with her, chastising himself for being so soft, but her eyes held such despair he could not ignore them.

"Well now, it's you again. What have you for me this time?"

He held out a hand twisted with rheumatism and fingernails long overdue for a trim.

Eliza reached into her drawstring bag and took out a small package. She unfolded the paper and placed in his hand Adelaide's pretty brooch. She looked at him hopefully.

"This is very nice, very nice."

Mr Solomon turned the piece over in his hand, took an eyepiece out of his pocket, and pushing aside his spectacles, he studied it. He was gratified to see it was of no great value. The young girl would have had to have stolen it if it was. No, it was inset with marcasite and a cultured pearl to each of the intertwined hearts. The bond for it would be very little and he looked at Eliza.

"How much are you hoping for my dear? Do you have a sum in mind?"

At this, Eliza gulped back the tears which constricted her throat, and trying to sound composed, replied, "Two guineas, if you please, Mr Solomon."

She had reckoned that with that amount she could keep her family from the workhouse for a short while at least. The future she didn't dare think about. The old man sat down heavily on his stool. He wanted to ask the girl why she needed such an amount, but kept silent. The brooch was fashionable enough: the sort a beau might give his girl as a token of his constancy. They were manufactured in their thousands. She must have fallen out with her young man to be willing to sacrifice it. The clocks ticked urgently as if pressing him to make a decision. He watched the girl as she fidgeted from foot to foot, trying to hide her impatience.

"You still have items to redeem you know. Still, I'm sure you have a very good reason for parting with it. Never mind, the next admirer who comes along might be more to your liking."

The few trinkets she had brought with her from Ireland were now with Mr Solomon.

Eliza frowned, then she realised what the old man was thinking. She pursed her lips together to prevent an admission. He mistook the look to be one of disapproval of the errant lover and he made up his mind to give her the sum she needed.

With his stiff inflexible fingers, he unlocked the heavy door of his safe and took from it a small cash box. Eliza glimpsed the folded notes beneath the tray of coins as he took out two guineas. He was about to hand it over when his hand returned to the box. Eliza's heart sank, thinking he had changed his mind. Mr Solomon poked about amongst the coins and took five florins out, adding them to the guineas, before putting them in Eliza's outstretched hand. He held her hand briefly, bending her fingers around the coins. She felt his bony fingers through her glove and resisted the urge to pull her hand away. His kindness puzzled her. She was sure that other pawnbrokers would not have been so obliging. She thanked him for his generosity and left the shop.

The old man, who put the fear of God in most of his customers, sat deep in thought on his stool, remembering his own long-lost love. That was a time long ago, in a far distant country. The clocks chimed one. He must close the shop and have a bite to eat. He heaved himself stiffly from his stool, put the brooch on display with the others and locked the shop door.

CHAPTER TWENTY-TWO
ELIZA IN TROUBLE

Adelaide dozed on the chaise longue and awoke when she heard the kitchen door closing. Glancing at her fob watch, she realised it was time for lunch. She rang the bell for Eliza and the girl soon appeared, flushed and breathless. Her mistress decided not to question the girl again but instructed her to bring lunch to the conservatory and inform Mr Harper, who was still in the library. Eliza bobbed a curtsey and disappeared.

Nathaniel joined his wife and they chatted as they ate game pie with chutney followed by dainty slices of fruit cake. Adelaide poured tea into the china cups then said, "Nat, dear, have you noticed Eliza's behaviour of late? She seems to be miles away and I must repeat my orders to her constantly."

She took a sip of tea, and brushed imaginary crumbs from her skirt.

"I can't say I have. Mind you, I have little to do with Eliza besides handing her my coat and hat. She is fulfilling her duties satisfactorily I hope?"

Nathaniel took another piece of the pie. He did enjoy Mrs Tunstall's baking.

"Oh yes. No doubt about it. She just appears preoccupied. I can't get anything out of her, although I have tried."

Her husband wiped away the pie crumbs from his moustache.

"The problems back home in Ireland must cause her great anxiety. Do you know how her family is faring? I'll do my best to wheedle it out of her, see if we can help in any way."

"That would be so kind, she may feel more obliged to open her heart to you, as the master of the house. Thank you, Nathaniel."

Adelaide stood up and began examining her plants. Satisfied that they required no watering, she waited while Nathaniel finished his lunch and then rang the bell for the dishes to be removed.

While her husband took an after-lunch nap, she took a stroll around the garden to gather roses for the sitting room. She had been concerned about Jessica the day before, imagining wrongly that Nat had feelings for her. Now she found she could concentrate her thoughts on Eliza and her problems. The perfume from the roses pleased her as she carried them indoors, and she rang for Eliza to fetch a vase for the flowers.

"Ma'am, might I have a few moments of your time please?"

Eliza smoothed her apron as she spoke while Adelaide arranged the flowers in the vase.

"Of course, come in here, child. We can talk in private."

She ushered Eliza into the sitting room and closed the door behind them.

"Sit down, sit down," Eliza sat down on the edge of the seat.

"I need to visit my family as soon as possible, ma'am."

Adelaide waited for Eliza to continue but she remained silent.

"Is it really urgent, Eliza?"

The girl nodded, not trusting herself to speak.

"Is there any way we can be of help to you, or perhaps your family?"

Eliza shook her head. She knew the time might come soon when she would need to plead her family's case but not yet. She blushed with guilt, remembering what she had done. Adelaide saw her colour rise but was kind enough not to pursue it.

"Very well. Now then, this evening we are going to the theatre. I will need you to help me dress later, so I will ring for you when I need you. Tomorrow we can make arrangements for you to visit your home."

Later, as Eliza assisted her mistress, she was terrified Adelaide would ask for the brooch but fortunately Adelaide chose a cameo to wear with her rust-coloured taffeta dress for her evening at the opera.

***

It came as a complete shock to Mrs Tunstall when, a few days later, she heard a commotion from the library. Mr Harper flung open the door in anger and called for Mr Tunstall to fetch the local constable to the house. Mrs Harper appeared, with a furious expression on her face, leading Eliza by her wrist. Eliza appeared terrified, her face swollen from crying, and she averted the cook's concerned looks.

The police constable was in the library for some time with Mr and Mrs Harper and Eliza. When he left he took Eliza with him, carrying a small bag of clothes she had been allowed to pack.

The supper was returned to the kitchen that evening with very little eaten and Tunstall shrugged his shoulders at his wife's questioning look, none the wiser as to the reason for Eliza's hasty departure. The following week, the Liverpool Mercury recorded what had happened. Tunstall read it out loud to his wife in the kitchen.

"Maidservant Stole Brooch"

"Eliza Walsh, employed as housemaid at the residence of Nathaniel Harper Esq., was brought before the magistrate's court accused of stealing from her mistress an item of jewellery, being a brooch set with marcasite and pearls. The accused took it to Mr Solomon, the pawnbroker, where it was exchanged for cash. As the defendant had previously had an unblemished character, when found guilty, Walsh was sentenced to twenty-one days hard labour and five years in a reformatory in which time she should contemplate her behaviour and reform her ways. Walsh broke down sobbing when she was led from the court and Mrs Harper was seen to be also distressed. She was comforted by Mr Harper as they left the court."

The young reporter on the local paper who had followed Eliza's case, Thomas Hall, had decided to pursue the sad tale to the end. He interviewed Jack Tunstall and wrote the following article.

"The Sad Tale of Eliza the Maid"

"Eliza Walsh has stubbornly refused to admit her reason for the theft. Mr and Mrs Harper had taken Walsh into their home and trusted her. She had betrayed them and must suffer the consequences. Eliza Walsh remains incarcerated."

Two weeks later another report by Thomas Hall caught Tunstall's attention.

"Eliza the Maid, New Developments"

"Eliza Walsh, who is serving time for theft as reported two weeks ago, has broken down and admitted the reason for the theft. Her family, back home in County Mayo, Ireland, have been reduced to abject poverty caused by the failed potato crop and have been threatened with the workhouse. Walsh hoped to send them what money she could and had naively thought she could redeem the brooch from wages still to come and return it before it was missed. She has since heard from her Parish Priest that sadly, her family has suffered great loss while seeking Government relief, both her father and baby sister expired on the road near Doolough and her family are now in the workhouse, but for one brother who works on the road-building programme which provides a small income for himself alone. I can report that when Mr Solomon was told of Eliza's dilemma, he offered to return the brooch to the owner. On questioning Mrs Adelaide Harper, I was told that she was so moved by the appalling news of Eliza's family and so overjoyed to have possession of her favourite brooch again, she promised to speak to Mr Harper. Subsequently, Mr Harper has asked the magistrates to review the case."

Then the story took a dramatic turn.

"Maidservant Back in Court"

"Eliza Walsh has been summoned to appear in court again. The Governor revealed to this reporter that this was most uncommon and had no idea what was to happen to the girl. When Eliza Walsh appeared before the magistrates for the second time, she was seen to have lost a great deal of weight and looked ill. Although she was dressed in clean clothes, they were ill-fitting and she displayed signs of neglect. She stood in the dock, gripping the rail tightly. She seemed surprised to see seated in the court, Mr Solomon and Mr and Mrs Harper. Mr Solomon then stood up and revealed that the stolen brooch had now been returned to Mrs Harper. Mrs Harper stood next and it was noticed that as she spoke, she fingered the said brooch which was pinned to her collar. She told the magistrates she was perfectly happy to take Eliza back into service. At this, Eliza Walsh broke down, weeping. The magistrates put their heads together, glancing occasionally at Nathaniel who nodded encouragement, and came to their decision. 'The felon before us, Eliza Walsh, will not now complete her sentence and it will not be necessary for her to attend the reformatory. This decision has been reached after careful consideration and with the blessing of Mrs Harper, the owner of the stolen goods. Let this be a lesson, however, to all who steal. Not every wronged person will be so generous. It is most unusual for a sentence to be commuted in this way. Court dismissed.' Eliza then joined her employers outside the court where I witnessed Mrs Harper approach the girl and embrace her. She told Eliza to spend the rest of the day recovering from her ordeal and return to work as usual the following day."

Thomas Hall, the young reporter, had taken more than a passing interest in Eliza. The young girl with her hair of dark curls and shy smile had captured his heart and they soon became good friends. He began reporting the shocking news from Ireland with complete honesty in the Liverpool Mercury to be sure the people of the city understood the plight of the starving Irish. It came as no surprise to the Harper household when the young man began to call on Eliza of a Sunday to go walking. Mr Harper began raising money from his wealthy friends for Father Murphy's parish to help prevent more unnecessary fatalities, and Eliza's cheerful demeanor returned.

Eliza wrote to Bridget.

Ma, I pray for you each night and as soon as I am able I will visit you all. The family here are good to me; I am allowed each Sunday off duty as long as I attend Mass. If I lived close enough to you I could visit you on Sunday afternoons but I have been promised a week's holiday and I have saved up my fare to cross to Ireland. Just let me know when it would be favourable, I miss you all. Kiss Pat, Joseph and Bridget for me,

God bless you all,

Your loving daughter, Eliza.

CHAPTER TWENTY-THREE
LIVERPOOL 1851

The front parlour of the terraced house where Thomas and Eliza lived was their best room, only used when the young couple had visitors. Eliza was looking forward to seeing Father Murphy from her home parish and Thomas had to press her to stay calm, sit down and think of the baby she was carrying. A fire burned in the grate and the smell from the coal mixed with the musty odour of a room little used was barely disguised by the fragrance from the vase of flowers standing near the window. Thomas refused to open a window as he feared his wife might catch a chill. Eliza crossed the room, pulled the heavy lace curtain to one side and looked out onto the street, hoping to catch a sight of the priest. It was four years since she last saw him on a brief visit home.

"Watching out for your priest won't make him come any sooner, my love. Come and sit down again, take the weight off your feet. I will answer the door when he knocks."

"Oh Tom, I feel like a child again. I do hope he has good news of my family. Ma writes so seldom and when she does she tells me very little. I try reading between the lines but it is difficult, she has a way of always sounding cheerful. Father Murphy is sure to be honest with me, don't you think? He will not lie to me surely?"

"Don't get so anxious, Eliza, stay calm for the baby's sake please! Oh, was that a knock I heard? Sit still now, I will see who it is."

Eliza sat by the fire, twisting her wedding ring as she did when she was agitated. She heard Thomas speaking as he closed first the front door then the vestibule door. He ushered their guest into the parlour and Father Murphy entered, beaming when he saw the heavily pregnant young woman about to get up to greet him.

"Dear Eliza, please, do not get up on my account in your condition. My goodness, I last saw a girl, now you are fully grown into a beautiful young woman, marriage obviously suits you."

He shook her hand then removed his hat and cloak which Thomas took to hang on the hallstand.

Tears of joy welled up in Eliza's eyes but she quickly brushed them aside.

"Father, how good to see you after all this time. Tell me, how are things back home? How is Ma, and my brothers and sister? It seems an age since I was last in Ireland."

"Your mother is well, coping admirably under the circumstances. Your brother has worked hard to get the land back growing crops again now that he has finished school for good. Bridget and Joseph are still getting an education. I see them at Mass some Sundays but I'm afraid your mother still stays away. She keeps busy, taking in sewing when she can. I have had occasion to benefit from her skills with a needle a few times myself."

This news seemed to satisfy Eliza.

"Tell me, Father, does she still hear from John?"

"John? Not recently I fear but he did write to tell her he was going prospecting for gold in California with one of his military friends. It has been reported in the papers that people from the world over have left their homes and livelihoods hoping to make fortunes there. Some do but sadly, others barely survive."

"The priest shrugged his shoulders and sighed.

"He has sent no money for quite some time so I fear he has not had much success."

"Oh dear, I hope that after all he has been through, seeing our Daniel die and all, he makes a small fortune at least."

Thomas excused himself to put the kettle on the fire in the back kitchen.

Father Murphy sat back in his chair.

"I want to ask you, Eliza, about Mr and Mrs Harper. I plan to visit them to thank them personally for their magnificent efforts in raising funds for the impoverished people back home. They were very trying times, very trying as you know. Your father's death and the baby too, were just too distressing for your mother. And others, of course," he quickly added, not wishing to appear to favour Bridget.

"Perhaps you can give me directions as to where I might find them?"

"Oh Father, Mr and Mrs Harper would love to meet you! I will ask Thomas to draw you a map, it is a long walk or a short hansom cab ride. They have a son now after years of fearing they would never be parents."

"And you, Eliza? When is your baby expected?"

Eliza stretched her back in an effort to get comfortable.

"I have just three weeks to go, Father. It will be a blessing not to feel so big and clumsy anymore. Tom has been an angel, taking over many of my housewife duties, even cooking meals. He has proved to be an excellent cook."

She smiled as Thomas entered, carrying a laden tray. He set it down on the table in the bay window and proceeded to arrange cups on saucers and pour tea. He offered one to Father Murphy who accepted milk from the jug but declined the proffered sugar. Thomas returned to the kitchen to collect scones and plates. The priest passed a cup to Eliza when he saw she was about to get up from her chair.

"Let me be mother, it will be a change from being Father. Milk? Sugar?"

Eliza had both and thanked him.

"Well, now Thomas, don't tell me you have been baking too?"

"Oh no, Father, Eliza enjoys baking, she made these yesterday especially for you."

They fell silent for a while as they enjoyed the scones.

Eliza asked, "Do you have a place to stay while you are in Liverpool, Father?"

The priest waited until his mouth was empty before answering.

"Have you heard of a Father Nugent?"

Thomas and Eliza nodded.

"Well, you must know that he does a lot for the Irish poor who came to Liverpool because of the famine. He is parish priest Of St Nicholas church. We are on good terms, writing to one another and he has kindly offered me accommodation with him at his rectory. His passion is ensuring that the waifs and strays, many of whom are orphans, receive an education and he opened a 'Ragged School' at Copperas Hill."

Thomas nodded.

"Hasn't he helped in the founding of a middle school in Rodney Street too?"

"And now a school for girls in Mount Pleasant, I believe" said Eliza.

"I can see he is well known here then, did you know he is half-Irish himself? His father has a greengrocery business here in Liverpool. Fathered nine children too; in fact, Father Nugent has a brother who is also a priest. I am eager to meet him face to face, and expecting many interesting discussions on his valued work."

Father Murphy brushed crumbs from his lap.

"Those scones were delicious, Eliza, you should set up a bakery one day. Not just yet, obviously, but when your child is a few years old."

"Thank you, Father, you are too kind, I might just do that. However, we hope to have more than one child and Tom makes a comfortable living as a reporter with the Liverpool Mercury so my work for some years will be looking after the little ones."

Thomas interrupted.

"Of course we also plan to move to a bigger house and then we can invite Eliza's family to stay. It will be so good for her to see her mother again."

The thought of Bridget silenced Father Murphy for a while. He knew that Eliza was not aware of his feelings for her mother and he meant to keep it that way. He emptied his cup and placed it on the tray before he stood up.

"No, stay sitting, Eliza. Thank you for the directions, Thomas, I will pass on your good wishes to Mr and Mrs Harper. Now, I must go and make myself known to Father Nugent. God bless you both, I will see you again before I return to Ireland."

When Eliza heard the front door shut on the priest, she rested her head on the chair-back and closed her eyes, a smile of contentment on her face.

***

Baby Clara was born a week after Father Murphy sailed from Liverpool back to Ireland but before he left he had arranged with Father Nugent that he might perform the baptism for Eliza. Thomas was happy to go along with his wife's wishes. He had attended his local Anglican church as a boy but had not been inside a church since his wedding day, quite happy to mind the baby on Sundays while Eliza attended Mass.

Eliza was a natural mother after helping with her siblings before leaving home for a new life in Liverpool. The disturbed nights lasted only for the first three months then Clara settled into a routine where she slept through the night. Thomas had moved temporarily into the small spare bedroom but he found the narrow iron single bed most uncomfortable and was relieved to join Eliza in their much larger brass bed.

All their furniture had been bought second-hand but this bed was their pride and joy. It had a small fitted mirror at the head, with a star-shape cut into the glass. On each corner of the bed ends was a brass ball, lovingly polished by Eliza. She had worked on a patchwork quilt from before she was married and completed it soon after they moved into the little house and this kept them warm. The baby slept in a cot alongside the bed close to Eliza so that the first sign she needed feeding Eliza could do so without disturbing Thomas.

***

By 1855 there were two more additions to the family, a boy they named Daniel and another girl, Margaret. The idea of a bakery was long forgotten, the only baking Eliza did was to feed her growing family.

One morning a letter arrived from Eliza's mother to let them know she had booked a passage to Liverpool for herself, Joseph and Bridget and that she hoped they could stay with them. Eliza was torn between excitement and dismay.

"Where will we all sleep, Tom? We only just have enough room for ourselves but I can't refuse my own mother. What are we to do?"

Thomas shook his head and thought for a while.

"Maybe Father Nugent would help?"

"Oh, I don't think that's a good idea. Ma no longer goes to church and I don't think the little ones do either. Where on earth can we put them?"

"Hey, how about the attic? It's quite roomy up there although it's a bit gloomy with only having that one small window."

The attic was never furnished because of their plan to move to a larger house when the children were older. That evening when the children were asleep, Thomas and Eliza pulled aside the curtain which hung at the foot of the creaky wooden staircase leading to the top floor. Eliza coughed from the disturbed dust as she followed her husband, carrying an oil lamp. The new gaslights fitted in the house did not extend this far. Cobwebs caressed Eliza's cheek as she paced the dimensions of the room to judge the size of beds it would accommodate.

"I think if we bought two small beds like the one downstairs they should fit and still leave room for a blanket box. What d'you think, Tom?"

"I can go to the big second-hand warehouse on the dock road, they are sure to have something we can use."

"I tell you, it is almost as roomy in this one small space as it was back home in Ireland for my whole family!"

"The beds we buy will be useful in our next house so it is not an unnecessary expense. I will call after work tomorrow, see what I can find."

"And when the children have their afternoon nap, I will get rid of all these cobwebs and clean the floor and window to let the light in. At least it won't need curtains as it is in the roof."

Eliza rubbed her hands together and her eyes shone with excitement.

"Oh Tom, I will write back straight away and tell her we are looking forward to her visit. I have missed them so, you don't know what a blessing it is for me to have you and our dear children chase morbid thoughts from my mind of my poor dead Pa, Daniel and baby Margaret. Still, their names live on in our own little ones."

Eliza wiped tears away then took a handkerchief from her apron pocket and blew her nose. She shook herself and smiled at Thomas, all feelings of self-pity banished.

***

The reunion was a joyful occasion. Everyone wanted to talk at once and the small crowded house was filled with laughter and squeals of delight from the youngsters. Joseph was now twelve and Bridget sixteen but they enjoyed playing with their two nieces and nephew. Clara was four now and happy to have Aunty Bridget to help her dress her doll. Joseph had brought with him toys he had outgrown and little Daniel followed him like a shadow.

One night, as Thomas was telling his children a bedtime story, Bridget shouted down the attic stairs to Joseph. He raced to see what she wanted and found her on the blanket box, straining to see out of the small window. He climbed up alongside her and was just in time to see a man on a bicycle slow down almost to a stop and with the long rod he held in one hand, he lit the gas streetlamp. Immediately, a warm orange glow illuminated the cobbled street below as the man slowly pedalled to the next lamp.

"Don't you just think that is magic, our Joe, we've nothing like that back home for sure unless they have it in Dublin. D'you think they'll have such lamps in Dublin, Joe? What if we could stay here?"

"And leave Ireland for good? Where would we live and what about school? That's not for me. Yes, it's good to visit but I'd miss the Gaelic and the soft rain blowing in from the sea. Here is too busy for me."

Thomas appeared at the door.

"Well, as well as being magic, what d'you think of the lamplighter? Isn't he clever, doing it without even stopping? Now you two, back downstairs while the little ones sleep and you can tell me all about Ireland. I've never been there so you will have a deal of talking to do."

CHAPTER TWENTY-FOUR
THE WANDERER RETURNS

The fortunes of the Hall family and the Walsh's improved over the years. By 1861, John Walsh had at last returned to Ireland with his good friend, O'Reilly. They had found enough gold for a comfortable living and had left California to cross America. In New York, they befriended a fellow Irishman, John O'Mahony. He belonged to an organisation for Irish in America which they had joined before they had sailed home to raise money towards payment for the return of the body of a valued friend, Terence McManus, to his mother country. John told them how McManus had fled Ireland in 1848 after taking part in an uprising in Ballingarry which sought to gain independence for Ireland.

As they sat around the fire in the family home in Ballybray, Bridget listened to her long-lost eldest son as he told them of his adventures. She told him what she remembered of the failed revolution.

"Do you know, I remember it as if it was yesterday. It was when times were really hard, men would meet secretly and talk of what could be done to put things right. There was more talk than action though because upmost in the men's minds was how to feed their families. Some men in County Limerick did try at Ballingarry. It was at a remote farmhouse and their action is called to this day "the battle of Widow McCormack's Cabbage Patch."

John listened intently as his mother continued.

"A small band of men besieged a group of Irish constables but it didn't last long as reinforcements arrived and two of the rebels were shot dead and more wounded. The rest fled. I imagine McManus was one who escaped but I never heard he had made it to America."

Her two other sons, Patrick and Joseph sat wide-eyed listening to the two Johns as they regaled them with tales of Mexico and the goldfields of California. They regarded the two adventurers as true heroes, men who were prepared to go anywhere to fight for the freedom of the oppressed.

Bridget's heart sank. The last thing she wanted was to face the possibility of losing two more sons to insurrection. There was growing unrest amongst the young men of Ireland who resented the presence of the British. She decided there and then that it was time for her to follow Eliza's lead and settle in England. With luck, Joseph would be willing to go with her.

Her other son, Patrick, had already carved out his future by working hard at school and his master was so impressed that he encouraged Patrick to continue with his studies after leaving school so that he could become a teacher. By studying every evening and working at labouring, farming or whatever casual work he could find during the day, he could afford the books he needed. Once he had passed the necessary exams, he was able to take over the teacher's post at his local school when his old teacher retired. At the age of twenty-three, he had married the daughter of a teacher from Cork and the young couple had left Ballybray to settle in the schoolhouse of a new appointment he had taken near Cork. His wife, Maisie, had not accompanied him on this visit as she was expecting their first child.

When Bridget first raised the possibility of leaving the home they had extended and made so much more comfortable, she met with strong protests.

Joseph was now the farmer, following in his father's footsteps. Bridget could see her dead husband in Joseph's features more than any of his brothers. Just like Patrick senior, he was very popular with the young girls of the neighbourhood, but unlike her husband, Joseph had not yet had his heart captured. He was in no rush to settle down. He attended all the fairs and fetes, enjoyed dancing and flirting with the girls, drinking and exchanging news with other young men and often arriving back home late and more than a little inebriated. Bridget never let him know that she lay anxiously waiting for his return before falling asleep once she knew he was home.

Her daughter, Bridget, had married young to an older man, a widower who lost his wife in childbirth and left him to raise his young family. Her mother had not approved of the marriage but bit her tongue, remembering how her own parents had disapproved of Patrick until he proved to them what a hard worker he was and they had finally warmed to him. Her youngest daughter had taken a position as a live-in housekeeper with the widower initially but their romance had blossomed and they were married very quietly with little expense. Kevin Pierce always appeared to his mother-in-law as a little grand, too arrogant. She had noticed when she visited them how he corrected her daughter's English even though he knew her first language was Gaelic. On one occasion as mother and daughter sat chatting, Kevin had drawn his wife's attention to the fact that the fire needed stoking and she had immediately jumped up and taken the peat bucket to fill it.

The disapproval of his mother-in-law almost led to her interfering when he had deposited a muddy pair of boots at his wife's feet for polishing. No words were exchanged, young Bridget meekly stood up and took the boots away to clean them.

Her mother watched, tight-lipped, afraid that if she showed her anger at the attitude of Kevin to her beloved daughter whose dedication to the care of his young children was the saving grace in the marriage, she might cause such friction as to make her unwelcome in their home again.

***

As they sat down to dinner the evening before John and O'Reilly left for America, Bridget announced that she had finally made up her mind and she had decided to move to Liverpool.

"But, Ma, what can you be wanting in England? All your roots are here, your children too. What will you do? Where will you live?"

"All my children are not here, no longer, anyway. You, John, are about to leave again, poor Daniel is buried in a grave I will never see, baby Margaret barely lived before she died and Eliza has a growing family in Liverpool."

"But what about this place?" asked Joseph.

"I want you to have it, Joseph. You are the one who has expanded it by buying up the farm of our poor deceased neighbours and building extra rooms to give us a more comfortable living. And who knows, once the place is your own, you will find a girl to walk out with and hopefully marry. I can picture you now carrying a pretty young girl over the threshold."

This caused hoots of laughter from everyone around the table, including Joseph.

"But Ma, I'm only nineteen! I'm not ready for marriage yet!"

"At your age I was already married to your Pa and with a baby, John. Anyway you will have a far better chance of attracting a wife if you have no family living with you. It is said that in-laws should always live at such a distance that to visit they need to put on a coat and ride on a pony or better still, take a pony and trap."

Joseph fell silent as he digested this news then his face lit up.

"I know, I can go to the Hiring Fairs, try before I buy sort of thing, and take on a housekeeper for short-term assessment. Ha! Yes, that's what I'll do!"

Bridget tut-tutted and stood to clear the table. John O'Reilly helped her carry the dishes through to the scullery. While they were alone, Bridget spoke to him in confidence.

"I understand you made quite a name for yourself in Mexico. I want to thank you for all you did for my boys."

"How can you think thanks are needed. If I had not encouraged the two of them to follow me to Mexico, Daniel would most probably still be alive."

Bridget shook her head.

"No, I believe our time to die is in our destiny and naught can change it. My faith in the church was lost long ago but I have accepted that what will be will be."

She hesitated before continuing, "As for your current obsession, for that is what it is, I understand your reasons for joining the Fenian Brotherhood but I do not support it. After what we Irish have been through in the recent past, I believe that what we need now is peace and harmony."

She looked him in the eye to see what his reaction to her views were.

"I would never argue with someone kind enough to have me as a guest in their home, but we must follow our hearts, Mrs Walsh, as simple as that."

"But what of your own wife? What does she make of your continued absence? And your son, you can barely know him?"

O'Reilly grimaced.

"My marriage is over, Bridget. A report was sent home stating that I had been killed in action in Mexico and my wife accepted the news with little regret. She was able to marry the man she was living with and he adopted my son. I avoided meeting with her. The fact that she is a bigamist can remain a secret. Anyway, it suits me well not to have my presence known. John assured me of your discretion."

"Promise me one thing, Colonel John. Do your best to stay on the right side of the law. My John has always been a serious young man since he was fourteen years old and followed his hero, Daniel O'Connell. Help him to have some fun in his life, he has known too much sorrow."

O'Reilly put his hands on her shoulders and looked earnestly into her beseeching brown eyes.

"Bridget, he is a fully grown man now, one with ideals too firmly engrained in his conscience for me to have any influence on him. I honestly believe that had he not left home he might have taken the cloth."

Bridget's eyes flashed.

"I am aware that the first-born son is often expected to become a priest but my true feelings are that it is a most unnatural life for a young man. Better to join the military, at least, then a man might enjoy the company of a woman."

"He has had experiences of that nature I can assure you. Did you know about Daniel's friend, Jane, he met on the passage to America? John keeps in touch with her, even after all these years. She never remarried but John tells me she keeps the memory of Daniel in her heart to this day so his friendship with her will no doubt continue only by letter."

He looked around to see their work in the scullery was done.

"Well, the others must be wondering what keeps us, I think we should join them, don't you?"

As they entered the sitting room, all eyes were fixed on the tall handsome colonel and their mother, still attractive, her face flushed and her long hair swept up with tendrils of curls framing her face. John noticed for the first time what a handsome couple they made. He glanced at Joseph to see his reaction. Joseph smiled and winked, both gestures noticed by their mother. However, their hopes of romance between their mother and the colonel faded as their lives took different paths.

.

PART TWO
JOHANN'S STORY

CHAPTER ONE
A CASTLE IN BAVARIA 1867

Johann Nicklas was helping the hairdresser attend to the ladies of the court prepare for a concert of music by Wagner being held at the castle. King Ludwig II was a great admirer of Richard Wagner but the composer was unable to conduct the concert personally as the king had very reluctantly banished him from Bavaria on the insistence of his ministers who objected strongly to Wagner's political radicalism. This was not going to prevent the King from enjoying his favourite composer's music however, and the castle buzzed with the preparations.

Johann had been chosen by the court hairdresser, Alfonse, to act as his assistant when he discovered that the boy had an invaluable knowledge of the benefits of herbs, learnt from his father Karl, the head gardener at the castle. After collecting the herbs for the physician, the chefs, the housekeeper and the hairdresser, Johann would prepare the different infusions which Alfonse used to treat a variety of problems. For dandruff, young nettle tops were boiled and massaged gently into the scalp while dull hair was treated with a preparation of rosemary or nettle oil. In return, Alfonse instructed Johann in the hairdresser's art. Johann gained his experience, practising on the kitchen maids who would giggle with delight at having their hair in the latest fashion. They prepared vegetables in the kitchen whilst looking rather grand with their hair piled on top of their head and sweet curls on their forehead or in soft bouffant styles fastened at the nape of the neck with a clasp; this caused them much merriment. The footmen, coachmen and grooms also benefited by having their hair cut and face hair trimmed in the style of the times.

One girl had caught Johann's eye; Marie had arrived at the castle with the fiancée of the King, Princess Sophie of Bavaria, to serve as her lady in waiting. She lived in the Ladies' apartments in the castle, close to her mistress and would attend the concert. While Alfonse looked after Princess Sophie's hair, Johann was allowed to arrange Marie's beautiful auburn hair. As he brushed her long curls, he caught Marie stealing a shy glance at him. Her large brown eyes sparkled with amusement when she saw that her attention to him had caused him to blush. Johann dropped the hairbrush in embarrassment and Marie turned in her chair to face him. When she smiled she revealed perfect white teeth. She tapped his hand in mock admonishment.

"I do believe you would much rather be out with the huntsman or the hawker than in a salon of ladies doing their hair, would you not – I do not know your name – Johann? Am I right, Johann, or maybe you have a maiden you wish to visit?"

Johann blushed even more, and denied there was anywhere he would rather be, stating honestly, "My lady, I can think of nowhere I would rather be than in the presence of yourself and to have the privilege of holding such beautiful hair in my hands – forgive me for being so bold but I have been admiring your hair as I have been brushing it."

Then it was the turn of Marie to blush, having looked Johann full in the face as he talked and found herself liking what she saw. He was tall, with blond hair and blue eyes and the physique of an athlete, but she noticed that although his hands had been gentle as he stroked her hair whilst brushing it, they were strong hands and obviously used to other work besides hairdressing. He was dressed simply in breeches and an open necked shirt and was close enough for her to be aware of his clean, masculine smell not disguised by cologne in the manner of the gentry. She found it was a pleasant, comforting smell and she daydreamed briefly of being held in his arms only to be brought abruptly back to the present when Alfonse approached them with urgency in his voice.

"Johann, you must work faster, the concert is due to begin shortly. There are several more ladies waiting to have their hair dressed and in more intricate styles than Marie here, if you will excuse me, Marie, as they are older and require grand styles to flatter them and belie their age."

Johann turned back to Marie, once again expressing regret at his clumsiness and deftly twisted her hair into a chignon then fastened it with the jewelled clasp she handed him. She stood up, shaking her skirt out and thanked him for his skilful work. One by one the ladies left the salon satisfied with their hairstyles while Johann tidied away the bottles of herbal preparations and collected dropped hairpins before finishing for the day.

As Johann walked through the herb garden in the castle grounds the next day, he could not get the image from his head of the girl he had met the previous evening. He went in search of Karl, his father, in the gardens. His father looked up from his work and asked,

"Johann, do you have the herbs for chef yet? Have you remembered what he asked for? He has a large house party to cater for tonight and needs marigolds and nasturtiums for the salads, a mix of herbs for the meat dishes and he particularly needs the elderflower as soon as possible for the jelly he is preparing for dessert."

Johann quickly gathered the herbs into the basket he was carrying and returned to the kitchen to hand them to the kitchen maid and collected an even larger basket for the elderflower. He looked forward to leaving the gardens to go out into the surrounding fields where he would find the elderflower growing in abundance in the hedgerows.

As he walked through the formal gardens to reach the gate leading out into the fields, he heard faint laughter coming from within the yew tunnel. He peered into the cool shadiness of the overhanging trees to find Marie stooping forward with her hands clasped in front of her, as she watched intently something on the ground. The object of her scrutiny suddenly hopped away and Johann could see it was a large toad. Marie turned her head to watch it and then she became aware of Johann's presence.

"Ah, my clumsy hairdresser," she exclaimed playfully, hoping to disguise the pleasure in her voice at seeing him and trying to compose herself and assume the dignity that she felt sure would be expected of her.

"You like toads?" said Johann with surprise. He was impressed that here was a young lady who did not shriek in horror at the sight of what some considered an ugly creature although he himself thought of it as the gardener's friend.

Marie stood up and with a tilt of her head, she assured him that she found it a fascinating creature and was disappointed that he had caused the toad to hop away.

"Now I must find another distraction to pass the time before I am needed once more for instruction by my mistress on how to be a lady-in-waiting." She said this with such a lack of enthusiasm that he felt obliged to ask was she not happy with her prospects.

"How would you care to be at the beck and call of a lady of such nervous disposition that she has never lifted a finger to so much as dress herself, fetch a book from the library or even open a window when she becomes stifled? These are to be my duties and for this privilege I am allowed to attend functions and be introduced to boring young men who just might wish me to become their bride, with little choice of my own in the matter."

She sighed and slowly walked from the shade of the yew tunnel into the bright morning sunshine.

They walked slowly side by side toward the gateway to the fields. As they walked they talked about the benefits of toads in the gardens and of the different birds they spotted, with Johann identifying them by their song. They stopped to watch butterflies settling on the plants then flying off as they searched for their favourite flowers.

They had arrived at the gate.

"This is where I must leave you. I must collect elderflower for the kitchen."

He opened the gate leading to the meadow beyond, bordered by an abundance of elder trees draped in creamy heads of elderflower, ripe for picking, and their perfume heavy in the air.

Marie hesitated, then casting a glance back toward the castle where she was expected in an hour's time she said impulsively,

"May I come? Perhaps I could help? I could carry the basket while you cut the flower heads from the trees."

She studied his face to see his reaction to her suggestion and her heart jumped with joy when she saw the delight on his face. However, his face clouded over as he felt he should not encourage her, thinking for the first time of their different roles at the castle and concerned that they would be in trouble should they be observed. When he told her he thought it was not a good idea, she countered by saying,

"I am still a free agent and besides, what harm can be done? It will be apparent to anyone who sees us that it was just a chance meeting."

Not too reluctantly, Johann acquiesced and so they passed through the gate, closing it behind them. It was a beautiful morning and as they walked around the perimeter of the field, they laughed as they disturbed grasshoppers, bees and more butterflies which flew up in front of them as their feet and Marie's skirt hem brushed them from the grass stalks and the wild flowers. Overhead, the skylarks celebrated the season with their song.

They chatted happily as Marie held the basket while Johann collected the elderflower, finding pleasure in each other's company as they discovered they shared a common joy in their surroundings. Johann had always felt the castle was a special place and although the cottage they lived in was close by, he spent all his waking hours in the castle grounds or inside the castle helping wherever he was needed. He described to Marie how he had become familiar with every room in the castle including the apartments of the King as he had assisted Alfonse when he attended to King Ludwig's hirsute needs. He had even had a rare glimpse of the view of the surrounding countryside which meant so much to the King. He told Marie of the large picture windows which had been installed at great expense in the King's private rooms. This breathtaking view was from the balcony of the throne room which overlooked the lake and the mountains beyond. Marie shared his appreciation of the architecture and admired the fine furniture and wall hangings along with the decorative panels used to great effect around the castle.

Soon the basket was full to overflowing and Marie and Johann headed back to the gate. On passing through it, they became a little awkward with each other. Now that they had returned to the confines of the castle, they no longer had the freedom to be so relaxed in each other's company and so they bid each other a self-conscious farewell.

That evening, as Johann walked back with his father to their cottage, his mind drifted back to the happy hour he had spent in the company of Marie and he was unaware of his father's troubled glances in his direction. He was not to know that his father had seen the young couple going through the gateway together and had watched the gate periodically until their return, two young people, happy and blind to the fact that they had been seen.

* * *

Princess Sophie complained constantly of missing her family, particularly her sister, affectionately known as Sissy, who was Empress Elizabeth of Austria. She and Sophie had been very close until Sophie had been introduced to Ludwig and eventually moved into his court when they became engaged. She and Ludwig were cousins, but had been attracted to each other when Ludwig spent part of the summer of 1864 in Bad Kissingen. He had proved very popular with all the young ladies but Sophie had pleased him most of all and on becoming King, he proposed to her and invited her to join him at his castle while the preparations for their wedding went ahead.

The whole kingdom seemed to be involved in the preparations, and there was an excitement in the air which was almost palpable. A special wedding coach was commissioned, commemorative medals were struck and smart new uniforms ordered for the Guard of Honour. The summer of that year was the busiest time the castle had experienced, with builders, carpenters, woodcarvers and other artisans making improvements to the castle. The approach road, which was steep and winding, was widened to accommodate the many coaches of visiting monarchs from all over Europe. Artists were busy decorating the Great Hall with scenes from Wagner's 'Parcifal', a favourite opera with Ludwig.

The elaborate throne room was where the wedding ceremony itself would take place, and no doubt would cause gasps of wonder from the assembled congregation on the day. It had been designed to be both a throne room and a church, suitable for all solemn occasions and from the exotic mosaic floor depicting animals from around the world to its high-domed ceiling painted with stars, it was staggering in its beauty.

Johann's father, Karl, and his team of gardeners were busy throughout the summer growing plants which were new to Europe, having been sourced from many countries. Young men who had taken to the current passion for finding previously unknown plant species, had shipped them home. Karl was enjoying the challenge of displaying to all the distinguished guests a feast for the eyes of amazing colour and variety of plants not seen by them before the wedding day.

The court dressmakers had many samples of silks, satins, brocade and damask sent to them for inspection and a variety of ribbons, braids, beads, feathers and other trims were examined for suitability for the outfits to be designed and made for the ladies of the court. It was necessary to call on extra help other than the employees of the castle, and the residents of the surrounding villages were eager to assist as the extra income was most welcome. Johann's mother, Augusta, and his sister, Catherine, were thrilled to show off their sewing skills.

The summer seemed to Marie to be passing too quickly and she was determined to seek out the company of Johann at every opportunity. They snatched precious moments together, usually early in the morning when only the servants of the castle were up and about and far too busy with their own duties to pay much attention to the young girl slipping quietly out into the garden when their backs were turned. She would meet Johann at the place in the garden pre-arranged during their previous clandestine meeting. This way they hoped they would be less likely to be discovered, and after all, Marie said to herself with a defiant shrug of her shoulders, what harm were they doing?

The time spent in Johann's company was treasured by Marie above all else in her daily routine. Princess Sophie was becoming more and more agitated as the day for the wedding drew nearer. She grew extremely demanding, finding fault with everyone around her, including Marie. Ludwig was visiting Sophie's apartments less and less frequently and he seemed to be avoiding spending time with her. Sophie would catch sight of him from her chamber window with his groom heading for the stables for his lengthy rides into the surrounding countryside or sometimes to take solitary walks and she stamped her feet in frustration.

It was during one of his walks that Ludwig, deep in troubled thought at his growing doubts about his impending marriage, decided to rest on the edge of a clearing in the forest where the sunlight filtered through the branches overhead, casting soft pools of light on the shaded ground below. He settled comfortably on a mossy patch with his back against the trunk of a tree and closed his eyes in order to appreciate more intensely the sounds and smells around him. The birds which he had startled into scolding cries had settled back to their scratching in the undergrowth in their search for food and the soft sounds of the wildlife with the rustle of the gentle breeze in the tree canopy overhead soon lulled Ludwig into a gentle sleep. He was awoken by the muted sound of two people talking quietly, unaware that the spot they had chosen to rest was within earshot of anyone as they had seen nobody else as they walked through the trees. Slowly, he raised his head sufficiently for him to see the heads of the couple sitting with their backs to him. The blond head of the boy and the auburn-haired girl seemed familiar to him.

Marie and Johann were completely oblivious of the presence of their monarch, sublime in their new-found recognition that they had fallen in love and nothing could spoil their joy. They were chatting as new lovers do about their daily activities, chuckling at Marie's accurate mimicking of Princess Sophie and Johann's of Alfonse the hairdresser. As Ludwig strained to hear them, he felt a pang of regret that his relationship with his fiancée was not as intimate and comfortable as the one he was witnessing. When the two young people (not much younger than himself he thought wryly) bent their heads together in a long, slow kiss, he realised that he had never before witnessed people truly in love. The behaviour between couples in his circle seemed very reserved and formal in comparison and he sighed deeply, feeling a great sadness overcome him. He stayed quietly out of sight until the lovers stood up, brushing the grass from their clothing, and walking hand in hand, strolled slowly back towards the castle, casting loving glances at each other as they left the clearing.

Ludwig waited a little while before he too set off in the direction they had taken, being careful to stay well behind, as he now felt like an interloper and he would have been mortified for them to know they had been observed. As he walked, his mind wandered to the story of Tristan and Isolde, the tragic lovers in Wagner's opera who could only be together after death and he tried in vain to shrug off the deep melancholy that now engulfed him. At least the young couple ahead of him were so at ease in each other's company that surely they were destined to be together? Little did he know that his desire for true love like theirs was to impact on their future as well as his own.

***

When Ludwig was not out on his horse or walking due to inclement weather, he would spend time supervising the work he had authorised to make the necessary improvements to the castle. He retained his enthusiasm for the ongoing work by reminding himself that the castle deserved the refurbishment not just for the occasion of the wedding but for his future comfort. The work was vital also to the prosperity of the region as it created much needed jobs for the locals and ensured that skills and craftsmanship were being taught to a new generation of artisans. The woodcarvers working on his bed chamber were creating masterpieces of furnishing and the scenes from "Tristan and Isolde" which were being painted on the upper walls were breathtaking. He dismissed from his mind the mounting cost of the work, justifying it to himself by the fact that it was not just for his pleasure the work was being done but also for the benefit of all of his people.

As summer turned to autumn and the preparations for the wedding were almost complete, Karl, Johann's father, was becoming more and more anxious about his son's behaviour. He flicked a wasp absent-mindedly from his brow as he glanced around the garden, straining for a glimpse of Johann who had taken to disappearing more and more when he should have been working. One day he caught sight of him just as he was slipping through the gate out of the garden. Karl frowned and decided to follow him as he felt that Johann was in danger of losing his livelihood if he kept up this behaviour and he, his father, would not be able to speak in his defence unless he knew his reasons. On seeing him being approached by one of the young ladies of the court with a radiant smile on her face, Karl guessed now that his son was infatuated and not wishing to draw attention to his presence, he returned to the garden with a troubled frown. He decided he would challenge Johann on their walk back to the cottage after work that day. The rest of the afternoon he had difficulty concentrating on his labour as he tried to work out in his mind what the outcome of such a friendship could be. He grew more and more troubled, his heart sinking at the thought of the inevitable pain he would cause Johann when he told him what he must do.

Johann heaved his bag higher on his shoulder as he walked alongside his father down the steep path to the village below and noticing his father was quieter than usual, he glanced at his face trying to gauge his mood. Karl was looking down at his feet as he walked briskly then catching Johann's glance, he coughed ready to speak and slowed to a stop.

He looked Johann in the eye and asked, "What is it that takes you from your work for such long periods of late? I am finding it more and more difficult to find excuses for your absence."

He did not hint that he knew the reason but waited for Johann to tell him.

"I have been fulfilling all my tasks more quickly to make time to take strolls with a friend." Johann smiled at his father as he spoke, hoping to allay any fears his father might have regarding his recent behaviour. He waited, knowing that his father would ask him who was this friend and Johann decided that he must be truthful. Karl did just that, and on being told Marie's name, his father, with shaking voice, said,

"Do you not realise that the young lady you call your friend can never be more than that? In fact, your very friendship is a danger to you both! She is very close to your future queen and if your secret meetings were to become court gossip, the reputation of the young lady would be severely compromised and could lead to her being banished from the court! Your future would be jeopardised, and who knows what would become of my position? If I were to be dismissed as head gardener, we would lose our home! Have you not considered the implications of your selfish actions?"

His father's usually quiet voice had risen as he spoke of his concerns and now his face was tight with suppressed anger. Johann had seldom faced the wrath of his father who was normally of a placid disposition. His work had a steadying influence, the patience required with plants was followed by a satisfaction in work well done. He was at one with nature in the gardens and not easily roused to anger.

They continued down the hill with the boy deep in thought and slow to reply, struggling to find an answer as the full enormity of his actions dawned on him. While he was with Marie, the difference in their positions at the castle had become insignificant. Once they had overcome the initial awkwardness, they had found they shared so many interests. He tried to explain this to his father, but Karl shook his head and grasping his son by his shoulders, he turned Johann to face him, saying,

"You must realise the friendship can no longer continue, you must tell - what is her name? – Marie, that you are unable to spend any more time alone with her."

When he saw the anguished look flick across his son's face he gently shook him, saying in a softer tone,

"If she is a true friend she will understand, she would surely not wish us to lose so much on her account?"

They were almost at the cottage where Johann's mother, Augusta, would be preparing the evening meal with the help of his young sister, Catherine. His father stopped, asking Johann to promise there and then to end the friendship the next day in order that the threat of an eviction could be averted. Johann nodded almost imperceptibly, fighting back tears, but enough for his father to believe his son understood what was being asked of him. Karl put his strong arms around his young son and hugged him roughly to try to ease the pain.

"There are lots more maidens waiting to enjoy your company before you need settle down, enjoy your youth while you may, and one day you will meet the right girl for you and find the same contentment your mother and I have found - but take your time, don't rush it!"

Karl walked the few remaining steps to the door of the cottage with a spring returned to his step. Johann realised his father was no longer concerned about his behavior, having had the assurance that he would act on his promise the next day.

CHAPTER TWO

Marie was choosing the undergarments for her mistress and humming softly as she did so, thinking that when Sophie was dressed and taking breakfast, she would swiftly run down the stairs leading to the garden and join Johann for a brief rendezvous. The very thought of him holding her in his arms hidden from prying eyes in the arbour sent a thrill through her. She chose quickly from the chest of drawers and laid the garments out on the bed ready for her mistress who was bathing with the aid of a chambermaid in the small room adjacent to the bedroom. Sophie had chosen the gown she would wear, a pale blue cotton dress with an embroidered bodice, not too ornate and most suitable as a day dress, especially as she was not expecting a visit from Ludwig. He was becoming more and more distant which perplexed her. She frowned as she compared her disposition to that of Marie who always seemed so happy these days.

"Perhaps if I were to take more walks in the garden, my spirits would be lifted."

She turned to Marie.

"Marie, would you open the window so that I might decide if the weather is warm enough for me to take a stroll in the garden?"

As Marie flung open the window, a breeze outside caused the curtain to stir, and Sophie shivered a little as she dressed.

"Perhaps not this morning. You may close the window again. I shall write a letter to my sister instead and tell her how the wedding plans are progressing."

Marie heaved a sigh of relief and helped Sophie to dress. Her mistress had never suggested walking in the garden this early before and for a moment, Marie had thought her precious moments of escape would be curtailed forever. As she deftly fastened the minute pearl buttons on the bodice, she gave silent thanks that her mistress did not have her own strong constitution. It would take a snowstorm to prevent her from meeting Johann.

With all her duties performed, she excused herself from the room as a maid came in with the breakfast tray for Sophie. She let herself out of the side door quietly and ran swiftly to the rose garden, their pre-arranged meeting place. As she breathed in the heady scent from the flowers, thinking to herself how perfect life was, she spotted Johann waiting with his back to her, so she crept silently up and slid her hand through the crook of his arm. He smiled briefly down at her, but the expression on his face instantly became solemn. She felt the gladness ebbing away as she anxiously tried to read his mood.

"Do you have time to walk to the field beyond the gate?"

he asked, squeezing her hand in his which helped allay the fear mounting inside her.

She nodded. As she looked into his eyes she was unable to anticipate his thoughts and she fell into step beside him with her mind imagining all sorts of possibilities. Maybe a member of his family was ill, maybe he had angered his father with his disappearances from the garden, or (and her next thought almost brought tears to her eyes) maybe he had tired of her!

As they walked he disengaged his hand from hers, worrying her even more and thrust his hands deep in his pockets. She dropped her hand to her side, feeling a knot tightening in her stomach as she realised everything was not as sunny as it had seemed earlier. They walked without talking until they were through the gate and it was closed behind them. Here they usually kissed but not this morning.

"What is it? What has happened?"

She turned to stand in front of Johann, preventing him from going any further, wishing for the first time that the birds would not sing so joyously, it hardly seemed right that they should sound so happy while she was feeling more and more miserable. Johann replied, "I don't know where to start."

He looked into the distance as if he might find the answer there, then he took hold of her hand again and held it to his lips, slowly bringing his gaze up to her face. Still holding her hand, he led her to a small secret place they had found where they could not be seen from any direction. He took off his jacket and laid it on the ground, signalling for Marie to sit down while he knelt in front of her. He began to tell her of his father's concerns, and how they could no longer meet like this, that from now on they must act like strangers to one another.

She listened, her eyes widening in disbelief as she tried to gulp away the tears which were welling up inside her, feeling the lump in her throat constricting her breathing as she tried desperately not to cry. Eventually she could hold back no longer and she gave in to her emotions, and nodded dumbly to acknowledge the fact that she understood the gravity of the situation, realising that his family could lose their home. The tears ran down her cheeks and as Johann lifted his hand to wipe them gently away, she took hold of his hand and kissing it gently lowered it to her breast where he could feel her heart beating rapidly. He then attempted to kiss away her tears, kissing her face until he found her quivering lips, and slowly the gentle kiss grew with increasing passion until they were locked in a firm embrace They slowly reclined until they lay down on the jacket, still kissing but with more and more urgency as they accepted that this would be the last time they would be spending together.

Slowly his kisses crept from her face down her neck. She was taken to an ecstasy she had never before experienced. It was obvious to her that this was a new experience for him also as he trembled with excitement. Marie whispered that she wanted him to take her completely and soon they reached the point of climax, wrapped in each other's arms as the waves of passion slowly subsided. They stayed in their reverie not speaking, but stroking each other's face, and gazing rapturously at each other at the enormity of what they had done. They felt as one, no longer two individuals but one unit. Then they remembered that this meeting was all about separating, not uniting.

They adjusted their clothing and swore they would love each other forever, come what may, then with their arms around each other they started back towards the castle, walking as slowly as they could to delay the final parting. When they slipped through the gate in the castle wall they were not aware that two people had seen them re-enter – Karl, who was working in that part of the garden, and Sophie, who had decided after all to take a stroll in the hope that it would lift her spirits.

**

Marie ran up the flight of stairs leading from the lower courtyard to the upper courtyard on her way back to the Ladies' apartments and kept her head bowed, afraid that anyone who passed would see that she had been crying. She did not notice the King himself descending the steps from his personal quarters. Ludwig, however, noticed Marie, and remembered her as the girl he had seen only days before happily walking hand in hand with her young man. He was disturbed to see she was in a distressed state, and although the young couple were obviously not suited socially, it had cheered him to see two young people so happy. He decided he would not involve himself in any way.

Marie suddenly noticed the king and she dropped a quick curtsey before darting quickly into the doorway of the Ladies' apartments hoping he had not noticed her grief. Ludwig acknowledged her curtsey, at the same time not showing her he had seen her tear-stained face. He made a mental note that he must ascertain the reason for her unhappiness as he was saddened that her earlier joy had been short-lived. He knew that she was an attendant to Princess Sophie and he frowned as he thought Sophie might be the cause of the young girl's distress.

Ludwig walked down the steps to the lower courtyard in search of his groom but he saw Sophie heading towards him with a face like thunder. He sighed as she approached, sensing he was about to find out why she was so put out.

"Sir, may I have a moment of your time?"

With a barely noticeable curtsey, she stopped in front of him. His heart sank as he thought of his mount waiting to take him away from his troubles beyond the fields which skirted the castle. Whatever could it be this time? Well, it would have to wait he decided, the morning was too good to waste and his horse would be champing at the bit.

"Not at present but I will see you before dinner this evening. I have urgent business now which cannot be delayed. I will then devote my whole attention to you, my princess."

He lifted her hand to his lips, noticing that she withdrew it more quickly than was polite, but he chose to ignore it. Sulkily, Sophie agreed. She needed longer than a passing encounter anyway to discuss her concerns with him.

Ludwig bowed and quickly strode off hoping that by this evening whatever was troubling his bride-to-be might have resolved itself and anyway, his prime consideration now was his horse. He intended to put him to full gallop today in an attempt to dismiss from his mind the impending risk to his peaceful kingdom. The Prussians were pressing for a united Germany to combat the ever-existing threat from France. Ludwig had reluctantly agreed to join the Alliance of the four southern German states with Prussia to form the North Germany Confederation. Each Sovereign would retain their throne, but all troops would be under the command of Prussia in the event of war. His kingdom of Bavaria feared and disliked the Prussians but with the countries of Europe constantly behaving aggressively to one another, by joining with Prussia he hoped Bavaria would be spared the need for war.

The young king had a very romantic outlook on his role as ruler. He admired the heroes of history and mythology. His favourite hero was Saint George who was depicted slaying a dragon on the wall of the throne room. Ludwig likened himself to Parsifal, the hero of the Wagner opera of the same name. Parsifal was of royal blood but chose to live a simple life. One day he met a knight and from that day, he strove to become one himself. He had to complete a number of tasks to achieve his knighthood and ultimately became king. This romanticism was to prove the downfall of Ludwig as his ministers shook their heads and whispered together that the king needed to be brought down to earth if he was to be a ruler upon whom they could depend.

The groom appeared leading two horses, one for Ludwig and one for himself. On this occasion Ludwig was happy to be accompanied. He intended to ride down into the valley and along the shores of the lake and did not intend returning to the castle until dusk. Although he would be tired physically, he would be refreshed mentally. They mounted their horses and trotted out through the gate and onto the road where they broke into a canter, eager to enjoy a day of freedom.

CHAPTER THREE

In Sophie's bedchamber, Marie, although still desperately unhappy, had composed herself and was busily tidying up after her mistress when in marched Sophie. Looking up, Marie was startled to see her expression as she slammed the door and crossed the floor swiftly. Sophie raised her hand and struck Marie across the face.

"Harlot! What do you think you are playing at!"

Her eyes blazed and her face was flushed and contorted with rage. The look of contempt she gave Marie as she brushed past her to close the window in order that her chastisement of her maid should not be heard outside her chamber alarmed Marie. She quickly thought back to how she might have offended Sophie, but no, she had made no clumsy mistakes of which she was aware, and what did she mean, harlot?

Suddenly it dawned on her that her mistress had been outside judging by the hem of her dress. It would require a good stiff brushing to remove the dust and mud from the garden.

"What do you think you are up to, cavorting with a peasant? Do you not realise that this calls for instant dismissal from my service? Now what am I to do? Who will carry out your duties? Even though you were hardly the best lady-in-waiting, I will have great difficulty replacing you at such short notice."

Marie flinched at the tone of Sophie's voice as she went on, "You have been so selfish and inconsiderate. I have already informed the king I require an audience with him. I shall leave him to decide your fate. When I tell him of your behaviour, I expect him to banish you from court. What have you to say to that?"

Marie's eyes had grown wide with horror. How much had she seen? Had she witnessed the passion she had shared with Johann? Surely Sophie had not ventured beyond the gate without someone in attendance?

"I saw you hand in hand, coming in through the gate in the castle wall. Who is that boy?"

Sophie said "that boy" with such disdain, Marie flushed with anger.

"Your behaviour is totally inappropriate for your rank. Well, explain yourself."

She sat down on the daybed and waited expectantly for what she thought would be an apology. She wondered if she should be magnanimous after all or take the high ground which was her normal course of action.

Marie meanwhile had gathered her composure and having felt the sting of both Sophie's hand and tongue, she now drew herself up and faced her mistress with her heart beating fast. She knew that she had agreed to be separated from Johann to save his family from destitution so she felt she had nothing to lose by standing her ground. At least Sophie was not aware how deeply she had been involved with Johann so she hoped to bluff her way out of trouble.

"Ma'am, what you saw was just a little skylarking. I had stepped through the gate to chase a butterfly when I met the young hairdresser. You must remember, he helps Alfonse? He pretended he had caught the butterfly and that is when I took his hand to free it from his grasp. No harm was done, it was just a playful interlude, and I can promise you such a thing will never happen again."

Marie felt uneasy at telling such an untruth but for Johann's sake she would lie through her teeth if necessary.

The doubt that showed on Sophie's face gave Marie hope. Perhaps Sophie believed her and would not be too harsh.

"Well, I will await the decision of the king on this matter. As I have already been granted an audience with him, I must tell him why I requested it and your fate will lie in his hands."

Sophie turned away and Marie stood in awkward silence.

"For now we will put it aside and you can help me change my dress. This one will require attention, I feel I have carried half the garden in with me. Then you can carry my paints and sketch pad outside. The walk has inspired me to do a likeness of some of the roses to send to my dear sister. Mind you, she has far grander gardens in which to walk but it will help pass the time before I meet with Ludwig."

She stood up for Marie to unbutton her dress, allowing her to step out of it. Marie lay the soiled dress over a chair for the chambermaid to remove for cleaning.

Sophie then chose a blue dress with a high neckline and long sleeves in soft cotton with a dainty floral print. With a large bonnet to protect her from the sun and a parasol to attach to the easel, which she reminded Marie would need to be taken out by one of the footmen, she was confident she would maintain her pale complexion.

Marie took heart from the change in Sophie's demeanour and was only too glad to do as she was bid. Soon they were settled in a quiet spot in the garden with the sweet smell of roses and lavender filling the air. Distant noises of people going about their duties soothed her senses and Marie relaxed, feeling that all would be well in the end.

Later that afternoon, Marie moved around the room quietly as Sophie rested. After spending time in the fresh air she had exhausted herself. Before retiring to her bed, she had instructed Marie on which gown she would wear for dinner that evening. After all, she was to see Ludwig, and despite being a reluctant bride (more to do with the kingdom than the king), she had to admit to herself that Ludwig was a very attractive young man. He stood six feet six inches, with a shock of dark curls, and had an amazing presence. Sometimes she felt she could easily be drawn into his fantasy world, and she would imagine herself as a medieval princess being courted by a knight in shining armour.

She returned to the present and reminded herself that it was Ludwig's yearning to live in the past that was filling her with doubt about their future. That his ministers mocked him behind his back was known to her and she felt that she would need to be the voice of reason on his part once they were married. However much she tried though, she had little influence on him and this caused her to be prickly, resulting in a feeling of mistrust between them.

Sophie sighed, resigning herself to the fact that she would need to try even harder once they were married. Meantime, she must look her best for him. Closing her eyes, she drifted off to sleep.

*****

Marie was deep in thought, sitting on the window seat staring out at the view. Usually the beautiful scenery raised her spirits but not today, nothing could dispel her gloom. Her heart felt like a great, leaden weight inside her chest and her throat was tight with emotion as she fought back her tears. Her earlier sobbing had left her with swollen, reddened eyes and when she looked in the mirror she hardly recognised the face looking back at her. How different she had felt that morning! She ached to be held in Johann's arms but she knew his family's livelihood depended on the two of them never meeting again.

When Sophie awoke, the chambermaid was summoned to assist with her bath. After having bathed and dried, Sophie called Marie to help her dress and arrange her hair with soft curls framing her face. Sophie was pleased with her reflection in the mirror. She needed very little rouge as the walk in the garden had given her skin a healthy glow and a sparkle to her eyes. She softened towards Marie and when she saw the distraught look on her maid's face she took her by her hands.

"When I took you as my maid and companion I was only too happy to be of help to your father. As you know, Papa always thought highly of him and when sadly your mother died, and your father was at a loss to know what was to happen to you, naturally I had no hesitation about agreeing to your appointment. Have I been a kind and fair mistress?"

Sophie lifted up Marie's chin as she spoke and searched her eyes for an honest answer. Signs of the tears shed earlier remained, but Sophie gently wiped Marie's cheek then put her arms around the unhappy girl.

"Yes, oh yes, my lady," Marie replied, wiping away the last, stubborn tear.

Sophie pretended not to notice, hoping that by doing so it would prevent further tears. She turned away.

"I will speak highly of you to the King this evening and beg him to allow you to remain in your position. As for the boy – well, I can do nothing for him as I know little of him."

She studied her reflection once more in the cheval mirror then asked, "Now. How do I look? Ravishing, I hope? Call me a footman to escort me to dinner and when I return I hope to bring you good news."

Marie ran from the Ladies' apartments out into the inner courtyard and up the steps of the Royal residence. There she spoke to a footman who went in search of King Ludwig. On his return, he informed Marie that the meeting between the king and his fiancée would be held in the room referred to as the living room on the third floor. Marie returned slowly to Sophie's room.

The footman came to fetch Sophie then the two of them crossed the upper courtyard, up a flight of steps and entered the large door leading to a cool interior. Stairs leading to the third floor brought them to the private quarters of the king and Sophie was shown into the living room. Never before had she seen this room. Aware that it was on the same floor as the King's dressing room, she felt a tremor of excitement at the intimacy of his presence and let her mind wander to thoughts of their wedding night. A door in the corner of the living room puzzled Sophie and as she speculated on what may lay behind it, the door suddenly opened and out stepped her fiancé. She looked past him into the interior and was amazed at what she saw. The room had the appearance of a cave and to her astonishment a waterfall, sparkling as it fell down the wall lit by coloured lights. Ludwig watched her reaction and took her hand to lead her into his secret room, his inner sanctum, his grotto. Sophie could hardly believe her eyes. When Ludwig pressed a switch on the wall, the grotto was transformed into a magical place as the lights played on the cascade and what appeared to be a fine mist rose from the pool giving the same effect of a natural waterfall.

A table and chair stood in the room and on the table was a small cask of wine and one glass.

"This is one of my special places."

Ludwig watched Sophie for her reaction.

"I come here when I need respite from the pressure of my position. Sitting here quietly helps me to put my thoughts in order without fear of interruption. What are you thinking?"

Sophie had difficulty maintaining an inscrutable expression. She was filled with a dread she could not explain as the full realisation of her future with the king filled her with horror. Was she really to be married to this strange man in a few weeks' time? Did other monarchs carry their fantasies this far? She had seen the throne room in all its magnificence and the Great Hall was an amazing spectacle like no other she had ever seen. But a cave? Near the top of a castle with running water and fancy lights? She half expected a character from Ludwig's favourite opera, Parsifal, to materialise out of the mist. No longer able to hide her true feelings she turned away but not before Ludwig had seen the disbelief, the doubt as to his sanity. He had seen such expressions before but never on the face of someone dear to him. He led her from the grotto and switched off the lights before closing the door. He had hoped to delight her with the fairy-like effects he had created, not shock her. He signalled to her to sit opposite him. With a raised eyebrow, he intimated she should begin to explain why she had requested this meeting. Sophie felt most awkward. She had hoped to impress him, not alarm him but she could see that he had read her feelings accurately and it was going to be difficult to win back his affection.

"Sir, I cannot find words to describe my gratitude to you for sharing with me your very private sanctuary."

Her voice trailed off as she saw his stony expression. She felt she would have to initiate conversation by retelling the events of the day.

As Ludwig listened to her condemning the young couple for flaunting their friendship (she no longer felt like being lenient towards them), he cast his mind back to the occasion he had witnessed them in the woods. At that time he had not been aware of the difference in their positions in his court but he admired them even more for considering themselves equal and free to fall in love.

Sophie was still complaining.

"I feel that Marie should be dismissed as soon as my family can arrange a replacement companion and that the gardener, for that is all he is, should be discharged from your service. Do you not agree?"

She felt with this appeal he would regard her more favourably as his future queen.

Ludwig now saw Sophie in a new light. She was a spoilt princess who would never be as comfortable as he was in the company of his people. She would always be arrogant and distant with them and that was not at all what he desired in a wife. His role as monarch and ruler was not to be that of an autocrat like other European royals. He wanted a soulmate, a companion, someone at his side to share his duties and to be loved and respected by his subjects. Outraged at her lack of compassion, Ludwig suddenly stood up, taking Sophie by surprise. She immediately stood as was court protocol.

"Leave this matter in my hands. I will advise you in good time of my decision as to what action I choose to take. Now we must go into dinner."

Fortunately, they were not dining alone. Seated around the table were a dozen or so members of the court whose conversation continued around the betrothed couple, the diners unaware of the silence between them.

Sophie was impatient to escape and as soon as she was able, she excused herself and was escorted back to her apartment. Marie was waiting anxiously for her return but Sophie's grim expression warned her not to enquire how the evening had gone. She felt apprehensive as to what would be the outcome of this calamitous day.

CHAPTER FOUR

Ludwig spent several days pondering what to do about the two young lovers. His head told him they had no future together but his heart reminded him of the predicament of Tristan and Isolde and he anguished over a solution. Finally, he made up his mind and went in search of Karl. He had spoken to Karl on several occasions, usually with a botanical query or about the weather prospects. He was aware that folklore was invaluable to gardeners and more often than not Karl's predictions had proved correct. On this occasion, however, he was not looking forward to the meeting.

Karl and Johann were not working together that day. Johann had been expecting to help Alfonse as a banquet was to be held in honour of a visit from Sophie's father. However, Alfonse had called Johann to him in the salon early that day and he had told him that, on instructions from the King, he, Alfonse, would attend to the ladies unaided. He had studied Johann's face for any clue, but Johann just shrugged, thinking it was because there was too much work to be done in the garden. Ludwig found Karl in the formal garden, trimming the low box hedges and he summoned him to follow to where seats were arranged for courtiers to take the air and gossip. Karl quickly removed his hat and turned it between his hands in discomfort. He stood before his king, inwardly shaking, thinking that the indiscretion between his son and the young lady must have reached the ears of Ludwig and naturally displeased him. Surprisingly, Ludwig indicated to Karl to sit down beside him and he did so, nervously.

"Be at ease, please."

Ludwig watched Karl as he relaxed a little.

"I need to know a little about your son."

Karl shifted and his face looked strained.

"He helps in the garden and also the court hairdresser, does he not? How old is he?"

Karl answered, "He is eighteen, your Majesty. I hope his work is satisfactory?"

Karl hoped this would divert the talk away from his son's sweetheart.

"Yes, yes of course. At least, I've had no complaints on that score."

Karl glanced at the king, his heart sinking, waiting to hear the worst.

"No. It is more to do with affairs of the heart."

Now it was Ludwig searching Karl's face, causing the gardener to shuffle uncomfortably in his seat, still turning his hat in his hands.

"Don't alarm yourself, I am well aware of the friendship between your son and a young lady of my court. I have been giving the matter some thought and I have a course of action that I feel will satisfy everyone concerned. That is, except for the young couple of course, but they in time will see the wisdom of my actions."

Ludwig then outlined his plan without disclosing too many details of his concerns regarding matters of state. That Napoleon III was demanding the return to the frontiers of 1814 as compensation for supporting the North German Federation and that Bismark in Prussia was considering a war in France, was not yet for his subjects to know.

Bavaria was growing increasingly concerned about the superiority of Protestant Prussia over Catholic Bavaria. Economics played a large part in maintaining links with Prussia as Bavarians resented the increase in their taxes and consequently began to support the formation of a greater Germany. Bismark felt that a war with France would increase his chances of unifying parts of Germany on Prussian terms and Ludwig and his ministers were considering introducing conscription into the armed forces.

Turning to Karl, Ludwig continued, "You must impress on your son that to pursue his friendship any further cannot be tolerated. However, I am persuaded by my ministers that we must enlarge our armed forces, and if Johann were to volunteer to join one of my regiments, I can promise that providing he passes out from his training period with good reports, I will personally ensure that he will have a good career in the army. If, however, he is only willing to serve a conscription period, providing we have no cause to go to war, God willing, he will be free to return here to work beside you once again. In the intervening period, the young couple will have made new friends and slowly will forget one another. Now, do you think Johann will accept my proposition?"

Karl was hesitant before replying. He needed time to grasp for himself the idea of his son in uniform. Having always been in the service of the ruling family in a peaceful occupation (his father and grandfather before him had also been gardeners to the Monarch), he knew very little about the armed forces.

Eventually he said, "Your Majesty, I know that my son will always be an obedient servant to you and he will comply with any plans you may have for him. How soon would he need to leave us to start his training? Will it be before or after the marriage celebrations?"

"I think that under the circumstances, he should leave as soon as possible. I will have the necessary arrangements made and one of my officers will call to see you both at home in the next seven days. The sooner we separate them, the sooner Marie will return to giving full attention to her duties and Princess Sophie will have no reason to complain further."

Ludwig cut himself short at that point, realising that he had never before hinted at any criticism of his future bride. He hoped Karl had not noticed it. He would be most vexed if any gossip were to spread through the castle that he was anything less than happy with his matrimonial plans.

Karl gave no hint that he had understood the King's indiscretion, but he and others in the castle had noticed how awkward King Ludwig was around his bride-to-be and that he seemed to enjoy his own company far more. It was being whispered that the marriage was destined to be a failure before it had even begun.

The King stood up and Karl immediately rose to his feet as Ludwig said, "Fine, now that is arranged, I must prepare for the visit of my future father-in-law. Be sure to tell Johann I have only his best interests at heart."

Ludwig strode back to his quarters.

***

The following day, as Johann worked in the garden with his father, he felt the wall of silence between them almost tangible. He desperately wanted to tell his father that the matter which concerned him had been resolved. They continued to deadhead the flowers in the herbaceous borders, gently coaxing stray growths of honeysuckle back against the wall as they worked. Soon it was time for a brief rest to take some refreshment. Augusta always prepared a basket containing sausages, cheese and bread, simple but nourishing enough to sustain them through the day until they went home to supper. When the sun was directly overhead, Karl straightened up and stretched to ease the ache in his back from bending all morning.

"Time for a break I think, son. Let's find a shady spot. Are you ready for a bite to eat?"

Johann rubbed the loose soil from his hands and wiped his brow.

"I'll fetch the basket and fill the mugs from the tap."

He collected their lunch from the spot by the wall where he had left it earlier that day. He busied himself with finding a suitable place to sit and they settled down with their backs against a low wall in the shade of a lilac tree which had long since blossomed. Father and son sat together eating the bread and cheese in silence, washing it down with the cool water.

Johann broke the silence after swallowing his last piece of bread.

"Father, I am sorry to have caused you such concern by my friendship with Marie, but you will no doubt be pleased to learn that it is over. I met her this morning for the last time and although it causes us much sorrow, we realise that it would cause more sorrow to others for us to remain friends."

Here he sighed and bowed his head, determined his feelings would not get the better of him.

Karl recognised his son was distressed and put his arm around Johann's shoulders, hugging him roughly to him.

"You cannot know how relieved I am to hear that. It has weighed very heavily on me and I am so glad that your mother and sister need never know about it. The King sought me out yesterday and we discussed your future."

Karl had spent a sleepless night wondering how he could tell his son he was to become a soldier.

"The King insists you must enlist in his army as he is to increase Bavaria's military strength to satisfy the Prussians. We feel that once you are parted, you two youngsters will find new loves and eventually you may be able to be employed at the castle. Your mother and sister need never know the reason for you leaving, it will remain a secret that just we three share."

Johann was dismayed at this proposition but if the King commanded he go then he had no choice.

Once the food was all eaten and the crumbs scattered for the birds, the two men continued with their work in the garden until the sun cast long shadows. Gathering up their tools, they stowed them away after cleaning them in the small shed concealed behind a high box hedge. Karl locked the door and they headed off in the direction of the road leading to the village.

As they walked home side by side, tired from the long day's work and looking forward to the tasty supper awaiting them, they fell into step together and this time the silence between them was comfortable for Karl but not for Johann. Ahead of them, they heard the sound of horses' hooves drawing nearer. They stepped aside as the King and his groom rode by and Ludwig acknowledged them with his hand raised. Johann noticed the King gave him more than a passing glance but was unable to see from the King's expression if he had displeased his master in any way. He shrugged and continued on his downward journey, his father unaware of the exchange of glances.

CHAPTER FIVE

Marie was kept busy on the day Sophie's father arrived. Her mistress was even more petulant than usual. She was naturally excited that she was seeing her father that afternoon and she took great care in choosing her outfit, a two-piece costume in a soft shade of lavender with a cream lace collar. The colour flattered her and enhanced her blue eyes. Presenting herself well to her father was important to Sophie. She wanted to impress him that she was indeed ready for the role of Queen of Bavaria. Her father had always thought of his younger daughter as being a little hot-headed and lacking the discipline of her older sister. Sophie was determined that today he would see that she was a mature woman, no longer the girl who had thrown tantrums for no reason.

Ludwig had excused himself from the emotional reunion of father and daughter as they took tea together then strolled around the garden, chatting and exchanging news. Sophie realised that her father was tired after his journey and they eventually parted so that he might rest before dinner with the King.

Sophie's gown for the evening was an elegant satin dress in a dusky shade of pink with a low-cut neckline and short sleeves trimmed with a matching lace. It had a fashionable bustle which emphasised her small waist. Alphonse had arranged her hair in a chignon with small curls falling softly onto the nape of her neck. She asked Marie to fetch her jewellery box so that she could decide which of her necklaces suited her dress.

Marie was trying hard to concentrate on her duties but thoughts of Johann brought her almost to tears. To be forbidden from seeing him ever again was unbearable and she was worried as to what Sophie might have planned for her. Their usual chatter had ceased as Sophie was too preoccupied with her own thoughts to pay any attention to Marie when a knock on the door startled them and Marie went to open it. A footman had arrived to announce that the king requested Princess Sophie's presence. When the door closed behind Sophie, Marie tidied away the clothes her mistress had discarded. The chambermaid would come later to turn down the bed so Marie went to her own room and closed the door. Only now was she able to give way to her feelings and she threw herself onto the bed, sobbing bitterly. She had grown so fond of Johann that she could not imagine life without him. To be forbidden to see him ever again was more than she could bear but she had to accept that to disobey would cause a great deal of trouble for Johann and his family. Her own family might also be told of her behaviour and she knew they would consider her a disgrace to their good name.

Eventually her tears subsided and she was washing her tear-stained face when there was a knock at Sophie's door. Relieved that daylight was fading and the room was in partial darkness, she crossed to the door and opened it to find Alfonse standing there.

"Excuse me, Marie, but I have left behind some of my hair preparations. May I come in please?"

She nodded, keeping her head turned away, hoping he would not see her distress. He went to the dressing table where Marie had tidied his bottles amongst those belonging to Sophie without realising what she was doing, too preoccupied with her misery.

Alfonse looked around, checking for anything he had overlooked then, looking Marie directly in the face, he said, "If I offend you with what I am about to say, I can only apologise, but I know of your friendship with Johann and how you have been forbidden to meet. I just want you both to know that should you wish to get a message to him, or he to you, I am perfectly willing to be a courier for you both. In my position, I am able to do this for you in utmost secrecy so please be assured that my offer is genuine."

Marie raised her face and gave a little smile. She reached for his hand and shaking it, she thanked him profusely; fresh tears, this time of joy, welled up in her eyes.

"Would you do this for us? Oh, how you have eased my pain. I could write a short note now if you do not mind waiting while I write one?"

"Of course, I can wait a few minutes."

Marie crossed to Sophie's writing desk and began to write.

My beloved Johann

How I miss you already now we can no longer meet. For your sake and that of you family, I was made to agree never to see you again but please believe me when I tell you that the memories of our wonderful times together will always live in my heart.

She signed her name with a quick sketch of forget-me-nots beneath it then she folded and sealed it before handing it to Alfonse with a trembling smile. He held her hand to his lips and promised his amity if she ever needed a friend then left her to her thoughts. The next day, Alfonse returned with a brief note from Johann with the startling news of his departure. Marie was distraught and ran into her room where she flung herself onto the bed, sobbing.

***

As Sophie entered the anteroom she flushed with pleasure at seeing her father again.

"Sophie, my darling daughter, you look radiant, my child, just as a young bride-to-be should look."

She hugged her father who, despite his age and position, was not at all stuffy and had always shown great affection for his large family. Maximilian Joseph, Duke of Bavaria, seemed not to notice the brief frown that formed on his daughter's brow at the reminder of her impending nuptials. He then explained his sudden arrival in hushed tones.

"The King is seeking advice from all quarters regarding the Unification of the German States. Accompanying me is a young

French diplomat, Ferdinand, the Duc d'Alencon. Although he is a Frenchman, he is here to persuade Ludwig that unification will benefit France as well as Germany and he believes that this path will lead to a long-lasting peace between our two countries. Come, let me introduce you to him."

He took Sophie by the elbow and guided her towards the dark-haired young man. Ferdinand had his back to them as he talked to other guests while awaiting the arrival of the King. He turned as they approached and Sophie was astonished at her reaction to his gaze, she felt herself colouring and quickly opening her fan, she rapidly cooled herself though her heart was thumping.

The handsome stranger before her had been equally impressed by the sight of the young daughter of his travelling companion. He quickly reminded himself that this vision was soon to become Queen of Bavaria and he lowered his eyes as he bent over her hand to kiss it. Sophie could not help but notice how long and thick his eyelashes were, how his dark hair shone and when he opened his eyes how they revealed obvious approval. She dropped a curtsy, fanning herself even more vigorously. At that point, Ludwig entered and moved around the room greeting his guests warmly. As he drew near Sophie and Ferdinand, he noticed the flustered state of his fiancée and the attention she was receiving from the Frenchman. The couple drew apart as he shook Ferdinand by the hand then took Sophie's hand to kiss it. Sophie could not help but think that Ferdinand had made her heart beast faster than Ludwig ever had. However, she brightened when Ludwig arranged for her to be seated next to Ferdinand at dinner.

While the other guests discussed the impending unification of Germany, Sophie chatted about the beauty of the surrounding countryside to the Duke and asked him in which region of France he lived. He told her that Alencon, his dukedom, was west of Paris on the River Sarthe. His chateau was in a valley with gentle hills and forests sheltering it from the north winds. As he talked more and more about his life in France where he enjoyed hunting with his friends in the forest and boating on the river with his sisters, he was aware that her eyes never left his face. She asked him question after question and soon they were oblivious to the other diners. Sophie was so enthralled by his attention that she did not notice Ludwig casting questioning glances her way. Had she noticed, she might have been relieved to see that he was not vexed. On the contrary, he seemed to be approving of their growing friendship.

When the gentlemen rose to leave the table, bowing courteously to the ladies before withdrawing, the Duke took Sophie's hand and raising it to his lips once more while searching her face with his eyes, he thanked her for her pleasant company and expressed a wish that they might continue their discussions while walking in the garden the following day. Sophie blushed with delight, dismissing his boldness and told him that she would be delighted.

"Whenever it is convenient for you, send a manservant to my quarters and I will join you as soon as I can."

She returned to her apartment feeling that she was walking on air and she hummed softly to herself as she climbed the stairs. This was the happiest she had felt since she arrived at the castle and when Marie opened the door to let her mistress in she was amazed at the transformation in Sophie's behaviour. She naturally thought it was because of her father's visit and hoped fervently that his stay could be a lengthy one.

The days passed and Marie found Sophie making excuses for not needing her constant companionship. It soon became apparent to Marie that the young duke was responsible for Sophie's joyfulness, not her father. Marie was concerned that Ludwig might notice his fiancée's change in demeanour, but whenever she saw Ludwig with Sophie he seemed more at ease than ever, and if anything he was encouraging Sophie to entertain the duke while he spent time with her father and members of his government.

The meetings eventually drew to a close and it was time for Duke Maximilian and the Duc d'Alencon to leave. Sophie was distraught. Marie found her sobbing on her bed after waving them goodbye at the castle gate. Nothing she could do or say would console her mistress. The two young women were grieving for their absent lovers and the apartment became a quiet refuge where they both silently went through their daily routines deep in their individual thoughts.

***

Summer passed and autumn arrived. The trees were proudly displaying their vibrant colours and where the surrounding fields had been harvested and replanted, they were already showing signs of new growth. Karl enjoyed this season in the gardens. The fruit had been picked, vegetables lifted and stored and bunches of herbs had been gathered and hung drying for use through the winter months. As he tidied the borders and took seed heads for the following year, he wondered how Johann was enjoying his new life as a soldier. His son had accepted his fate without argument. In fact he knew it would be easier not seeing Marie when he couldn't be close to her and he had thrown himself into his training with vigour. Karl and Augusta had received few letters, and it was difficult to tell if their son was truly happy as he wrote only of how his training was going and that he had been told he would make an excellent soldier. He asked after his mother and sister, how were the plants growing from the seeds he had planted and was he missed in the garden?

Karl wondered if by this he meant did Marie still walk in the garden and if so, did she inquire after him? He sighed and continued his weeding with a heavy heart. He knew his agreement regarding Johann and Marie had been the correct measure to take, but he felt for Johann and hoped and prayed that time would truly be a healer.

One morning in early September when Marie woke to find everywhere very quiet, she realised something must have disturbed her sleep. It was still dark and already there was a chill in the air. She lit a candle, took a shawl and wrapped it around her shoulders. She slipped her feet into her slippers before crossing quietly to the closed door leading to Sophie's room where she hesitated, listening for any sound. After opening the door silently, she was shocked to find the room empty. In the flickering light of the candle, she could see that all personal possessions of Sophie's were no longer there. The dressing table was bare. Hair brushes, Sophie's musical box which played a haunting tune whenever its lid was raised by a melancholy Sophie, and perfume bottles had all gone. Marie realised that lately the musical box had played often through the day.

She passed through the dressing room and found the closet doors ajar, revealing the fact that many of the clothes had been removed.

It became apparent that she must have been woken by Sophie trying to leave the apartment stealthily so as not to disturb her. Marie wrapped the shawl tightly about her and hastened to the door leading to the outer staircase. As she ran down the steps and across the upper courtyard, she could hear the sound of horses' hooves galloping towards the outer gate. Muffled orders could be heard followed by the groan of the heavy gates being thrown open. She looked anxiously about as she ran across the lower courtyard, hoping to see someone she could ask about what was evidently the hurried departure of her mistress. Before she could reach the outer gate, she saw the gateman returning to his post after closing the gates firmly.

Gasping for breath, she blurted out, "Who passed through the gate? My mistress is missing. Please, I must inform his majesty."

"Now then, miss, don't alarm yourself. Yes, it was Princess Sophie, accompanied by a groom. They have left on urgent business and have the King's full permission, he is aware of their departure."

At this, the gateman withdrew into his sentry box.

Puzzled, Marie walked quickly back to her room where she tried to make sense of her mistress's actions. She washed and dressed after making up her mind to seek an audience with the King. Approaching the King's apartments, she hesitated. His Majesty had always shown her kindness but how was she to begin? Did he really know about Sophie leaving?

She waited to be summoned into his living room and was pleased to see him welcome her with a warm smile. He beckoned her to draw nearer and his large frame was almost as intimidating as his position. He stood at six feet six inches and towered over her. She trembled a little in awe but he waved her to sit on a chair opposite him.

"Now, young lady, what is causing you concern?"

"Your Majesty, my lady, Princess Sophie, is no longer in the castle. She told me of no plans to leave. I would usually help her to pack, to prepare for journeys and I woke unexpectedly to find her gone. It is so unlike her I was alarmed."

Clasping his hands behind his back, Ludwig strode back and forth.

"I have realised for some time that the Princess was unhappy here at the castle. I have no desire to keep her here against her will but it seems her feelings for me have changed. She has my full consent to seek her happiness elsewhere."

He crossed to the window to watch dawn break.

Marie was confused. He did not seem at all unhappy, in fact he looked happier than she had seen him for a long time. She had imagined that the coming wedding was praying on the minds of the engaged couple and that had been the cause of their preoccupation.

"I insisted that if she was to leave, it would be in the dead of night when most of the castle slept and few people should know of it. Can you keep secrets?"

Knowing that she had kept her own secret about Johann for many months.

"Sir, I am your obedient servant and anything you tell me will be locked in my heart."

"Well, Sophie has given her heart to another. When I questioned her about her assignations with the Duc d'Alencon which had not gone unnoticed, she broke down in tears. Naturally, this was a great shock to me, but I offered to release her from our engagement. I had known for some time that we were of different minds and that our union would have been one without love. I tell you all of this because of your own tragic love affair."

Marie went crimson at the memory of Johann.

"I would rather we parted than go through life acting parts for appearances sake. When I confirmed with the duke that he wished to make Sophie his bride, I helped make the necessary arrangements."

He stood deep in thought while Marie tried desperately to understand what he had told her. Her mistress, Princess Sophie, was to become a French Duchess and had gone to live in France!

CHAPTER SIX
1870

Europe was once again facing turbulent times. France was seeking reassurance from Prussia that the throne of Spain would not be relinquished to Prince Leopold of Hohenzoller – Sigmaringen, who was a nephew of King Wilhelm I of Prussia. The offer was accepted, much to the chagrin of the French government who demanded that the Prussians renounced their claims to the Spanish throne or prepare for war. This response delighted Chancellor Otto von Bismarck who wanted the French to be the first to declare war and an offer of mediation by the British was declined by the French.

In 1867, Napoleon III had demanded that the frontiers of 1814 be restored as compensation for his support of the North German Federation which had only served to alarm Bismarck into wanting war. During this period, the Bavarian government was growing anxious at the rising superiority of Protestant Prussia, but for economic reasons they felt it necessary to maintain ties between the two states.

Support for the formation of a greater Germany grew in Bavaria as a means of decreasing Prussian power. Napoleon believed war would reunite his nation behind him while Bismarck was sure that war would increase his chances of unifying Germany on Prussian terms.

Johann had enlisted in the Bavarian Army as instructed by his father on the command of King Ludwig and spent the first week having a medical test which he passed with no problem, being fitted with his uniform and undergoing constant drilling with his fellow soldiers. With his comrades he listened to the rumours in the taverns of the menace of war once again. From the talk it was initially thought likely that war would be averted by diplomatic means, but word rapidly filtered down through the ranks that Bismarck was doing his very best to ensure that war would eventually be the outcome.

Ever since 1866, the railway network in Germany had been expanded on Bismarck's orders. He had planned for war and the rapid movement of troops was vital. From all over Germany the army moved swiftly towards the Rhine, taking advantage of the fact that France, having declared war, did not attack immediately. The French, in fact, were totally disorganised. They were transporting huge quantities of supplies into Metz but they had few men available to disperse them. Subsequently, even high priority stores such as ammunition failed to reach their troops. An offensive could not be launched until Napoleon III himself arrived on 28th July. The French officers were misguided in believing they would cross the Rhine and the fighting would take place around Frankfurt.

On 16th July 1870, Bavaria and Baden began to mobilise their troops while French troops gathered on the German – French border. On 19th July, France had declared war knowing their troops were outnumbered by the Germans but confident that with their more recent battle experiences they would triumph. Their weaponry included the new breech-loading rifle which they called the "Chassepot" and was far superior to the German rifle.

As the Bavarian troops travelled towards the French border on the crowded trains Johann, sitting astride his kit bag with his gun slung over his shoulder, thought longingly of the castle he had left behind. His heart ached for Marie, the love he had been forced to give up. While some of his comrades displayed boyish enthusiasm for the exciting times ahead and others sat with staring, unseeing eyes as they imagined the possibility of defeat and maybe death, the battles to come held no horror for him. His future seemed grim enough without Marie and he followed the strict routine of a soldier's life like an automaton. His professional attitude earned him praise from his commanding officer who noticed that here was a soldier able to perform any duty with a single-minded approach which resulted in all his assignments being completed with top grades. Johann's skill with his rifle was particularly outstanding.

The train sped quickly through the countryside of Baden. The young soldier sitting next to Johann broke the silence between them by offering his hand and introducing himself.

"Nice to meet you, I am Lukas Schmidt from a small village near Nuremberg. I am – well, I was – an apprentice carpenter but when I was conscripted to save Bavaria I was overjoyed. Carpentry in a small town can be very boring. What about you?"

Johann shook the proffered hand but hesitated before replying. He was reluctant to tell his companion that he had been ordered by King Ludwig himself to join the army. He smiled.

"Like you I too had no military ambitions. I am a barber by trade, Johann Nicklas is my name."

He thought that by claiming to be a barber he might be of some use to his fellow soldiers where a gardener would not.

The train slowed to a stop as they arrived at the last station before the border with France. Officers passed through the train advising the men that there would be a thirty-minute halt for the locomotive to take on water and giving the men an opportunity to stretch their legs.

As the men climbed down from the carriages, they were greeted by local townsfolk cheering them and offering food and drink to the delight of the newly conscripted troops.

The engine hissed patiently while the crew attached the water supply to the tender and stoked the fire for the onward journey. The station platforms were filled with noisy, laughing people and a band which had assembled played patriotic and popular tunes. There was such a carnival atmosphere. Johann turned to Lukas who was close by.

"Anyone would think we are a victorious army returning from war! How cheerful everyone is."

He returned the smile of a passing girl wearing her Sunday bonnet.

"Maybe they know something we don't," replied Lukas.

"Perhaps the French have seen the error of their ways and have realised the strength of us, the opposition."

Johann tilted his head thoughtfully then shook it.

"I doubt it."

He thought it most unlikely but then life just recently had shown him that the unexpected does happen.

They thanked an elderly man as they took bread and cheese from him then a young woman pressed them to take a cup of wine. Others had steins of frothy beer which thirsty soldiers accepted gratefully.

With the tender full of water and the fires burning well, the engine driver pulled on the whistle to let the troops know they were ready to move. Steins and glasses were quickly drained, pretty girls offered kisses and young children waved their flags with extra enthusiasm while the elders of the town slapped the young men on their backs wishing them a safe return, tears in their eyes because they remembered going to war themselves and knew the horrors that awaited these brave youngsters. Packages of food were handed to the troops before they boarded the train once again to hang from the windows and doors, waving farewell to their new-found friends. The wheels skidded until momentum moved the train slowly forward as it drew out of the station, the whistle joining in the noisy cheering for both the passengers and the people on the platform fading into the distance as it picked up speed.

"What an adventure we are on Johann!"

Lukas's eyes sparkled as he squeezed between two of his comrades.

"Imagine what a welcome we will receive on our return! All those pretty girls waiting for us! Oh, maybe you already have a particular girl waiting back home for you?"

Johann watched the fields speeding past the carriage window.

"No. No one special. Do you?"

Lukas laughed and winked.

"Like you, no one special but several maybes."

Another soldier who told them his name was Tobias Hofmann joined in the conversation.

"Conscription has done me a big favour. I got too close to a young lady if you take my meaning. Now her belly comes between us and her father is on the warpath!"

Laughter in the carriage told them others had been listening. Soon fellow soldiers began to exchange similar confidences and Johann retreated into a daydream in which he and Marie were once again strolling through the castle gardens with no thought of prying eyes.

Their sergeant, Wilhelm Muller, stuck his head around the door.

"Right lads. We are now approaching France. Our orders are to march across the Alsation border and camp not far from a town called Wissembourg. Gather your belongings and prepare to disembark."

Dusk was falling as the men fell into line beside the railway track. Dark rainclouds burst over them as they marched, their new boots hurting their feet while the wine and beer they had drunk was causing nausea. The noisy friendly banter was replaced with groans and mutterings of dissatisfaction when they stopped to camp. The ground on which they were to sleep was sodden, they were beginning to miss their families and it was dawning on them the war they were about to fight was one that the Bavarian people really did not support.

After a restless night of very little sleep, they were awoken by the bugle. Breakfast, for those who could stomach it, was rushed and the gunners were already in place and loading the cannons. The first shots were fired soon after eight o'clock to allow the infantry to advance through the vineyards where they had scant cover and came under French fire. Johann and his comrades fell to the ground and stayed low. They had been told that the more experienced Prussians were soon to join them.

Members of the international press lived with the soldiers, sending news home to interested readers. Johann was surprised when he heard cursing in English from the civilian by his side. The stranger was ducking and diving, moving forward stealthily with the troops but carrying no arms.

"Damn and blast the French, always ready for a fight."

Shots whistled past their ears and Johann raised his gun and returned the fire as they moved towards the retreating enemy.

The English reporter stepped over casualties lying injured on the ground without regard while Johann, Lukas and Tobias fought the urge to stop and assist the wounded soldiers. They had been trained for battle but not for the consequences which surrounded them. Scattered amongst the bodies was enemy kit, abandoned by the French soldiers in their hasty retreat. Knapsacks and muskets were strewn around as their owners fled to the surrounding pine forests for shelter. French civilians were amongst them, families piled high on top of their possessions on slow moving carts and cattle being driven into the trees for safe keeping by the worried farmers.

A squealing pig ran across Johann's path, startling him. His reaction was to lift his gun to shoot but he lowered it without firing. This was not the pig's war.

As night fell and the gunfire ceased, the German troops, exhausted, prepared to camp. The sergeant walked among his men congratulating them on a victorious fight.

"We had the better of them today men, may it always be so. The cowards have left us many prizes, not least their weapons."

Lukas was fighting back tears as he spoke.

"What about those poor farmers, animals scattered and wives and children frightened witless?"

"That's war, boys, that's war. Your folk back home have faced just such perils when we fought Napoleon remember."

Johann spoke next.

"What I don't understand is why we are fighting them now? We are the attackers; after all we are on French soil, not defending from our side of the border."

The sergeant shook his head.

"Not for us to wonder about, we just obey orders. It is something to do with the Spanish throne I have heard but…"

He shrugged and continued.

"Old Bismarck got his way anyhow. We are all German now though I for one will always be Bavarian first."

"I bet the Prussian soldiers feel the same. Pity King Ludwig accepted the terms though."

The men fell silent and sought a place to sleep before the next day's operations.

The following morning, fighting was furious but by midday the Prussian and Bavarian soldiers had the French retreating once again. The Germans soon captured the railway station and the French troops scattered, leaving the town of Weissenburg in the hands of their enemy. There were heavy casualties on both sides but the Germans had taken one thousand French prisoners with a further thousand French dead and dying awaiting collection while the remaining French soldiers fled along the road to Soulty.

The German army took Weissenburg on 4th August, outnumbering the French by three to one. Saabrücken remained in French hands briefly but confusion reigned within their ranks as orders were contradicted from one day to the next which resulted in the troops marching all day through heavy rain, camping overnight then retracing their steps the next day. This resulted in them falling back to Spicheren and Forbach. With the intention of crossing the Saar, they realised that their supplies would have been taken by the Germans and they became strung out along the frontier, too scattered to be of much use.

Johann's unit was part of the V Corps of the III Army and on August 6th he was one of over seven thousand Bavarian soldiers facing six thousand three hundred French riflemen at the battle of Woerth, forty miles south-east of Saabrüchen. There were heavy losses on both sides but the German troops had found smouldering fires left by the French who had abandoned their positions and fled to the Spicheren Heights a mile to the south. The two German commanders then ignored the plans set out by Moltke, Chief of Prussian General Staff, and they reported back that the French were retreating. This was not strictly true, as the French regrouped as once again their supplies would be lost to the enemy and they did in fact have an excellent vantage point from the Rotherberg which overlooked the whole valley and the heights above Saabrüchen. Down in the valley they deployed men to prevent an attack on Forbach via Volklingen. By not leaving behind any attachment to warn them of a German approach however, they were taken by surprise early on the morning of the 7th August, when they were horrified to see Uhlan patrols above Saabrüchen. This battle lasted throughout the day until seven-thirty when the French abandoned Forbach even though their losses were only half the number of German casualties.

***

The German troops moved relentlessly further into French territory with their cavalry leading the way through the Vosges Passes. Johann and his new friends were part of the Third Army which travelled through Saar-Union and Dieuze with difficulty. The ground was sodden from heavy rainfall causing their morale to sink along with their boots. Sickness was prevalent amongst the new reservists but slowly they advanced to the Moselle where their cavalry occupied Nancy by 14th August and the infantry arrived two days later. Soon orders were received that they were to destroy the railway line between Nancy and Metz, to cut off the French supply lines.

Under cover of darkness, two squads were chosen to attack the railway at different locations to be sure of at least one successful break in the line. Sergeant Muller led Johann along with eight other soldiers including Lukas and Tobias. The men moved forward making very little sound to a point on the line hidden by trees. With prearranged signals they took the explosives from their knapsacks and with shaking fingers, prepared the fuses. The rain had ceased falling and the moon showed from behind clouds so the wet track could be seen shining until the moon was hidden once again. When Sergeant Muller was satisfied with their work he signalled for them to fall back and head for a safe vantage point. The men remained silent, just expelling breath slowly with relief. Once they were safe Sergeant Muller, who had remained to light the fuses, could be seen with a glowing cord bending to ignite the explosive. He then ran towards them, glancing over his shoulder to check the fuse was still lit. As he threw himself down amongst his men there was an enormous boom and the smell of cordite. All the soldiers had covered their heads with their arms until the dust ceased to fall on them. When they looked up, they sat still in silence as the wrecked railway line came into view and the dust cloud dispersed.

"Mission accomplished boys."

Muller stood and could be seen in the glow of the burning foliage to have a huge grin on his face.

"Back to camp, well done, a good night's work."

The following day Trevor Evans, the English reporter who Johann had heard cursing, reappeared with news gleaned from time spent with the French.

"The French are running scared. Rumours abound that you Germans have large numbers of troops not yet deployed. In all honesty they don't know which way to run for safety. They listen to the gossip in the cafes and hotels where some of the staff are English and take pleasure in making mischief."

Johann asked, "So they speak French and German these English waiters? And you, Trevor, you are fluent in all three as well?"

"Four languages if you include Welsh, the language of my family back home in Wales."

He saw the three young friends were puzzled.

"Ah, I can see you have no knowledge of Wales. You will think of it no doubt as a western region of England but Wales is a country within a country. Sadly, we do not have the prestige of Scotland or Ireland but we do have our own culture and language. Now that you are part of a unified Germany you may find Bavaria will have less individual identity."

They were sitting around a small fire.

"Tell us more about Wales, Trevor. Is it as beautiful as Bavaria?"

The reporter lay back, resting his head on his hand and watched the dark clouds in the distance move slowly nearer.

"In some ways. We have mountains with green valleys, castles, mostly ruins, lakes, we have more than our fair share of rain. There are forests where wild boar used to roam and beautiful beaches around our coast. Wales is called "The Land of Song" you know, wherever people gather, be it church or chapel, pub or temperance hall, folk love to sing."

"Would we feel welcome in Wales?"

Tobias had been listening intently to every word.

"Of course, most certainly. You would naturally be asked lots of questions, we Welsh love to mind other people's business if you take my meaning; we are naturally inquisitive, which in my case helps my career. One of the first questions you would be asked is "are you church or chapel?"

"Not are you Catholic or Protestant then?"

"No, not many Catholics in Wales see. High Church mind amongst the gentry but not too many."

The group fell silent then cursed as the rain began to fall once again. Another night of discomfort with little sleep beckoned.

CHAPTER SEVEN

It was the 14th August and dawn was breaking when French troops attempted to cross the swollen River Moselle but the number of men waiting to use the few pontoon bridges which had survived the torrential rain caused a major bottleneck. Access to these bridges was across water-logged fields and only the infantry could use them. The wheeled vehicles had to make their way to the permanent bridges beyond Metz. Behind them the sound of enemy fire alerted them to the close proximity of the Germans.

After all the rain the sun finally broke through and the day was sunny and bright. The Bavarian troops could see for miles across the Moselle with the cathedral clearly visible. French soldiers were preparing to camp but by evening, battle had once again commenced. By nightfall the Germans were so confident of winning, their bands struck up and played rousing tunes of victory, raising the general morale of the weary troops. The morning of the following day, however, they were not so self-assured.

The light of day revealed the carnage from the previous day. Five thousand Germans lay dead and three to four thousand Frenchmen. It was a bitter victory, claimed by both sides. The French had already regrouped and were on the road through the narrow streets of Metz heading for the plateau of Gravelotte.

The Germans themselves were busy closing the road to Verdun at Mars-le-Tour. They found abandoned carts and waggons left by fleeing French troops and desperate civilians blocked the road. There were many carts piled with bodies of dead and dying French soldiers. On 17th August, the French were marching along the Verdun road to Metz from Mars-le-Tour, not realising that the Germans lay ahead, waiting. Massive numbers on both sides fought long and hard throughout the day of the 18th with the French gaining the initiative with their superior chassepots but eventually with the arrival of the Saxon units coming to the assistance of the Germans, the French once more fell back to Metz. The victory of this day's fighting was once again disputed.

***

For two days the guns fell silent while the armies of both sides reorganised, attended to the dead and dying and refreshed the exhausted men. Supplies were checked, guns cleaned and ammunition was distributed while some of the men attended to their own wounds. The spirit of adventure they had shared on their train journey to France had totally evaporated. Smiles were seldom seen, grim determination showed on their faces and boys had turned into men. Before they became too relaxed though, Field Marshall Moltke ordered the advance to recommence. The Third Army was south of the River Meuse. By the 23rd August they approached two fortresses at Voul and Verdun and they bombarded them with little success until the siege artillery arrived accompanied by many more troops, allowing them to break through the enemy lines. The French fled towards Reims with the Germans in pursuit.

Trevor reappeared from his latest mission behind enemy lines. With him he had smuggled out copies of French newspapers.

"The latest I can tell you boys is that according to their own press releases, the French Commander, Marshall MacMahon, is planning to go to the aide of Marshall Bauzaine at Chalons. From what I have learnt, your Commander, Moltke, tends to believe these press reports and intends to act on them."

Sergeant Muller grunted.

"I can well believe he does."

The young men looked to their sergeant for explanation.

"It has ever been my experience that the sharing of information amongst the upper ranks can be lacking in detail. You would be surprised at the arrogance and egos of your 'superiors'. They are all seeking personal glory and have been known to turn deaf ears to orders they find disagreeable. The press on the other hand, being neutral, tend to report the true facts."

A soldier named Gunther, who had half-succeeded in growing face hair, turned to the reporter.

"Trevor, good to have you with us. I know you share your time between the two sides but your company is not just enjoyable but also valuable. How do you stay safe, crossing from one side to the other? It must put you in grave danger."

"I like to travel under cover of darkness. One man can go unnoticed with little difficulty and it can be seen clearly that I carry no weapons. I thrive on the excitement which is all the better for not having to take lives as you do."

The bugles sounded, alerting the men to prepare to move. The Germans, one hundred and fifty thousand men in total, began their pursuit of the French through the forest of Argonne. The routes along which they travelled were almost impassable after all the heavy rain with traces of all the boots of the trudging soldiers but by 27th August, the German scouts reported sighting the forces of Marshall MacMahon. The cavalry of both sides clashed but the French Commander soon realised he was left with just one escape route, to the north via the river crossings on the Meuse at Remilly and Mouzon but it was too late. The Germans had encircled them.

Two days later, fighting began in earnest in the valley of the Wiseppe. When darkness fell, the French dispersed into the forest to Beaumont where they pitched a hasty camp close to the town and collapsed, exhausted. The next day Bavarian scouts discovered them.

Sergeant Muller held up his hand to signal his men to halt and take cover. Below them was the enemy camp and their artillery were ordered to fire. The French guns replied, their drums could be heard encouraging the troops.

Lukas whispered,

"God Almighty! What a shambolic sight! Look! Officers pulling on their tunics as they run from their billets! And see, they have the townsfolk running amongst them, poor devils. Surely we cannot fire on sitting ducks!"

He soon cursed however when French snipers, hidden in the houses, fired their chassepots at them. His pity evaporated and he raised his gun.

Slowly the French were pushed towards the Meuse with the Germans driving them back, through woods and down steep banks. The desperate French sent their cavalry charging at the Germans, hoping to buy time for their men to cross the river. Cries of men and frightened horses falling into the river in their panic to cross, filled the air. It was seven o'clock in the evening when what remained of the French had either crossed the bridges or drowned. Daylight was fading when Johann and his comrades reached the riverbank and found the remnants of the fighting – supplies abandoned, guns, dead and dying French soldiers, and men holding their hands above their heads who were quickly taken prisoner. The sight of so many casualties from both sides brought tears to the eyes of the young recruits. Two days before they had been admiring the scenery, enjoying the spell of sunshine and rejoicing in their victories.

***

The French retreated towards Sedan, a fortress town close to the Belgian border. The location was considered excellent by the officers in charge. Behind the town there were hills and to the south the valley of the River Meuse with excellent views of any enemy movements. By the 31st September, the French felt they were fully prepared for battle but when the Bavarians began firing from across the river while Prussians and Saxons encircled the town, the following day the only escape route for the French would mean crossing into Belgium.

Johann's battalion approached the bridge to cross the river where they discovered French soldiers frantically preparing to blow it up. His squad was ordered to charge at the enemy immediately and for the first time the young recruits were involved in close combat. With no time for hesitation they charged, bayonets fixed, and fell upon the French soldiers attempting to light the fuses. As some of the young Bavarians tackled the French, others heaved the barrels of powder and hurled them into the fast-flowing river. Protesting French soldiers followed the barrels and were soon swept away. While this was happening, other squads of Bavarians were erecting pontoon bridges to enable the large number of troops to cross as quickly as possible. The French were now truly trapped.

It was four in the morning, not yet light and the valley of the Meuse was shrouded in low-lying mist when the Bavarians entered the village of Bazeilles stealthily so no alarms would sound. Some of the buildings were still burning from the artillery fire of the previous day but others were fired deliberately by the attackers to flush out snipers. Barricades had been erected hastily by the locals who joined with their Marines in fighting off the enemy and the ferocious battle lasted well into the afternoon. Because the villagers had fought alongside their troops, they were captured as unlawful combatants, executed and the village was set on fire. A few of the French, mainly cavalrymen, managed to escape into the Ardennes Forest.

Johann and the other members of his squad had watched in disbelief as fellow Bavarians volunteered for the firing squad.

"This was not at all what I expected war to be. If I was faced with such an attacker as these people were, I too would fight to the end to save my home."

Lukas's face was flushed with anger as he spoke.

Johann could only nod in agreement but others shook their heads.

A soldier nearby named Jacob pointed to the casualties in German uniform.

"But just look at our countrymen lying dead, slaughtered before they could even raise their guns! I would have no problem killing the French bastards."

Sergeant Muller approached, wiping blood from his bayonet.

"We have just learnt that Napoleon III has been captured and has been forced to surrender."

"Does that mean the war is over?"

283

Johann had been quiet but now beneath the grime of dust, blood and sweat on his face, a glimmer of a smile expressed his hope.

"Oh, if only I could tell you the answer is yes but not yet, boy, not yet. Did any of you see our superiors sat upon their horses on a hilltop across the river overlooking the village? What fun they had, cheering us on as we fought for our lives, watching through their field-glasses, no doubt fortified by local brandy. It is said that the King of Prussia himself was amongst them."

Muller did a quick head count.

"Now you men, have a break. Get some food and drink down you then we all have the grim task of attending to the casualties, dead or alive."

The young recruits had little appetite for food but ate anyway. After several hours of carrying corpses for burial and transporting the injured men to their field hospital on makeshift stretchers, the camp that night was sombre. Sleep came quickly as they had no fear of their enemy who had been dealt a heavy blow. Once again mist rolled over the valley as if to hide the evidence of the atrocities and occasional sparks from smouldering buildings coloured the mist in a rosy hue.

CHAPTER EIGHT

Trevor came with news that because of the surrender of Napoleon to Moltke and the Prussian King, France now had no government therefore the Germans had no one to declare peace with. He told his eager listeners that Napoleon had been exiled to England and an emergency provisional government had been installed in haste but that the new commanders refused to accept defeat. In late October, the French at Metz finally gave up the besieged town but sporadic fighting by the French kept the German troops from acting as victors. Consequently, the city of Orleans fell to the enemy who plundered the city's supplies but the French fought bravely and took it back. Paris was held by French troops but was surrounded by Germans. The troops in the city hoped that the French soldiers outside Paris would soon come to their aid. They had no way of knowing that the armies outside Paris were ill-equipped and too few in number to be of any real assistance. That would have meant challenging the Germans who were waiting for them to attack. The late November weather changed from rainfall to frost on the ground which enabled the Germans to move their guns with less difficulty and the Bavarian troops were billeted in barns and farmhouses, quite comfortable while they waited impatiently for the order to attack.

The news from Paris was that the French presence had been boosted by sympathetic foreigners. Among them were British, Italian and Belgian residents who had displayed their support with a large gathering in the Champs Elysées. All Parisians not in the military armed themselves with whatever weapons they had available and joined with the foreigners as flags were waved, bands played patriotic music and women and children cheered. The rationing of food and fuel was stoically accepted as the Parisians felt confident it would not be for too long. However, as the temperatures dropped and heating was scarce, they prayed for an early attack by the Germans. They were not to know that Moltke was in no hurry. His troops were comfortable in their billets, the homes left empty by French civilians who had fled the countryside for the safety of Paris. Empty chateaux were used by the officers as observation posts and forts. The German sentries willingly exchanged some of their rations for brandy, newspapers and information and a local boatman offered his services to any neutral passengers such as Trevor and his colleagues even though some of the crossings were terrifying.

The beleaguered citizens of Paris were soon growing restless and demanded action from the commanders. Their attempt at attacking the German armies on the 29th November had been a disastrous failure and on 1st December a truce was called so that both sides could bury their dead. With grim faces Johann, Lukas and the other men in their squad gathered the bodies from where they had fallen. The sight of the horrific injuries suffered by their comrades made them question their presence in France once again.

"How is it we are killing our French neighbours, for what? Look, here is poor Gunther, such a sweet boy, always had such a cheery face, nothing seemed to disturb him. Now he hardly has a face at all."

Tears ran down the cheeks of Jacob as he spoke. He wiped them roughly without embarrassment with his blood-stained tunic sleeve.

"Only yesterday he was telling me of his hometown and how his family would be preparing for Christmas. He and his father would be going out into the forest to choose the prettiest Christmas tree for their house and his mother and sisters would be baking festive dishes. Damn the war!"

He dug deep with extra vigour even though the ground was hard from the frosty morning.

Johann had just shoveled his last scattering of soil onto the grave he had been digging.

"So far from home. This man's dog tag shows he was a Prussian. It was difficult to tell his age but my guess is he had fought in other wars."

They were desolate when they learnt that their sergeant, Muller, had been severely injured and was already on his way to the field hospital.

Meanwhile, the French were also burying their casualties but unlike the Germans they had no comfortable shelter to retire to at night and no hot food. The night mists blanketed their shivering bodies as they lay exhausted on the hard ground praying they might live through the night. After three days, mission completed, they took advantage of the mist to retreat back into Paris. Twelve thousand French had died.

***

In the luxurious Palace of Versailles, the senior members of the German command were gathered. They were in no hurry to continue the fighting, quite prepared to wait for the French in Paris to capitulate. Bismarck had even invited King Ludwig of Bavaria to join them while foreign dignitaries came and went. The Bavarians were garrisoned at Villacoublay awaiting supplies to be railed in from Germany. There was only one railway line and shipments were slow. This delayed any attacks on Paris being considered by the German command until at least the New Year. After a trial bombardment it was decided to shell Paris on 5th January. This continued with little retaliation from the French until the night of the 18th. Unfortunately for the French, everything that could go wrong did so. The weather was no longer frosty but heavy rain once again muddied the fields and the bridges which allowed but a few men at a time to cross were fiercely guarded by the Germans. When darkness fell, the French were ordered to retreat but they were hindered by their own supply wagons and extra guns blocked their way. Once again, the sight greeting the Germans next morning when the mist lifted revealed the abandoned remains of the retreating French troops. Exasperated, the French General Trochu called for an armistice to clear the battlefield yet again. On 22nd

January, with just two days' worth of flour left in Paris, the French surrendered and requested talks to discuss terms.

The King of Prussia had been declared Emperor of Germany, or Kaiser, at Versailles on 18th January. Then an Armistice was finally signed on the 28th January with the Government of National Defence which was effective for Paris immediately and by February 19th for all of France. In this time, a new Assembly was elected with the responsibility for deciding whether the war would continue or peace could be agreed. During this period, German troops would remain in Paris to assist in providing relief to the citizens. Negotiations for peace included the forfeit of Alsace and Loraine to Germany and compensation to be agreed of five milliard Francs. The Germans also insisted they had a triumphant entry into Paris on the understanding they would only leave when the full reparation had been paid. The occupying force in Paris would be limited to thirty thousand men.

It was 1st March before this was voted on and ratified.

The Bavarian soldiers were amongst the remaining occupying troops and many were camped in the Gardens of the Tuileries including Johann and his comrades. The parade was surprisingly good humoured, the French citizens enjoyed the military bands of the victors. After all their recent hardships, they were only too ready to have some joy in their lives. The happiness was to be short-lived. When the excess German troops marched out of Paris, the revolution which had been festering amongst the lower classes ignited and power was seized by the Commune. This was now civil war, French against French.

Back home in Germany, the people wanted the return of their troops but it was the 10th May before the Treaty of Frankfurt was finally signed and the war was officially ended. The German casualties were twenty thousand killed and ninety thousand wounded.

In the grounds of the wrecked Palace of the Tuileries, the young soldiers pitched their tents in orderly lines, more relieved than triumphant that the fighting had finally ceased.

"Have you noticed the poor wretches, how they look like walking skeletons? Trevor said the Parisians had been reduced to eating dogs, cats and even rats!"

Johann adjusted the guy ropes on the six-man tent he would share with Lucas and four other soldiers then unfolded a canvas stool ready to act as barber for any comrades needing a trim.

One of them, a tall young man with a permanent woeful expression named Rolph Bergman said, as he rolled the canvas door open and neatly tied it back,

"What I cannot understand is why these people have accepted peace with us but insist on continuing to fight amongst themselves! It beggars belief, they are causing far more damage to their city now than we ever did."

He stepped back and inspected his handiwork. With a few adjustments he was satisfied that their tent would pass the eagle-eyed inspection of an officer. Then he became Johann's first client.

"Well I can't wait to get back home now to the mountains of Bavaria. I wish now I had not volunteered to remain here with the occupying forces. I hope we won't be here too long, that's all."

"Johann, what made you volunteer to stay? Didn't you say you were employed at one of King Ludwig's castles? Surely you would rather be there than here?"

Johann turned to answer Conrad, one of his new comrades.

"I heard that the news back home is not good. There are large numbers of people unemployed and in the court of the King his government officials disapprove of his excessive spending. They think he will bankrupt Bavaria if he continues."

Karl, Johann's father, had written to his son with this news. He had also told him that Marie was no longer in Germany but had joined her mistress, Duchess Sophie, in France now that hostilities had ceased. When the other men discussed what they intended doing on their return, he was considering a course of action which did not involve him going home at all.

Later that evening he walked in the gardens with Trevor and he asked him about life in England.

"What chance is there of me being accepted into your country should I choose to leave France on a ship bound for England instead of returning home to an uncertain future? Where should I go and what would I do? I am just a gardener after all."

Trevor smiled at his young companion.

"You are seriously considering doing this? Well, I can say that now I feel I know you well, you should grasp the opportunity while you can! Anyway, you are also a skilled barber, there is always a need for barbers. But what of your family? Won't you be missed?"

Johann slowed to a standstill.

My father tells me the King has been forced to reduce his staff so my position is no longer available and my sister is to marry, she and her husband will move in with my parents. So you see, I have no reason to go home."

"But didn't you confide in me that you had a sweetheart? What of her?"

There was a long sigh from Johann as he averted Trevor's eyes and looked away into the distance.

"That romance can no longer blossom. It never had a chance if I am honest with you. Marie, the girl of my dreams, is from a different class. She too worked in the court of King Ludwig but as a companion to his fiancée, Princess Sophie, not in a lowly occupation such as mine."

Trevor put his hand on Johann's shoulder.

"Ah, the class system. It is much the same at home in England. At least we can congratulate the French in their efforts to rid society of such impediments. For all their faults and shortcomings, they are pursuing the correct path with their republican ideals.

"Well, if you have given this plenty of thought I will help in any way I can. Unfortunately, I will leave France before you but I will write out for you details of how you might find me."

The more he talked with Trevor, improving his English as he did so, the more excited he became at the idea uppermost in his mind. He planned to head for England when he was demobbed, not join the others on their trains bound for Germany. He would make his way to

Calais and board a ferry. From there he would head north to Liverpool where he would meet up with Trevor. That night, their first night under canvas in the city of Paris, as his companions snored and tossed in their sleep, he lay with his hands behind his head and smiled to himself as he planned his future.

CHAPTER NINE
JOHANN TRAVELS TO ENGLAND

When the day arrived for Johann to make his farewells he had no regrets. Some of his companions were returning to Germany while others planned to remain in France until all the reparations had been paid by the French. A few had already formed relationships with French girls and were enjoying life now that hostilities had ceased.

With his kitbag slung over one shoulder and his final pay of wages owed safely stowed in a breast pocket of his uniform tunic, he bade farewell to his closest friends and waved goodbye before heading for the station where he would board a train to Calais then sail to Dover.

As the train sped through the countryside, he ignored the curious glances of the other passengers. They were whispering, wondering why a German in uniform was travelling north and not east to Germany. Johann understood most of what they were saying but feigned ignorance. Soon they became bored and conversed amongst themselves with no need to whisper. Johann intended to replace his uniform with civilian clothes in Calais before boarding the ship.

He found a stall which sold second-hand clothes in good condition amongst many stalls selling goods to the thrifty travellers about to leave France. His uniform he rolled up and fastened to his kitbag securely after transferring his money into his new jacket pocket.

Once he was aboard the cross-channel vessel, Johann spent the duration of the crossing watching the shores of France dwindle into the distance and pacing the deck, too excited to feel hungry. The small amount of food he had taken on board the train sustained him until his arrival in England. As the sky darkened and the waves grew, the ship began to roll and sent most of the passengers into the public salons not to venture out again until they felt the ship slowing down.

Trevor had told Johann his first sighting of England would be of the impressive white cliffs of Dover. Now Johann felt even more excited as he leant on the ship's rail, watching the wash from the bow diminish as they slowed and when the ship's whistle sounded one long, one short and one long blast for the pilot to come alongside and guide them into port, he covered his ears. The ship bumped gently against the quayside under the expert handling by the ship's captain. Ropes were thrown ashore by the deckhands and the passengers emerged from the salons, some rather green of pallor, crowding around the disembarkation area in readiness for the gangway to be lowered. Rain was falling as the passengers all filed onto the gangway and shuffled their way onto English soil. Johann was careful of the slippery deck of the pier as he watched others passengers struggling not to fall. The staircases were equally treacherous but soon he was safe on the flag-stoned promenades lit with ornamental gas lamps where horse buses waited for passengers. Johann searched for the way to the railway platforms. Even though it was now evening, he was able to exchange his money for sterling at a kiosk on the station and once he had done this, he purchased his ticket for Liverpool Lime Street Station via Euston Station London as Trevor had advised him. A porter pointed to the platform for his train and soon Johann had found a seat in a carriage where several were still available. He relaxed when the doors slammed, the smoke from the funnel blew in clouds past the windows and the wheels slipped as the engine picked up speed. The day had been long and Johann's eyes closed as they travelled through the English countryside with the murmurings of the other occupants of the carriage soothing him asleep. When he awoke, the train was travelling through suburbs of smoke-grimed houses, back to back with others and tall factory chimneys spewing more smoke over the rain-soaked streets. This was his first impression of London. He had mixed feelings now. Bavaria was so clean and green in comparison. He decided that Liverpool could only be better than London and with that thought to cling on to, he stood as the train drew into the station and stopped. The doors were thrown open as a porter shouted, "Euston Station everybody off."

Johann approached the man and asked him, "Platform for Liverpool please?"

Without looking at him, the porter pointed vaguely so Johann followed the direction but before he boarded the train with thin wisps of steam coming from the engine he sought out someone else to confirm it was indeed the train he was to take. A man about his age was just climbing into one of the coaches so Johann quickly said,

"Excuse me, is this train bound for Liverpool please?"

"Yes, I am going to Liverpool myself, perhaps you would care to join me, there are plenty of seats in this coach."

The young man had a friendly face so Johann thanked him and shook his hand.

"You are too kind."

They both stowed their luggage in the overhead luggage rack and sat down.

"I'm Bill Gregory, by the way. Pardon me for asking, but you are from foreign parts?"

"Yes, Johann Nicklas, from Bavaria in Germany."

He had noticed Bill had no knowledge of Bavaria but he had heard of Germany.

"I have read about your war with France. It is all over now?"

Johann nodded but pointedly changed the subject.

"The scenery here is so different from the mountains of home. Are there mountains here in England?"

"Yes, of course, but down here in the south they are just rolling hills while further north we have mountains which might impress you."

The two chatted for a while then the movement of the coach rocking gently as the wheels click-clacked on the lines lulled them to sleep.

Johann was woken up when the train was motionless. He wiped the condensation from the window so that he could read the name of the station: CREWE. Bill stretched and yawned before joining Johann at the window.

"Ah, I see the engine is thirsty, we have a short time to stretch our legs. Care to accompany me, Johann?"

"Maybe we can get some food?"

Johann was now feeling hungry.

"Let us find out, shall we?"

The platform was bustling with passengers using the waiting rooms, queueing for food from the café or just walking the length of the train for exercise.

"Oh, something smells good."

Bill pointed to a pie seller doing a brisk trade.

"I will join the line, do you want one?"

"Yes, please."

Johann had noticed another trader selling hot potatoes.

"Would you like a potato to go with your pie?"

Bill's smile answered for him.

"A meal in a bag, good idea."

With their piping hot purchases, they made their way back to the carriage to eat them in comfort. On the way they bought bottles of ginger beer to wash down the food.

When they had finished eating they sat waiting for the rest of the passengers to return to their seats.

"May I ask you why you travel to Liverpool if it is not too impudent for me to do so?"

Johann told him of his friendship with Trevor and how he had met him on the battlefields of France.

Bill's eyes widened with interest but before he could ask too many questions Johann was reluctant to answer, the young Bavarian told him, "Trevor has given me the address of his family and he hopes to be home himself before too long. I have a trade which I hope to find work with; I am a gentleman's hairdresser with some years of experience."

"A barber, eh? Well, there is always work for a good barber with all the face whiskers an' all, you should do well, I wish you every success."

"How about you? Why do you go to Liverpool?"

"My aunt and uncle run a shop and as I recently lost my father who had been ill for some time with consumption, my mother is now alone. Her sister, my aunt with the shop, kindly offered me a position so I could return to live with my mother nearby. I know little of hosiery but my uncle is willing to teach me. So here I am, left London for pastures new."

Johann took a while to translate for himself what Bill had just told him.

"Liverpool has pastures then? I imagined a busy town."

Bill laughed.

"Ah, pastures new you mean?"

Johann nodded.

"That is just a way of saying 'new places'. Liverpool is a very large city in fact. Hang on, I have a postcard in a pocket somewhere."

Bill searched each pocket, eventually pulling out a crumpled picture postcard. He handed it to Johann.

A paddle-steamer was berthed in a dock with an imposing building in the background. The "Custom House" was printed on the card.

"Liverpool is a lot different from my home town. I must take care not to get lost."

"Where does your friend, Trevor, live?"

Wavertree Road. Do you know it?"

Bill clapped his hand on his thigh.

"Know it? My Ma lives in Marmaduke Street, I have to walk down Wavertree Road to get to it."

Johann took Bill's hand and shook it vigorously.

"This is so good I met you, Bill. Such a relief. Now I have two friends in Liverpool. How lucky can a man be?"

The train was passing over a river and Bill explained to Johann the bridge was newly built to cross the River Mersey at Runcorn.

"Not too far now, I must confess I am so happy to be back north again. The people here are so friendly, just you wait and see."

When the train was approaching a station, Bill said,

"We should get off here, this is Edge Hill; we don't need to go all the way to Lime Street Station. Get your bag, Johann, we can wait near the door."

Daylight was fading fast as they made their way out of the station. The first junction they came to was with Wavertree Road.

"What number is your friend's house?"

Johann stopped walking to confirm the number on his scrap of paper.

"Thirty."

The two new friends chatted as they walked until they arrived at thirty. Bill shook Johann's hand once again and wished him good fortune in his new life.

"When I am settled in my uncle's shop I will call and see you, maybe get a haircut, eh? We must keep in touch, don't you agree?"

Johann watched Bill until he turned to wave and disappeared round a corner. He suddenly felt very alone. With a sigh he raised the polished knocker on the door and waited.

A light showed through the fanlight and the sound of the bolt being slid back made Johann straighten his back and exhale slowly.

The door opened to reveal a young man who was as like Trevor as two peas from the same pod.

"Ah, Johann, come in, come in, we have been looking forward to making your acquaintance ever since Trevor wrote asking if you could stay with us. Here, let me take your bag."

Trevor's younger brother, Simon, led him through to the sitting room to meet his parents.

"Look who I found on our doorstep, Johann Nicklas, all the way from France!"

Sat either side of the fire burning in the fireplace were Trevor's parents. His father stood up to welcome Johann and his mother smiled and extended her hand to him.

"You must be so exhausted after all your travelling. Here, sit down at the table, let me offer you some refreshment. Do you drink tea? Or is coffee preferred in Germany?"

"Please, I will have whatever you have. We drink a lot of coffee, and also in France, but tea is also popular."

"Tea it is then. Do you like cream and sugar?"

Johann shook his head.

"No, just tea please will be nice."

Mrs Evans went into the kitchen and returned with a tray bearing a teapot, jug and sugar bowl. Simon followed behind her with tea plates, cups and saucers. On the sideboard was a biscuit barrel which was offered to Johann. He was no longer hungry but he was too polite to refuse so he helped himself to one piece of shortbread and nodded with satisfaction at the first bite.

"This is very good."

Trevor's mother beamed.

"You like my shortbread? It is an old family recipe, please, have another piece, do."

Having tasted one, he had no difficulty accepting another.

The family asked him about his journey, pleased to hear of his new friend, Bill, but avoided questioning him about his war experiences. Trevor had told them many harrowing tales of the loss and bravery on both sides and reminding Johann would be too unkind.

Johann tried to stifle a yawn but Simon noticed.

"Shall I take Johann to his bed, mother, he must be so weary."

Mrs Evans apologised to their visitor for keeping him from his rest and nodded to Simon.

Sleep came easily that night and Johann did not stir until the next morning when he heard the family up and about.

***

By the time Trevor made it home for a brief visit, Johann was part of the family. Mr Evans had introduced him to his barber who had a business at 40 Wavertree Road, on the corner with Winifred Street.

The barber offered to give Johann a trial period in which time he could show his skills. The young man demonstrated haircutting and facial hair trimming and old Mr Pemberton was sufficiently impressed and his customers likewise, so he gave Johann a permanent position. One customer, on learning that Johann was German, asked him if he had found the German Church in Renshaw Street. When Johann told him he had not he was given directions on how to get there and he became a regular worshipper. Every Sunday he felt he had returned to Bavaria for just a short while as he conversed in his native tongue. Life was indeed good. His English improved daily as did his popularity with his customers who listened with interest to tales of Bavaria and occasionally a light-hearted reference to France. The letters he sent home to his parents comforted them with the knowledge that although it was unlikely they would ever see their son again, at least they were confident he was happy.

CHAPTER TEN

Johann was settled and happy. He enjoyed his work, the family he lodged with treated him as they would a son of their own and he had made friends with fellow Germans at the church where he was able to speak his own language.

One Sunday as the congregation gathered outside church after the service, one of them suggested they all have a day out together.

"My customers tell me of the fun they have had, they took a day trip to New Brighton. The ferry sails from the floating landing stage so the boat crossing itself would be an adventure."

Hans Gerber was a waiter at Liverpool's smartest hotel, The Adelphi.

"That is an excellent idea but we would need a whole day to get the most out of it and for most of us that would mean going on a Sunday. Don't you sometimes work on Sundays, Hans?"

"Yes, but not always, we will need to find a day which is free for us all."

The third young man in the group was Rudolf Kramer, a clerk with the shipping line.

I only work Saturday mornings and never Sundays so I can fit in with you two."

The three finally settled on a date in early April and early one Sunday morning with the sun shining, they made their way to the landing stage with money in their pockets and briskness in their walk. The crowds waiting to embark on the ferry 'Heatherbell' were all in high spirits and when they heard the rush of water from the huge paddles of the ship as she slowed to allow the ropes to be thrown to the waiting shore crew, a loud cheer went up from the passengers.

Once the gang plank was lowered, they waited patiently for the few passengers on the journey from New Brighton to disembark then the crowd surged forward to find a good vantage point on the decks. Johann and his two pals went up to the promenade deck which soon filled with other travellers. When the captain received the signal that all passengers were safely aboard, the funnel's fine wisps of smoke from the two funnels changed to billows of darker smoke as the engineer responded to the telegraph to increase speed. The boat shook as the paddles began to turn faster. The three young men shouted excitedly to one another to be heard above the noise of the vessel. Two blasts on the ship's whistle announced to other shipping that the ferry was leaving her berth and she slowly turned to head back across the Mersey bound for New Brighton. The river was bustling with boats of all sizes. Steamboats, tugboats, schooners and brigantines, even a transatlantic migrant ship with four masts and a topsail flying the 'Blue Peter' was waiting at anchor for her passengers to be shipped out in tenders. Sailing skilfully amongst the larger ships were small yachts and rowing boats. The river was lined with docks for miles and ship's masts were so closely packed they resembled a forest.

The happy travellers took deep breaths of fresh sea air and talked rapidly in their own language, baffling the other passengers. The river crossing was soon over and once more 'Heatherbell' slowed as she approached the sandy shoreline of the Wirral Peninsular.

"Look! How thrilling, see, there are donkeys on the beach and children playing in the sand!"

Rudolf leaned over the rail, mesmerised by the sun glinting on the wash of the paddles. Hans was busy watching the deckhands preparing to throw the rope to the waiting shore crew before the gangway was lowered to the deck once more.

"Well, wasn't that fun! Let's wait for most of the passengers to land before we do. That way we can take our time and decide which direction we should go."

Hans pointed to the families on the sand.

"Well, I have never been on a seashore before, I suggest we take a walk down to the water's edge. Either of you two coming?"

Johann and Rudolf needed no encouragement.

"Race you then!"

Johann set off with his friends in hot pursuit as they dodged around the family groups building sandcastles and the gentle donkeys patiently carrying their young novice riders on their backs.

The three of them only slowed down when the waves rippled near to their feet.

"Who's for a paddle?"

Rudolf was sitting on the sand removing his boots and his two friends followed suit. They rolled up their trouser legs and tied their polished boots together before hanging them round their necks and running into the sea.

The chill of the water did not detract from their enjoyment. This was the first paddle ever in the sea, the sky was a clear blue and the sun was warm on their faces. Around them were other people paddling and some daring swimmers. When their feet began to get cold, they returned to the sand and threw themselves down to spend some time watching the smiling children and listening to their squeals of delight. Elderly folk sat primly on deck chairs, some men with newspapers over their heads or knotted handkerchiefs whilst the women shaded themselves from the spring sunshine with large hats or parasols.

When their feet were dry they put their boots back on, rolled their trouser legs down again and stood up, brushing themselves free of sand. They walked away from the sea to the Lower Parade wall where they had noticed cafes and shops. The Lower and Higher Parades had been newly built to cater for the large numbers of visitors to New Brighton by ferry or train. The locals called the Lower Parade the Ham and Egg Parade because of the large number of refreshment rooms serving hot meals.

The sea air had given the three young men an appetite. It had been a long time since they had eaten breakfast so when a pretty young lady approached them with a beguiling smile to entice them into the café where she worked, they were only too eager to comply and followed her inside. The success of the young lady was obvious because almost every table was occupied. She found them a table by a window and once they were sat down, handed them a menu and wished them "Bon appetite", mistaking them for French visitors.

Soon a waitress appeared to take their order. They all chose the famous ham and eggs, a plate of bread and butter and a pot of tea for three. Their choice had been influenced by the diners at a neighbouring table who were tucking in with gusto.

Hans looked around.

"It is good to be in the company of people such as these. At the hotel where I work, all the guests are too civilised if you understand. They would never laugh out loud as these people are doing. See how they are enjoying themselves?"

When their food arrived, they tucked in ravenously. The ham was thick cut and juicy with crisp rinds and the eggs, two on each plate, were cooked to perfection. Once all the plates were cleared and the bread and butter eaten, they drained their cups.

"Well, that filled a little corner or two as my father used to say. Roll on supper, eh?"

Hans beamed at his companions.

Rudolf patted his stomach. He had a waistline which clearly showed his love of food and was larger than those of his friends. Sitting at a desk all day in the shipping office at Albion House meant he had less exercise than his friends but he enjoyed his work as the owner was a fellow German, Gustav Christian Schwabe, who had his nephew, Gustav Wilhelm Wolff, a designer of ships, also in his employment.

To pay for their meal, they divided the cost between them and paid at the desk by the door, adding a tip which prompted a big smile of thanks from the waitress.

They strolled back out into the sunshine and headed along the parade to see what the shops had for sale. They were fascinated at the variety of colourful souvenirs, from miniature lighthouses to painted shell necklaces and sugar sticks called rock. There was also an oyster bar doing a brisk trade for passing individuals with not enough time to sit in a café. They could see the lighthouse ahead and decided to walk to see it.

"We have plenty of time to get there and back to the pier before our return ferry."

Johann stepped up the pace. He wanted to make the most of this wonderful day.

The tide was still out so they were able to walk around the base of the ninety-foot edifice with other curious visitors. The lighthouse stood on Perch rock, a sandstone outcrop which would be underwater when the tide came in. Nearby, was the battery known as Fort Perch Rock which had been built to defend the port of Liverpool from attack in times of war.

As they walked back on the sand towards the pier, they saw a small brightly-coloured tent with children sitting in a semi-circle watching a puppet show. The smiling parents watched as their pink-cheeked youngsters laughed, squealed in horror at the appearance of the crocodile, shouted warnings to Mr Punch and clapped at the antics of the puppets. With large bonnets, the women shielded their faces from the heat of the sun while most of the men had ruddy complexions from their outdoor labouring in all weathers. They stood in groups smoking pipes, smiling benignly at their happy families.

The young Germans continued walking amongst the family parties seated on the sand. The older visitors were sitting on rented deck chairs, their eyes closed as they dozed. Women with baskets of drinks, paper windmills, necklaces made from shells, postcards and other souvenirs walked amongst them, offering their goods for sale. Parents indulged their children and boys raced around with their new toy windmills to make them spin fast while girls proudly displayed their necklaces.

It was late afternoon when Johann and his friends arrived back at the pier. The access to the promenade pier was from steps from the ferry pier and the cost was two pence each to enter. Couples, arm in arm, strolled leisurely the length of the pier or sat in the saloon drinking fine ales. There were cafes serving other refreshments and bazaars with seating down both sides of the pier. A band struck up on a raised platform which reminded Hans of the popular bands back home in Bavaria.

"Shall we sit a while and enjoy the band? It is so like the bands back home in the parks."

Johann looked around.

"There are very few seats available, how about we go up a deck? See, it is a penny more to pay but we should get seats there and good views too."

Hans checked his pockets.

"I have a spare penny, how about you, Rudolf?"

"Me too, let's go."

This one day was like a holiday for them. Once on the top level, they found themselves in the company of more well-to-do visitors waiting in line patiently to use the fixed telescopes which enabled the viewer to watch the ships sailing on the River Mersey. When it was the turn of the friends, they scanned the river sharing the sightings of particularly impressive vessels with one another.

Hans was first to see the paddle steamer 'Heatherbell' leaving the Liverpool landing stage for her return journey to New Brighton.

"I can see our ferry on her way back. Shall we get this one? It has been a long day and I have an early start tomorrow at the hotel."

Rudolf and Johann nodded in agreement.

"It has been a grand day boys, we must do it again in the summer. Right, let's be sure we don't miss the boat."

Johann led the way to the ferry pier, ready for embarkation.

On board, tired but contented families rested, huddled together after their exhausting day at the seaside. The three young men stood on the upper deck watching the wash from the paddles spew into the air with the last of the sunshine making it sparkle. They were silent, each deep in their own thoughts. The new life they had all chosen in a foreign country was becoming increasingly more pleasing. Thoughts of Bavaria no longer made them feel melancholy. England was now their home.

CHAPTER ELEVEN
1877

Not far from the barber's shop where Johann worked was a haberdashery store. He passed it almost daily when he took his midday break. It happened that he often encountered a pretty young lady leaving the shop punctually at five minutes past twelve. Soon they were exchanging shy smiles and he would raise his cap to her. On one occasion, the young lady dropped her gloves as she pulled the shop door closed behind her. Johann quickly darted to pick them up for her and she blushed as she whispered thank you to him. He took his chance and asked, "Would you mind very much if I walked with you? We seem to be going the same way."

"No, I have no objection. Tell me, you are the new assistant at the barber's I believe?"

Johann stopped walking and extended his hand.

"Yes, that is so, my name is Johann. I arrived in Liverpool some months ago from Germany to make a new life here."

"How do you do. I am Clara Hall, I work in the haberdashery shop but of course you know that already."

She stopped outside the baker's shop and studied the mouth-watering display of bread, cakes and pies in the window.

"The buns look appealing. Are you buying too, Johann?"

Johann nodded.

"I think I might treat Mr Pemberton to a cake, he has been so kind to me. Which do you suggest he might like, Clara?"

Clara went pink at his use of her name.

"They do delicious custard tarts, my own father's favourite."

"Then I shall buy two, one for me and one for my boss."

With their purchases made, they left the bakery and strolled slowly back, reluctant to bring an end to their time together.

"Would it be possible for me to see you again, maybe if you are free after church on Sunday? Or do you have a young man you walk out with already?"

Clara stopped walking and turned to face him. She found this young man very attractive and so polite!

"No, I have no young man and yes, I would be happy to see you on Sunday. At what time?"

"Just after one o'clock perhaps? Do you live close by?"

"Not too far, Botanic Road."

Johann knew the road and if he left church at noon he could make it to meet her by one.

"I could wait for you on the corner?"

Clara agreed that would be fine.

Johann held out his hand once again and waited as she went into the shop before walking back to the barbers.

Their friendship grew and by the time autumn had arrived, Clara had invited Johann to meet her parents. Eliza and Thomas were delighted with the pleasant young man who had been making their daughter so happy over the summer months. It came out in conversation that Thomas, still a reporter with the 'Liverpool Mercury' knew Trevor and his family. The family listened with interest while Johann told them a little of his time spent with Trevor and how it was thanks to Trevor that he was here in Liverpool. Clara's two younger brothers sat enthralled at the amazing tales of the war in France while Charlotte, the youngest member of the family, listened intently to the stories of a castle far away. Clara's mother, Eliza, still had her soft, Irish accent and interrupted Johann when she could to ask about his family. She could sympathise with this amicable young man far from home and the family he loved. Her memories of Ireland were a mixture of happiness and sorrow too.

One Sunday, after the family had eaten, Johann asked Thomas if he might have a private word. Clara blushed and stared at her feet while Eliza smiled and nodded to her husband as he led the young man into the front parlour. The younger members of the family looked at one another with puzzled expressions. It was not too long before the two men returned to the kitchen with Thomas patting Johann on the back and smiling at Clara.

"Well, Clara, this young man, your Johann, has just asked me if I would agree to you becoming his wife. How do you feel about this then?"

Clara went crimson.

"Oh father, you would make me so happy if you gave your consent."

"Eliza, and you? What do you think?"

Johann stood quietly waiting for Eliza to reply.

"Thomas, Clara, I have come to like this young German very much. He is so polite, so obviously smitten with our Clara, I can assure you I can think of nothing which would make me happier. Clara, if it is really what you want you have my full blessing. Now Thomas, don't make the poor girl wait any longer, what about you?"

Thomas clapped his hands together and his smile widened.

"Of course you may have our beautiful daughter as your bride. You can start the preparations right away. I think we need a celebration of your engagement so next week invite your friends over and we will take a drink to your good health and longevity. For now, we will toast you with tea, eh, Eliza?"

"I have only one request, Clara and Johann. The wedding should be held in St Peter's church. I know you are a member of the German Church, Johann, but I hope you understand? Now that you are so familiar with English, a ceremony in English will not be a problem for you. Will you both agree to this?"

Clara knew that her mother struggled with her faith so this request was quite unexpected. She looked at Johann.

"Mrs Hall, wherever I marry Clara will be fine with me. We will visit the church to make our arrangements as soon as we agree to a date."

Clara nodded her head and smiled at her parents.

As they drank their tea they discussed how soon they could marry. Thomas had no parents or siblings but Eliza wanted Clara's Irish uncles and aunt to travel over for the wedding. Bridget, Eliza's mother lived in Liverpool with young Bridget so naturally she would be at the ceremony.

Johann said he would write to his parents and ask them if they could attend but he stressed he thought it most unlikely. His father still worked at the castle but he was no longer as fit as he had been and his mother would refuse to travel without her husband. His sister had moved away with her husband and son, Jacob, to a remote Alpine village and Johann had received no replies to his recent letters. He had lots of friends in Liverpool of course, Trevor and his family, Bill who he saw rarely but was still a good friend and his fellow Germans from Church. Also of course, Mr Pemberton and his wife. Before the evening came to a close, quite a list of expected guests and a date had been decided: March 28th 1878.

***

Karl replied to Johann's invitation with the reply his son had expected.

Dear Johann

If it was at all possible for us to celebrate your marriage you know we would be delighted to accept your invitation but times are still hard here and money is short. However, be assured that your mother and I will be with you in spirit and may your union be blessed with a large and happy family.

Your Loving Parents

Johann pictured his father sitting at the kitchen table writing ever so slowly with his arthritic hands, his tongue protruding oh so slightly from his mouth as he concentrated on his words. His mother would be hovering over him, reading as her husband wrote and correcting his spelling. The room would be warmed from the tiled stove while outside the winter snow would still be blanketing the ground. Karl's wood pile would be as neatly stacked as ever and the lights from the neighbouring chalets would be shining like stars on the crisp snow while wood smoke curled lazily from the chimneys. The lowing of contented cows, snug and warm inside for the winter months would break the silence now and then.

Johann suddenly felt very far from home.

CHAPTER TWELVE
1878

March was a wet and windy month but the sun broke through the clouds as Clara and Johann left St Peter's church as a married couple. Their assembled guests stood as Clara, in her lavender dress with a small bustle and becoming hat trimmed with a small veil, and Johann, in a smart new suit, walked slowly back up the aisle to the church door. Grandma Bridget, now sixty-six years old with her long grey hair in the fashionable chignon topped with a hat decorated with flowers, was accompanied by Colonel John O'Reilly and Clara's eldest brother, John. The two men had been visiting Ireland from America after receiving the wedding invitation. Patrick and his wife, Mary, came without their children and had crossed to Liverpool with Joseph and young Bridget as she was known by family members. She had returned to the family home in Ireland to help her youngest brother farm the land and keep house for him after he tragically lost his young wife in childbirth and had never remarried. The other guests included Trevor and his family, Bill, with a pretty girl on his arm, Rudolf and Hans and Mr Pemberton. They all returned to the home of Thomas and Eliza where a wedding breakfast had been prepared by the women of the family.

Everybody managed to squeeze into the house with youngsters sitting on stairs, the elderly seated in the front parlour and the kitchen and scullery busy with the girls filling plates. Eliza and Thomas made their guests very welcome. Eliza joined the young couple as Clara was introducing Johann to her uncle John and the Colonel. The men avoided talk of war except for exchanging the locations of their battles. War, for the present, was history. As evening fell, the friends and family slowly bade farewell to their hosts, wishing the young couple every happiness once more before leaving. When the last guest had left and only their immediate family remained in the house Clara thanked her parents for all they had done to make their special day such a success. Johann stood beside her, smiling and nodding.

"May I say too, how grateful I am to you all for accepting me as one of your family. I miss my own mother and father but if you will allow me to call you mother and father you would make me an even happier man."

Thomas clapped Johann on his shoulder

"Well, if we may call you son? Let us raise our glasses to each other as true family."

The glasses, almost empty, were raised and everyone said,

"To our one united family, may we always remain so."

The children were yawning and sent off to bed while the scullery was tidied before the adults retired for the night. Clara and Johann left for their new home above the barber shop. Mr Pemberton had become very frail and he had moved out to live with his younger sister who was glad of his company and the financial support he provided.

The business continued to prosper and when Clara became pregnant with their first child, Johann was able to buy the business from Mr Pemberton. Their son, Thomas, was born in 1878 followed a year later in 1879 by a daughter, Margaret. Another son, John, was born in 1881, daughter Carolina in 1882 and Philip in 1884. Life was good. Clara was so happy with her young family keeping her busy until tragedy struck. Thomas, their firstborn, caught measles and died when he was just five years old. And when their daughters, Margaret and Carolina, were struck down aged 6 and 8 with tuberculosis, Clara, who was pregnant again, was absolutely heartbroken. Johann did his best to comfort his wife but one night after the boys had been tucked in their beds, the two of them sat at the table lost in their own thoughts. Johann, who had been even more quiet than usual, reached out and took Clara's hand.

"My sweet love, I have been considering for some time that maybe living in a big city is not ideal. What would you say to us moving out, perhaps to the countryside? We must think of our boys, and our next child. The open fields and country living must surely be a better place for raising a family?"

Clara frowned and did not answer immediately. She eventually asked, "Where do you have in mind? What about your business?"

Johann moved closer to her and put his arm around her shoulders.

"I chat to my customers as you know and I have heard them speak about moving away to the mill towns or to the mines where there are plenty of workers needed."

Clara interrupted.

"But you are a skilled barber not a miner or millworker."

Johann smiled.

"Yes, but don't you see? Miners and millworkers need haircuts too? I would soon have many new customers."

Clara shifted in her seat trying to get comfortable as her unborn baby kicked her.

"I will be happy to leave here, we have such sad memories. So I say yes, why not? I will leave everything to you, Johann to arrange though, if you don't mind. The sooner the better."

Johann took a ride out into Lancashire and stopped in the town of Golborne which was a growing market town. Nearby was the colliery and cotton mills but green fields surrounded the town. Johann found in Heath Street an empty shop with living accommodation, ideal for his barber's business and promptly sought out the owner to arrange a tenancy. It was 1888 with only weeks to the imminent birth of their child when Clara and Johann moved everything they had, with the help of Eliza and Thomas, to their new home.

The move to Golborne was not without tragedy, however, as Clara became pregnant again in 1890 but baby Kate was sickly and died soon after birth. Gertrude followed in 1891 and sadly lived for one short year. Emily, born in 1892, thrived followed in 1893 by Florence but Johann and Clara accepted their lot with stoicism as other families fared no better. They took solace in the continued good health of John, Philip and Clara. The loss of children was common whether the parents were princes or paupers. Another boy, Charles, was born in 1895 and did not live to be one-year-old then Beatrice arrived in 1897, announcing her arrival with her powerful lungs, as robust as her sisters. Clara's last child was born in Christmas of the same year, 1897 when Clara was thirty-eight years old but May died, aged two, from cholera.

Johann and Clara wrapped their remaining children in love and cherished all six of them. Some grief-stricken families found comfort by attending Mass or Chapel, three times on Sundays while others cursed the Almighty and abandoned attending services completely.

Life at their new home was one of contentment. The vegetable garden at the rear of the barber's shop was Johann's pride and joy and the family soon made many new customers who became friends. The two boys, John and Philip, were enrolled in the school recently built in Heath Street and Clara was busy at home with their precious new baby, Beatrice. The family enjoyed the social life of the town community. The local annual show was always well attended where the keen gardeners showed their prize vegetables, wives baked cakes and made preserves, skilled knitters and needlewomen made garments hoping to pick up prizes and even the children showed off skills in drawing, writing poems and model making.

Every year May Day was celebrated with the townsfolk making their way to the common where a maypole was erected. A fairground was set up with swing boats, hoopla stalls and a coconut shy to entertain youngsters and old folk alike. For refreshment there was a tent serving beer and soft drinks and stalls offering sweets and confectionary were very popular. When the lucky girl who had been chosen to be 'Queen of the May' was crowned, her attendants would be transported around the field on a beautifully decorated cart drawn by the shire horses from the local brewery. At the maypole, excited children danced their ribbons into an intricate plaited pattern until the pole was covered then the dancers took the ribbons in their other hands and reversed the dance until the ribbons were free once more.

Proud members of the local brass band, with their instruments gleaming in the sunshine, played popular music with an occasional well-known hymn to pacify the local clergymen. At the end of an exhausting but happy day, the revellers slowly made their way home carrying sleeping babies with the older children following slowly behind, struggling with baskets full of their purchases. The fairground travellers were already packing up ready to move on to other fairs.

***

John and Philip helped their father with his garden and between them they built a pigsty at the bottom of the plot where a rear gate led out into the lane running behind the houses. Chickens clucked in contentment from the safety of their wire enclosure which served to keep them safe from predators and to ensure they did not escape into the vegetables. Clara tended the rows of vegetables and taught her younger sisters how to collect the eggs from the laying boxes and carry them carefully in their aprons back to the kitchen. They enjoyed feeding the hens but when asked to weed between the carrots, onions and potatoes would often find a caterpillar to distract them or squeal with delight if they found a spider's web glistening with dew in the early morning sunshine. Johann loved sharing his gardening skills with his growing family and by the time John was working as a railway porter and Philip had left school to train as a barber, the girls were all well accomplished in the duties of their two brothers. Clara proved to be a keen seamstress and as she had helped her mother, Clara, make clothes for her siblings she too had no difficulty finding work at a local haberdashers where she did alterations for customers. The family thrived, the business grew and Johann seldom thought of his home in Bavaria. However, life was about to change once more for him.

CHAPTER THIRTEEN
WAR IN EUROPE

By 1914 Johann's business provided a comfortable living for the Nicklas family. The two boys were now married men with families. John and Sarah, his wife, had a son aged nine, named Alexander. Philip's wife was Lydia, their son was four-year-old John William Thomas (known as Bill when he was older).

Throughout the year, the newspapers had printed disturbing articles about an imminent war with Germany. When his sons tried to discuss the possibility of war, Johann would not listen.

"Why would we fight one another? What is there to gain from conflict? No, the politicians, the two kings will surely never allow it to happen."

"It is talked about in the ale houses, father."

John wore the expression of a fearful man. He had not told his father how some of the locals who knew that Johann was from Germany were muttering about him and threatening to make his life difficult should war break out.

"The ale houses? Am I to believe every bit of nonsense spoken when men are no longer sober? My customers have said nothing to me of fearing war."

Philip replied,

"Father, we have our faithful regular customers who I have known all my life but the new incomers, some of them no more than ill-educated troublemakers, are trying to stir up hatred against us. We were reluctant to tell you but one evening John and I were enjoying a beer when an angry mob threatened us."

"Words. Just words, that's all. You see, it will all be forgotten by Christmas."

Two weeks passed and John and Philip were enjoying an end of week drink when the same angry mob as before became aggressive so the two brothers left their pints and headed for home. However, they were followed and when they arrived at their father's shop one of the noisy pursuers began shouting.

"Go back to where you came from you filthy Hun, we don't want your sort here."

This was taken up by the others in the gang. Then the one who had shouted first picked up a stone from the road and hurled it at the shop window. The crash of broken glass sent the crowd fleeing in all directions and the upstairs window was thrown open by Johann who spotted his sons about to give chase.

"John! Philip! Back here and explain, now! What was all that commotion about?"

John grabbed Philip's arm as he was about to follow the troublemakers.

He shouted back to his father,

"Get back to bed, father, we can handle it, don't you worry yourself. Let us in and we will secure this broken window for you."

When they were inside they fetched some wood from the shed and made a temporary repair to the window. As they worked, they talked.

"You do know the government is now recruiting for the army, don't you? War is more than a possibility now, it is a certainty. If me and you, Philip, were to enlist this coming week as volunteers, those cretins will see which of us is a real man. What d'you say, brother?"

Philip studied his brother's face before replying.

"I can see you mean what you say, you're not just rising to the bait. If we get first in line at the recruiting office in Warrington, we will show how British we are. Mother and father will be proud of us too, and it should keep them safe."

They shouted up the stairs to tell their parents all was safe and they were off to their beds.

As Philip climbed into bed alongside Lydia, she stirred and asked if he had had a good night.

"After a fashion, yes. Go back to sleep, dearest, we don't want to wake the boy."

Next morning after his breakfast, he left the house at his usual time but instead of going to the barber's shop he called round for John and the two men caught a train for Warrington.

When they found the army recruiting office a queue had already formed. Although most of Britain had believed war would never happen when it became a certainty, men of all ages and class demonstrated their patriotism by enlisting. Philip was ahead of John in the queue and was soon called for questioning.

The officer finished what he was writing then raised his head as Philip stood nervously in front of the desk.

"Name?"

"Philip Nicklas – spelt n i c k l a s, sir."

The officer looked up at him but said nothing.

"Nationality?"

"British, sir."

"Age?"

"Thirty, sir."

"Profession?"

"Barber, sir."

"Join the line for the doctor. Next!"

Philip passed the medical and the eyesight test then joined a line of men waiting for a sergeant to group them into a dozen at a time for the recruiting officers to rush them through their oath of allegiance. Each man spoke his own name then the oath was taken all together.

I do make Oath, that I will be faithful and bear true Allegiance to His Majesty King George the Fifth, His Heirs, and Successors, and that I will, as in duty bound, honestly and faithfully defend His Majesty, His Heirs, and Successors, in Person, Crown and Dignity, against all enemies, and will observe and obey all orders of His Majesty, His Heirs and Successors, and of the Generals and Officers set over me. So help me God.

Relieved to have been accepted, Philip winked at his brother who was still being questioned. He turned to chat to another recruit when he felt John tugging at his sleeve and looking agitated.

"They won't take me, Philip! Because I work on the railway he said it is a protected industry, vital to the smooth running of the country in time of war! So brother, you will have to go without me."

The brothers left the recruiting office discussing the outcome of their interviews and as they passed men still in the queue, they recognised two of their assailants from the night of the attack on their father's shop.

One of the men nodded approval to Philip and held out his hand for a conciliatory greeting. At first Philip was reluctant to take the man's hand but John whispered, "Think of Dad, make things right for him, eh?"

Philip obliged, the four men smiled and nodded then John and Philip headed home to see their parents.

Johann sat in silence as his two sons told him their news. He bowed his head to hide his feelings but Clara cried inconsolably. Eventually she wiped her tears on her pinafore and sniffed and looked from one son to the other.

"So, one to go and one to stay is it? Well, the Lord be praised for small mercies. What the war is for I'm sure I don't know. Why can't we all just live in peace? Your father had his fill of war in France."

Johann looked up, eyes filled with unshed tears.

"John. I am truly thankful you are not to be a soldier, I really am. Philip, I only wish you had gone down the mines now instead of taking up my trade as a barber then you too might have been excused. We could have had you both safe at home with us. Oh, the futility of war. Will the powers that be never learn? May it be short and swift."

Clara asked, "Do Sarah and Lydia know where you went this morning?"

"No mother, we should go now to tell them. We saw some of the crowd from last night waiting to enlist so they know now that Nicklas men do not shirk their duty."

Clara hugged Philip and promised to pray for him every day he would be away.

"And you, John, be thankful you must stay behind. One fighting man in the family is one too many."

Johann stood up, suddenly looking frail and older than his years.

"God be with you, son, I just hope you have a better war than I had. When do you leave for training camp?"

"They gave me three days to do anything I need to do then we will be off to the barracks at Warrington where we will board trucks to take us to a new training camp out in the countryside."

"What about your uniform? Do you get that in Warrington?"

"The officer just told us we would be issued with our uniforms in due course; that could mean days or weeks I suppose. Right, must be off to tell Lydia and young William. You coming, John?"

"Aye, I'll walk with you. I imagine Sarah will be relieved I shall be going nowhere but I feel bad we can't be together, I'll miss out on all the fun!"

Johann's face flushed with anger.

"Hear this my boy, war is not fun at all. Be glad you will not be killing or maiming boys who could be related to you, strangers with lives and wives of their own. As for you, Philip, we will pray the war is short and by Christmas, God willing, it could be all over."

He hugged his son.

"Come home safe and sound boy, we will pray for you every day. Be sure to follow instructions, use the training they give you wisely and stay out of trouble."

He turned to John and shook his hand.

"You, John, will be needed here to look after your mother and me so don't go wishing you were in foreign parts. Now off you go."

Clara hugged Philip again and swept the hair from his face as she had done for as long as he could remember.

"Goodbye my lovely boy, I will count the days until you return."

Philip pulled away gently, wiping tears from his cheek which might have been his mother's or his own.

"I will write when I can, look after Dad. I will be back being a barber again before you know it."

Johann sat down heavily, his chest heaving from breathlessness and emotion.

"Well then, we will say our goodbyes when the day comes. May your enemies be my friends and friendly with it. Now away and tell Lydia."

Clara noticed her husband's grey pallor and was concerned for his health.

"You do realise that Philip enlisted to save you, his father, from being interned as an alien because you have never been naturalised as a British citizen. Johann, he did it to save the business for you. He is afraid that the next time men with strong anti-German feelings will turn up even nastier. We must be pray that his enlisting in the army will keep the local thugs away from our door."

Clara walked to the door with her sons and watched them until they reached the street corner where they turned to wave and disappeared from view.

***

Lydia was becoming worried at Philip's absence. He had left quietly that morning before she was awake. As she assumed he had gone to the barber's shop she had only started to worry when he failed to arrive home at his usual time which came and went with neither sight nor sound of him. She peered out of the net curtains hanging in the parlour, hushed William when he broke into song and remembered the report from one of her neighbours that the barber's shop had been attacked. Philip had made light of it, told her it was just drunken men doing what drunks do on a Saturday night. She moved the pan of stew from the hob and set it on a trivet to keep warm. The table was laid for tea and she could see that William was patiently waiting to eat. As she busied herself dusting, yet again she thought fondly of how she and Philip had met. At the time she lived in Wallasey and she and her friend Rebecca had gone down to the pier one Sunday. Philip had been on a charabanc excursion to New Brighton with some of his pals when he spotted Lydia as she strolled past them, her arm linked through Rebecca's. The girls smiled at the boys and soon they had been chatting away as young people do. Lydia recalled Philip's shy attempt at a kiss and how he promised to visit Wallasey regularly. They had courted briefly before marrying in Wallasey in 1910 then settling in Golborne.

CHAPTER FOURTEEN

The hands on the mantle clock seemed to have stopped but when Lydia put her ear to it, the gentle ticking assured her the clock was working. She paced the floor, trying not to worry young William by pretending to dust the furniture. When she heard the front door close she stood still but as Philip entered the kitchen, she hid her anxiety by demanding to know how he was so late. Her husband had expected this homecoming to be awkward and he turned his cap in his hand in the manner of a youth caught misbehaving. Young William glanced from one parent to the other, his Mam and Dad seldom had cross words but his grumbling, empty stomach offered a reason for his Mam's anger. She too must be hungry.

"Where have you been out so late? I have been worried sick wondering what harm might have befallen you. Teatime was ages ago and we have waited to eat with you."

She swung the pot back over the fire to heat it again.

"Lydia my love, and you, young William, sit down I have something important to tell you."

Lydia and the boy sat at the table, Lydia still fidgety, began to sweep imaginary crumbs from the tablecloth.

"Now that war between Great Britain and Germany has been declared the government are in need of recruits, they need soldiers, lots of soldiers."

Lydia waited for him to continue, her heart beating faster as she guessed what it was he was about to tell her.

"This morning, instead of going to the shop, I met up with our John and we caught the train to Warrington to enlist."

"What? Both of you? Your poor Mam and Dad, what will they do without you both? The shop needs you and William's got his job on the railway, what will poor Sarah do?"

Philip interrupted her.

"No, it's not as bad as it seems, they only took one of us."

Lydia leapt from her chair and threw her arms around her husband's neck in relief.

"Oh merciful God, they took John but not you? Still, hard on Sarah and Alexander, but we can take care of them, can't we?"

"No love, you've got it all wrong. John was told that because he works on the railway which serves the coal mines he is in a reserved occupation. The coal is vital to the war effort, it is crucial all the steam engines in ships and factories have a plentiful supply of coal so it is me who is off to war. I am the chosen one, not John."

Lydia was shocked and shouted,

"You say that as if you have been blessed! That's not how I see it!"

She turned away and busied herself filling the bowls with stew and setting them down on the table.

"Sit down, eat it while it is hot."

Philip stuffed his cap into his pocket, removed his jacket and went into the scullery to wash his hands. As he took his place at the table he smiled at his son who was eating his long-awaited tea. Lydia sat, grim-faced and pushed the food around her dish without tasting it.

"So, what now? How soon before you leave us?"

Philip swallowed a mouthful of the delicious stew before answering,

"I must return to Warrington in three days' time and we will be taken to training camp somewhere out in the country I think. I will write and let you know as soon as we know ourselves."

Lydia threw down her knife and fork.

"Three days? That soon? Then when will we see you again?"

She began sobbing.

Philip stood and put his arms around her.

"Hush, my love, we get a week's leave before we leave for France, don't distress yourself."

Lydia dried her eyes.

"What will your father think, his boy fighting his fellow Germans?"

Philip sat down again to continue eating. Young William had already emptied his bowl and was waiting patiently to see if there would be a second helping.

"Me and John have already broken the news to Mam and Dad. Well, as you would expect, they are both in shock but when I explained to them it was for their own good, I think they understood."

"What do you mean, for their own good?"

"Don't forget my love, Dad is a Bavarian, which means he is German and there is already a lot of bad feeling towards the so-called 'Hun'. The fact that he has lived here since 1871 matters little to some folk who just see a German name or hear a German accent and get mean."

"So the broken window we talked about was more serious than you let on, is that it?"

"Well, it could get a lot more serious but some of those men who did the damage saw me and John enlisting and indeed they shook our hands in recognition of our patriotism. Our John will be around to ensure Mam and Dad's safety which makes me feel easier."

They ate in silence until William spoke.

"Daddy, will you be a soldier then, in a soldier's uniform?"

Philip wiped his dish clean with a chunk of bread and sat back in his chair, his meal finished.

"Yes son, I have joined the South Lancashire Regiment, and I am a Prince of Wales Volunteer."

"And will you have a gun Daddy?"

William's eyes were wide with wonder.

"I suppose so, but not straight away. When I come home on leave we must get a family photograph taken, perhaps Mummy will arrange for that, eh love?"

Lydia nodded, too choked to speak. Philip was going to war.

***

325

Three days later Philip woke early. His few belongings had been packed neatly into his kitbag the evening before by Lydia. Breakfast was a quiet meal, William and Philip ate well as always but Lydia pushed her plate away, her boiled egg half eaten and her toast untouched. Philip refrained from commenting, emotions were at breaking point. They had decided before bedtime the previous day that Philip would go unaccompanied to the station and they would say their goodbyes in the privacy of their own home. Lydia was relieved, she was afraid she would not be able to keep her feelings in check and dreaded the thought of crying in public. She had broken down when they had visited Johann's parents the day before. Her ability to keep a stiff upper lip had been tried too far. Philip finished eating and rose from the table. William was still dipping his toast soldiers in his egg so his father bent to kiss his cheek and ruffled his hair.

"You must mind Mummy now, William, help her around the house and be very well behaved for her, promise me?"

William nodded his head, the gravity of the situation was not felt by the young boy.

"I will go to school Daddy while you are away. I will be learning, same as you."

Philip and Lydia exchanged glances and smiled.

"Of course! Perhaps you will learn to write and you can send me letters or even drawings, that would please Daddy."

The boy nodded again and wiped egg-yolk from his chin with the back of his hand.

This gave Lydia the excuse to fetch a cloth from the scullery to clean his face. She was able to wipe away her tears before returning with a weak smile at her husband.

"Right, I will be off then, I am meeting John who offered to see me onto the train on behalf of you all."

He took Lydia into his arms and kissed her tenderly. She hung onto him until he had to take her arms from around his waist then he put his cap on, hoisted his bag onto his shoulder and hugged his son before leaving the house with a last slam of the door. Young William watched, puzzled, as his mother sank back into her chair and with her head on her arms cried all the tears she had fought so hard not to shed.

***

At the station, John turned to Philip.

"Just as well Lydia and young William didn't come, look at the crowds!"

The platform was packed with tearful wives, mothers and sweethearts, all there to send their loved ones off to a war they knew very little about. There was an air of patriotism, with children flying Union Jacks and a local band played stirring hymns and popular tunes. Fathers patted the shoulders of their departing sons, many of them close to tears.

The young recruits were flushed with excitement and fear in equal portions but managed to maintain a carefree demeanour in front of their peers.

The train stood waiting, steam issuing from the funnel, hissing impatiently while the fire was stoked by the fireman. The engine driver glanced out of his cab to watch the porters as they checked and shut all the doors after the troops had hastily climbed into the carriages. Each door window had been lowered to allow for final brief kisses, prolonged handshakes and hasty goodbyes to be exchanged then the steam whistle blew urgently, smoke swirled around the station platform and the driver pulled on the whistle again signifying the train's imminent departure. As the wheels slipped, the crowd watched the train pull slowly from the station, nobody leaving until it was out of sight.

John joined the throng as they all headed home, the sound of sobbing mingled with the sombre exchanges of the families and friends of the troops now off to training camp.

CHAPTER FIFTEEN

At Warrington the new recruits were assembled in the barracks and a sergeant did a roll call to satisfy the officers all the men had arrived. After a break for refreshment and latrine visits, the young soldiers were head-counted once again into the waiting trucks for transport to Heaton Park, Manchester, where their basic training would begin.

The gated entrance to the camp was guarded by two sentries who emerged from their sentry box when they heard the trucks pull up. Philip admired the smartness of the uniforms. Brass buttons gleamed against the khaki tunics and so did their cap badges. Their belts had been khaki-blanco'd and boots were highly polished while puttees were tightly wound around their legs. He promised himself that he would strive to be well turned out in his uniform so that Lydia and young William would be proud to be seen with him.

The new recruits were impressed to find a tented city, rows and rows of white bell tents, each one to house six men. The officers had them line up to be assigned to a numbered tent, then they were marched between rows of tents until the sergeant called,

"Halt. Now you lot, when I tell you to fall out, it is six to a tent and your bedding is a palliasse which you will find inside your tent which you will take to fill with straw at the barn near the entrance, understood?"

The men nodded their heads, hoping someone amongst them knew what the sergeant was talking about.

"When you have done that you will fall in ready to be introduced to Company Sergeant Major Cross, cross by name and cross by nature, so don't run foul of him or by God you will wish you were in France already fighting the bloody Hun, believe you me."

Philip found himself with two other men from Golborne, customers of his father's barber shop. The other three were familiar but not known to him personally. Inside their tent they introduced themselves. Bob Hooper and Victor Gibson knew Philip and patted him on the back.

"Good lad, joining up. We all did wonder about your family, you know."

Philip replied, "I was almost first in the queue, my dad knew nawt about it until I got back to the shop. Our John tried too, but his railway job is necessary to the war work he was told so here I am on my own."

The other three listened, curious to know what was being talked about. Philip turned to them to explain.

"My name is Philip Nicklas, and just so's you know, that's a German name. My Dad came here after fighting for Germany against France so let's see, 1871 to 1914 – forty-three years he's been here and settled happily in Golborne where he has a barber's shop. Bob and Victor here are customers, know us well."

Two of the other men shook his hand and introduced themselves.

"I saw you at the recruiting office, I'm Joe Wilson, farmer's boy, luckily number two son as my older brother is same as yours, 'vital for the war' he was told."

"Francis Kelly, call me Frank. Originally from Ireland so I know what it's like being foreign."

He laughed.

"Not too foreign to fight though, eh?"

Philip smiled then turned to the last man who had stood back, a grim expression on his face.

"And what do we call you?"

"For the sake of the others I'll tell you. But if you think I will shake the hand of a Hun, think again. Charlie Proctor, that's me, ready to fight for my own folk so who will you be fighting for, eh?"

"That's a bit strong, Charlie. He's like me, fighting for his country, same as you. Give it a rest, we all know Germans are the enemy but not this lad."

Frank waited for an apology but none was coming.

Charlie held his hand out to Bob and Victor. They grudgingly shook it and shrugged as they saw Philip turn his back on them all and bent to collect his palliasse from the pile.

Just then the sergeant drew aside the tent flaps and entered.

"Not ready for inspection yet I see? Hen's teeth, three months won't be long enough to get you lazy rabble ready for service. Right, get your beds stuffed, get back here at the double then bedding down, blankets folded neatly, kitbags stowed on your left, boots on your right. Tomorrow we will get you kitted out with uniforms. The cooks are preparing supper so come to the cookhouse for food when you hear the bugler. At all times stay in groups of six until we tell you otherwise. Any complaints?"

He had sensed the atmosphere was strained so he waited for an answer.

Frank spoke for them.

"None sir, just getting to know each other's names that's all."

Sergeant Harold Owen looked at each man to be sure then left the tent as quickly as he had entered it. They heard him going through the same drill with the next tent. When they returned from stuffing straw into their palliasses under the watchful eye of the Quartermaster, they set their gear out as instructed except for their boots and waited for further orders.

Philip had spent an uncomfortable night on the straw-filled bed. The blanket was thin and the snoring of the other men made it difficult to fall asleep. The enormity of his present situation prayed on his mind as he thought of his young wife and son, also the danger his parents might encounter. When he eventually fell asleep, it seemed like only minutes later the bugler was sounding reveille. The other men in the tent stirred, yawned and threw back their blankets, grumbling at the early hour. They dressed quickly and tidied the tent ready for inspection then joined a queue of soldiers waiting patiently for a welcome mug of tea. They had barely time to drink it before Sergeant Owen appeared and barked orders at them to fall in on the parade ground in double quick time for exercises. As the men had been enlisted from all walks of life, not all were used to such physical exertion and puffed and panted until they were red in the face, flinching at the derogatory insults hurled at them by the sergeant. At his order to stand at ease, their relief was obvious to him as he strode up and down, his back erect and his uniform immaculate.

"Right, you lot of nancy boys, it looks like we have a deal of work to get you ready for soldiering. This morning, however, you must report to the Quartermaster's stores where you will be issued with your uniforms, on receipt of which you will return to your tents and be back here dressed as the fighting men we intend to turn you into. Before that you will be pleased to know, breakfast is served in the mess. Dismissed."

He strode off to get his own breakfast in the Sergeants' mess while Bob Hooper led the other five men at a run in the direction of another growing queue of hungry, impatient men.

"Thank God for that, my belly was beginning to think I had fallen out with it. I'm fair starving."

Victor ran alongside Philip.

"Do you smell bacon? Just fancy bacon and egg and a large fried slice, eh?"

A cook was standing behind a trestle table on which stood a large pan of bubbling porridge. He dealt it out with a ladle, splattering the men with it as it hit the dishes and ignoring their protests, he indicated with his head to them to move along to the next cook standing with a tray of toast. Two slices were issued to each man who then collected a mug of tea before finding a place at a table on which were large tins of jam.

Philip sat with Joe to his left and one space to his right for Charlie who was just getting his tea. When he approached the others already seated he looked at the empty place and his face could not disguise his displeasure. Without a word, he turned on his heel and headed for a different table.

"What's that all about?"

Victor looked to his fellow men for an explanation.

"Ah, that will be my fault."

Philip spoke between mouthfuls of porridge.

331

"He thinks I am his enemy. Just wait until he meets the real enemy, that's all I can say."

"The man's an idiot! Has he never met a German before?"

"Well, I'm born and bred in Lancashire so strictly speaking I'm only German by name. My whole family are English but for my father as you two know."

He turned to Bob and Victor who both nodded assent.

"My father had enough of war with France and chose to settle here in England. My mother, my brother and my sisters are all proud to be English, same as me. I enlisted as a patriot but if Charlie can't accept me, I for one will give him a wide berth so as not to cause any trouble between us."

"Good on you. We'll not encourage him in his bigotry, let him see for himself how wrong he is."

Frank bit into his toast and took a swig of tea.

Victor wiped the crumbs from his chin and looked around.

"Not exactly the Ritz, boys, but can't be choosy. As long as we get enough to fill our bellies each day I won't be complaining."

Joe had finished his porridge and was enjoying his tea and toast. Bob turned to him and said, "Said you were a farm boy? This food should be home from home eh? I worked in a bank until my mother and sister persuaded me to enlist. Right now they will be enjoying bacon and eggs no doubt followed by toast with marmalade or honey. Lucky them."

The sergeant reappeared, shooting a puzzled look at Charlie, sitting alone. He made a mental note to watch that one, he smelt trouble.

"Not finished yet? Get your arses off those benches and get yourselves over to the Quartermaster for uniforms. Follow me."

He marched quickly away as the six men scrambled to fall in behind him.

At the Quartermaster's stores, corporals were measuring men and sending them to where the uniforms were stacked in piles according to the size. Each man was issued with two khaki tunics and trousers, webbing belts, undergarments, boots, putties and socks. Once their arms were full, they stood in line to have a cap slapped on their heads then they were ordered to return to their tents and get changed.

"Then back to the drill yard at the double where your training will begin in earnest."

Sergeant Owen marched away, accompanied by the two corporals.

Philip changed into his uniform and was lacing his boots when a voice outside the tent shouted, "South Lancs. Let's be having you, you lazy bastards. Fall in outside at the double now and I mean now!"

"Jesus," said Joe. "This must be him!"

Men scrambled from twelve tents to stand at attention at the sight of Sergeant Major Cross waving his pace stick accompanied by two corporals.

All the recruits had changed from their civilian clothes into uniforms and marched to the drill yard where they stood to attention in neat rows. The Sergeant Major walked up and down the rows, frowning. On his tunic sleeves shone brass crowns, denoting his rank. He stopped in front of random men, filling them with dread as he studied them from cap to boots. When he had inspected the men, he stood before them and finally spoke.

"Now, you horrible rabble, you want to be soldiers and fight the Hun do you, well I will tell you now not to believe what you hear about the war being over by Christmas. People who think that are deluding themselves. I have served in the army for twenty-one years, in India then in South Africa where we fought the bloody Boers. I saw many good men killed and maimed. War is no bloody picnic. If the young women who feel it is their duty to present any man they see of fighting age with a white feather, denoting cowardice, could see for themselves the carnage of battle, they would weep at their own ignorance."

He studied his feet before continuing.

"I had left the army in 1911, had a nice pub in the country and was enjoying a quiet life when these bloody Huns decided to kick off and I was recalled for service once again. I am determined to make soldiers out of you lot, good ones at that, and when I am finished you will be ready to go to France or wherever you get posted and start killing the bastards."

He turned and pointed his pace stick at Sergeant Owen.

"The sergeant, here, and the corporals will be your squad leaders. Each tent will have a corporal or lance corporal who will be your section leaders. They will show you how to wear your uniform correctly, how to wind your puttees so you don't look like some Egyptian mummy, and how to get a shine on your boots so I can see my face in them. You will be instructed how to lay your kit out for inspection when I come round accompanied by your Lieutenant, Hough-Smith. He is still wet behind the ears, fresh out of public school but he is a superior officer so watch your p's and q's.

"Reveille is at 0530, you will parade in squad order then march to the cookhouse for your breakfast after which you will be shown how to make up your kit in military fashion, no mummy dear to do your beds for you. Then at 0800, I will carry out my inspection and God help any man whose kit is not up to scratch."

He held his pace stick in both hands before roaring,

"Company, fall out."

CHAPTER SIXTEEN

The weeks passed with constant squad drill, learning to march, form fours and turn, also musketry and physical drill with lectures. By the third week they did night work training, in the fourth week route marching and the fifth week did outposts practice.

Over the twelve-week training course they also covered entrenching, bayonet fighting, platoon drill and more lectures.

Woe betide any man who didn't come up to scratch. Sergeant Major Cross never missed a thing; a brass buckle that wasn't polished at the back as well as the front ended up with the poor victim running around the parade ground with full pack and holding his Lee Enfield rifle above his head for an hour. The recruits were told only once and very few made the mistake of not conforming to any orders issued. The result was the men were becoming real soldiers and learning to obey orders and take a pride in themselves.

Lieutenant Hough –Smith did seem like a schoolboy in uniform and totally in awe of the Sergeant Major, hanging on his every word with a 'yes, sergeant major, if you say so, I respect your judgement in these matters'.

To which Cross replied with a wink at Owen, "Very good, sir, if you say so, sir."

It was announced that at last they would do some shooting with the rifles they had cleaned, oiled and polished for weeks just to do rifle drill - sloping arms, presenting arms and royal salutes along with bayonet practice which involved lunging at straw filled sacks. When a poor lad got his bayonet stuck, the Sergeant Major grabbed his rifle from him, put his boot on the sack and pulled the bayonet out. Yelling at the men to stop and assemble around him he said,

"This is a Lee Enfield 303 rifle. It has a magazine holding five rounds and one up the spout but if you can kill the bastards with your 18-inch bayonet do so but do not get the bloody thing stuck in the Hun like Jenkins here! If it won't pull out then put your foot on the bugger and if that don't work pull the bloody trigger, that will blow it out! That way you can deal with the next one that's coming for you!"

Sergeant Major Cross continued,

"In the morning you will be going to the butts: after parade each man will draw thirty rounds of ammunition from the Quartermaster and you will be marched to the range two miles away."

The men were excited the next day when after the brisk march, they were detailed off into their respective squads ready for shooting practice. The sergeant explained again,

"This is the Lee Enfield 303 which I have already told you has five rounds in the magazine and you will have one in the breech in battle. Now load and make sure your safety catch is on."

The men took a clip of five rounds out of their ammunition pouches and loaded their magazines.

"Right you boys" Sergeant Owen said, directing Philip's group.

"Lie down in the firing position, the target will come up for thirty seconds, set your sights to two hundred and fifty yards and when you take aim, deep breath, hold it steady and fire. Now, let's see what kind of soldiers we have here."

The targets were wound up and the command 'fire at will' was given. Philip couldn't believe the bang after he pulled the trigger. The recoil was like being kicked in the shoulder by a mule. No pointer went to the target; in fact, only one boy from the group hit his target and that was Joe Wilson, the farmer's son who had done plenty of shooting on the farm. There was a roar from Sergeant Major Cross.

"Those bloody Huns are going to love you lot firing away at them, missing all the bleeding time while they pick you off like sitting ducks. You, Nicklas, I'll show you how to shoot."

He took Philip's gun, laid prone on the ground, his right leg straight with his body and his left leg at about forty degrees.

"Watch carefully you lot, this is how you shoot. You don't pull the bloody trigger, you squeeze it gently! Pull the rifle into your shoulder, that way you won't suffer the effects of the recoil so much."

The Sergeant Major held the rifle to his shoulder, squeezed the trigger and the gun cracked; he pulled the bolt back, ejecting the cartridge case and then cracked again and again until the remaining four rounds that were left in Philip's magazine were gone. The pointer went up to the bull to find four bulls. With that the Sergeant Major got up, threw Philip his rifle shouting, "Don't drop it, laddie! There, four bulls that was expected of a British soldier in the Shropshire Light Infantry when I was shooting at those Dutch German bastards the Boers in Africa. Otherwise it would be you copped it not them! It's the same now, kill or be killed, so show me what you are made of!"

After recruit training, the men were to begin collective training but in the case of Philip's squad and one other they were summoned by their Lieutenant with the Sergeant Major for new orders. Lieutenant Hough-Smith and Sergeant Major Cross had been so impressed with the speed at which the twelve men had performed they did not hesitate to put them forward for immediate posting overseas where more men were already desperately needed. They were given a one week pass to visit their families before they sailed for France.

***

When Philip arrived back in Golborne, he was physically so much fitter from all the training that the walk from the station took much less time than he was used to. As he approached his house he could see the net curtains were pulled aside and Lydia's anxious face peered out, searching for a sight of her husband. He waved to her and ran the last few steps. The door was flung open wide and an excited young William shot from behind his mother's legs and threw himself into his father's outstretched arms.

Lydia stood in the doorway with a big smile on her face and rosy cheeks.

"William, my boy, you have grown already in just three months!"

Philip lowered him to the ground and hugged his wife with William holding on to his leg.

"Come in, both of you, it's parky out here and we have a roaring fire in the kitchen. Anyway, what will the neighbours think!"

Lydia was always shy of showing her feelings in public but once they were inside and the door shut on the outside world, she wrapped her arms around Philip's neck and kissed him passionately.

"Oh, we have missed you so much, it is good to have you home again."

"I have a whole week off to make up for being away."

He pulled his kitbag off his shoulder and went into the kitchen.

"Daddy, you are a real soldier now! Can I try your cap on please?"

Philip placed his cap on his young son's head where it fell down over his eyes and caused his parents to laugh. William pushed it back on his head hoping his ears would hold it in place but he giggled as it fell down once more so he took it off.

"What a handsome soldier you have become, Philip, you fill out your uniform well. Now, sit down while I check the dinner."

He sat on his rocking chair beside the range and looked around the familiar room, thoughts of which had filled many of the hours of training or resting at camp. The flames shone on the brass fire irons and the trivet with the kettle keeping warm for tea later. The table was set for three and a smell of baking reminded him he was hungry.

"What is that you are cooking? It isn't one of your lovely pies is it?"

Lydia smiled

"Rabbit pie, one of your favourites. With mashed potatoes and leeks from the garden and some chutney I made from the windfalls. Then for afters, an apple cake."

"Well, William, have you had any part in this cooking?"

His son climbed on his knee and his father rocked as they talked.

"I gathered the apples, daddy, and pulled the leeks. Uncle John gave the rabbit to mummy 'cos he said you like it."

"To the table you two, dinner's ready."

Lydia set the pie on the table and began to cut and serve it. She handed their plates to them and they helped themselves to the vegetables from the dishes used only for special occasions.

"Mmmm, this beats the cookhouse food which is filling but nowhere near as tasty. As usual, Lydia, you have made your husband so grateful to have such a good cook for a wife. What d'you say, William? Isn't mummy clever?"

William could only nod his head in answer as he had a mouthful of dinner.

After the apple cake, Philip undid the top button of his trousers and sat back in his chair.

"By gum, that was good! I could not eat another mouthful."

"Well you sit there and I'll do the pots. Maybe you have one of your stories you used to tell William before his bedtime?"

The boy's face shone with enthusiasm.

"Oh, yes please, daddy, you tell such good stories."

Philip returned to the rocking chair but William sat on the fender stool facing his father.

Lydia busied herself in the scullery, listening contentedly to the story of the early bird and the worm which was a favourite of the boy. By the time she was satisfied everywhere was tidy, she undid her pinafore and returned to the kitchen where William was yawning and rubbing his eyes, the story told.

"I think it is past your bedtime, lovely boy. Kiss daddy goodnight and up the dancers with you."

William did not protest. He went before his mother up the stairs and was soon tucked in his cosy bed. Lydia drew his curtains, kissed him on his forehead and crept back downstairs to find Philip had nodded off. She gave a contented sigh and sat with just the sound of the wall clock ticking, making her feel sleepy. It had been a long day.

***

The week passed far too quickly for Philip and his family. He discussed his training with his father and brother and their reaction to his pride in being chosen for immediate deployment could not have been more different: his father was worried it was far too soon to send his son to the front, he had believed the normal training period of at least six months was barely enough. His memories of the war between Germany and France had never dimmed. John, on the other hand was proud of his younger brother and took him in a bear-hug while he congratulated him.

"Well done, our Philip! You can fight for the two of us being as you are such an excellent soldier, well done!"

Johann sighed.

"Well who would have thought that a son of mine would fight in France as I did but with my enemies against my countrymen. The world is such a puzzle…"

He too hugged Philip, reluctant to free him.

Clara said nothing, just smiled weakly at her son and nodded her head before retreating to the scullery where she wiped an unwanted tear from her eye.

Lydia had been torn between feeling proud of him and wanting to shout in anger at him for being so diligent in his efforts. To be rewarded for his excellent results with an early deployment was an anathema in her eyes. Young William was just sad his Daddy was going far away for a long time this time but he cheered up when Philip promised to send him stories for Lydia to read to him at bedtime.

Once again John saw his brother off on the train. He would meet his fellow soldiers back at the training ground from where they would be transported by train to Southampton for embarkation to France.

Philip's platoon was joined by soldiers from other regiments who had travelled on the same train and after lining up outside the station, they marched down to the harbour. As they passed through the Bargate in the centuries-old city walls which had stood as part of the defences for more than eight hundred years, the locals lined the street on both sides to show their support for all the young troops. Young women threw flowers in the path of the troops, waved and cheered until they marched out of sight to board the waiting ships.

The Army Service Corps was responsible for not only transporting the men but also ammunitions and supplies for the front including horses, carts, motorised vehicles and everything required by the troops in the trenches. A twin-funnelled vessel, 'Brighton' was laying alongside the quay with men from the ASC busy loading and stowing equipment and supplies. The number of soldiers waiting patiently to go aboard swelled to two thousand or more but eventually they were climbing the gangways, excited to be on their way at last.

Joe Wilson was alongside Philip.

"I just heard some lads saying there might be submarines in the channel. I've never even been on a boat before but to be on one likely to be attacked scares the shit out of me."

Philip was about to answer when the Bosun of the 'Brighton' who had overheard the young lad's remark, patted him on the shoulder.

"Nowt to worry yourselves about boys, we make the crossing at night, escorted by two destroyers. This ship is only a couple of years old, her turbine engines give her a speed of twenty-two knots so we'll be there on the other side before you know it, take it from me."

And he hurried off to prepare for sailing.

A man wearing four gold bands on his sleeves was shouting through a megaphone from the bridge.

"That'll be the Captain, I'll bet."

Bob Hooper had joined Philip and Joe.

"All officers and crew to single up fore and aft and hold on to a forward back spring."

From the stern came a shout.

"All clear aft."

The sound of the telegraph bells rang out and from the propeller wash, they could see they had slowly begun to move. The stern started to move out from the quayside and the recruits watched in awe as the captain shouted from the bridge, "Let go forward!"

Once again they heard the response from the officer operating the telegraph, the inside propeller sent wash against the quayside and the ship was free, moving astern into open water.

Three sharp blasts of the ship's whistle made the recruits jump as 'Brighton' went rapidly astern until the telegraph rang again. The ship stopped briefly then white water kicked up from the stern. Anxious young men held on to anything within their grasp as the vessel shook and vibrated before moving ahead through the water, quickly gaining speed.

"What about that? I wish I'd joined the navy now."

Bob grinned and his eyes shone.

"Beats being a bank clerk any day!"

The young soldiers watched as the land was soon left behind.

"Look how far we have sailed already, the shore lights can barely be seen and the people gathered on the quayside waving look no bigger than ants."

Nearby, the other three men from their tent stood peering over the rails watching the wash, fascinated.

They waved at them and Victor Gibson and Frank Kelly waved back. Charlie Procter lifted his head but as he caught Philip waving to him, he turned his head and looked back at the sea.

Philip ignored the snub and turned his thought to Lydia and William. What tales he could tell his son when he returned home. If the rumours were true, it could all be over by Christmas.

CHAPTER SEVENTEEN

Evening was drawing in as they approached the coast of France. The Port of Le Havre was busy but the experienced captain of their ship skilfully manoeuvred them alongside, the engines set to go astern as she moved slowly alongside the quay. The soldiers heard the telegraph ring instructions down to the engine room and the noise of the engine ceased. The ship's crew sent the mooring lines ashore to secure the 'Brighton' fore and aft then the gangway was lowered in readiness for disembarkation. The newly-arrived troops stood with their packs on their backs and their rifles slung over their shoulders ready to land in France.

The South Lancashire section lads from Golborne shuffled forward, eager to join the throng of men already ashore.

Frank Kelly nudged Philip.

"Jesus, Mary and Joseph, will you look at all the ambulances! And see how many men are lacking arms by the look of their greatcoats. Poor bastards."

The motorised ambulances were lined up in convoy with horse-drawn vehicles all marked with a red cross, waiting to discharge the wounded men they had carried from the front. Stretcher bearers loaded up the worst of the wounded and carried them onto the deck of the 'Brighton' which was to return to Southampton as soon as all the wounded were aboard.

The new recruits saw the empty expressions on the faces of the casualties. None of them responded to any form of question or greeting but just turned away.

"Fuck! But everyone said we were winning the war!"

343

Philip stood in silence finding it difficult to take in the reality of war, so different from the patriotic fervour they had all felt. Somebody shoved him and growled, "Look what your lot are doing to our boys, happy now?"

Charlie Proctor was glaring at him, his eyes full of hate.

"Eh, watch it you, what's this uniform I'm wearing? Same as you mate and I'll be fighting twice as hard as you when the time comes, just you wait and see!"

He joined Bob and Frank who had witnessed the unfriendly exchange as they moved forward to disembark.

"That Charlie has a problem, be sure to take care when he is around, Phil."

Bob put himself between Charlie and Philip as they made their way down the gangway and soon felt land beneath their feet.

The gruff voice of Sergeant Major Cross carried over the noise of the assembled men.

"Men of the South Lancs, in orderly formation, four abreast, stand at attention. We are to march to the station in double quick time so when I give the order, quick march. You don't want to miss the train, lads, or you'll be marching all the way to the front. Ready? Left, turn, left, right, left, right, heads up, you're proud Lancashire boys, ready to take on the Hun."

Steam and smoke filled the station as the locomotives stood, hissing impatiently while the men climbed aboard. The young recruits of Philip's squad had been so proud when they had learned they were being fast-tracked to Belgium because they had been the best trainees. What they were to learn was that the fighting at Ypres had been so savage that their regiment had suffered severe losses and had called urgently for replacements. Some of these men who had survived the battle but had been badly injured were being disembarked on yet more stretchers waiting for the ambulances to return for them.

"Come on, South Lancs. Get on board as fast as you can, never mind looking at those lucky buggers, they're off home to their mothers and sweethearts. They've left the trenches all spick and span for you, ready for you to take on the Germans. We'll give them a taste of their own medicine, right lads?"

Sergeant Major Cross was last to climb aboard and the porter saw that all the troops were on the train, doors slammed shut and he blew his whistle for the train driver's attention.

Their destination was Poperinge, behind the front line and the closest town to the Ypres Salient, vital to the Allied troops for distribution of supplies, providing billeting for soldiers and a casualty clearing station.

The train slowed as they approached the station where waiting officers and NCOs stood in readiness for identifying their own regiment's replacement troops. Sergeant Major Cross leapt down from the train and found the commanding officer of the South Lancs. Regiment. He raised his hand and summoned his boys to follow him. Once the officer was satisfied he had the correct number of new men, they lined up behind other regiments ready to march through the town to join their regimental companions already billeted. It was dark as they marched smartly through the streets. The locals spilled out from their houses and young girls hung from the upstairs windows to cheer on these brave boys who had left the security of their homes back in Britain to fight for and alongside their own soldiers.

At tables outside cafes and bars, British officers sat drinking wine or cognac, relieved to be away from the trenches for a brief period of relaxation. The new recruits straightened their backs as their stature grew with renewed pride.

Outside the town was the holding area camp of wooden barrack huts and hastily erected tents to allow for the unexpected emergency arrival of new troops. A dozen or so field kitchens could be seen, their presence indicated by their smoking chimneys. As the men passed between the rows of tents, the smell from the huge cooking pots lifted their spirits. Cooks stirred the contents with heavy spoons and grinned at the recruits as they rubbed their stomachs in anticipation.

"I hope they've got enough for us, I'm bloody starving."

Victor licked his lips as he salivated.

Philip winked at him and was about to reply when the order to halt came from their Sergeant Major. They had arrived at one of the long wooden huts.

"Right men, you've fallen lucky, they have a hut empty and available just for you. None of you will be sleeping under canvas for tonight at least."

The squad gave a cheer of approval. After they had stowed their rifles and equipment alongside each allocated bed, the officer gave the order to fall in outside.

"Attention! Here come your officers."

A major and his lieutenant appeared and Sergeant Major Cross saluted.

"Men ready, sir!"

The officers returned his salute.

"Very good, Sergeant Major, stand them at ease."

The men obeyed instantly.

"Well men, I will introduce myself to you; I am Major George Hamilton and my fellow officer is Lieutenant Hough-Smith who you already know. From now on, you will be under our command with your Sergeant Major. You are now in Poperinge, but no doubt you will soon be calling it 'Pops' as all the lower ranks do. From here we will move on to Ypres where the battle is fierce and unrelenting. The men have their own name for Ypres as well, they call it 'Wipers' after the way it is spelt."

The men listened attentively.

"Tomorrow you will join the rest of the brigade for the march to the reserve trenches. You will be held there for a week or so before going on to the frontline trenches where you will finally get the opportunity to do what you have all been waiting for over the months of training – get to confront the Germans. We will be ready to start the move up to Ypres at 0700 hours tomorrow morning and once there, we will wait for nightfall before leaving for the Menin Gate. This being a walled town there are two gates we will pass through, the other being the Lille Gate. Hopefully our enemies will not be aware of our movements and so they will not announce their presence with a welcoming barrage from their artillery. However, occasionally, they fire sporadically in case we are on the move and in range."

Major Hamilton turned to Sergeant Major Cross.

"That's all for now, Sergeant Major. Fall the men out and see they get fed. Up for breakfast at 0500 hours and all ready to move by 0630 with full kit."

"Sergeant Major Cross saluted.

"Very good, sir."

He called the men to stand easy.

"So now you know where you're going tomorrow lads, let us get some vittles in you and then hopefully a good night's rest. Bugger, here comes the rain. Fall out!"

It had rained all night long so when morning came and the men were ready to move out, the ground was sodden and muddy. The platoon of forty-eight men was accompanied by pack horses carrying shovels, pickaxes, billhooks, saws and crowbars. These horses were followed by horse-drawn carts laden with the heavy weapons and ammunition, barrels of water and timber for essential repairs. The men would learn at the trenches how and when they would use these tools. The raw recruits were ready to march, rifles slung over their shoulders and packs on their backs.

At precisely seven in the morning, all the vehicles began to move followed by the troops to begin the eight-mile march to Ypres. To the watching Belgians it was obvious these were new recruits, their uniforms were still smart, their caps not yet shaped to the wearer's head and their boots still intact.

The mood of the men was jovial, they smiled at the Belgian civilians who waved to them as they marched past on their way out of town. As they got nearer to Ypres, the number of locals passing in the opposite direction dwindled. The cobbled streets of Ypres rang with the sound of marching men and the buildings looked deserted except for those taken over to billet the Allied officers. The old medieval part of town had been badly damaged and Cloth Hall, which had stood since the thirteenth century, had been set on fire by German incendiary shell fire. After the bustle of Poperinghe, Ypres seemed mostly free from civilians. Many of the townspeople had fled to the relative safety of 'Pops' In silence the men marched with a better understanding of the enormity of the war they were now part of.

When they arrived at the holding camp, their spirits lifted as they saw the welcome smoke from the field kitchens lined in a row. The men released themselves from their backpacks, stacked their rifles and joined the queue of hungry soldiers, mess tins and mugs in hand. Stew was the ideal meal to cook as once the meat and vegetables had been prepared they could all be cooked in the giant pot while the bread was kept warm in the ovens. An urn of strong tea sent wisps of tea-scented steam into the air, wetting the men's appetite even more.

After their hunger had been satisfied, the men collected their packs and weapons and the Sergeant Major introduced them to the reserve trenches where they would spend the night with the weary soldiers taking rest after an exhausting week on the front line. From this trench, the recruits would move up to the support trenches in readiness for their turn at the front. From now on the men would have lukewarm meals at best, cold mostly because the field kitchens were well away from the frontline as the smoke from their chimneys would give away the allied position to the enemy.

"Jesus, Mary and Joseph, I never expected this."

Frank looked down at his feet, barely remaining dry as the duckboards, which were in place to keep men's feet dry, were sinking into the mud.

Bob and Victor shook their heads, too overcome to speak. Charlie cursed.

"Fuck! Is this the best they can do! I've seen dogs with better shelter than this."

"Hang on, what's this?"

Philip had noticed a dugout in the side of the trench.

A soldier, wearing corporal's stripes, laughed nearby.

"You must be the new boys, eh? Just arrived? Well, that posh bit is for officers and NCOs only so you lot have to rough it, ok?"

The recruits looked up and down the trench.

"So where do we sleep, corporal?"

Philip's question was met with a hearty laugh.

"See where you are standing?"

Philip looked down at his feet and nodded.

"Well, you will be provided with a groundsheet, maybe if you're lucky a small tent and the duckboards serve as your bed, see?"

"What? Out here under the stars?"

Charlie frowned in disbelief.

"Out here, yes. Under the stars? Well, we've had so much rain I cannot remember the last time we saw stars. Not exactly the Hilton I know, but war is war and discomfort is something you are going to have to live with."

"Or die from," muttered a man to himself.

The corporal ignored the remark.

"Tomorrow prepare to move to the supply trenches but not until after dark. We pass through Hellfire Corner, so named because the Germans hold a good position from where their artillery constantly fires at anything that moves. If, however, we do need to move in daylight, we do so with the accompanying horse-drawn carts taking it at the trot or often at the gallop. The first week you will be supporting the frontline boys with any ammo they need or supplies and do any repairs necessary. Then, when your week there is done, the present frontline men will be relieved by you while they take their well-earned break from the firing line. You will finally get to meet the enemy face to face. Any questions?"

He didn't wait for a reply but left them to make themselves as comfortable as they could. They said very little, each man was lost in his own thoughts. Philip remembered his excitement as he kissed Lydia goodbye and wished he was back home with her and his darling boy.

CHAPTER EIGHTEEN

The following day, the men prepared for inspection by the officers who ensured their equipment was short of nothing. When they stopped for a midday meal, their spirits lifted when the mail from home arrived and those men who were fortunate enough to receive some settled into as quiet a spot as they could find to read the messages from loved ones. Philip waited anxiously for his name to be called and he breathed a sigh of relief when a small package was passed to him. Inside, with a letter, was a pair of woollen socks, knitted by Lydia. Her message read,

My Dear Philip

We are told here at home that small items of clothing are much needed by our men in the trenches, so let me know your preference for socks, gloves or scarves. I will be so happy to knit for you and with every stitch I will be thinking of you so you will be warmed not only by the socks, but by my love for you. William misses you so much but we visit often with your parents and John's family. On the back of this page is a picture William drew for you, I do believe he has an artistic talent, don't you?

Philip turned over the page and smiled. William had sketched a good likeness of their small house with smoke curling from the chimney.

Are you getting well fed? We are told the best of the country's groceries and meat is shipped out to you fighting men so I must not grumble if we get second best. I will wait as patiently as I can for your reply, just a line or two assuring me you are safe and well will soothe my anxious thoughts,

All of my love and more
Your loving wife
Lydia

When evening began to fall, the men were ordered to stand to as a hazy sun set behind dark rain clouds. They formed ranks with their packs and rifles slung on their shoulders ready to continue the march to the front. As they approached Hellfire Corner, the Sergeant Major ordered them to march at the double. A howl and the shriek of shellfire was followed by an orange glow from the exploding shells lighting the sky. An old regular soldier who introduced himself as Jim marching with Philip's squad, told them,

"That's the bloody Hun, let a few off hoping to catch us on this stretch of road. They just fire for the hell of it. Sometimes they get lucky, other times we get lucky."

Jim adjusted his goatskin jerkin which he wore over his tunic and began to run.

The men could make out alongside the road netting fastened between the remaining trees.

Frank asked, what purpose can that serve?"

Victor shrugged his shoulders as he ran. The older man heard the question.

"They screen the road in the day from the German gunners so they don't get sight of any necessary daytime movements but the bastards shoot randomly and cause casualties. So keep running boys!"

In the distance, bright magnesium flares lit the sky as bright as day followed by the rat-a-tat of sporadic machine gun fire. A strange howling noise was followed by dull, thumping explosions.

"That'll be the trench mortars the Hun use to clear any obstacles. Including us."

He assured them this happened every night and both sides used flares to illuminate 'No Man's Land'.

"They often catch a raiding party or a wiring party out in the open just to keep us on our toes. What you've got to watch out for at dusk and again as dawn breaks, the Bavarians and Saxon soldiers have bloody good snipers in their ranks and if some poor sod needs to use the latrine trench he'd better keep his head down while his trousers are down or he's likely to cop it."

Smashed wagons lay at the side of the road with dead mules and horses. Wounded men were being attended to by medical orderlies. One man was screaming in agony then fell silent. Bile rose in Philip's stomach, making him retch as he ran past the casualty. He saw that the poor man's belly had been ripped open.

"Christ, please don't let me die like that."

The head of the company turned off the road and the Lancashire boys were astonished to read a road sign 'East Lancashire Road'. They laughed when the sergeant said, "Nearly home, boys, let's hope they've got the tea brewing."

Under cover of darkness, the platoon arrived at the front-line trench where each man was allocated a section to stow his equipment in small dug-outs in the walls. The weary troops that had held the position for several days gladly handed over to the column of raw recruits who had been sent to relieve them. Philip saw the haunted look on their faces as they passed, the exhausted men ignoring the sympathetic smiles of the newly-arrived replacements. Someone from the South Lancs said,

"I thought it was all supposed to be over by Christmas!"

"Not bloody long to go then," replied one of the leaving men.

"The trouble is, the bastards didn't say which Christmas!"

Sergeant Major Cross walked through the trench.

"Well lads, looks like we are going to be the lucky ones to spend Christmas right here so let's get cracking. I need fatigue parties for the following duties. Some of you will fill sandbags which others will use to strengthen the walls. You five will be posted as sentries."

He pointed at Bob, Philip and three men from another squad, including Jim.

"You can use the fire steps but do not be tempted to poke your head out; you will draw enemy fire and they have some good snipers. I will also need volunteers to crawl forward under cover of darkness to the listening posts. All of you, whatever your duties are, must stay perfectly still when the Hun send up flares. Night will become day and the merest hint of movement will make them trigger happy, understood?"

As if the enemy could hear every word, the crack of a rifle bullet followed by a bang confirmed the sergeant's warning.

The floor of the trench was permanently under water, even the duckboards could not prevent the men's feet from becoming cold and wet. The arrival of some hot food and drink cheered the men for a short time and they hunkered down to eat, temporarily ignoring the enemy's sporadic attacks.

None of the men slept well that night and as the first light of day slowly crept through the trenches, the Major and Lieutenant moved along the trench with Sergeant Major Cross.

"Except for the lookouts, stand the rest of the men down Sergeant Major for them to have breakfast. The sentries can eat later. Then I want you and Lieutenant Hough-Smith to inspect the men and their equipment before daybreak. Have the men fix bayonets to be prepared for any enemy activity, don't want to be caught off guard."

Major Hamilton returned to the relative comfort of the officer's dugout which was larger than the others and was sheltered by a corrugated iron roof.

"You heard the major lads, fix bayonets and you, sergeant, detail five replacement lookouts."

He repeated his warnings.

"You sentries, keep your eyes peeled! You have three periscopes between you, use 'em! Never ever be tempted to stick your head above the parapet because Fritz is just waiting for you to do that so that he can put a bullet in it so look through the firing gaps between the sand bags. Most important of all, anyone caught sleeping on sentry duty will be court-martialed and very likely shot for dereliction of duty, understood?"

The men nodded their heads.

"If any of you get caught short and need the latrines, first you need the permission from me or any NCO, but if it's just a piss you need, you pee where you stand, right?"

The men were feeling more and more miserable at their conditions but replied, "Yes, Sergeant Major."

"Ok, you four, go to the reserve trench to fetch breakfast. If we get lucky it might be salty, fatty bacon but if not you will have to make do with bread and jam. With luck, the tea carried in an old petrol can will still be hot and at least it will fill your bellies."

Two of the young soldiers returned carrying old petrol tins with the tops cut off and rope handles attached full of tea along with mess tins of bacon swimming in greasy fat. The others carried between them a sack full of bread and some tins of jam. The breakfast was shared out down the trench with the ravenous men each taking a helping of bacon into their mess tins along with a mug of lukewarm sweet tea and a couple of large slices of bread. Although the tea had a slight petrol taste, Philip and the others slaked their thirst and wolfed down the bacon wrapped in one slice of bread followed by a doorstep of bread and jam. They had just finished eating when there came the thunder of artillery fire followed by the howling shriek of shells passing over. Great mounds of earth were thrown up behind their positions and the men were showered with it. The next barrage came followed by German trench mortars.

"Stand to the Lancs," shouted the sergeant major

"Man the fire step."

The sudden attack flushed Major Hamilton and the Lieutenant from their dugout.

"Have the men fix bayonets and stand by for an attack, Sergeant Major."

"Yes, sir. Fix bayonets and weapons at the ready lads, looks like the buggers want to play and see what you boys are made of."

From his position on the fire step, Philip suddenly saw movement about a hundred yards away then dozens of soldiers in field grey uniforms appeared and advanced towards their positions. The Major shouted, "Open fire, lads, fire at will!"

The crack and thud of rifle fire was heard all down the line followed by the rat tat tat of the Vickers machine guns as the machine gunners sprayed their fire into the oncoming figures in field grey.

Some wore pickelhaube helmets while others had grey caps with red bands. They slowed as they encountered the barbed wire that had been replaced by the previous occupiers of the front trenches and which the enemy artillery had failed to destroy. Philip fired instinctively, not sure if the men falling had been hit by him or if it was the fire of his comrades. The deadly fire from the machine gun positions in the line joined in then above the deafening din of their gunfire was the scream of shells overhead. Thankfully, this time the shells were not falling on them but amongst the advancing Germans. The enemy were caught in the wire by shellfire, machine gun fire and the rapid fire from the South Lancs rifles. Philip saw men and earth being blown up no more than thirty yards in front of him; orange and black explosions and shrapnel bursting overhead. The German attack faltered then broke as men struggled to get back to their own positions and the safety of their own trenches. Some unfortunate soldiers were caught in the wire, their mouths screaming without being heard, such was the deafening noise of the firing and the shells bursting amongst them. One man was firmly in Philip's sights, struggling to help a comrade who was badly wounded. The Lancashire boy could not bring himself to pull the trigger. He willed the soldier to make it back to the safety of his own trenches but Charlie Proctor climbed onto the top of the trench shouting,

"The bastards are running. Let's get 'em, boys!"

The unmistakable burst of a German machine gun stopped him in his tracks and he fell back into the trench watched by Sergeant Major Cross. The Major ordered Lieutenant Hough-Smith to get on the field telephone and call off the artillery barrage immediately. Two medical orderlies attended to Charlie but he was too far gone. Blood was coming from his mouth and Philip noticed the vacant look in his eyes. He spoke just one word,

"Mother."

Sergeant Major Cross looked at him and shook his head.

"What a stupid bugger! Let that be a lesson to you all. Never break cover unless you are ordered to."

Eventually the noise abated and the exhausted men leaned their rifles against the sandbags and rested.

To lift the spirits of the frontline soldiers, the second batch of mail for them had been held back and now was the time to distribute it. This time Lydia had sent a larger packet so Philip found the driest spot of the trench available on a firing step to unwrap his parcel. Lydia had been busy. In it was a warm woollen scarf which he wound around his neck straight away and another pair of socks. He stuffed the socks into his tunic and searched for a letter from home. As much as he appreciated the gifts, the letters were most valuable to him. Buried under a fruit cake, a piece of his favourite cheese and a bag of humbugs were two sheets of paper. One was another drawing by William, this time the young boy had drawn what was obviously meant to be a cat with enormous whiskers. For a four-year-old boy, it was very good. He then unfolded Lydia's letter.

Dear Philip,

Because life is very quiet now with you gone I decided to add to our little family by taking in a kitten to entertain us. It has done wonders for William, he is so happy having a playmate. He has called him 'Buttons'. If you look very carefully you can see why, he has a white bib with two small patches of black which do indeed look like buttons. We are both well although it is cold here but we keep the fire burning just like in the song. Everyone in your family is well, although your father says little these days but I feel he thinks a great deal about you. My parents are also in good health and they all send their best wishes for a hasty end to this dreadful war. When you wear your scarf, imagine it is my arms around your neck and enjoy your cake with a bite of cheese as you like it. The cake should keep well if you store it somewhere safe, away from the rats you wrote about. Stay safe my love, I will pray for you. Have the best Christmas you are able to and think of us.

All my love,
Lydia

CHAPTER NINETEEN

The remaining few days before Christmas were without incident apart from the usual bit of sniping around dawn or early evening but the boys had learnt to keep their heads down. Both sides took advantage of the period to repair trenches, shore up the trench walls with timber delivered by men from the support trench and fill more bags with sand. Water was bailed out and duckboards raised in the hope that their feet might dry at last. The men dug further into the trench sides so they got more cover using timber and corrugated iron sheet to protect them from the elements when they were stood down and allowed to sleep. Weapons were cleaned and oiled and ammunition handed out so each man was able to refill his pouches. On Christmas Eve the weather turned cold and misty with a heavy frost and as they huddled together for warmth, Philip and his comrades heard singing from the enemy trenches.

"What have they got to sing about?" asked Bob as he peered through a firing slit.

"Shush."

Philip listened to the words of the song.

"It's a Christmas carol, much like one we sing at home. Let's give them a carol of ours, eh, boys. Who knows 'Good King Wenceslas'? OK, ready?"

After the two sides had taken turns singing, Philip heard one of the Germans shout across to them, "Tommy, no shooting, eh? We get our dead and you get yours."

Lieutenant William Hough-Smith appeared

"What's happening?"

Sergeant Major Cross replied,

"It's the Huns, sir, they have been singing carols then asked if they can recover their dead and for us to do the same."

The two men looked across no man's land and were surprised to see a German soldier climb out of their trench with a white flag held above his head and carrying no weapons of any kind. "It's an officer, sir."

"Alert the Major will you, private," the lieutenant said, addressing Philip.

"Yes, sir."

Philip headed for the officers' dug out and climbed down the wooden steps to find the Major writing a report. He looked up as Philip saluted.

"Yes, Nicklas, what is it?"

"Begging your pardon, sir, but the Lieutenant feels you should know that there is a German officer in no man's land heading this way and carrying a white flag."

The major stood up and pulled on his cap, heaved himself into his greatcoat and followed the private out of the dug-out up into the trench.

"What's going on, Andrew?"

"The German officer shouted across that he wants to speak to our commanding officer. He is carrying a white flag, sir."

"Right. Let us see what this is all about then. Have the men cover me will you? Here, take my revolver as he is obviously unarmed."

With that, the Major climbed out of the trench and slowly walked towards the German officer.

Philip and the other men watched in silence as the two opposing officers were having a conversation. The two men then shook hands before returning to their own trenches.

The men waited to hear what Major Hamilton had to say.

"Well, the Germans have proposed we agree to a truce for today and Christmas Day to give us all the opportunity to reclaim our dead and allow us to bury them. There is to be no shooting from either side for the duration. I have agreed to their terms so now, Sergeant Major, you can detail burial parties from the men. I have to warn you it is pretty awful out there. Some of the men that were killed in the attack before we arrived are lying where they fell and what is left of those unfortunate men is barely recognisable as human remains."

Philip looked across to the enemy trenches. He told his pals,

"They have started already. They are approaching the wire with their hands up, not carrying their rifles either. Hang on – one is carrying something. Oh, he has wire cutters that's all. Now he is cutting free the poor bastards who got caught in the wire and the others are taking them down and carrying them off."

Sergeant Major Cross gave the men their orders.

Victor was first to climb up the ladder, closely followed by the rest of the men. They crossed no man's land as far as the wire and lost no time in releasing their fallen comrades still trapped. Other bodies lay decomposing in muddy shell holes, eaten away by the rats as big as cats that roamed the battlefield and the trenches. The men worked in silence with some wearing cloths to cover their noses in a vain bid to prevent the stench from making them retch. As bodies were placed on stretches to be carried away from the scene of battle for burial, their rescuers searched around to retrieve the dog tags to accompany them. Not enough tags were found and identification was almost impossible. However, the dead from both sides were buried with as much respect as possible in the mud of Flanders. When the grim task had been completed, the weary men were given extra rations of rum ordered by the Major. They learned later from the Germans they too had been given brandy to settle their nerves. An unusual camaraderie grew between the men of both sides who, just a few days ago had been trying to kill one another. As they chatted, the English soldiers learned that some of the German soldiers had been working in England when war broke out and had been recalled to fight. They had been waiters, bakers and like Philip and his father, barbers. They agreed they knew very little as to why they were fighting each other and men from both sides exchanged gifts: the Germans had sausage, chocolate, cigars, wine and beer to offer while the British soldiers gave rum, cigarettes, tobacco and cake. The officers promised each other that they would desist from shooting for at least the next day.

Christmas Day dawned under a shroud of mist but when the sun rose in the sky it soon cleared to display a frosty landscape. In the middle of no man's land the Germans had stuck a Christmas tree into the mud and when they spotted the English soldiers emerging from their trench, they waved their hands and cheered.

"Merry Christmas, Tommy."

All the men climbed out of the trenches once more to exchange Christmas greetings. The dry but cold weather was such a welcome change from the incessant rain of the last few weeks. Even though the hardened earth was pockmarked with deep shell craters from all the bombardments, it was much easier to move about and cold feet were better than wet feet. The agreed truce brought a welcome period of peace to both sides and although their officers had mixed feelings about the situation they saw how the men's morale had lifted so turned a blind eye to the fraternisation. After the normal morning duties had been performed and while the men enjoyed a Christmas dinner sitting in their rough dugouts, the officers arrived with gifts for the men from Princess Mary. They had already received greetings cards with photographs of King George V and Queen Mary so the small tins containing pipe tobacco, twenty cigarettes, a pipe, and tinder lighter complete with a Christmas card and a photograph of Princess Mary were an unexpected treat. The few men who did not smoke were pleased to receive a tin with a packet of acid drops and a khaki writing case holding paper, a pencil and some envelopes, again with a card and photo. The brass tins had been designed to fit in the pockets of the men's tunics which suited the soldiers in the trenches because of the limited space for personal objects.

The men were feeling almost happy. The dinner had not been as good as their families were having back home but they had supplemented the meal provided with cake and puddings sent by their families and shared between the other members of the squad. They sat in the small dugouts in the trench walls and lit their pipes or cigarettes. The smoke curled upwards but nobody feared the enemy today, the Germans were enjoying their Christmas too. Conversation avoided all mention of the war, men related stories about their wives or children, jokes were exchanged with the more risqué ones causing loud guffaws of laughter and men wiping away tears running down their grimy faces. Popular songs were sung but as evening fell, they spontaneously began to sing Christmas carols and from the enemy trenches they could hear the enemy joining in. Philip wrote a brief note to Lydia before the light dwindled completely.

My Darling Lydia and little Bill

We have spent a most enjoyable day today with Christmas dinner followed by singing. The Germans have been very friendly so we all live in hope that soon the fighting will cease altogether and we will come home. It is getting dark so I will send you both my wishes for a Happy New Year and kisses to you both

Your loving husband

Philip

***

The following day, the South Lancs battalion was relieved from the frontline and returned to Poperinghe for their rest from duty. Philip and his friends found the town to be little changed, the war could have been many miles away as the locals carried on with business as usual. The first place the men were taken to was the bathhouse. Large tin baths were filled with luxurious hot water, they were given bars of soap and clean towels and left to enjoy themselves while their clothes were washed or disposed of if they were beyond repair. For the first time since they had arrived in the Ypres Salient they were free from lice. Doctors checked their feet for trench foot, a debilitating condition caused by never having dry feet because of the incessant rain and the inability to bail the standing water out of the trenches completely. Cafes and bars were open, full of exhausted men intent on making the most of this precious time. Philip's young pals heard of the brothels doing plenty of business and egged each other on to visit one.

"How about you, Bob, fancy a pretty young Belgian girl to be your first?"

Victor dug his pal in the ribs and winked at him.

"What makes you think she'd be the first, eh? I'll have you know I have quite a reputation back home in Golborne, walked out with several lasses from the town."

Victor laughed at Bob's reply.

"I think you will find the lasses here are not interested in 'walking out' more like 'lying in' if you get my meaning."

Philip smiled at the friendly banter but declined the invitation to join the boys seeking sexual adventure. He was happy to remember Lydia, so loving towards him once she had overcome her shyness as a new bride. Memories of their lovemaking warmed him and he remained at the café table quite content with his own company, happy just to watch the world go by. When he had drunk as much coffee as he was able, he took a stroll around town in search of presents for his wife and son. The women of the surrounding area had been busy with their embroidery making patriotic pictures featuring the flags of the allied nations. He chose one of the Union flag draped around the shoulders of a young Belgian boy and bought it for William. The region was famous for its lacemaking and he searched for a pretty lace collar for Lydia. He decided against the lace handkerchiefs on display; the association of tears and handkerchiefs was too emotional and anyway, he knew that Lydia would make good use of a new lace collar for a favourite dress.

Joe Wilson arrived and stood beside him as he paid for his purchases. The young farm boy had surprised them all by being the worst affected by the experience of burying their dead comrades. As a farm boy he had seen many animals slaughtered for meat. He had killed and skinned rabbits, helped at the annual pig killing so his reaction was most unexpected. He was so close to Philip that the strong smell of alcohol on his breath made Philip cough.

"D'you fancy a drink with me, Phil? The others have all gone in there."

He pointed across the road to a building with girls sitting provocatively at tables.

"Not interested myself, no good will come of it, you wait and see. Bloody officers in there too somewhere, I've been giving some of them a piece of my mind. They threatened to put me on a charge just for speaking the truth. This war is a disgrace, that's what it is."

His voice had risen and passers-by were looking at him and shaking their heads. Just then Sergeant Major Cross came over to speak to him.

"Now look here, Private Wilson, if you persist in this aggressive behaviour I'll have you sent back up the front where it will be appreciated as long as it is aimed at the enemy, right? Now, you Private Nicklas, as the oldest man in your squad, I trust you to keep young Joe here in order for his own sake. I know he's a good lad but threatening officers with his fists is serious insubordination and he's lucky they were well in their cups themselves and laughed at him."

"Yes, sir, and anyway he is our best sniper. I'll do my best."

He led Joe back to the café where he had been earlier and sat him at a table with his back to the passing soldiers. He signalled to the waitress and sat down opposite his comrade.

"Coffee, Joe? You can have it black or with cream, how d'you like it?"

"Can I have a large mug of hot sweet tea please, I'm not partial to coffee, we don't have it on the farm. Milk we have and cider at harvest and ale of course…"

His eyes were heavy and he sat with his elbow on the table and rested his head on his hand.

The waitress stood poised, waiting for their order.

"Do you serve tea?"

The girl smiled and nodded.

"Then make it two large ones with sugar and milk please. How about a cake or some bread and cheese, Joe?"

"Yeh, bread and cheese sounds good."

The waitress repeated their order and went to fetch it.

Once the youngster had eaten his food and drunk most of his tea he calmed down and was happy to hear Philip's tales of his family. The big farm boy and the dapper young barber became good friends that day and vowed to look out for each other when they were returned to the front line.

***

The routine of moving from relief to support then to the frontline continued. Fighting had reached the point where, apart from sporadic shell fire and sniper fire causing limited casualties, both sides were just dug in, holding on to the territory they already had but advancing no further. Much of the time was spent bailing out the water-filled trenches and repairing the regular landslips in the walls of the trenches and hurdles. At night under darkness they reinforced the communication trenches. On the night of the 26th January, all men were alerted to the fact that the next day was Kaiser Wilhelm's birthday and the British commanding officers were expecting renewed patriotic attacks to commence. Thanks to the prior warning, the British troops kept their heads down while the fresh activity from the enemy led to no more casualties than usual.

It was the first week of February when Philip's squad returned to the front line. As before, the officers had retained mail for distribution at the front to help morale. This time the packages were larger, some of it included Christmas gifts from home. It was obvious that women back in Blighty had got the message loud and clear that the soldiers were suffering from the cold weather. Men were tearing open parcels and finding long woollen scarves which they immediately wrapped around their necks. Others had balaclavas and gloves but the most popular items of clothing were socks, the longer the better.

Every so often gunfire from the enemy trenches reminded the men of their presence but it did seem to be less enthusiastic since the Christmas truce. It was returned with equal reluctance and neither side suffered many casualties. The biggest threat was from snipers as any man forgetting to keep his head down soon found out when he heard the crack of a rifle and felt a bullet whistle past him. German troops wore hard leather picklehaube helmets or soft caps; the British troops had only their soft peaked caps, none of which offered any protection at all.

Their midday break of Maconochie stew was carried to them in dixies packed in hay boxes meant to keep the food hot but seldom achieved: the food was usually cold with lukewarm tea to wash it down. The men lit up after eating their food and chatted or reread their mail. Philip lit his cigarette and held it between his teeth as he groped in his breast pocket for his letter from Lydia. He had read it several times already but he enjoyed picturing Lydia sitting at the kitchen table, the cosy fire warming her legs as the kettle came to the boil and William sitting beside her, head down, drawing the picture to send to his Daddy. The latest family member, Buttons, would be curled up on the brightly coloured rag rug Lydia had made from old worn-out clothes. He puffed on his cigarette and opened the folded paper carefully.

My Dearest Philip

I hope your presents are keeping out the cold, it must be dreadful to be out in all weathers at this time of year. We are all well here although your father is very quiet, he spends many hours rocking in his chair just gazing into space and sighing. Your dear mother does her best to cheer him up but we think that this awful war is reminding him of his wartime experiences in France. Whenever we visit them I take some home-baked scones and it is so rewarding to see his eyes light up and to hear him say 'danke' with a smile. William tried to draw a picture of him for you smoking his Bavarian pipe. Can you see how well he has done a likeness? Our little boy spends many happy hours drawing and he is also learning to write. The town is very quiet, almost empty of young men and your barber's shop does very little trade as many of your customers are over there with you.

Well my darling, I must get back to my knitting so I will bid you goodnight and God-bless with an X from William

Your ever loving wife

Lydia

Philip folded it carefully and put it back in his pocket before taking out the drawing to look at once again. He puffed on his cigarette and with his free hand tried to unfold the sheet of paper. As he did so a gust of wind blew through the trench and snatched it from his hand. Without thinking he leapt up to retrieve it but it was snatched again to lie just out of his reach. Fearing it might blow away to no man's land Philip climbed out onto the parapet intending to grab it quickly then return to the safety of the trench. It was to be a fatal error on his part. Forty yards away, an ever-vigilant sniper spotted a Tommy raising his head in full view. A sharp crack startled Philip and he fell backwards, clutching the precious drawing, just as Joe was about to pull him down from harm's way. The two men fell in a heap on the floor of the trench and Philip felt a stinging sensation in his neck.

"What the hell d'you think you were doing, Phil? Want to get yourself killed?"

Philip was dazed and shook his head. He felt his neck thinking he had a graze but Joe stared in horror when he saw the amount of blood his pal was losing. He fumbled in the pocket sewn into his tunic containing dressings and pulled one out then began applying it as a compress to the wound.

He shouted, "Stretcher bearers, we have a casualty here, bleeding like a stuck pig. You hang on in there, Phil, mate. We'll get you to a doctor who will put a stitch or two in your neck and you'll be back with us in no time. Or, if you got lucky, you might get shipped back to Blighty, eh?"

The urgent call was relayed down the trench and in no time at all two medical orderlies appeared and soon had the wounded soldier on the stretcher and being carried away to the comparative safety of No7 Field Ambulance.

***

The sombre news of Private Philip Nicklas's death was related to them by Major Hamilton who spoke a few words in recognition of the gallant soldier with his family background and reminding his men of their dead comrade's dedication to duty. Frank, Victor, Joe and Bob kept stiff upper lips until the officer left then wept freely. Two down, four to go.

Philip had not regained consciousness and had died on the morning of the 9th February.

The letter informing his wife, Mrs Lydia Nicklas, of his death was sent to the Vicar of Golborne.

"No 7 Field Ambulance, 3rd Division, B E F, 10th February 1915

Dear Mrs Nicklas – I am sorry to have to write and tell you that your dear husband, Philip, 11757, 2nd South Lancs, was brought in here the night before last suffering from a severe wound to the neck. I think a bullet had struck him on the right side of it. He was unconscious, but the doctor dressed the wound, and did everything for him that was possible, and I read the commendatory office over him. He lived during the night, but passed away perfectly peacefully, and without regaining consciousness the next morning at about 8.45am. I buried him later in the morning in the churchyard at Lochre, which is 8 or 9 miles from Ypres, in Flanders, and a wooden cross with his name burnt upon it marks the grave.

I know it will be a great sorrow for you, and just as he has laid down his life for others, so now you are being asked to give up what is dearest to you on earth, and I like to think you will do so ungrudgingly, in the knowledge that he is in God's keeping, and that God asks this sacrifice of you. May God bless you, and grant him everlasting rest –

Yours sincerely Harold T A Peacey, Chaplain."

***

Lydia was numbed by the news. She asked the vicar, "Why Philip? He told me he was being so careful, he even said the Germans and the British soldiers had become friends and promised to aim high? My little boy needs his father. We will never see him again, and we can't even visit his grave to take flowers. It is all so cruel."

She wept bitterly but dried her eyes and turned her face away as young William ran into the kitchen to see who was visiting. When he saw the vicar, his smile faded. He could see by the man's face that he had brought bad news.

"Mummy? Is it about Grandfather Johann? Has he been taken ill again?"

Lydia composed herself and knelt to hug William.

"No, darling boy, not grandfather. We have bad news about Daddy, he has been shot."

The young boy freed himself from his mother's arms.

"Has he been hurt, Mummy? Will he get better?"

Lydia found her throat had tightened and she was unable to speak so she turned to the vicar who spoke for her.

"William, the news is very bad I'm afraid. Your Daddy will not be coming home, he died peacefully in Belgium and he is now at rest in a churchyard. He fell asleep and never woke up."

The boy was too young to understand much of what the vicar had told him but he had heard the words 'he died peacefully' and without making a sound, tears welled up in his eyes and ran down his face. Lydia hugged him again then they sobbed quietly together. Eventually with a huge sigh Lydia stood to shake the vicar's hand and see him to the door. He offered to tell the parents of Philip but she recovered her composure and thanked him.

"No, I must tell them. It has been their greatest fear. Philip was half German you know but a more patriotic man you would never meet."

"Will you be at church on Sunday? I will tell the congregation of his death and we can all pray together for his soul."

"That is very kind of you, we will do our best to attend. Thank you for all your kind words."

They shook hands and the vicar strode off. He had letters to write.

The editor of the Wigan Observer and District Advertiser, the local paper for Golborne, printed the following tribute to Philip after interviewing the vicar.

"Private Nicklas is the son of a Bavarian, who fought for Germany against France in the war of 1870, and who was one of the army that marched into Paris, in 1871, passing under the Arc de Triomphe, and encamping in the gardens of the Tuileries. Immediately after the war the father left Germany and came to England, and married an English wife. He has been in this country ever since, and for the last 26 years has resided at Golborne. He is the only registered alien in the township, but is confined to bed and too ill to be moved. It is a remarkable coincidence that Private Nicklas is the first Golborne soldier killed in the war, and moreover it must surely be unique to find a son fighting against the compatriots of his father, and on the side of the enemies his father engaged against more than forty years ago."

Lydia had broken the news of Philip's death in the kitchen of her parents-in-law with Philip's brother and sisters present. The young grandchildren had been allowed in the front parlour to play or look at books. Johann covered his face with his hands and said nothing. Clara wept on her son John's shoulder while their daughters Clara, Emily and Beatrice comforted Lydia. The vicar greeted them all when they attended church the following Sunday. Johann was too ill to attend so his youngest daughter, Beatrice, stayed at home with him. The vicar told them about his interview with the local paper's editor and that Johann would be proud to see his story in print. The following Saturday, 20th February Lydia went to buy two copies of the paper. The newsagent had read the story and recognised Lydia so gave her enough copies for the family to have one each, and he refused payment. The whole town was in mourning for their popular young barber.

The months following saw a rapid decline in Johann's health and by August he had been admitted to the Union Hospital in Leigh where he died on 4th August 1915. His family believed he had died from a broken heart.

EPILOGUE
FEBRUARY 2015
BELGIUM

The couple had planned this visit for some time. As her husband Dave was the driver, Beryl was the map reader. She had studied the map of Belgium and had highlighted their route but somehow it seemed they had taken a wrong turning. She was starting to regret not taking her son up on his offer of a Satnav for the car. After all, they had taken many holidays with her doing the navigating and she had never lost their way before.

"Turn here, at least we will be heading in the right direction."

Dave signaled and turned left onto a small country road. As they drove in silence, not too sure they should have left the major road they had been on, Beryl pointed.

"Look, there's a church in the distance. We can find out which village it is and consult the map again."

Dave knew how important this trip was to his wife so he didn't argue with her. The church ahead had an imposing square tower and stood in the village of Loker according to the sign.

"This is it! Pull over and park, we will take a look, be sure it is the right place. The spelling is different, I was looking for Lochre."

They parked near the church and put on their coats. After the warmth of the car, the air was damp and chilly. Beryl pulled on a hat and gloves but her husband braved the weather by turning up his collar and stuffing his hands in his pockets. They took with them a bunch of flowers from the back seat.

They gazed around the churchyard in awe at the number of war graves, then began to count them and reached more than two hundred.

Row after row they searched until they found the one they had travelled so many miles to see. As the graves were so well tended by the War Graves Commission, Beryl felt their flowers were redundant so she placed them on a much older neglected grave. With their heads bowed they stood in silence, then straightened up to read the details on the headstone. Beryl wiped away her tears as Dave put a comforting arm around her. He knew that ever since she had learnt of Philip's war, Johann's war and her Great-great-grandmother Eliza's brothers, John* and Daniel's* war in Mexico, Beryl wanted to tell their story. The couple represented the family who Philip never knew. His son, young William had married, had nine children, fourteen grandchildren and fourteen great-grandchildren.

*John and Daniel are fictitious characters.

Printed in Great Britain
by Amazon